# STARTING
# FROM
# AMELIASBURGH

## Books by Al Purdy

### Poetry:

*The Enchanted Echo* (1944)
*Pressed on Sand* (1955)
*Emu, Remember!* (1956)
*The Crafte So Long to Lerne* (1959)
*The Blur in Between: Poems 1960–61* (1962)
*Poems for All the Annettes* (1962)
*The Cariboo Horses* (1965)
*North of Summer: Poems from Baffin Island* (1967)
*Wild Grape Wine* (1968)
*Love in a Burning Building* (1970)
*The Quest for Ouzo* (1971)
*Hiroshima Poems* (1972)
*Selected Poems* (1972)
*On the Bearpaw Sea* (1973)
*Sex and Death* (1973)
*In Search of Owen Roblin* (1974)

*The Poems of Al Purdy: A New Canadian Library Selection* (1976)
*Sundance at Dusk* (1976)
*A Handful of Earth* (1977)
*At Marsport Drugstore* (1977)
*Moths in the Iron Curtain* (1977)
*No Second Spring* (1977)
*Being Alive: Poems 1958–78* (1978)
*The Stone Bird* (1981)
*Birdwatching at the Equator: The Galapagos Islands* (1982)
*Bursting into Song: An Al Purdy Ominibus* (1982)
*Piling Blood* (1984)
*The Collected Poems of Al Purdy* (1986)
*The Woman on the Shore* (1990)
*Naked With Summer in Your Mouth* (1994)

### Editor:

*The New Romans: Candid Canadian Opinions of the US* (1968)
*Fifteen Winds: A Selection of Modern Canadian Poems* (1969)
Milton Acorn, *I've Tasted My Blood: Poems of 1956–1968* (1969)
*Storm Warning: The New Canadian Poets* (1971)
*Storm Warning 2: The New Canadian Poets* (1976)
*Wood Mountain Poems* (1976)

### Other:

*No Other Country* (prose, 1977)
*The Bukowski / Purdy Letters 1964–1974: A Decade of Dialogue* (with Charles Bukowski, 1983)
*Morning and It's Summer: A Memoir* (1983)
*The George Woodcock–Al Purdy Letters* (edited by George Galt, 1987)
*A Splinter in the Heart* (novel, 1990)
*Cougar Hunter* (essay on Roderick Haig-Brown, 1993)
*Margaret Laurence–Al Purdy: A Friendship in Letters* (1993)
*Reaching for the Beaufort Sea: An Autobiography* (1993)

# Starting from Ameliasburgh

The Collected Prose of

## AL PURDY

∾

Edited by
SAM SOLECKI

Harbour Publishing

Harbour Publishing
Box 219
Madeira Park, BC V0N 2H0

Cover photograph by Kevin Kelly
Jacket design by Roger Handling / Terra Firma
Page design & layout by David Lee Communications

Published with the assistance of the Canada Council and the Cultural
Services Branch of the BC Ministry of Tourism and Ministry Respon-
sible for Culture.
Printed and bound in Canada by Friesen Printers.

Canadian Cataloguing in Publication Data
Purdy, Al, 1918–
    Starting from Ameliasburgh


    Includes index.
    ISBN 1-55017-127-5


    I. Solecki, Sam, 1946– II. Title.
PS8531.U8A16 1995    C814'.54    C95-910416-X
PR9199.3.P87A14 1995

# Contents

## I No Other Country

## II The Writing Life

## Poetry Chronicle 1958–1990

# Contents

# Editorial Note

**D**ESPITE AL PURDY'S NOTE OF SURPRISE in his introduction about reprinting these pieces, I assume that most readers of this book will share my assumption that his stature within Canadian and contemporary literature is a sufficient justification for the volume. I also hope that most will agree with me that the pieces are interesting in their own right. I had two criteria in mind in deciding which essays and reviews to include. On the one hand, I was looking for pieces that would be representative of the kinds of non-fiction prose Purdy wrote (everything from travel pieces and memoirs to reviews); on the other, I was looking for work that would illuminate the poetry and shed light on the evolution of Purdy's poetics, individual poems, and vision of life ("Charles Bukowski," "Rudyard Kipling," "Cougar Hunter"). The overall intention was to put together a volume that would be representative rather than comprehensive ("collected" rather than complete).

For the most part, articles and reviews are arranged chronologically within each section except for those instances where thematic juxtapositions seemed to make more sense. The pieces are reprinted, again for the most part, without changes or significant revisions, though errors of spelling, grammar, quotation and citation have been silently corrected. A few sentences or paragraphs repeating material present elsewhere in the volume have been cut. And although I have attempted to standardize some aspects of the style (capitalization, spelling, punctuation, for instance), I have not allowed standardization or house style to take precedence over some of the personal idiosyncrasies of Al Purdy's prose style. As a result, I have regularly retained some idiosyncratic spellings ("thru," "gonna," "altho,"), compound words joined by hyphen even where the usage isn't sanctioned by the OED, and the author's very liberal use of the dash and colon.

Some of the titles have been changed, but the originals are listed in the acknowledgments. Since this is not intended to be a scholarly edition I have not listed variants either in the prose or in the quotations from the poems, nor have I footnoted all of the author's references and quotations; instead, most of the relevant information has been included in the essays and reviews themselves. Quotations from other writers and from Purdy's own work have been checked against the originals. Anyone interested in the essays, articles and reviews not included here should consult the Purdy bibliography in *The Annotated Bibliography of Canada's Major Authors* (Volume Two), Robert Lecker and Jack David, eds., (Toronto: ECW Press, 1980). The most notable omission is "Disconnections" (*Essays on Canadian Writing*, No. 49 [Summer 1993]) which I decided to leave out both because it appeared recently and is therefore readily available and, more importantly, because it repeats material from other essays and *Reaching for the Beaufort Sea*.

Al Purdy was consulted at every stage of the editing, and he approved the final choice of materials as well as editorial decisions. I want to thank him and Eurithe Purdy for their cooperation and hospitality both at Ameliasburgh and in Sidney, British Columbia. I also want to thank Ursula, André, and Vanessa Solecki for various forms of encouragement; Professor W.J. Keith and Elias Polizoes for their continuing interest; Audrey McDonagh for retyping some of the pieces; Dr. Andrea Werner-Thaler of the University of Vienna for advice on Canadian poetry; Professor Joaquin Kuhn of the University of Toronto for help with Swinburne; and the staffs of the Libraries of the University of Saskatchewan and of Queen's University for helping me find my way through the maze of the Purdy Papers in 1994 and 1995.

Sam Solecki
University of Toronto
March 1995

# Introduction

**M**Y FIRST REACTION TO THIS BOOK IS SURPRISE. In my earlier days I never expected such a book to be published, and now that it is I still feel surprised. And I don't want to go back in time and read the reviews I wrote long ago; let them stand as they were written. Sam Solecki has chosen them, undoubtedly corrected grammatical mistakes and any obvious inaccuracies. I am content with that.

The reasons I wrote reviews in the first place are more interesting to me. Obviously a writer writes. Long ago I was eager to get into print, to comment on those authors who interested me, and some in whom I was not very interested. I said some things I thought were necessary to say; I indulged my enthusiasms and strictures; I tried to "call them as I saw them." Sam Solecki feels they are worth collecting and reprinting.

The travel articles, the other pieces I wrote for money or for love, that's something else. It was wonderful to go to those various other countries and the strange unknown places in my own country, to feel those things and then say them and feel them all over again. To stand on top of a mountain at Macchu Picchu, see another mountain a few miles distant, which Earle Birney later told me he had climbed.

To stand face to face with a llama in the high Andes, try to stare the snooty-looking creature down and fail and collapse laughing at myself. (Is that one in here, Sam?) To have the lights go out while you're writing something on the bed in your apartment in a little Mexican village, smoking a cigar whose red coal three inches away from your face is the only illumination anywhere—: and darkness blacker than light is light overwhelms the world.

---

What do I remember? I remember everything. It exists somewhere in my head waiting to be awakened, if I just knew the magic words to say that would trigger memory. And I am somehow composed and constituted of all those things that happened to me, a mosaic of additives and bits and pieces of all that is.

What do I remember most? Faces, faces. They fly into my sleep at night and say: "I am Jonesie, Inuit hunter on Baffin Island in the high Arctic. Do you remember the time we brought dead seals home in the boat, stripped them of their skins, kept the meat and threw the offal back in the sea?" And the hungry dogs leaped into the blood-reddened water to eat and fight savagely with each other over the liver? And I, the alien white guest, reached out my hand and touched the face of a dead seal. With the feeling this creature was nearly human. Yes, I remember.

And Japan. Hiroshima, in the atomic museum, watching shadows on concrete like photographic negatives of men and women who were standing alive at that precise spot when The Bomb exploded. Such things churn the guts. And in Lima, Peru, a public square, its buildings pock-marked with bullets where the Shining Path guerrillas made their wishes known.

I wanted my own feelings and the word-photographs of things to translate back into thoughts when I wrote these travel pieces. Did they do that? Well, perhaps, here and there I hope; like using a flashbulb in the mind whose power supply was faulty. And I have to say it, here and now, how marvellous it is and was for me to have gone to these places and done these things. I hope you get even a hint of that feeling here. "Arctic Places" says the same thing:

—they are mileposts of old passage
echoes of our hinterlands
plunging name-sounds
of things we felt or dreamed or imagined
this farthest earth
the shuffling roof of clouds
summers beyond our lives
with nothing of ourselves wasted
we used what there was
our bones flow onward
blood breaks and stops

Al Purdy 1995

# Part One:
# No Other Country

# The Cartography of Myself

IN EARLY SUMMER, 1965, I WAS COASTING ALONG in a Nordair
DC8, bound for Frobisher Bay, Baffin Island. It was about 4 a.m.
and most of the other passengers were asleep, but I was peering from
the window watching the small reflection of our aeroplane skimming
over the blue water and floating ice of Frobisher Bay, several thousand feet down. Low hills on either side of us were patched with snow,
like Jersey cows. The water was so blue that the colour looked phony;
the sun had been up for about an hour.

Far beneath the noisy DC8, ice floes reeled away south. Black-
and-white Arctic hills surrounded us. This was the first time I had
been to the Arctic, and I was so excited that I could hardly sit still. In
Cuba, England, France, and other countries I'd felt like a stranger;
but here, I'd never left home. And I thought what an odd feeling it
was in a region that most people think is desolate and alien. But I felt
that the Arctic was just a northern extension of southern Canada.
Baffin Island:

> A club-shaped word
> a land most unlike Cathay or Paradise
> but a place the birds return to
> a name I've remembered since childhood
> in the first books I read—

("The Turning Point")

I have this same feeling of enjoyment, of being at home, all over
Canada. Maybe part of the reason comes from an earlier feeling of
being trapped forever in the town of Trenton, Ontario, when I was a
child; then the tremendous sense of release when I escaped, riding
the freight trains west during the Depression. Also, I take a double

view of history, for then and now merge somewhat in my mind. Winnipeg is also Fort Garry and Seven Oaks. Adolphustown, not far from where I live in Prince Edward County, is the spot where the United Empire Loyalists landed nearly 200 years ago. The restored fortress of Louisbourg in Cape Breton makes me feel like a living ghost, especially when looking at the tombstone of Captain Israel Newton who died there, a member of the colonial army from New England. And driving along Toronto's Don Valley Parkway, I think of the old Indian trails that take the same route under black asphalt. In cities everywhere, grass tries to push aside the concrete barriers of sidewalks.

I think especially of people in connection with places. Working on a highway near Penticton, British Columbia, with a fellow wanderer named Jim, shovelling gravel atop boiling tar: a speeding car ignored warning signs and nearly killed us; the big road foreman blistered that driver's hide until his face turned dull red.

And walking through the Okanagan Valley with my friend, picking cherries from orchards for food, sleeping wherever we could: sometimes in vacant sheds, and once buried in the pungent shavings of a sawmill. Then going to work for two weeks on a mountain farm, for a man whose name sounded like "Skimmerhorn." I got five dollars for those two weeks, cutting down trees with Jim and splitting them with wedges. At night, we listened to John McCormack sing "The Far Away Bells Are Ringing" on a wind-up phonograph. Jim stayed behind to work for a stake, but I gave up and rode the freights west to Vancouver. I never saw him again.

One of my favourite Canadian places is the area around Hazelton and Woodcock on the big bend of the Skeena River in British Columbia. I was stationed at Woodcock in 1943, helping to build a landing field as part of the defences for an expected Japanese invasion. Snow-covered mountains surrounded the barracks sheds, with the Skeena River racing down the green valley on its way to Prince Rupert. Sometimes there were eagles, circling overhead nearly as high as the sun. And on weekend passes, airmen from the base would hop freight trains to Hazelton or Smithers to drink beer and terrorize pleasurably the local female population.

In 1960 I went back to the big bend of the Skeena to do some writing about the Tsimshian Indians around Hazelton and Kispiox.

I was driving a '48 Pontiac that coughed its way up and down the mountain roads, threatening to expire at any minute. But I managed to reach Kispiox on the Indian reservation, with its carved house fronts and rotting totem poles. The place seemed entirely deserted, so I drove past the village and down to the Kispiox River. Standing in the shallows, wearing hip waders and baseball caps, were some twenty American fishermen with station wagons parked nearby.

There are other places stored on my mind's memory tapes. Places where I feel comfortable, at home: the battlefield at Batoche, in Saskatchewan, where I camped in a trailer; the highline tracks of the CPR near Field, BC, where I'd walked after a cop kicked me off a freight at Golden, then became a CPR labourer on a landslide blocking passage east for forty-eight hours, then rode in legal luxury to Calgary on a work train. And once there was a mile-long Arctic island, my home for three weeks of summer: I lay with my ear flat against the monstrous stone silence of the island, listening to the deep core of the world—silence unending and elemental, leaked from a billion-year period before and after the season of man.

I think back to all the places I've been, the people I've met and the things I've done. Having written and edited some twenty books, I hope to write a dozen more—to follow all the unknown roads I have not explored, until they branch off and become other roads in my mind . . .

There is a map in my head that I've carried there ever since I left school, and I connect it, oddly, with Leo Tolstoy. He wrote a short story called "How Much Land Does a Man Need," in which a man was given title, free and clear, to as much land as he could encircle on foot between sunup and sundown. The man was too greedy for land, tried to walk around too much of it, and died of exhaustion just before the sun went down.

But I have as much land as I need right now. There is a tireless runner in my blood that encircles the borderlands of Canada through the night hours, and sleeps when day arrives. Then my mind awakes and the race continues. West with the long and lamentably undefended American border; north along the jagged British Columbia coast to the whale-coloured Beaufort Sea and the Arctic Islands; south again past Baffin and Newfoundland to the Maritimes and sea lands of the Grand Banks. This is the map of myself, what I was and what

I became. It is a cartography of feeling and sensibility: and I think the man who is not affected at all by this map of himself that is his country of origin, that man is emotionally crippled.

My own country seems to me not aggressive, nor in search of war or conquest of any kind. It is exploring the broken calm of its domestic affairs. Slowly it investigates its own somewhat backward technology, and sets up committees on how not to do what for whom. My country is trying to resolve the internal contradictions of the Indian and French-Canadian nations it contains. In rather bewildered and stupid fashion it stares myopically at the United States, unable to assess the danger to the south—a danger that continually changes in economic character, and finally confronts us from within our own borders.

This is the map of my country, the cartography of myself.

*(1977)*

# The Iron Road

Riding the boxcars out of Winnipeg in a
morning after rain so close to
the violent sway of fields it's
like running and running
naked with summer in your mouth
being a boy scarcely a moment and you
hear the rumbling iron roadbed singing
under the wheels at night and a door jerking open
mile after dusty mile riding into Regina with
the dust storm crowding behind you
night and morning over the clicking rails
("Transient")

THE YEAR WAS 1936, AND I WAS SEVENTEEN. I rode the freight trains to Vancouver, along with thousands of other Canadians during the Great Depression. In the Hungry Thirties it seemed that half the population was on the move. The unemployed workmen of Toronto and Montreal and all the other big cities swarmed over the boxcars, moving west to the Prairies, west to Vancouver, wherever there might be hope of finding work.

There were also the professional hoboes, who always went in the opposite direction from where there was any rumour of employment. They lived in hobo jungles beside rivers and near the towns, never far from the railway yards. There they lit camp-fires, cooked food, washed clothing—if it was absolutely necessary—and told tales of the steel highways while standing over the fires at night. Of towns where housewives always invited you inside for dinner when you asked for a handout, and never handed you an axe while pointing sternly at the woodpile. Of towns where you never had to work, there was always plenty of beer . . . But after a day or two in the jungles they got restless again, and boarded the train to Anywhere.

It was a dark night in early June when I caught my first train at the railway yards in Trenton, Ontario. It had chuffed in from the East an hour earlier, and was about to pull out for Toronto. The yards were full of shunting switch engines bustling back and forth in the night, red and green signal lights gleaming like the eyes of stationary cats, and every now and then you heard a hoarse, impatient scream from the whistles of the westbound train.

I'll never know how I had the nerve to board that train, for I was scared to death of it. I'd quit school a couple of years before, and there was no work at all in Trenton. But that wasn't the reason why I was heading west. The reason was boredom. I wanted adventure. That was why I crouched in some bushes beside the tracks, almost too nervous to breathe, wondering how I'd ever manage to climb onto that boxcar. Was it something like getting on a bicycle or a horse? And where were the railway police hiding?

Suddenly the westbound train made a peculiar "toot-toot" that signaled departure—a sound I've heard many times since. Hoboes call it "the highball." Then a great metallic crash came from the couplings, and the train grunted away into the night. I broke from cover and ran alongside, grabbing at the steel ladder of a passing boxcar, and climbed up onto the roof—collapsing on the swaying catwalk while all the vertebrae of the wriggling wooden serpent beneath me thundered west.

A few days later and miles from home, I received my first instructions from a professional bum about the proper method of boarding a moving train. A lean little man with a dark stubble of beard, he'd seen me swing onto a train by the rear ladder of the boxcar.

"That's the way guys get killed," he said. "Ya gotta do it the right way. I seen guys lose a leg or arm falling under them wheels. Ya always go for the ladder at the front end of the car, never the one at the back end. If ya miss yer hold on the rear ladder ya fall between the cars and yer a gone goose. Always the front ladder. An remember that, kid."

There were other famous bums who wrote their names and deeds on boxcar walls or on the supports of watertanks with knife and pencil—Regina Sam Jones, Montana Slim, Midnight Frank. There was also the immortal Kilroy, who wrote "Kilroy was here" the length and breadth of the continent.

Farther west, at Broadview, Saskatchewan, the Mounties had a reputation for being very tough on bums. The stories about their toughness alarmed me so much that I crawled down the trap door of a threshing machine mounted on a flatcar before going through town. I crouched in the darkness of that monster, nervously waiting to be discovered and hauled off to jail. I heard the police tramping around outside, making a tremendous racket, but they didn't find me. When the train pulled out on its way west, I was the only illicit passenger left of the three score or so who had ridden with me into Broadview.

When I first started out for Vancouver I had some money in my pockets. But it was soon spent. I had to forsake the aristocratic habit of eating in restaurants and join the other bums knocking on doors to ask for handouts. It was embarrassing, but I got used to it. You nerved yourself, knocked on a door, and waited, wondering what might happen. The dignity of man was, of course, a lesser consideration than being hungry.

You might get a sandwich from a housewife, perhaps even a full meal, a "sitdown" we used to call it; but you might also be given an axe and directed to the woodpile; or a man in shirtsleeves might come to the door and tell you to "Beat it, bum!" It was all part of the game, and you didn't really hold any grudges for a harsh reception. You just kept on trying.

Sometimes you went to the bakery of whatever small town you happened to be passing through, asking the baker if he had any stale bread or buns. Most of the time you got something to eat, but occasionally there were long stretches on the train where it wasn't possible to ask for a handout. At such times you stayed hungry.

On my first trip west I hitchhiked north from Sault Ste. Marie, and was disheartened to find that the road ended at a little village called Searchmont (at that time the Trans-Canada Highway was not yet completed through Northern Ontario). Near midnight I boarded a freight travelling north and west, riding in an open-air gondola used to transport coal. After an hour it began to rain, and the coal dust made things worse. My face and hands were streaked with it. We stopped around 5 a.m. and it was still dark. I had no idea where I was, but the rain and coal-dust were too miserable to be borne. I ripped the seal off a boxcar with my hunting knife and tried to get inside.

But the door was too big and heavy for me to move, so I went back to my gondola and huddled under the rain in silent misery.

A railway cop materialized out of the greyness not long after I got settled. He'd seen the broken seal, and knew I was responsible. He told me that the settlement was named Hawk Junction, then locked me up in a caboose with barred windows and padlocked door. And I thought: how would my mother feel now about her darling boy? At noon the railway cop took me to his house for dinner with his wife and children, gave me some Ladies Home Journals to read, and casually mentioned that I could get two years for breaking the boxcar seal.

When returned to my prison-on-wheels I felt panic-stricken. I was only seventeen, and this was the first time I'd ventured far away from home. I examined the caboose-prison closely, thinking: two years! Why, I'd be nineteen when I got out, an old man! And of course it was hopeless to think of escape. Other prisoners had tried without success, and windows were broken where they'd tried to wrench out the bars. And the door: it was wood, locked on the outside with a padlock, opening inward. It was a very springy door though: I could squeeze my fingertips between sill and door, one hand at the top and the other a foot below. That gave me hope, blessed hope, for the first time. My six-foot-three body was suspended in air by my hands, doubled up like a coiled spring, and I pulled. Lord, how I pulled! The door bent inward until I could see a couple of daylight inches between door and sill. Then, Snap! and screws pulled out of the steel hasp outside. I fell flat on my back.

Peering cautiously outside, right and left, I jumped to the ground, walking as slowly and sedately as I could make myself—toward freedom. The urge to run was hard to resist, especially when crossing a bridge over a wide river along the tracks, and continuing steadily in the direction of Sault Ste. Marie, 165 miles south of the railway divisional point. But that cop would be looking for me, and so would other blue uniforms! Two years! Walking the tracks would make me far too obvious, much too easy to find. So how about making the journey twenty or thirty feet into the heavy forest lining both sides of the right of way? That way I could see if anyone came after me, and duck back among the trees. Brilliant, positively brilliant.

But the trees went uphill and down, turned leftways and right-ways, without landmarks or anything to orient me with the tracks. I began to feel uneasy: better stay close to the railway. Too late. I was deep into the woods, not knowing in which direction to turn. I was lost—and didn't even feel stupid, just terrified. My heart began to pump hard, and I ran, with branches and leaves slapping my face, blundering into trees, splashing through little streams.

Finally I stopped, knowing panic was useless but feeling it anyway. The possibility of dangerous animals occurred to me: what about bears?—bears must live in these woods. I had no defence against them; the railway cop had confiscated my hunting knife. Besides, what good would such a feeble weapon be against an angry black bear? And the brown shape that flitted between the trees, not so much seen as realized, what was that?

I slept on the side of a hill, huddled around a mother-tree, and it was cold, cold. Morning was grey with a light rain falling, more mist than rain. By this time I'd thought of the sun as some kind of directional reference, but there was no sun. And just a couple of miles away I could hear engines shunting and butting back and forth in the railway yard, the sound seeming to come from all directions among the trees. Old logging trails meandered through the forest, but they were so old that when I tried to follow them they vanished in the vague greyness. Once I stumbled on an old hunting camp, so ancient that the lean-to logs were rotten. Later in the day, during my stumbling, lurching progress, I came on that hunting camp twice more, each time increasingly terrified about walking in circles.

At age seventeen I didn't believe in God, at least I told myself I didn't. But this was no time to take chances one way or the other. I prayed. Fervently, passionately, and with no reservations, I prayed to get out of that forest. And remembered the forty-some Sundays I'd attended church two years before, without listening to the preacher's sermon but in order to receive a prize for attendance. Since then I'd become a non-believer in that fire-and-brimstone God, but now for reasons of expediency I pretended to myself and to a possible Him that my backsliding was over—at least for as long as I was lost in this northern forest.

And maybe it worked: I still don't know. That railway bridge I'd crossed when leaving Hawk Junction popped into my head. Adolescent high school logic took over. The river and railway tracks would make two sides of a very large isosceles triangle. And carry it a step further: if I could finally walk in something close to a straight line, which hadn't happened thus far, then I must finally locate either river or tracks. And the sun, now becoming a pale spot in the overhead grey, gave me some small direction. I walked and walked, and two hours later nearly fell head-first down an embankment into that blessed blessed river.

That same evening I boarded a passenger train just behind the engine, and rode south to the Soo in style, careless of legal consequences. But no cops appeared on the smoky cindered horizon of fear. At the steel town I dived into a Scandinavian steam bath to stop the shivering chill that I'd picked up from two days in the woods. And sleeping that night in a cheap flop-house, I was still shuddering a little, in slow motion.

I think my first sight of the mountains was worth all the hardships—waking early in the morning inside an empty boxcar and gazing down into a lake surrounded by forest stretching for miles and miles—cupped and cradled by the white peaks. And myself crawling round the side of a mountain like a fly on a sugar bowl. For the first time I realized how big this country was. And, naively, because I was only seventeen years old, I felt a tremendous exaltation at the sight. How marvelous to be alive and to ride a bare-backed train through such a country. And, naively, forty years later, I've not changed my mind.

Vancouver was a sprawling, dingy, beautiful giant of a waterfront city even in 1937. I walked down Water Street, over the puddles and wet grey concrete in the early morning. An old Indian woman on an iron balcony called down for me to come up and see her daughter, mentioning explicitly certain delights that could be expected. Rather prudishly, I declined. I spent the afternoon at a movie, paying fifteen cents for the privilege of watching Dorothy Lamour disport herself in a sarong. But I'm not sure if the Indian girl wouldn't have been a better bargain.

After the movie I was seized with a realization of the immense distance I had come from home. Originally I had meant to get a job fishing on a purse seiner at Vancouver, but the smelly old harbour depressed me. The Lions Gate Bridge, stretching spider-like across First Narrows, seemed alien; the streets themselves were unfriendly and peopled by strangers. I was homesick.

On the same day that I had arrived I slipped under the barrier at a level crossing and boarded a freight train moving east. And all the immense width of the continent was before me again, all the lakes and rivers and mountains—and the green country of childhood lay behind.

> Riding into the Crow's Nest mountains with
> your first beard itching and a
> hundred hungry guys fanning out thru
> the shabby whistlestops for handouts and
> not even a sandwich for two hundred miles
> only the high mountains and knowing
> what it's like to be not quite a child any
> more and listening to the tough men
> talk of women and talk of the way things are
> in 1937—

("Transient")

*(1963)*

# Lights on the Sea

IN 1937 WHEN I RODE THE FREIGHT TRAINS WEST, I had intended to get a job on the fishing boats in Vancouver; but homesickness forced me to hop on an eastbound train on the very day of my arrival in Vancouver—without ever having tried to get a job on a fishing boat. I was seventeen.

Thirty-seven years later I rode a seiner fish packer west from Vancouver harbour at midnight. Enjoying myself thoroughly, standing with feet wide apart on the gently heaving steel deck, deciding that even if I'd written the script I couldn't have made things more dramatic: Vancouver lights all pointing toward the ship and myself, neon arrows on the black water; the packer, *Pacific Ocean*, a momentary centre of the universe. Red and white lights all around, Stanley Park a dark animal crouched low in water. Slipping under the Lions Gate Bridge, with soundless cars passing 200 feet over our heads and a white moon some 200,000 miles farther up. Ernie, the cook, is at the rail playing his harmonica—the Toreador song from *Carmen*, I think.

In the wheel-house Skipper Herb Shannon, a veteran of fifty years at sea, steers the packer toward Juan de Fuca Strait. (In the last century Herb's father sailed wind ships across the Pacific.) Herb Shannon, a little man in baggy khaki pants, reminds me of a retired railway engineer (nobody ever looks like what they are); he talks about fishing while the boat rolls queasily and I wonder about that last dish of blueberries at dinner.

"Well," I say, because I can't think of anything else, "how does your wife like you being late for almost all your meals?"

"She knew what I was doin' before I married her," he says. And behind us the blaze of lights is growing dim.

On a packer, two hours out from Vancouver, the transmitted motion of the sea is not the same rocking-chair dream it is at the Fraser's mouth. Dub, the engineer and half-owner of the boat, says, "You look kinda green." I hold onto cables at port or starboard, trying to keep my eyes on some fixed object, according to previous advice. There is no getting away from it, I am not a well man. Water slops over the rail with each sickening heave. At this point I lose a plate of blueberries right off the top of my stomach. I have not been so sick in all my damn life. Ernie plays the harmonica unfeelingly. I am dying.

At 3:30 a.m. we strike a floating field of logs in Active Pass, thirty miles or so south-west of Victoria. Motors stop, we drift among the logs on the sea's momentum alone, bumping gently toward clear water. Herb Shannon, in the wheel-house, guiding us to safety. Sunk in near-death unconsciousness in my quarter, I do not even lift my head from the bunk after we strike. Next day in the galley:

"Fine sailor you are," Dub says.

And Herb Shannon, sipping hot coffee: "You'll get used to it."

I'd better.

The area around here, north of Cape Flattery and along the southwest coast of Vancouver Island, is "the graveyard of the Pacific," thus named for good and sufficient reasons. The Japanese Current drives north along the American coast; eastbound ships get careless and don't watch their radar sometimes. Only eighteen months ago a Japanese ship with a cargo of Dodge Colt automobiles wrecked on the southwest coast of Vancouver Island, a few miles north. It's still here, stranded among rocks like great stone teeth.

"Of course, those Colt curb-jumpers disappeared damn quick," Herb Shannon says. "Miraculous the way things disappear off a wrecked ship. Barges pulled alongside and the cars got winched off . . ."

At Port Renfrew, a fine deep-sea harbour on Vancouver Island's west coast, seiners and gill-netters march toward us though the early morning mist— *Sun Burst, Sherry Joan, Sea Fair, Silver Luck, Joyce R., and Georgia Saga.* Most of them come directly from the "surf-line" boundaries, established by a 1957 unwritten agreement between the United States and Canada that no salmon fishing with nets will be allowed beyond the surf-line. The agreement covers the coasts of

California, Oregon, Washington, Alaska, and British Columbia. Its purpose is to conserve the salmon stock for each country, although the Canadian fishermen say that the United States almost invariably takes the eagle's share of salmon bound for spawning grounds on BC rivers. One reason for the disproportionately larger American catch is that, after the agreement was made, Alaska decided its fishing area would extend three miles seaward from the surf-line that had been established for the other coastal states and British Columbia. One might call this an international doublecross, but Canadian fisheries officials are rarely that impolite.

Now, this situation makes a lot of BC fishermen pretty resentful. One hears talk of blockading the Fraser's mouth with nets and simply cleaning it out of fish. But that is obviously self-defeating, for fifteen to twenty percent of the salmon must reach their home waters in the Fraser and its tributaries to spawn. If they were blockaded, the rich ocean harvest of the great river would vanish entirely. The only rational answer is further arbitration and agreement through the International Pacific Salmon Fisheries Commission.

*High Rose, Brilon,* and *Miss Jennie* swing bow and stern expertly alongside the *Pacific Ocean,* skippers joshing good-naturedly with the packer's crew. "Who's the city man?" Joe LePore wants to know, meaning me, of course.

LePore says he hates fishing, wants to quit. "Too many boats working here; you can't catch enough fish. But with a family, how can I quit?"

Rosemary Wilson, a fisherman's widow with no children, is alone on the gill-netter. "Why?" I ask her. She chuckles deep inside her windbreaker.

"There's more fish at sea than men ashore." Which is fair enough, but near the season's end there aren't enough fish, either.

The Pacific Ocean leaves Port Renfrew on a fish-pick-up trip to Sooke, some forty miles south. We move directly into the northward-driving Japanese Current, with a sneaky twisting slop striking us from the west, as well. Hastily I swallow seasickness pills, with a despairing look at Herb Shannon. Too late. Already my whole body feels like Lazarus seven days dead, arms and legs almost useless, brain active but hardly helpful. And watching a fixed object on the horizon doesn't work at all. I take to my bunk, holding onto the high varnished sides desperately, afraid that I might survive.

I try to think of something else besides my sick sick self. Albert Radil, for instance. I met him on the BC Packers' dock at Steveston. He's one of the fishermen's aristocracy. By contrast to Radil, gill-netters and seiners probably averaged $5,000 to $6,000 a year in 1971; whereas Radil's boat, the *Royal Canadian*, cost half a million to build, and his catch is correspondingly valuable. He isn't wealthy, in the same overwhelming sense as are people like E.P. Taylor and the Bronfmans: but his wealth takes the form of achievement—being a high-liner and among the top fishermen every year, being the man who comes to mind immediately when one thinks of the best.

Albert Radil is a nondescript, red-faced, middle-aged man in a faded checked shirt and work trousers. He's mild-mannered and far-distant from the image of Jack London's savage tyrant skippers. Unloading a ten-day record of ground fish—turbot, cod, sole, and ocean perch, caught by dragging long nylon nets over the sea bottom—Albert and his five-man crew have dumped 387,000 pounds of rainbow cargo into the black hold of the 105-foot *Royal Canadian*. Of course, ground fish fetch only five cents a pound, except for sole, which are ten cents. But the total value of that catch comes to around twenty thousand dollars.

What I want to know from Albert is exactly why he is such a good fisherman. He says it's because of all the ship's electronic equipment—sonar, echo sounds, net monitors, Loran radio, as well as the nearly standard radar; also, the ability to use them to advantage. Which isn't what I mean. Other draggers besides the *Royal Canadian* have the same slick devices, uncanny robot marvels that map the ocean bottom, actually outlining schools of fish—and even single lone-wolf fish—on paper in the wheel-house.

I think Albert is slightly bewildered by the fact that I prefer any other explanation besides the wealth of equipment and his own long experience. He knows he's a high-liner, is modest about it, and long years at the job enable him to fish where the fish are, and to use all the technological gimmicks as if they were familiar and trusted extensions of his own mind. But I am trying to make something intangible become visible—maybe some ability that he isn't aware of himself.

John Radil, Albert's eighty-year-old father, born in Yugoslavia, speech thickened by old age and remote traces of the sea-fringed Balkans, accompanies us around the boat. Albert says, "His life, you know. He's been a fisherman since he was a small boy, can't stay away even now." I look at the old man with respect, but can't understand his geriatric language.

Behind us, the crew is unloading tons and tons of varicoloured fish, winches humming, scrape and curse of metal on metal, buzz of words: and I'm still intrigued by Albert, the unassuming but confident man-of-the-sea, with a golden touch, with the admiration of everyone I talk to about him . . .

"All right then," I say, still trying to find the secret of expertise, "how do you know where to go to find those fish in the first place?"

Is there pity for my obtuseness in Albert's eyes? "We follow the edge of the banks," he says. "That's where the fish find their food." He means those undersea plateaus that are the rich feeding grounds of all west coast fish. And he shows me their location on the wheel-house charts, depths noted, rocks that might destroy nets marked, everything seemingly organized by an electronic file clerk in the computer of the human mind.

My own mind can see him there, dragging the seas south of the Queen Charlottes with his immense net, wind blowing and the water choppy, greenish light from the wheel-house radar deepening the lines in his face, waterproof brain thrusting below the surface to follow contours of deep-down feeding grounds, answering light in his eyes flashing acknowledgement of the machines' flow of information, all the various streams of experience and intuition coming together in a nearly magical kind of awareness.

"Knowledge and experience," Albert says again. Then he introduces me to Bob Giljiuch, who once walked on the backs of fish at the fifteen-foot-wide net mouth while it was being reeled inboard.

"Walked on the water?" I want to know, having some weird vision of Christ on Galilee, I suppose. Giljuich, a raw-boned youngster with projecting extremities, says no.

"There was so many fish in the net it was like they was solid, like on the ground almost."

Bob Giljuich goes back to work unloading fish. And I see that these pragmatic men are not going to give me any kind of mystical explanation. The radar, which Albert has switched on for my benefit, sweeps its circular light around under glass, outlining Vancouver Island, miles away across the Gulf of Georgia. He nods at me. That is how it is done. All right.

Once the *Pacific Ocean* is back at Port Renfrew the seasickness is gone, leaving me with the conviction that I'm a confirmed landsman. In mid-afternoon a Cessna 180 lands a few hundred yards from the *Pacific Ocean*. It's taking me to Tofino, along the west coast of British Columbia. Pilot: Bobby Wingham, manager of Canfisco at Tofino. And there's nothing to make the flesh feel so vulnerable as these flying baby carriages, powered by twisted rubber bands. Farther north along the coast we spot that wrecked Japanese freighter, now shorn of its automotive cargo, creamy waves lapping its sides. The pilot glances at me sideways, perhaps meaning to be reassuring. I hold onto the handle dingus installed for nervous passengers. Am I nervous, am I reassured? Yes. And no.

Tofino is a fishing village with one main street, two groceries, and a hotel. Its location might be described as west of nowhere: but nowhere has miles and miles of white sand beaches, sounding whales off the blue lace-fringed sea's edge if you're lucky enough to see them, and maybe 300 trollers growing like a watery forest from the harbour. Trollers because the surf-line agreement prohibits net fishing for salmon. And a scarcely touched primeval paradise all around the village.

But Tofino for me is mostly Gil Sadler. He's a troller, age thirty-three, ex-carpenter, married with kids and owns his own house—kind of a gee-whiz, gosh-all-fish-hooks sort of guy. I mean the fortunate kind who strikes you as partly a kid still, even though physically a man. Five years ago Sadler decided to be a fisherman, despite the more than 6,000 licensed fishing boats operating in British Columbia. He did some soul-searching about it with his wife, bought an elderly thirty-six-foot troller, and renovated her, calling her the *Promisewell* since fishing seemed to promise a better life for his family.

But here was the rub: Sadler had never fished before in his life, except with hook and worms off the dock. Then what about Joe McLeod, the brash, confident record-setter and pacemaker for all the local fishermen? No doubt the fish were actually afraid not to bite his hooks, or else McLeod might speak to God about it. Gil Sadler knew McLeod slightly, and was sure of help from him. And he got it, too, but not exactly as expected. He described himself sailing the *Promisewell*, to McLeod, following the edge of a shoal feeding ground where salmon ought to be, should be, must be feeding, and using a particular kind of bait. McLeod would grunt enigmatically and say of that, "Should be a different colour!" To which Sadler would respond eagerly, face lighting up at a word from the master, "What kind of bait do you think is best, Mr. McLeod?"

But McLeod never gave him a direct answer, letting the younger man figure it out for himself, dropping tantalizing hints on where and how and when things should be done. The old master fisherman, kindly but not too kindly, wise but not relinquishing his hard-won wisdom too easily so that someone who hadn't earned it over the hard experience of years could pick it up and profit by it. But kindly, nevertheless. How could one not respond to such open admiration for himself in the fresh-faced young fisherman?

Gil rode the elderly *Promisewell* into the open Pacific, fishing with spoons and butterflies sometimes, the colour of the lures changed to match changing colour of the water. High winds blowing, hurricanes lifting knouts of swirling water in columns out of the frantic, whip-lashed sea. And running—sometimes running like a scared fool—in hundred-mile-an-hour winds for the safety of a little opening in the rocky shore, a cove like the biblical house of refuge. And twelve-foot sheets of water ripped from the sea's face, rigging literally torn off the boat like clothes from a scarecrow, leaving only the stripped-down hull.

Once in a fog in a dream, a 300-foot Russian trawler loomed over the *Promisewell*, and the little boat quivered with fear. The trawler's whistle blew deafeningly, continuously. But which way was the damn thing going? Is that the bow I'm looking at or the stern? What shall I do, what would Joe McLeod have done? Then, what use my eight measly trolling lines against this giant floating claw that snatches whole schools and tribes of fish from the sea? Only the comparatively high price for fish caught with hook and line—ranging at that time from $1.40 to $2.15 a pound for coho and spring salmon—made it worthwhile; and the desperate drive toward excellence, as well, excellence embodied in Joe McLeod.

Listen to other fishermen on the radio: voices talking without bodies on the solitary sun-blinded sea. Now the Loran radio signal whispers; match that with a corresponding number on the chart where shoals and fish are waiting! How long will the fish wait? You're there, all eight lines out, trolling the bank: rush back into the wheel-house to check the Loran, check the echo sounder for fish, glance at the depth-finder and all those little flashing lights and sounds connected with electrodes fixed in a human brain.

And salmon, their long gleaming silver bodies flopping out of the sea, coho transformed into dollar bills and groceries; spring salmon become a new room built onto the house, mortgage paid off, desperate anxiety about being a loser changed to the elation of a winner. Then laughter? Amusement at one's self, the half-phony laughter soon silent when salmon disappear, fading to nothing but the blood's whisper and murmur of your own breathing, defeated sound of feet scuffing a worn deck slippery with fish scales.

But riding home to Tofino in the elderly *Promisewell* with 1,700 salmon—stern awash, deck awash, bow juddering and trembling from the engine's feeble efforts, the whole worn-out Rube Goldberg contraption not quite sinking—veteran fishermen mutter, "Throw some o' them fish back, boy, or you'll never make it to hum, boy!"

Under your breath: "Well, old boys, I'm making it, somehow, home!" After which a new record is weighed and counted for one year's fishing out of Tofino, the cash value: $18,500.

And weaving a little with good tiredness up the town's main drag, clothes covered with blood and fish slime, covered with dirty glorious triumph. And the woman seeing you at the house door, knowing it all from the look on your face, how the uncertainty ends in you as it ends in her.

And Joe McLeod? But, of course, McLeod will be pleased, happy you've learned what you had to learn, and the dollar bills stacked in one corner of his mind will move aside, allowing generosity and friendship to take over.

Lights at the Co-op Grocery come on, people inside moving toward the cashier's counter. Sun dimming beyond green pop-up hills and clustered familiar islands. Home is a warm blanket all around, an order of priorities for everything known and established, friends waiting to say "Well done!" and shake your hand. It's almost too much, or nearly too little, like a picture on the living room wall that says, smugly, "God Bless Our Home" and has to be straightened after the kids knock it sideways playing inside on a rainy day. Sadler laughs softly, walking toward Joe McLeod's house in Tofino. A woman with a brown bag of groceries cradled in one arm looks at him, thoughts elsewhere from her eyes, and moves on toward her different destinations.

The stone backside of Canada is not the mainland Coast Range, but the savage bare peaks of Vancouver Island, surrounded by forests nearly as inaccessible as another planet. Riding a different Cessna 180 we swing over them, east-bound for a fish cannery at Namu, about 180 miles south of Prince Rupert. Again this feeling of being stranded in mid-air, hanging onto a wriggling piece of two-by-four. Below us the lumbering town of Gold River belches anal dregs into the sky. I think of ex-Premier Bennett's comforting words: "I like the smell of pollution, it's the smell of progress!" In which case we have a lot of progress here. Whole mountains stripped of timber in a wilderness so vast it seems that the last green tree could never be destroyed. But we're trying.

We lift over the BC Inland Passage to Alaska, uninhabited green islands "more like a kingdom than a province"—high half-frozen lakes feeding their overflow to other lakes farther down the mountains, then still other lakes in shimmering necklaces strung together on top of the world. And fishing boats far below are water-beetles, their mile-long wakes reduced to seeming inches. Then Namu, a four-million-dollar cannery with its machinery silent and only the refrigeration plant in operation.

It's country so beautiful that nobody deserves to die without having seen it. Bald eagles fly over the bunkhouses; salmon throng in the harbour, unable to ascend the low-water river until the next rainfall. Raised boardwalks wind through the trees, connecting bunkhouses, cannery, refrigeration plant, and deserted Japanese village nestled at the edge of the rain forest. A BC Packers' company town in 1971, it employs only about eighty people instead of the 500 it carried in its heyday years ago.

Fishermen—gill-netters and seiners by scores—swarm around the floating docks—Indian, Japanese, and various breeds of Europeans now become Canadian. All have a non-urgent air about them, no hurry to do anything, for the best fishing is over. But Indian kids make long casts with bare hooks into the harbour, and snag a fat coho when their luck runs good. Carlo Politano lounges on his boat, dark, heavy-set, big nose dominating his features. Carlo is sixty-three now, and thirty-six years a fisherman. He started years ago because of owing $360, and paid that debt in his second year. It's a lonely job now, for all his friends are gone.

"In the old days you'd see a boat chimney smoking, and three or four guys would row over for coffee or rum or breakfast." A sadness shades his thickening face. "I can't take the rough weather any more."

On a float nearby, two Indian girls work skilfully to repair nets: Ena and Lorna, who make $3.60 an hour.

"Good girls," Carlo says. "They're invited to white people's houses."

Les Brown is sixtyish, brown from sun and sea, shop steward at the refrigeration plant. "Workers at Namu average about three dollars an hour and pay sixty dollars a week for room and board at the bunkhouse," he tells me. Brown worked at a whaling station owned by BC Packers on Vancouver Island in the early fifties, introduced a union there, and lost his job. Now, ironically, he works for the same company at Namu.

Alonzo McGarvie, gill-netter and dangerous-tempered ex-fighter, was said to have knocked five men cold when they attacked him one memorable night for allegedly stealing their fish. I saw him as we left Namu, weaving along the dock and swinging a case of beer, with a bottle of whisky sticking out of his pocket.

We're riding the supply boat, Canadian Number One, north from Namu to Bella Bella and Klemtu before we head back to Vancouver. George Radil, son of Albert, the son of John, is wearing carpet slippers and steering expertly with his feet. On the starboard side of the boat a humpback whale blows and dives. When we reach Bella Bella a dozen Indian youngsters swarm over the boat. If the crew hadn't shooed them away, they might have sailed away to the South Sea island.

Back in Vancouver, Barry McMillin, brisk young manager of J.S. McMillin Fisheries, says that his small company (six million dollars gross sales a year—is that small?) is more efficient and has less overhead than the bigger ones. "Besides, we don't have the ill will that those big companies sometimes generate." McMillin owns three boats and contracts six more. He estimates that the four-man crew of a dragger can make up to $30,000 per person per season. And adds, "Give us an even break, and we'll beat the big boys every time."

John Wolff is a halibut long-liner out of Vancouver, seventy years old and looking about fifty-five, black hair only slightly sprinkled with grey. He has fished all his life and doesn't expect to spend the rest of it any differently. His halibut long-liner operates north of Banks Island in Hecate Strait, the halibut feeding grounds. (A long-liner is a 300-fathom-long cable to which are fastened short lines for bottom fishing.) Wolff talks about a time when a pod of 150 killer whales was on both sides and behind the long-liner.

"When whales blow they smell awful bad, and it was like being in the middle of a big garbage dump. Most of them had their mouths open. You could see their teeth. I was never so scared before or since."

Wolff thinks that Canada should have a fifty-mile continental limit, the same as Iceland. "Most fishermen I know feel the same. Just look at it this way," he says seriously. "Take the salmon and halibut; they're on their way to BC coastal rivers to spawn when we catch them, so in a manner of speaking we paid their board and lodging. It isn't right that other countries like Japan, Russia and the United States should catch those fish."

At the Campbell Street wharf I meet Vance Fletcher, bearded tuna fisherman, long dark hair, age thirty. A slim, athletic animal in his movements, bubbling excitement held just under the surface of his talk. Fletcher operates a fifty-foot long-liner with a three-man crew, who've just returned after ten days out with a catch of more than $7,000 worth of tuna. But listening to him, all is not beer and skittles (or fish and chips?) in the fishing industry.

Cape Chacon, he explains, is a southern point in Alaska, three miles from the Canadian Nunez Rock. "Now, the International Boundary should run right in the middle of those two points, and it does. It does. And yet the Alaska Fisheries people claim a three-mile limit from Cape Chacon, which takes in the Canadian Nunez Rock. What it means is that our fishing boats are chased by American patrols in Canadian territorial waters." Fletcher's eyes flash a little. "Of course, we don't stop, but someone could get killed out there if the Americans get trigger-happy—as they are sometimes."

Fletcher lives and eats fishing; on this last trip he took a hundred tuna in forty-five minutes. And that's $600. "In the last few years I've been tryin' to get outa debt; before that I blew more than $150,000. What for? Well, maybe I wanted to regain the life I missed as a kid because of fishing." He says that a fisherman works on instincts and reflexes, and those make the difference between a good man and a loser. The *Island Queen*, his present boat, is six years old. The one before that went down in a storm in Hecate Strait. He says of himself, "They say I'm a legend in my own time." I wonder if he knows how he sounds.

From Norman Safarik on Fisherman's Wharf I hear of Anton Kowalski for the first time: an ex-soldier from the Polish Army, a loner and a wild, unpredictable oddball. Kowalski operated a seventy-foot, one-man dragger ten years ago, always with a girl or two for company, and generally with a bottle whose contents he sampled freely. When the federal fisheries people were in the process of seizing his boat for illegal halibut fishing, he revved the motors to full speed in reverse, broke his mooring lines and escaped into Vancouver harbour. Once in open water he threw all the halibut overboard by hand, thus providing no evidence of poaching—even though the uniformed officials watched the whole procedure with open mouths on shore.

Safarik, a fishing company owner, tells of Kowalski's boat going down in a storm twenty-five miles from Prince Rupert. "But he managed to get ashore with his girl in a skiff he'd borrowed from me. There were no oars; he'd forgotten to take them. The crazy bastard had to carve oars from driftwood and row all the way to Rupert in early winter." Safarik shakes his head in amazement. "After that he disappeared for a long time. Everyone thought he was dead. Then I got a phone call, and a kinda ghostly voice says he's Anton. 'But you're dead,' I tell him. 'Maybe so,' he says, 'but I got 20,000 pounds of rock sole to sell you before they bury me.'"

After screwballs like Kowalski it's no surprise to hear about another one, for British Columbia has more of these than any other province. The name Alvo von Alvensleben still evokes amazement, even if I can't pronounce it. A young immigrant, scion of German nobility, he came to British Columbia in 1904, married an Okana-gan-peaches and Fraser-Valley-cream girl, and got involved in the fishing industry. In 1910 von Alvensleben built a cannery called "Pacofi" on Selwyn Inlet off Hecate Strait, using foreign money for its construction. Nothing unusual about that.

When World War I broke out, von Alvensleben disappeared for parts unknown with his Canadian wife. "Pacofi," the cannery he left behind, went through several different owners, eventually winding up as the property of BC Packers in 1938. Its machinery being long out of date, the plant was torn down. Below the building were found mysterious and elaborate concrete installations, whose purpose puzzled the wreckers so much that measurements and pictures were taken. These were submitted to experts in structural design, who revealed that a submarine base had existed under the cannery for twenty-eight years, right to the brink of the Second World War.

In the character of the fishermen I've met there is some quality I keep trying to define. Not something that will make a man stand out in a crowd, but more like a composite of Vance Fletcher's arrogant inde-pendence, the sturdy, undeviating lifestyle of John Wolff, and a wrapped-around loneliness that comes from driving their boats along the intricate, indented coastline of British Columbia in summer and winter, storm and calm.

Through these coastal wanderings, I've somehow caught up with some of my own life that should have been lived before. On my final trip, aboard a Canadian Fishing Company power launch, early-morning gill-netters at the Fraser River's mouth lower their 200-fath-oms-long nylon nets like undersea fences into the grey-green water. These are manned by drowsy, half-awake men, and one by a woman. There's Roy Morimoto, born in Japan in 1920, come to Canada as a child, and moved east during the war with Japan, away from the vulnerable-to-sabotage Pacific coast; and George Woods, hauling his net aboard with the hydraulic gurdie to remove—eleven crabs, one empty milk carton, and two salmon. "The way to make a living, boy," George says.

The floating town of gill-netters lifts lazily on the tide; we rock into daylight sleep. Just as I'm leaving, Roy Morimoto gives me a big silvery sockeye: and he caught only four all last night! The life I should have lived before has been lived for the first time—among people that I seem to have known for all my lives.

*(1974)*

# Cougar Hunter

**R**ODERICK HAIG-BROWN WAS A PROFESSIONAL bounty hunter for cougars on northern Vancouver Island at age twenty-two, in the early 1930s. He told me about Cougar Smith, then the official predator hunter, when the price paid for a dead cougar was forty or fifty dollars. Smith was about fifty-eight, lean and spare as a lodgepole pine, generally with a roll-your-own smoke hanging from his lower lip. Dogs are always used to trail cougars, but sometimes, over logging slash on dry ground—such as on this occasion—the dogs are baffled and show no interest. So there's Cougar Smith following the trail himself, specs sagging low on his nose so he can peer over them, picking one cougar hair from a log, noticing faint paw prints on dusty ground, moving from one sign to another with a kind of informed intuition. And it's quite likely that there's a 200-pound cougar holed up for the day in heavy timber beyond the logged area, waiting for the prowling night.

There's something attractive and yet uncanny about this woods runner and tracker, Cougar Smith. It brings to mind Dan'l Boone, also the fictional detective in *Les Misérables,* trailing his criminal through the sewers of Paris. Ridiculous, of course. But Cougar Smith's reputation had preceded him when he visited the Nimpkish River country to hunt with Haig-Brown. The young man, only a few years out from England, and the old bounty hunter roamed the woods companionably together, chasing the big cats.

Cougars, sometimes called "mountain lions," may reach nine feet in length. They can weigh up to 250 pounds. Their ordinary prey is the mountain deer population. But sometimes they become outlaws when old or crippled, and they kill sheep and cattle. The procedure then is for the farmer to get in touch with a professional hunter, who arrives on the scene with dogs. They bark and yap on the trail, generally treeing the cougar. And shortly thereafter the hunter arrives with his rifle. But cougars, grown old and wise, have been known to double back and forth across a river to confuse pursuers, refusing to be treed, occasionally turning on tormenting dogs to kill them with one swipe of a powerful paw. They kill deer in much the same way, leaping on the terrified animal's back, reaching around with one paw under its nose, and wrenching backward and up to break the gentle creature's neck.

And yet they are valuable and beautiful and fascinating to watch. I've seen and admired them in zoos, and once one of them passed me in the night, rousing all the town's dogs and cats in Fernie, BC. Cougars keep the bush ecology in balance, eliminating older or crippled deer. Inquisitive animals, they sometimes follow people through the woods like a tame tabby, without anyone knowing they've been followed. Cougars are polygamous, with no fixed mating season. Males run, play, and mate with one female for several days, then hunt alone and look for another female later in their wild roaming among the mountains of northern Vancouver Island. It's a free life, a hedonistic and carefree existence that very few humans have been able to live, without the guilt and culture-pressure of being "useful to society."

Haig-Brown hasn't killed them for years, won't kill any other animal, either. There comes a time in some men's lives when killing anything is distasteful and ugly, when you take pleasure in life rather than death. As novelist and nature-writer (specializing in fishing), judge and magistrate at Campbell River, and perhaps a kind of wilderness father-figure now at age sixty-seven, that non-killing time has arrived. A medium-sized, brown-faced, balding man, he's quiet with the quietness of natural things that aren't noisy for the sake of making noise—as one must be to hear woodsmoke messages, the whisper of trees, water, and sky. He's so respected by other people that I felt incredulous when talking to them, and said to Haig-Brown himself when I met him, "You ought to have a halo, an angel's halo quivering over your head."

The catalogue of Haig-Brown's achievements runs on like a roll-call of honours. He's written some twenty-five books, all but one still in print, and considers himself a writer above all else, although he hasn't written a book in ten years because of his duties as a judge in Campbell River. He feels a little guilty about that, because "a writer's business is to write. It is a defeat not to be writing." (One of the low spots in his life was when half a dozen publishers turned down a synopsis and several chapters of his fourth book, refusing to give him the $500-advance he needed desperately at the time.)

He is a literary fisherman with wide knowledge of both fish and fishing. But more important, Haig-Brown has a deep emotional involvement in all the things he writes about. He has lived and is still living a life nearly fused with nature. He's a member of the International Pacific Salmon Commission, which involves being a kind of ecology detective: "Our first objective, preservation of Pacific salmon." Among other things, " . . . we count fish—out at sea, in the catch landings (commercial fishing), on the way through the straits (Juan de Fuca and others), off the mouths of the rivers (Fraser, Adams, and Columbia), on their way up the river, on the spawning grounds—and all the way back again as the young migrate outwards. At the Adams River we stand on the bank and gloat, behaving politely to our 100,000 guests."

As a youngster in England Haig-Brown was fascinated by and in love with nature. His grandfather gave him an early affection for the woods and for the wide variety of English trees. The old man in his mid-seventies knew when particular forest stands were planted, who planted them, and why. Haig-Brown and his brothers were required to go along on extended trips through the forest, while their autocratic ancestor imparted the lore of natural things. The kids were expected to listen, respectfully attentive. Haig-Brown remembers that he learned without knowing that he did at the time.

When he was eighteen years old, Haig-Brown wanted to join the Colonial Civil Service, but was too young. Impatient to be older, he came to the United States, Washington State, in 1926, and worked at logging camps near Mount Vernon. He worked as scaler and rigger (a rigger is the guy who climbs trees and clips off their tops)—among all the other jobs like choker and chaser and faller, levermen and whistle punks. (Logging jargon clogs into unintelligible lumps in your ears, except for the whistle punk, who is a boy "who relays the hooktender's shouted signals by electric whistle to the donkey." Now do you know?)

Haig-Brown must have been some physically exuberant, gung-ho, cock-a-doodle-doo kid in those days! A rather small middleweight boxer, he fought semi-pro in smokers at Sedro Woolley: you got twenty-five dollars if you won and nothing but a beating if you lost. In those days he could walk all day and climb mountains all night. He fished and hunted the lakes and forests of Washington State—and chased girls. He wrote articles for sporting magazines in England and the United States. And since he had entered the land of the free as a student and wanted to get back in legally, he went to Vancouver Island to work before returning to the States. And thought about writing his first novel. And returned to England.

Living in a rented room in London, England in 1931, he did write that first novel. It was/is *Silver*, the story of an Atlantic salmon. He also worked in London film studios as a "wilderness expert" and "chased girls from hell to breakfast." The book was written in longhand in ruled scribblers. And here enters the villain (or hero) that changed his life: name of *Oplopanax horridus*, the botanical term for "devil's club," a BC thorny plant cursed by early travellers and explorers in that province. While writing *Silver*, the spines of *Oplopanax horridus* festered in his arms and shoulders, popping out on the table in front of him. The discomfort in Haig-Brown's body made him homesick for Canada. He went back home to British Columbia.

In Vancouver Haig-Brown was locked up briefly at the old immigration building on Burrard Street until he could convince authorities that he wasn't a twenty-three-year-old tenderfoot Englishman who couldn't find his way in the woods from one tree to the next pub. After release, he guided tourists in the Nimpkish River area on Vancouver Island, where he had worked previously. He built his own lodge there, too, and had a registered trapline. In 1932 more logging, beachcombing, bounty hunting for cougars, sport fishing, and above all writing. He was working on his next book at that time, *Pool and Rapid*.

Once he and his friends, Ed and Buster Lansdowne, heard of a freighter holed by rocks and sunk in forty feet of water off the coast of northern Vancouver Island. The three friends thought it a good chance to make some money. They bought salvage rights to the *Chackawana* from an insurance company, and devised a plan to raise the sunken ship. It was more than fifty feet long, a huge dead weight, puzzling in its salvage problems. The method finally used was pretty simple: Haig-Brown and the Lansdownes cut four huge cedar trees, hitched a steel cable under the bow of the sunken ship, and secured the other end to the logs. They repeated this procedure at the *Chackawana*'s stern—all at low tide. When moon-magic raised the tidal water and cedar logs, it also lifted the sunken freighter, whereupon the logs were shoved and towed shorewards until the *Chackawana* came to rest in shallower water.

At low tide the process was repeated, then repeated again, until finally the wrecked hulk was salvageable—a triumph of ingenuity for the three friends. Also a hard job in winter weather with high winds and the logs ice-coated, ice that sometimes caused the cables to slip and patience to explode in cuss-words. Haig-Brown lived those three or four winter weeks so intensely that he remembers them well long afterwards.

Once, on the fishing boat *Kathleen* with Buster Lansdowne, they ran it into breakers in bad weather. Haig-Brown went overboard at the stern to help push the boat off, levering with the tow-post. The *Kathleen* came free suddenly and unexpectedly, leaving him hanging precariously onto the stern tow-post. Buster didn't know he was there; he assumed that Haig-Brown had enough sense to stay on the beach, safe from churning propellor blades. It was only because Buster then took the very sound precaution of walking to the stern to see if he could holler to Haig-Brown on the beach that he found him and pulled him aboard. Otherwise Roderick Haig-Brown would have been in some small danger of never writing those two dozen books.

The roving woods life began to fade away in 1934. Haig-Brown married Ann Elmore of Seattle; they bought a small farm near Campbell River and settled in to raise a family. Eventually there were four children. In 1941, at age thirty, Haig-Brown became a magistrate: "I was the only guy with time and education for the job." Hearing his first case, which involved possession of an unregistered revolver—and hearing it on the day he was sworn in—for fifteen minutes his body seized up with something like terror. "My hands shook, my eyes blurred, and my mind struggled with the spoken words as though they were a flood that would drown me."

Normally he gives the impression of a brown, quiet man, in such complete charge of himself and his own reactions that nothing flusters him: his coolness would chill beer. So it pleases me that Haig-Brown was so absolutely human on this legal occasion, and felt responsibility so strongly that he went rigid.

I kept trying to get inside this cocky kid in the woods, wearing logger's raintest with waxed knees and shoulders, chasing cougars; a small man fighting in smoky arenas and dramatically knocking out huge loggers and professional boxers. The guy who could walk all day in the bush and climb mountains all night, could haul out a 200-pound deer on his back ("I cheated and dragged it a little sometimes"), and could learn complicated things so quickly that he made the experts blush with shame. It relieves me to hear Haig-Brown say: "I get acrophobia quite easily and have to crawl in the mountains where others walked; it made me sweat to learn to climb and rig a tree and I was never easy with it."

The magistrate and judge deserves some credit for his very human wisdom: "For the most part, crime is a sad little thing, shoddy, explainable, foolish, sex-starved, or hasty, but almost never wicked." I have been all those things myself, and if I ever meet again such a heavenly judge may hope for forgiveness or at least clemency.

There is a passage in his book *Measure of the Year*, describing a 200-foot Douglas fir tree in a field near Haig-Brown's house. It is rotting to death, and has been dying for many years. "I have watched a hundred, perhaps a thousand, eagles perch in its topmost branches. I have seen it plastered with snow from ground to top . . . and watched flickers and pileated woodpeckers search its crevices for grubs." The tree is perhaps five hundred years old. It was a seedling before Shakespeare and the Wars of the Roses, before the American Revolution. It was probably born around the time Jacques Cartier slipped up the St. Lawrence River on his voyage from St. Malo to the New World. Haig-Brown speculates in his book that the tree will probably be dying still, long after his own death. But shortly after that lyrical and elegiac passage for the tree and for himself was written, the big Douglas fir blew down in a storm. "It was most embarrassing," he says, without any appearance of embarrassment.

During the early part of the Second World War Haig-Brown was turned down for service because of varicose veins. A woods runner and cougar bounty hunter with varicose veins? It doesn't seem right. But he got into the army anyway (good man!), became a captain, then a major, and as personnel officer was loaned to the RCMP. If peace hadn't come along, I'm sure he would have eventually become commanding general of the Allied Forces in Europe. He's that sort of person, he makes me think that about him just listening and watching him while he knows I'm doing it. The gung-ho kid still lives in that middle-aged body, the cougar hunter roves in his brain, the books slide out regularly in longhand, the brown face impassive, unbetraying any pride. And myself, watching, am stirred with a trace of envy. Because, despite being very human, Haig-Brown also seems just slightly Olympian. As well, there is a maverick quality about Haig-Brown, a refusal to be pigeon-holed into anything, despite all the ruts and crevices and quiet desperation we humans generally fall into.

Once, having a drink with J.H. Bloedel, the west-coast lumbering tycoon—a man who collected all sorts of valuables—Bloedel said, "I hear you're the worst trouble-maker on Vancouver Island." Which remark came as the result of Haig-Brown's outright hostility to logging companies because of their ravaging the land to a naked membrane by razoring off the tall trees for timber and toothpicks.

The awkward moment passed. Bloedel showed Haig-Brown his valuable collection of what-nots and what-ises ("They're all collectors," Rod said to me later, referring to all tycoons). Then Bloedel asked him to do some writing on behalf of his lumber company.

"I don't want to be collected," the writer told the tycoon. I like that.

Haig-Brown's study-cum-library and work room is often just a place in which he can talk with friends. Today his thirty-year-old son, Alan, is there, and Alan's Indian wife. Both now live in the Chilcotin country of north-central British Columbia. Alan's father is discussed in Haig-Brown's very presence, dad remaining discreetly silent. Alan, who has worked at commercial fishing all up and down this coast of multiple bays and inlets, said: "About half the fishermen I've met had been up in court before father. They told me it wasn't the sentences he passed that bothered them so much. It was the lectures he gave them afterwards."

"Did he lecture you, too, the same way when you were a kid?" I asked Alan.

"Well, yes, so he did," Alan said.

Haig-Brown himself, depleted scotch in hand, sits like a brown Buddha through this passage-at-arms, halo not even slightly askew.

The discussion turns to salmon, in all their several varieties, which have been an interest and passion for Rod Haig-Brown most of his life. His books on angling and fly-fishing are classics of the genre; some are collector's items that fetch high prices in antiquarian bookstores. Arnold Gingrich says about these books: "His writings are read, as Izaac Walton's are, as much in spite of as because of being about fishing." Which is to say that the man lives inside his writing, and outside.

In talking with Haig-Brown his opinions come across as positive—sort of radically conservative, in the sense of conserving what we have in this country. He believes that American encroachment in Canada will sort itself out: "Most countries tighten their laws about that sort of thing, as we are doing now. Eventually, if necessary, they take over foreign industry. We've been timid here in Canada, afraid of frightening away capital. The result is that we haven't made enough money from our own resources. I think that Premier Dave Barrett has the right idea about this. Profits from British Columbia industries flow south from Canada to Seattle and San Francisco—which isn't right."

About the charge that Canadians are provincial: "Of course they are! What does the cockney know of rural England, or the countryman of London? I'm not at all sure that provincialism is such an evil thing at that. No man becomes a great patriot without first learning the closer loyalties and learning them well: loyalty to the family, to the place he calls home, to his province or state or country." Haig-Brown has no patience with the recurring questions of identity that Canadians ask themselves: "That's a question manufactured by writers and intellectuals." A larger population for Canada? "I'm afraid so. We're going to have to take some of the Earth's excess people here. The world's future lies in an eventual abandonment of sovereignty." And this means world government? "Yes, we can't go in any other way. I'm not optimistic right now, but we have to work in that direction—especially when you see problems seemingly insoluble in human terms.

I mean Ulster, and the Arabs and Israelis. Peace will have to be imposed." A Canadian citizen most of his life, Haig-Brown has a feeling for the country that is undefensive and unapologetic. He becomes irritated at the inferiority some Canadians claim is Canada's international status, and believes such people really have a very poor opinion of themselves.

I have two outstanding mental images of Haig-Brown. One, the kid in London, writing his first book longhand in school scribblers, while devil's club thorns pop out of his arms and shoulders. You might call that a painful reminder of citizenship. The other image is of Haig-Brown watching the old tracker, Cougar Smith, pull out the makings for a roll-your-own, then follow the trail of a mountain lion across logging slash with specs low down on his nose. Haig-Brown the judge watches the bounty hunter, watching the logger watching the married man watching the fisherman and writer—like the picture inside a picture inside a picture on the cornflakes box.

One of those pictures shows Judge Haig-Brown rushing into the court room late. He's been out fishing, and hasn't had time to change from the hip-length black rubber waders fishermen wear to whatever a judge wears. The fisherman is superimposed on the man of juris-prudence: a local citizen of Campbell River with his world view not to be destroyed by mountain storms. And not to be collected.

Near the end of 1976 Roderick Haig-Brown died at Campbell River. I thought he would live for years, and that I'd be talking to him many times. He was a friend, and a friend to all the creatures of river and forest.

*(1974)*

# A Place by the Sea

I'M DRIVING THE PACIFIC RIM HIGHWAY on Vancouver Island, between Port Alberni and Tofino on the west coast. It's a mountain road, full of reverse twists and steep climbs. A heavy rain is beginning to fall. I'm doing the driving, my wife a bit tired from sleeping on a bad mattress the night before.

We pass Sproat Lake on our left, the sound of rain a steady drum on the car roof. Clouds and mist hang over and between the mountains, and you can see yellow splashes of deciduous trees among the evergreens. And places where all the trees have vanished from logging, as if earth itself had been shaved with a very sharp razor.

It's 120 kilometres from Alberni to Tofino, not very far on a good stretch of the Trans-Canada Highway—but, come to think of it, this is the far western leg of the Trans-Canada. Four or five silver necklaces decorate each mountain—temporary waterfalls created by the rain. They give me the feeling that they bind earth to an invisible sky. And I'm in danger of wrecking the car. Peering through rain at the encircling mountains, trying to think of words to describe all this. There are none. The annual rainfall in this area is four or five metres—that much water would be well over the head of the tallest basketball player.

The weather is clearing a little when we pass the turn-off to Ucluelet, stopping at Long Beach, facing the open Pacific Ocean. When I was here before, eighteen years ago, writing an article on West Coast fishing for *Maclean's* magazine, I remember seeing grey whales breaching far out in calm water. This time there's nothing but empty sea and a few gulls wheeling above rock castles along the shore. You think of beaches as long uninterrupted stretches of sand, but here the sand is interspersed with rock formations of all sizes and fantastic shapes, sculpted by weather and waves.

Tofino is a fishing and logging community of about 1,100 people on Clayoquot Sound. It has, alas, become a tourist centre, with more than half a million people visiting the Pacific Rim area in season, many of them for whale-watching. At the local library I ask for names of people familiar with Vancouver Island's west coast and its history. At eight o'clock in the evening, climbing a long driveway to Ken Gibson's house, perched on a high hill in complete darkness, feeling like a burglar with my flashlight, I wonder if this was a good idea.

But I am expected. I tap on a porch window and am ushered into the living room. Ken Gibson is a large greying man in his mid-fifties. He grows prize rhododendrons for a hobby and writes about them. Glancing at the colour pictures of lush blooms in his magazine articles, I see that he knows his stuff. Dot Gibson, Ken's wife, is slightly younger than her husband.

Ken is a marine contractor. He builds fish pens for piscatorial farming, wharfs, piers and the like. Fortunately I feel comfortable with these people, something that doesn't always happen when you meet strangers. We plunge immediately into talk about nearly everything. I know this place has nearly the highest rainfall in Canada; Ken says the Pacific Rim has the mildest climate as well.

"When you cross the mountains at Sutton Pass everything changes. The weather gets much milder; we had the same average temperature here last winter as Oakland, California." I goggle a little unbelievingly at this information. "It's true," Ken insists. "Arctic weather blows south down the valley of the Columbia River, then west to the US coast. West of Sutton Pass is true rain forest as well, not the same trees.

"Before Sutton Pass [I hadn't even noticed that pass while driving west] the trees are fir, dogwood, arbutus, maple and so on; after the pass you get hemlock, balsam, cedar and no fir. And very few deciduous trees either," he finishes triumphantly.

I make appropriate noises of surprise and marvel, privately deciding to get some verification of all this from books.

"The warm Japanese current flows north along this coast, and that's what makes our winter weather so mild," Ken goes on, a bit smugly, I think. "We've even got a 10-metre palm tree growing at my mother's house."

There is a kind of scratching noise at the front door. When Dot turns on the porch light, a whole family of raccoons is standing there waiting, their face masks making them look like begging bandits.

"They're just moochers," Dot says, throwing them dry dog food and grapes.

"But wild animals still," Ken says a bit warningly.

"And they love grapes."

Until the mid-sixties there was no highway over these mountains. Before that people relied on the coastal ship *Princess Maquinna*; it served the entire western area. "Young couples who wanted to get married waited till the ship arrived, because the captain was empowered to marry them. There was no local minister then. After the marryin' was done there was always a wild party, with both ship's crew and the local people joining in to celebrate."

"Who paid?" I want to know.

Ken grins. "The bride's parents, of course."

Over the past few years there has been an influx of newcomers the townspeople call "hippies," free spirits who live as best they may in the surrounding forests. I'm a bit intrigued by the notion of "hippies" (which I had thought to be an outmoded term) on the Pacific Rim. Meeting one on the street I say "Hi." He responds with "Yeah, man." (Does that mean I'm elected to the tribe?)

Tofino is a town dominated by the sea. Visitors are aware of this immediately; local people probably take it for granted. Nearly all the streets, wherever they are, provide at least a glimpse of the sea, bright blue in sunlight or lead-grey in wet weather, among the misty offshore islands. The sight, the smell, the taste, touch and sound of the sea.

There is, of course, a forest of fishing boats in the harbour, as well as docks and quays, all at the service of Lord Salmon and Lord Halibut, not to mention the tourist visitors. And there is an unmistakable living rhythm of lunar tides here, which remains in our blood—like a memory of being born in the great rush of waters, a lost memory of peace.

Houses away from the waterfront are any houses, ordinary enough to pass without special remark. But when I call on retired fisherman Alf Jensen at Hagard Ho next to BC Packers, I feel bemused and amused by the place. Along the steep driveway running down to a waterside house, coloured vinyl fenders from fishing boats; in the rock garden, a white ceramic toilet with a pair of black boots sticking out, looking as it their owner had dived headfirst into the toilet. And there is a sign saying "First free trade—then GST: goodbye cruel world." Another unfriendly sign says "Keep out!"

I go down the driveway and ring the ship's bell outside Jensen's front door. Even though I am expecting a sonic boom, I can't help jumping at that end-of-the-world sound. Then for about a minute and a half I just stand at the door, thinking about Alf Jensen (later on, somebody tells me he has gone to Florida). The guy is obviously a conscious eccentric: he knows the house and he are being looked at and enjoys the attention. It would have been interesting to meet him. I wouldn't be surprised if he has vestigial gills.

On Strawberry Island, just across from our motel on Tofino Inlet, stands one of the local landmarks: a wooden sculpture called *Weeping Cedar Woman*, the right hand upraised in protest. The statue is three metres tall and sheds rivers of tears for the continuing devastation of West Coast landscape. And that means, principally, logging operations. Godfrey Stephens, the sculptor, certainly had that in mind when he created this imposing monument. Later on, a birch-bark skirt was added-for modesty's sake, I assume.

Sulo Hovi operates a fishing troller out of Tofino harbour. His wife, Judy, works at the Tofino Co-op. She is short, dark and vivacious, in contrast to Sulo, who is more measured in speech, with blond hair becoming a bit scanty at age forty. The daughter of the house, eleven-year-old Keane, is anxious that I read her stories and school narratives, while I disclaim all critical knowledge and authority.

Talking with Sulo, I want to know what it's like to be the skipper of a fishing boat. How big a crew have you? (Three.) What do you worry about most when outward bound? (Sandbars.) How long are you at sea? (Eight to ten days.) And how does it feel?

There is really no answer to that last one. Because we humans are all different, although all the same. Different in our reactions to danger and the way we think. The same in the basics—physical needs like eating and sleeping. I am, for instance, sometimes strung as tightly as a violin; my nerves twang at unexpected noises and situations. Sulo,

I think lives at a different level. Not a phlegmatic one, but existing in a calm ambience made necessary by a crew of three on the *Full Circle*.

"Last year," he says, "there was the quota to make. And only eleven days to catch enough sockeye salmon to fill that quota."

"How many lines from the boat?"

"Six. They've got flashers on them, twenty for each line. A flasher is a kind of plastic lure that imitates shrimp by wiggling in the water, goes 'hootchie-kootchie' to the fish."

"You mean they think the flasher is sexy? I thought flashers were exhibitionists at football games."

"Not this kind," Sulo says shortly. "Put yourself in my place. Here we are in heavy fog—"

"Fog?" I want to know. "How did fog get into this story?"

"You aren't listening. Anyway, there we are in thick fog, with eleven days to haul our quota of fish into the *Full Circle*, with fish buyers on shore waiting for us to get back. Time passes quickly. Then we've got a week to fill the quota, then just three days . . . "

And Sulo's face remembers the tension he felt then: will the full quota of salmon be caught before the cut-off date for fishing? The deep blue eyes regard me enigmatically.

Of course he knows the answer to that question, and I don't. But just for a moment, I can see him there: three days left until the cut-off date for trolling. And all around him fog, fog, FOG.

"Well, did you make it?"

Sulo grins at me. "Sure we did."

"On your boat, all those modern mechanical gimmicks, Loran, depth sound, radar . . . ?"

"Yep, we have them on the *Full Circle*. But the others, the other trollers, I mean, they're all around us. You can see 'em in the green light on the radar screen, but you can't see them with your eyes. Fifteen or 20 metres is the extent of your vision in the fog anyway.

"And once in a while, when we're about 100 kilometres out in fog, a big freighter, acting like it's not sure of its bearing, maybe doesn't even know we're there because we're so close—that freighter slams right through the trolling fleet."

"Like a fox among chickens?" I say.

"Yeah," and Sulo grins again. "At that point I'm liable to be a little nervous."

For a moment I have this displaced-in-time-and-space feeling: of being suspended in white darkness myself, while all the mechanical gadgets flash and murmur before my eyes. Below the *Full Circle* ghostly shapes of fish in their watery dimension; all around us the little electronic dots and dashes of other trollers. But nothing real and tangible except the Full Circle and its crew is actually present, nothing you can touch that all your senses can testify is real.

Next day I run into Ken Gibson again, at the Loft Restaurant. We drink coffee and talk a while, then he shows me this ten-metre palm tree at his mother's house. I'd swear that palm tree isn't more than five metres tall and kind of scruffy looking anyway.

"Are you telling me that tree is ten metres tall?" I say accusingly He smiles. "Would you maybe settle for eight metres?"

Walter Guppy is a retired electrical contractor, a prospector, author of a book on his mining experiences and very knowledgeable about the early days of Tofino. He is more than 70 now, greying and grizzled with mobile eyebrows.

We talk about the hippies and Clayoquot Indians, native to this area. The town site was surveyed in 1912, but homesteads existed even before that. Tofino became a municipality in 1932, settled mainly by Norwegians and Scots—names like Hansen, Arnet, MacLeod and Mackenzie still dominate the telephone book—but was cut off from the outside world, reached only by sea until Walter Guppy walked over the mountains in 1948.

"We wanted publicity," Guppy says. "Newspaper publicity that would tell the government this proposed road was perfectly feasible. And it was."

"No trouble at all, a stroll to the corner store?"

Walter twinkles at me. "Not much. A boat across Kennedy Lake and up the river from there. And this was in June. I was thirty years old then, lots of energy. And there was a Department of Mines trail to follow, windfalls cut down . . . "

"Where did you sleep?"

"At a lineman's cabin. Only trouble was the water for tea was full of mosquito wigglers. But that won't kill you."

He chuckles reminiscently. "Another boat at Sproat Lake. But after Sutton Pass on the return trip, the trail was grown up with three-metre alders. You had to push your way through."

"And the government paid some attention, the road did get built."

"Yes. MacMillan Bloedel and British Columbia Forest Products built sections of it in return for logging concessions from the government. And the road opened in 1964."

It occurs to me that so-called progress is generally balanced by something else: that road-building trade probably resulted in clear-cutting and an unsightly mountain landscape stripped of trees here and there. It also resulted in employment for many BC loggers. Take your pick: what's most desirable for prosperity and progress and our children's future?

On the morning of our departure the mountains across Tofino Inlet and Clayoquot Sound are draped in mist as if for a wedding. The town is a cliché of beauty. Green islands in the harbour and beyond melt into grey, intersecting and overlapping and surmounting one another, climbing into an invisible sky that has no ending.

I think of Housman's line, "the land of lost content," which is the past: when Walter Guppy was young and strode the mountain trails to Port Alberni; when the *Princess Maquinna* called at Tofino and its captain married the waiting lovers and wild parties went on all night; and even now I am leaving these mist-hung mountains behind me in the past, and do not expect to return.

I am already lonesome for what I have not yet lost.

*(1992)*

# Ghost Towns of BC

DRIVING THROUGH THE BRITISH COLUMBIA MOUNTAINS. In late April on the Hope-Princeton Highway, when spring has unlocked ice and snow on the heights, you notice streams of water falling down the mountains, and falling so near to the vertical that the water has scarcely any acquaintance with stone. And passing the nearby mountain walls you glimpse small flashes of purple rock, then realize it's purple flowers growing right out of the stone cliffs.

I say to my wife, who's doing the driving, "Eurithe, it's as if the earth was displaying itself, showing off all its best features for our pleasure."

"If you'd take the wheel once in a while, I'd have a better look at the landscape," she says.

"Sure, but you're a much better driver than me. And I learn just by watching you."

Our expedition into BC's interior high country is to visit ghost towns, preferably where gold has been found and the finders gotten rich as a result. And where visible remnants of the miners themselves remain.

In 1862, when news of the big Cariboo gold strike reached the East, a party of several hundred men and one woman started west from Toronto in quest of the yellow metal. They were called "The Overlanders," since the only other way to reach the Pacific coast at that time was by shipboard, around Cape Horn. And thousands of other gold-hunting hopefuls also travelled north from the United States, by ship and horse and shank's mare.

My wife and I had already tried to reach Leechtown, 40 kilometres from Victoria on Vancouver Island. We'd been stopped by "No

Trespassing" signs on a tangle of logging roads. Back in 1864 Peter Leech found gold-bearing gravel in the creek to which his name is now attached. Shortly after this discovery, hundreds of men slogged up the Sooke River to its junction with Leech Creek. A few weeks later six general stores and three hotels were open there for business. But within a year the instant town was pretty well deserted, although many Chinese miners were still patiently panning the gravel until very recently. At its peak, Leechtown and nearby Boulder City had a combined population of 4,000 people.

Beaver Dell and Hedley in the Okanagan area were similarly unproductive of whatever I was looking for. And what was I looking for exactly? Not just rotting log houses, shattered remnants of people's lives in the shape of things they left behind. I wanted the sense that actual people had once been here, men and women whose lives were understandable in terms of my own life. And how do I discover that feeling in these rather pitiful deserted places, among broken boards, useless household utensils, where nothing can touch you in any personal way? How do I discover that? I don't know.

On the mountainside at Hedley just beyond an angry little creek, you could see the remains of a factory that once processed gold-bearing ore. And the town museum has a weathered rocker for separating gold from river gravel. A few pictures of times long past inside the building. Nothing else.

Granite Creek, 20 kilometres from Princeton, was more promising. Once the third largest town in BC, behind Victoria and New Westminster, it had thirteen hotels, nine groceries, two jewellers, two blacksmiths, and some 56 cabins strung along two muddy streets in the late 1880s. Now it's only a dozen or so falling-down log houses, some with their backs broken; a few others well on their way to dissolution. Where other houses once stood, grass was a green cosmetic.

Granite Creek was "a wild swinging town," where everyone carried a gun—ranchers, cowboys and miners, all in search of the "royal metal." Gold was discovered in 1885 by a party of eight or ten men from the US. A young girl of that time remembered the strike much later, her reminiscences appearing in the Vancouver *Province* on May 17, 1931.

They worked hard, except one man, Johnny Chance, who was too lazy to work, so they made him cook, but as the weather got hotter that was too much exertion for him, so his partners gave him a gun and told him to get a few grouse. He departed and strolled about until he found a nice cool creek that emptied into the river. Here he threw himself down until sunset, his feet paddling the cold water, when a ray of light fell on something yellow; he drew it toward him, picked it up. It was a nugget of pure gold! He looked into the water again and there was another. He pulled out his buckskin purse and slowly filled it. Then, picking up his gun, strolled back to camp where he became a hero and the discoverer of Granite Creek.

The BC government erected a cairn to Johnny Chance at Granite Creek, with a metal plaque commemorating his fortunate laziness. When we visited the site the cairn was still there, but someone had pried off the plaque with a crow bar.

Over the mountains to Yale, the head of navigation on the Fraser River for Cariboo-bound miners in 1858. Twenty thousand men, Caucasian and Chinese, rummaged the Fraser River for gold in that same year. We met Bob Barry in his trading post at Yale. A heavily built middle-aged man with a moustache, Barry is the grandson of Ned Stout who accompanied Billy Barker to the Cariboo gold fields during the original gold-rush. In 1994 the town offers little besides the museum for history-conscious visitors.

But in the 1860s there was intense rivalry between Yale and Hill's Bar, a nearby mining camp on the Fraser. Two drunken miners, Farrell and Burns, went from Hill's Bar to Yale, where they got into an argument with a black barber named Dickson, and proceeded to beat him over the head with a pistol. Dickson, annoyed at the treatment, lodged a complaint with Magistrate Whannell. Warrants were issued for the two miners in Yale, but by this time they had returned to Hill's Bar.

Constable Hicks in Hill's Bar therefore arrested the miscreants, and took them back to Yale where they were thrown into the hoose-gow. But Hicks somehow offended Magistrate Whannell, and also got himself locked up for contempt of court along with the two miners.

When Magistrate Perrier of Hill's Bar got word of these goings-on, he lost his temper completely. He swore in special constables and dispatched them to Yale. They raided the Yale lock-up, freed Constable Hicks, brought back Farrell and Burns to Hill's Bar, and for good measure included Magistrate Whannell among their prisoners.

Magistrate Perrier, lord of all he surveyed in his own courtroom, fined Dickson's assailants $75 each. But more important, Perrier also fined Yale Magistrate Whannell fifty bucks and forced him to pay the fine. Whannell, frothing with rage at this insult to his high office, appealed to the colonial governor. A detachment from the British Army, Royal Navy Marines and police were quickly sent to Yale, where Matthew Baillie Begbie (the "Hanging Judge" himself) dispensed justice. Things kept getting more and more complicated between Yale and Hill's Bar. When the hullabaloo subsided, more fines were levied, Magistrate Perrier and Constable Hicks were fired, and the local honour of Yale appeased. Until next time.

And in 1994 my wife and I drove northward through the mountains toward the Cariboo Plateau. You can talk about Andean splendours in South America, the Tien Shans—the "Mountains of Heaven"—in Asia, or any other awesome molehills you can cite to make a point, I'll take the high Cascades of BC. These mountains uplift the soul, or where the soul should be in case you don't have one. If you could flatten out all these vertical highlands of the BC interior, press them flat into a horizontal position like a huge sheet of paper, you'd have a land mass that would fill the North Atlantic Basin (statistics available on request).

I mentioned this casually to my co-pilot. "You exaggerate," she said. "You always exaggerate."

I sulked until the next town, but humbled myself at lunch over a ham sandwich and coffee. Just the same, those mountains do something for me.

The Cariboo is ranching country, not flat exactly but the mountains have receded: gullies, ravines, wooded hills and grasslands. It's one of the big interior plateaus of BC, as the Chilcotin is also a high plateau farther west. The scenery is slightly less awesome than the Cascades, but more human, grazing livestock and cowboys well aware they're cowboys. Parts of the Cariboo are harsh, especially in winter; but it's somehow welcoming and gracious at the same time. I can't explain the apparent contradiction.

We branched off Highway 97, the main north-south artery, at 150 Mile House, and onto a wilderness road that led eastward to the stars, or seemingly did. Our objective now was Horsefly, one of the earliest mining camps in 1858, with not much left in the way of ghost town ruins. Then why Horsefly? Mainly because we like the sound of the name. (Just say it to yourself, "Horsefly, Horsefly." Doesn't it rival Tombstone, Dodge City and all the other American western shoot-em-up towns?)

The guidebooks were right about Horsefly. We went searching for an old log cabin, supposedly dating from the earliest times, but encountered only a friendly dog. All we got from Horsefly was two orders of poached eggs on toast (twelve bucks) at the local restaurant, and that half-comic name to whisper in the mind.

Far north by this time: bright and sunny by day, much colder at night due to increased altitude. From Horsefly cross-country to Likely: range country, following a wandering gravel road with cattle guards at intervals to prevent the critters from straying. (The brown and white animals are probably like me: in a phone booth I have to dial the operator and ask how to get out.) The calves we saw here didn't look more than a few weeks old, and stayed close to their mothers.

Small herds of deer lifted their heads in wonderment to watch us go by.

From the motel at Likely to Quesnel Forks, an old-time mining settlement twenty kilometres over the hills. Hills? Hell no, huge mountains. Our Chevy Lumina clung to a road scraped from the sides of overhanging cliffs as if it loved the earth below. You could see places on the road from which mountain landslides had taken a bite and were hungry for more. It occurred to me then: a single raindrop might trigger a thousand tons of rock and gravel onto the roof of our car. You don't dare spit!

Higher up, snow had disappeared: spring was coming in the mountains. Deciduous trees in little groups spread lacy nettings to catch the sky. Evergreens remained apart, gowned in darkness.

Quesnel Forks amounted to a dozen or so log buildings, broken-backed, tumbling down and caught in the act. I had no sense that people had ever lived there, despite the indubitable remains. Wong Kim, the last Chinese miner, died in 1954. In its heyday, the town had been half Chinese and half Caucasian, along with Horsefly the first of the Cariboo gold towns in the 1860s.

Here at this deserted place, near the junctions of the Quesnel and Cariboo Rivers, came Billy Barker of later Barkerville fame. Here as well came the greenhorns and veteran California miners, with fever in their veins, searching for the last big strike. Many of them remain here, part of the earth.

Barkerville itself is now government-restored, but still a ghost town despite the arrival of 80,000 noisy tourists every summer. It's also a cold country at this early season, with nearby lakes hard frozen. In 1862 the above-mentioned Billy Barker made the richest strike here that "anyone had ever seen" until that time. Overnight a wilderness city with mining camp was born in order to rummage Williams Creek and adjacent streams for gold. Saloons, groceries, brothels, blacksmiths, drugstore, bakery, everything sprang up magically here in the mountains north of nowhere.

When my wife and I arrived at the hinge of April/May, great heaps of piled snow shouldered among the log frame buildings. At the administration office we were expected and welcomed. Brian Fuegler, a genial moustached man in his mid-forties drove us around Barkerville in a GMC panel truck. The town has three main rows of buildings and two main streets between them, with Williams Creek supplying obbligato music.

"The town used to flood every spring," Fuegler mentioned. "The buildings had to be constructed on stilts because of silt and mine tailings left behind."

"But there's no flooding now?"

"They diverted the creek around the town. It used to run right down the main street. The original Barkerville is about sixteen feet below where we are now."

Which makes me think of Troy and other ancient cities of the Middle East. When rubble and trash rose too high in those places, the people built another town right on top of the old one.

We drove past the hundred or so log and frame buildings, with the driver supplying commentary. The place gave me an odd feeling. Here where the miners drank their booze, shouting loud derision at each other, in a place so vividly alive it must have seemed like a backwoods carnival sometimes—there is now nothing. Oh sure, the dead remains of those people are here, buildings with signs and labels, etc. But once in this very place, five thousand people did and said everything that human beings can do and say, which includes "Cold Ass Mary" and her establishment on the main street. But nothing of the sorrow and laughter remains. And I have a desolate feeling. But, of course, that too will pass.

We drove to the end of the town, and Fuegler swung left, turning onto the other main street. Ahead of us there appeared to be nothing but snow, and snow that was quite deep. I looked at Eurithe, she looked at me. We looked at the driver and said nothing, with great effort. About forty metres down the snowy road we got stuck, and I wasn't able to even whisper "I told you so."

Fuegler tried to rock the GMC back and forth; it started to dig itself down to the road underneath. "Sorry, folks," he said. "I'll get some help."

Snow was falling from a dark sky when our driver disappeared in the white stuff. "You think they'll find our frozen bodies when spring comes?" I said to Eurithe.

"You're exaggerating again," she warned.

"This too will pass," I said mournfully.

Brian Fuegler was back with five men in less than ten minutes. They rocked us out of there in short order. Driving back our driver glanced at us, slightly apologetic. "Doesn't happen like this very often," he said.

Barkerville and its legends have now begun to overtake reality, replacing it with stories of the colourful past protruding into the tourist present. Billy Barker, described as "five foot nothing" with a bad temper, invested in other mining ventures after his first big strike. He went broke eventually, dying of cancer in Victoria at age 77.

"Cariboo" Cameron, who was then just plain John Cameron, left the family farm near Cornwall in Canada West for the gold fields of California, then north to the Fraser gold-rush. Cameron emerged from the wilderness moderately prosperous, returned east to marry his childhood sweetheart, Sophia Groves. The newlyweds then journeyed west again. Back in the Cariboo with his wife, Cameron went into partnership with Billy Barker on a Williams Creek claim. In October, 1863, with the temperature at minus 34 degrees and typhoid raging across the north, Sophia caught the disease and died. Cameron swore to carry out his wife's last wish: bury her back home in Canada West.

He preserved Sophia's body with alcohol, placed her metal casket inside a wooden coffin, and buried it beneath an empty cabin. Two months later Cameron and his partners "struck it rich." He then offered $12 a day and a $2000 bonus to miners helping him haul his wife's pickled remains through snow and ice to Victoria. She was buried there again, again temporarily, while Cameron spent that winter back on Williams Creek searching for more gold.

He went back to Victoria in the spring with $300,000 of it, retrieved his wife's body, and returned with it by ship around Cape Horn to Canada West. There he married again, this time to one Christianne Ward in 1865.

But rumors began to circulate about Sophia's body: was it really inside that metal casket? Or could the casket be filled with gold and not Sophia? Then a New York newspaper reported that the lady had returned from the dead: she'd been a slave among the Indians, escaped, and now was free and back at Cameron's grandiose new house in Cornwall, along with Cameron and Christianne. Immorality was implied. The bedevilled and angry Cameron was forced to exhume his wife's body and prove there as no skullduggery afoot or under.

The crowd gathered, both relatives and the rubberneck curious. Cariboo Cameron poured out the alcohol that had pickled young Sophia (she was 12 years younger than her husband). The body was identified; the casket sealed again; rumors ended. And one story has it that grass never grew again where Sophia's last drink drained into the earth.

In nearby Wells village, we called on Kathy Landry to ask her about present-day miners still searching for gold in the Williams Creek area. Kathy, a pleasant looking woman in her early forties, had lived in Barkerville until the BC government took it over in 1958 to make it a tourist attraction. Before that date people were still living here, and even today some buildings are privately owned.

"I object to Barkerville being a ghost town," Kathy told me vigorously. "It was a nice place to live before the government got involved."

Before we left, Kathy also talked about Mildred Tregillus. "Mildred is a widow now, but her husband was a miner for years. She's in hospital extended care at Quesnel, getting pretty old. But her mind is still sharp and clear. She'll be able to tell you about the old days."

From Barkerville to Quesnel, 85 kilometres on Highway 26, a good paved tourist road. But again there were places where the mountains closed in on us, more signs warning motorists not to stop because of landslide danger. Great bare slopes of rocks and gravel loomed above our little Chevy van. I felt as vulnerable as a mosquito on a bald man's forehead.

At the extended care facility in Quesnel, a nurse escorted me into Tregillus's room. She was sound asleep.

"Oh don't wake her up," I said. "There's lots of time. I'll come back later."

"No, she'll want to see her visitor," the nurse said. "They just live for visitors."

She shook the sleeping woman's shoulder. "Mildred, Mildred, wake up! Someone to see you."

Tregillus came awake almost without transition, a small dark-haired woman who didn't appear much older than me. She had alert intelligent eyes, and looked at me questioningly.

"Kathy Landry at Wells gave me your name," I said. "I'm writing an article about ghost towns. And since your husband was a miner, you might be able to tell me something about him and your life together."

There was an awkward pause, at least it was awkward for me.

"There are no stories," Mildred Tregillus said distinctly. And her self-possessed little face looked up at me calmly from the white pillow.

I was suddenly overcome by an enormous embarrassment. Those few words of hers had left me without a word to say. "I'm sorry to have bothered you," I mumbled, and scuttled out of there as fast as I could manage it.

Mildred Tregillus had immediately figured out my reasons for coming to see her. I wondered if my character was always that transparent.

On Highway 97, driving south through Cariboo ranching country, the Chevy van clocking a regular 100 kilometres an hour. And the people whose lives and deaths I had touched on passed through my mind again. Cariboo Cameron on his long journey around Cape Horn, lugging the pickled body of his dead wife; Billy Barker, "five foot nothing" with a bad temper; Wong Kim, the last Chinese resident at Quesnel Forks; Johnny Chance, the lazy miner at Granite Creek, whose laziness paid large dividends. But more than any of the others,

Mildred Tregillus in Quesnel extended care—alert and somehow indomitable, preparing for a long journey.

There is no happy ending to this kind of story. Nearly all of those long-ago miners who found the rainbow's pot of gold wasted their money on gambling and booze or whatever: but who is to say it was wasted. One has the feeling those ghost lives were lived so fully, their outpourings of triumph so wholehearted, their drunken howls at the moon so pleasurable—in some unexplainable way they are still alive. And the gold itself: even after the glittering yellow nuggets are sold, for dollars and groceries and booze, its fever-dream remains in the mind for generations to come.

*(1995)*

# Imagine a Town

IMAGINE A TOWN THAT SITS ON THE EDGE of a great blue inland sea, where polar bears roam day and night across the garbage dump (as many as eighteen have been sighted at one time, and part of the local taxes is used for cherry bombs that sound like the Kamchatka explosion to drive the great beasts farther north); where a Chipewyan Indian village, an Eskimo settlement, straggling Métis houses, and the white man's city stand close together but never quite mix; where white whales lollop and roll near the river mouth, in sunlight so brilliant that it makes shadows seem more real than buildings.

The town is Churchill, Manitoba, on Hudson Bay, with a population of 10,000 and a deep-sea port that shipped 25,000,000 bushels of wheat across the Atlantic in 1970. I arrived there near midnight, having taken the night plane from Winnipeg. Next morning I drove around the town with Ernie Senior, manager of the port of Churchill, as well as publisher of the local newspaper. Ernie is short, middle-aged, balding, and a bubbly enthusiast for the good things about this small Arctic city. The Arctic—or, in this case, the sub-Arctic—seems to abound with people like that, who love the North and want to publicize it. Three or four years ago he was an adviser to Warner Troyer when the latter made a CBC documentary about Indian social conditions in Churchill—which were not very good at the time, although they have become slightly, infinitesimally better now.

Ernie talks non-stop about Churchill: a new recreational centre for the Chipewyans, whale hunting for tourists (eighty bucks a day and a two-whale limit for each big-game hunter), the sheer exhilaration of breathing clean wine-like unpolluted air, and Ernie's own pet project of a northern university here, using the near-billion-dollars-worth of government buildings now gradually being phased out at Fort Churchill.

Years ago Ernie Senior was an Anglican missionary paid one hundred dollars a month, sometimes spending a large part of that salary feeding starving Indians and Eskimos. After leaving the priesthood he did a little of everything before coming to his present job. I had lunch with Ernie and his wife, a brisk, cordial woman who dispensed hospitality as if strangers like myself were old friends and never an inconvenience.

In the afternoon Ernie and I did the grand tour of Churchill again: visiting huge grain elevators on the edge of Henry Hudson's sea; cruising slowly through the garbage dump, where one cantankerous-looking female polar bear lifted her swaying head wickedly, then went back to eating delicious garbage; touring the Indian recreation building, whose functions were explained to me briefly by a Chipewyan youth with a stoned expression; and talking to a man building his own cottage near a shallow inland lake. "Just to get away from the crowds," he said. Crowds? I think that the arctic population works out to one-and-a-quarter bodies per square mile, give or take an arm or a leg.

Near the Churchill River mouth I stared across at the stone ruins of Fort Prince of Wales, on a narrow promontory jutting into the sea, with cannon peering across the empty horizon. The stone fort is 300 feet square and the walls forty feet thick. During the war between Britain and France in 1782, La Pérouse, the French admiral, captured it without firing a shot. At that time there were only thirty-nine men defending a fort meant to be staffed by 400. The immense empty stoneworks lie there in sunlight like a stranded grey whale, forever useless except as a magnet for tourist dollars.

Rattling around with Ernie over the bumpy roads of Churchill, I thought of Frobisher Bay on Baffin Island, where I had spent an Arctic summer six years before. It was barren, desolate, and all those other adjectives writers use about the North. But maybe there's something wrong with me, for I don't feel those things, as some others do. Sure, I'll be out of here damn quick after today, but the things I see are people, most of all—and the huge elemental map of land and sky and sea, on which everything is stripped to essentials. People are only and first of all people, and not executives and cost accountants; here they retain their humanity. Land is stripped to earth or to the bare stone of the Canadian Shield, and the sky and sea explode with their own blue being.

Not everyone feels this way about the North. And maybe all of us citizens of the southern north and the northern north are money-grubbers on the lookout for the big buck. Money is certainly necessary to life; we're realists and pragmatists in the sense that we live day to day and go where the money is to do it; but beyond that there has to be something; for some a god, for others a woman, and perhaps friends. Well, I don't despise those other things, but I think that the sheer concepts of land and country—contained by reality and echoed in the mind—these also are indispensable to myself.

I suppose that's one of the reasons I liked Ernie Senior, because of feelings similar to mine that I sensed in him. He's a talkative little man, a verbose publicist for the North, but I'm sure with a great emotional blaze in himself for things around him. The sky overhead, the rocky pancake land with its savage, arrogant, man-killing weather, the map in himself of summer and winter, the Anglican priest that he was and the Churchill port manager that he is now: and the human being that includes them all.

I was thinking of all this when Ernie drove me to the train, and as I travelled all night and the next day southward to meet my wife at The Pas. And of Churchill with its exhilaration and its squalor, parked beside Henry Hudson's sea; with the go-getting merchants and soon on-coming wheeler-dealers and fast bucks; and with Indians sitting out their exile from the just society. And of the strangeness of riding a train south from the barren ground and being myself. Imagine Churchill.

*(1972)*

# Dryland Country

I T'S LIKE COMING OUT OF A DARK ROOM—to leave the hills and leafless forests of an Ontario countryside on a dull April day, to find yourself under the white blaze of a Saskatchewan sky. Transport by Air Canada to the prairies in three swift hours requires some mental adjustments on arrival; my body has already made them, but the mind is still getting used to this new landscape. Then driving west from Regina along the Trans-Canada over some of the best wheatland in the world, flat as a table top, turning south on Highway 21 at Maple Creek and surrounded by low treeless olive-coloured hills, I'm feeling more at home. It's still Canada. Stopping to stretch my legs, I'm the one vertical thing in a country where all else is horizontal. I rather like the feeling; it gives some unique importance to myself. I think many of the people here must feel the same way.

The reason for my trip is to visit the site of a proposed Grasslands Park in the southwest corner of Saskatchewan. The joint Federal–Provincial park will occupy some 350 square miles in two separate parcels of land connected by a park road, an East Block and a West Block near the towns of Val Marie, Killdeer and Mankota. It will, that is, when and if the park proposals are fully implemented. Its purpose is to ensure that "a remnant of the prairies grasslands would be set aside and interpreted for this and future generations." Prairie dog towns along the Frenchman River valley are the only ones in Canada where this animal can be observed in its natural habitat.

But there's a fly in the ointment—for Parks Canada and the provincial authorities at Regina. The proposed parkland is already occupied by more than prairie dogs, golden eagles, hawks, coyotes and rattlesnakes. People live there too. Thirty-nine families of ranchers are directly dependent on this land, either living there on land partly leased, or in nearby areas. Their holdings include some 6,000 head of cattle; most of their sons and daughters were born and raised on this sunlit tableland. The ranchers object to being displaced in favour of prairie dogs.

I'm approaching the disputed rangeland through the back door, via the Cypress Hills. These Hills have what I think is the most interesting and colourful history in Canada, which is a flat statement of fact. They are situated on the Saskatchewan border, directly adjoining the US border, rising a little more than 4,800 feet above sea level, hence more than a thousand feet above the surrounding rangeland. Seventy million years ago a shallow body of water, called the Bearpaw Sea by geologists, covered the central continent from the Gulf of Mexico to the Arctic Ocean, including all of the area I'm now visiting. Dinosaurs romped at the edge of this Bearpaw Sea; exotic vegetation flourished there before and after the Rocky Mountains were born. The thirty-five foot king tyrannosaurus, with teeth like small swords, chased the gentle vegetarian reptiles along those shores. Later in geologic time, there were sabre-toothed cats, camels and titanotheres. All this long before the embattled ranchers and their dispute with Parks Canada.

During the last Ice Age, 20,000 years ago, glaciers blanketed these northern plains. But the Hills (which are actually a dissected flat-topped plateau) were never entirely covered by ice. It flowed around and crossed between them at an opening called "The Gap." An island of eighty or ninety square miles lifted above the frozen desert, and diverted the slow stampede of ice on either side.

Animals fled to this high plateau as ice groaned and splintered along the flanks of the Hills, warning that the Earth-Shaker was upon them. It was a refuge, a biological island, preserving Rocky Mountain plants and animals far into the plains, and southern species far into the north. In 1977, it's a park.

I stop at the park buildings, deserted except for one lonesome secretary, to eat sandwiches and drink a beer. Not far from where I'm having lunch, eighty Assiniboines under Chief Little Soldier were massacred by American wolvers and whiskey traders in 1873 at Moses Solomon's trading post. All around me spruce, pine and aspen stir peacefully in the April wind, as if nothing had ever happened here.

But as a result of the massacre came the Royal North West Mounted Police, the Mounties. And with their arrival things did stop happening, at least to the extent that full-scale wars between the Blackfoot and other tribes ended; the whiskey traders went out of business, or back south, or became mere bootleggers. When Sitting Bull fled to Wood Mountain, north of the border Medicine Line, after trouncing Custer at Little Big Horn, the Mounties told him to behave himself. And rather amazingly, he did.

Nobody quite knows how the Mounties were able to accomplish such sweetness and light in such a notably lawless country. But they did. And the US Army, those blue-shirted "Long Knives" watching their fugitive Indians escape the American way of death north of the Medicine Line, may also have wondered a little how the trick was done.

Fifteen miles south of the Cypress Hills with their relatively abundant rainfall, I turn east into arid semi-desert. Trees become a rarity; gophers popping up on either side of the road look thirsty. Prairie towns skim past, Robsart, Eastend, Shaunavon, and finally Val Marie. The landscape is low rolling olive-coloured hills, part of the hundred miles of rangeland country between the Cypress Hills and Wood Mountain. It's also part of Palliser's Triangle (he was a British explorer in this neck of the prairie in 1857, who said the country was entirely worthless).

Val Marie looks like most small prairie towns: population about 250, down from 500; a little more shabby than is usual; grain elevators are vertical coloured blocks against the sky; an early spring sun searing everyone off the street except a dog on the hotel porch, panting. In the pub I ask directions how to find the dissident ranchers. I turns out a few are in favour of the park, most notably Francis Walker.

Outside Val Marie I join Wally Carlier, his wife, and Merv Timmon, a rancher-farmer, drinking coffee in the Carlier kitchen. Mrs. Wally is the town clerk, and won't say much about the park because of her official position. Merv Timmon, sandy-haired and about forty-five, is more outgoing. He says the park is "the craziest thing I ever heard of." Well, that's more like it: a strong positive opinion. Timmon goes on, "Ranchers don't interfere with the natural state of the land, so why spend millions preserving it the way it already is?"

When and if the proposed park is implemented, it will directly adjoin the American border. And there's an International Agreement with the Americans that they will receive half the natural run-off from the creeks that drain south into the US. However, at the present time they receive much more than half of these downstream water benefits in this near-desert country. Reason: there are no dams north of the border. If the park is implemented (and a report of the Public Hearings Board indicated it will be), then such building projects as dams will not be permitted. The Frenchman River and several smaller creeks drain this area in southern Saskatchewan of precious water, and there's been no appreciable rain since August, 1976. The final yes or no decision about the park will be made June 30, 1977.

That's about the extent of my park knowledge until I talk to Norm Kornfeld and his wife Doris on their ranch about eight miles south of Val Marie. Norm is forty-two, heavyset, side-burned and slightly balding. Doris is thirty-eight, not very big and quite a pretty woman. The Kornfelds have thirteen sections of crown land under government lease (a section is 640 acres), and run 225 head of cattle. Norm and his family came here in 1964 from Verwood farther north, and operated the ranch in partnership with his dad, who is now retired. Son Glen, seventeen and daughter Gail, sixteen, both grew up on the ranch. They say they'd "feel a kind of emptiness if we lose the land."

"People ask why we need so much land," Norm Kornfeld says. "well, they don't realize that a section of land can only feed about two dozen cows in this dry country." I drink some more coffee and read the brief Norm presented at the park hearing in Val Marie: "I have spent the past twelve years, the most productive years of my life, transforming this ranch to its present modern state of corrals, barns, water and sewage facilities and a new home. Now I have less than ten minutes to present a brief about why I wish to remain in this part of the country and fulfill my childhood dream of being a successful rancher."

I can see what he means, and those dozen years out of his life are all around us. No, it doesn't seem entirely fair to me either.

The three of us, Norm, Doris and myself, board his four-wheel-drive truck to visit the prairie dog colony near the Frenchman River bottomlands. (And the only way you can get around in this country, aside from horses is by four driving wheels.)

We jolt over the winding road that's more track than road, and more trail than track, me braced against the bumps, stopping at a high butte where you can see the green-bordered Frenchman River snaking across the prairie. It's all the green there is. On the bottomlands a nation of black-tailed prairie dogs has pimpled the ground with earth beside their holes. Their heads pop up; they make a noise like some weird bird, going "cheep-cheep." I guess it means "Danger! Two-legged critters on the prowl. Watch yourself!"

Norm draws a map to give me directions for Bruce Dixon's ranch, twenty-five miles away. And says at the door, "We won't leave this ranch!"

Bruce Dixon is forty, his wife Stella, thirty-eight. We drink coffee in the Dixon kitchen. He says, "They protect prairie dogs, why not protect people?" It's a question with some resentment, and I can't answer him. They've been on the land since 1955, the year a very young Bruce and his dad built their first log house. Since then the son has gradually taken over ranch operations from his father. Bruce and Stella have two children, the usual heavy investment in buildings and machinery, without much return since beef prices have been low for some time. Like the Kornfelds, they're on call every three hours, to assist or provide aid and comfort to cows giving birth at this season of the year.

The Dixon's lease and own forty-two sections of rangeland, a much larger outfit than Norm Kornfeld's place. "What happens to you when beef prices are so low?" I want to know. "You ever feel like giving up and going to work in a factory?"

Bruce Dixon smiles. "We just tighten our belts. And wait." The smile is maybe a little forced, but he's right; all anyone can do is wait until things get better. "And we won't move," he says, "no matter what."

Every ranch house I visit gives me a map showing me how to get to the next; and I've drunk so much coffee I hate the stuff. I've seen no people on this dirt track that seems to lead nowhere. Then a string of about twenty horses sweeps around a curve, startled by the car, manes tossing and colours brilliant in the sun: chestnuts, greys, black and whites, half-wild and wholly graceful. A youngster on a black horse follows them and I think he can't be more than eighteen. The hat sweeps off in greeting, and they're gone around another bend in the road, a small cloud of dust rising and disappearing.

Occasionally there's a deserted house to arouse my curiosity. I stop at one of them, jump over a small creek, my feet nervous from possible rattlesnakes. The house is stone with mortar decayed, the shingled roof fallen in, its interior a mass of broken chairs, tangled bedsprings and household wreckage. It must be years since anyone has lived there. When I stick my head inside a broken window frame, a dozen birds nearly decapitate me in their frenzied escape outward.

As I reconnoiter for a non-muddy place to cross the creek again wind tugs at my clothes insistently. It is a prairie constant, that wind. Overhead clouds sail eastward before it like ships; here on the ground everything moves in brief unison, whether plant or animal; it handles grass and the most delicate small flowers, twitching the fur of rabbits and prairie dogs, a continual part of their lives. In winter it rides the Chinook across mountains, moving snow with invisible hands, and some snow still remains in early spring. And there are voices contained by the wind, non-human voices, as if it were the thing Shanley referred to in his verse:

Sancta Maria, speed us!
The sun is falling low;
Before us lies the valley
Of the Walker of the Snow.

Don Gillespie is balding and big, I'd guess about 210 pounds, and very quiet. Maybe that's because his wife, Norah, is vivacious and not given to long silences. They are both forty-eight. Four generations of the family live at the ranch. Norah's dad and his brother, Lloyd Way, came here in 1915, and built a 14' by 16' shack on the land. Norah's Uncle Lloyd is now eight-three, becoming a little pale and fragile. "But he still works," Norah insists. Lloyd grins. "Not now."

I mention the deserted house I passed on the way here. "It was abandoned in the mid-forties," Don says. Son Darwin, fourteen, says there's the remains of a sod house not far from here. "But there's not much left of it, only the four corners." No wonder it's vanishing into the ground it came from, built only of sod and grass roots. A man named Fred Hausman died there some time in the thirties.

About the park, Norah says, "We don't intend to leave, but they might starve us out. The government could cancel our leases at any time." The Gillespies are not precisely scornful about the park, since we all agree that preserving the prairie ecology is a good thing. But living where you've lived all your life, and where you expect your bones to be part of the land eventually—that too is important. Norah says that on their forty-plus sections of rangeland, "We want to raise the best bunch of cattle that ever roamed the prairies." Then she adds thoughtfully, "We grow live things." She means, I guess, that ranching is different from turning out plastic doodads or manufacturing steel automobiles in concrete factories; in fact, it's different from anything but ranching.

Leaving the Gillespie place, I take a wrong turn. It's several miles before I notice I'm somewhat lost, and that the dirt track over the prairie isn't taking me anywhere. Everything looks like everything else; no landmarks whatever. Of course it's no big deal, but I can't turn around in my rented car because of the shallow ditches and some ugly-looking rocks. Thirty feet from the road a brown and white cow is sleeping. How nice, how peaceful and rural! But when I pass by a little farther there's daylight shining through the cow's body from end to end; it's entirely hollow. Nothing there but hide and bones and hooves, a skin tent. It does give you a little chill at such times. Olive-coloured rangeland all around, with late patches of snow scattered here and there, nothing alive but prairie dogs and rattlesnakes—and myself for a while longer.

The Paris Hotel at Mankota is not exactly reminiscent of the City of Light, but it's comfortable. The town itself has about 400 people, with no livery stable despite it being cowboy country. Those are off the movie set in Hollywood. I have something to eat and a few beer, talk to the barkeep, play some pool and to bed.

Sometime in the night I find myself standing beside an encampment of Red River carts, the same kind used to help settle the nineteenth century prairies. I'm slightly aware that it's a dream, because I'm still tired in the dream after several days driving and talking in Saskatchewan. But a dream is something you can't swear isn't real when you're right inside it. The carts are stopped along a river valley, but too large a river to be the Frenchman. I walk around them, pleased they're not moving, because when they do move there's a noise like a thousand devils filing saws to cut off the legs of shrieking sinners in hell. Made entirely of wood, there's no grease in the axles, because dust would seize them up. And I seem to wonder: do these carts belong to Métis on a buffalo hunt in the last century? Or the

Overlanders of 1862 on their way across the plains, bound for the Cariboo gold fields?

There's moonlight, pale stuff tinging the encampment with dusty silver. No horses. Nothing alive that I can see. But they must have left a guard somewhere. No hunting party would sleep without one. And I'm right. He's down by the river, a dark hawk-nosed man, probably Métis, sound asleep. His long-barrelled rifle is held in his right hand, a Sharps, I think, the kind "that shoots today and kills tomorrow." They were a favorite of buffalo hunters. The rifle's wooden stock is beaded with condensed mist, and as I watch a small drop of water trickles irregularly down the polished wood, disappearing in grease.

A dream. Next I'll be dreaming of the Bearpaw Sea, with dinosaurs in full colour? Anyway, I make a note of it when I wake up in the morning.

The barkeep is a genial sort of guy, and invites me to visit a rattlesnake pit with him. These are depressed places in the prairie, into which gophers or burrowing owls have driven their own burrows. And since reptiles can't dig holes, they simply take over from creatures who can. But it's too early in the spring for snakes to be above ground; the spade-shaped heads and buggy-whip bodies are coiled sluggishly under the earth in reptilian dreams.

In May, 1976, one hundred and eight briefs were submitted to a Public Hearings Board, which was "appointed to advise the Government of Saskatchewan on the degree of public support for the proposed Grasslands National Park." These hearings were held at Regina, Saskatoon, Killdeer, Mankota and Val Marie. Obviously, the people who submitted briefs in Saskatoon and Regina were not generally involved directly with the area concerned (as some ranchers I talked to pointed out). Briefs from urban areas were almost entirely in favour of the park; ranching areas were largely against it.

And some insights into the situation might be derived from the briefs themselves. I found it interesting that the learned societies and ecology people presented papers in rather pedantic language, sometimes crowded with statistics which they felt proved their point in favouring the park.

Several of the ranchers' briefs were in longhand, and their grammar wasn't always perfect. They tended to be a little emotional at times, which is easy to understand. They were outnumbered by professors and civil servants; a few sound slightly paranoid, as if they've already lost the struggle for their land. And I think they have. I think the government has already decided, despite the deadline for decision on the park being June 30, 1977.

The rancher-wives are often more articulate than their men. Mrs. Marjorie Linthicum, from a ranch near Killdeer, says:

> I wouldn't like to see the ranches destroyed and their remains become a monument of the past, as are dinosaur bones, teepee rings of the Indians, and the many rows of rock piles of the early settlers which are all so familiar in some of the area I speak of. I have spent many days riding over this land. I know what it's like to ride all day and never encounter another soul; to have a faithful horse bring me sixteen miles home through a blinding storm; to drive cattle home in the fall and have them strung out for two or three miles heading for their winter pastures; to sit on a knoll and watch cattle graze on an alkali flat, or two mighty bulls battle over a harem of cows; to repair fence all day and pick wood ticks off all evening; to see bands of wild horses trailed out to packing plants because of modernization; to sit on a high butte and look south over the prairie for miles; to drive cows and calves to summer pasture and then sit on a hillside and watch till they mother-up; to dream as a young girl of riding south to the badlands and driving cattle with my dad and then having my dreams come true; to trail carloads of grass-fed beef thirty miles to the railway in thirty-five degree-below weather; to see buffalo horns on the prairie and wonder if it died from a winter storm or an Indian arrow; to have your horse get loose and leave you fifteen miles from home. Perhaps I am selfish, but I would like my family and their heirs to be able to enjoy this part of my heritage as much as I have. I feel I am as much part of this land as are the coyotes and gophers.

And that says it all.

Driving east to Regina the wind is blowing, a heavy gusting wind that scoops topsoil off the farmland, and turns the polished fields pale and ghostly. It makes you think of the bad dust bowl days in the dry thirties, especially when the white stuff you're driving through is the actual soil of somebody's farmland. It makes all our hopes for the future seem no more substantial than white mist, a floury dust that coats the car's interior plastic but can't be baked into bread. Only the gold stubble-land of last year's crop resists the scouring wind.

It's a strange and tragic feeling to be driving through somebody's dreams at about 65 miles per hour. It makes me think of the biblical Seven Lean Years in Egypt here on the prairies, with all the Pharaoh's storage houses and our own red grain elevators filled—filled with nothing but dust.

But that feeling is still only a dark mood, which may yet turn to silver in the falling rain. South-west of here, and all across the untracked ranges, cows are dropping their young in an orgy of birth. Thousands of calves are staggering to their feet and searching blindly for their mother's milk. The rancher midwives attend them: sympathetic, but cussing sometimes from lack of sleep. In the Cypress Hills, spring stirs, grass awakes. Soon the sun will trigger flowers like small red jewels nearly hidden in winter's brown slag.

It takes a small leap of the imagination to realize that all of this brown land, soon turning to green and gold, was once the Bearpaw Sea seventy million years ago. Hereford and Charolais and other cattle breeds have replaced the dinosaurs. As pronghorn deer have replaced camels and titanotheres. In a much later time, whites have replaced the Indians and Métis. It's impossible to conceive an equal leap into the future or whether there will still be men at all in that distant time. But if there are, I hope some may be ranchers.

*(1977)*

# Streetlights on the St. Lawrence

CANADA IS A COUNTRY WHERE the heartland centres of commerce and population are almost entirely inland. The Atlantic traveller approaching the United States is suddenly confronted with the whole North American continent—it lifts right out of the sea at New York, and you're surrounded by people with scarcely any transition. But the traveller or immigrant bound for Montreal may enter the great watery jaws between Newfoundland and Cape Breton and be surrounded by five provinces of the new country without even knowing it. Distances in the Gulf of St. Lawrence are so immense that there often could be no land within sight of the marine traveller.

Nineteenth-century immigrants, particularly, must have observed with alarm and sometimes fear the rugged olive-green hills of the North Shore and the mountains of Gaspé drifting past. Some of them may have known that Jacques Cartier called this place of water and stone "the land God gave to Cain"—which seems to me a little extreme, even for an explorer from sunny France. But after voyages sometimes lasting many weeks, cooped-up on ships that must have seemed prisons, the dispossessed Scottish crofters and survivors of the Irish potato famine surely had a right to hope for something better. And to the women and their sometimes half-starved children this new world must have seemed much worse than the old. They were lost in this desolate place, thousands of miles from friends and relatives without even control of their own bodies and destinies.

In late May, 1974, I reversed the westward track of those nineteenth-century immigrants. Boarding the 8,500 ton lake freighter *Golden Hind* at Thorold on the Welland Canal, Captain Cecil Freeman commanding, I travelled eastward through Lake Ontario and the St. Lawrence Seaway, eventually reaching Baie Comeau on the Quebec North Shore. The ship's cargo was soy beans and corn from Chicago; she carried a crew of thirty-one. At Baie Comeau I left the *Golden Hind* and flew back to Montreal, with the feeling of having added another thousand miles of previously unknown territory to the place in my mind that is Canada.

Traversing the seaway was like driving a car, then coming to a whole series of maddening red lights: stop and go, stop and go. We would enter a lock, wait, water pouring out of the concrete playpen with a whoosh, and drop some fifty feet. Then zoom-zoom go the engines and we're on our way to the next traffic light. Moving slowly down the Welland Canal, the whole green country of the Niagara Peninsula is dwarfed trees, houses, people, everything. The 620-foot-long ship is simply monstrous. And your mind has to handle it somehow. I managed that by saying to myself that lakers like the *Golden Hind* —as well as larger ships—are only boxes made of steel being pushed somewhere by wound-up rubber bands, or some other motive power invented by people. It's less grandiose that way.

The original *Golden Hind* weighed one hundred tons and was probably not more than seventy-five feet long, with a crew of around one hundred. Francis Drake circumnavigated the world with this ship in 1580, an age when many people still thought the Earth was flat and you'd fall off at the other side. Drake was an English pirate and patriot, a religious man who had prayers on shipboard twice a day, and who thought there was nothing irreligious about sacking a Spanish town in the Caribbean Sea between prayers. And yet when Francis Fletcher, his chaplain, criticized him slightly for poor sea-manship, Drake padlocked Fletcher to a hatch and excommunicated him in the sight of God and man and the devil. The fair-haired freebooter, sitting cross-legged on a sea chest, ordered that a band be placed around his chaplain's arm that proclaimed the wearer "Francis Fletcher, the falsest knave that liveth." Which seems to indicate that if you don't agree with a captain while at sea you'd better keep the disagreement to yourself.

But Captain Cecil Freeman is nothing like Sir Francis Drake, he's a six-foot-tall, heavily built middle-aged Newfoundlander, and with a nice sense of humour. In the wheel-house of the *Golden Hind*, between saying to the wheelsman, "Steer between those two buoys," he talks to me about getting a ticket for speeding from the US Coast Guard.

"I was master of the SS *Thorold* a few years back, and they told me on the radio-telephone that I'd exceeded the fifteen-miles-per-hour speed limit."

"And you hadn't?"

"It's like talking to the cops, they hear only their own side of anything. When you argue you make it worse. But I won this argument."

"How?"

"Well, they measure your speed by the period of time it takes for the distance between the ship's bow and stern to pass a fixed point on land. It's all done mechanically and pretty hard to disagree with. But in this case they had the wrong ship."

"Huh?"

"There happened to be another, earlier SS *Thorold*. It was a longer ship than mine, so it took longer to pass their speed-measuring devices. I pointed that out to them, very carefully of course. It's the only time I ever won an argument with the cops."

We have by this time passed through the misty expanse of Lake Ontario overnight; Wolfe Island glimmers grey behind us, the sun burning away early morning mist in the Thousand Islands of the upper St. Lawrence. Then more seaway locks and another set of traffic lights, with gay go up and gay go down, while loudspeakers and computers murmur electronic endearments to each other. An unexpected starling's nest is tucked in the lock wall, where someone must have slipped to allow anything but stone and steel. The mother bird doesn't bat an eyelash as the monster ship gurgles past, home free down the widening river.

On the American side of the seaway, castles of American millionaires are built on green islands, their scores of rooms empty in the late spring season: Heart Island, with battlements and dozens of stone towers, the Boldt Castle, built by a now-dead millionaire. (They die, too, of heart disease and cancer and a great deal of everything, the same way ordinary people do from having too little.) All the limestone and timber components had been hauled in by barge. Farther on, Mary Pickford's castle—she who was America's Sweetheart in the glittering and near-gold heyday of fairyland Hollywood—she who was once a Canadian. And cranes, dozens of the huge birds, rowing through darkening skies to inexpensive treehouses on Ironsides Island.

In many ways the ship is two floating towns, one suburb forward and the other behind. In between are some 450 feet of deck containing the cargo holds. For meals you walk aft to the dining room, where the crew's cabins and recreation rooms are located, one or two men to each cabin. After dark, streetlights illumine the deck, although I suppose they're called something else. Forward is the officers' quarters, also my own large cabin and bathroom, which fact makes me feel somewhat non-proletarian. There are probably a dozen television sets aboard, and nearly everyone has at least a radio. The meals? Well, the meals are ambrosia and nectar—in fact roast beef, steak, ham, ice cream, the best of everything. Three meat courses for lunch and dinner. Glynn Perry, the First Cook from Roseway, Nova Scotia, could give lessons to a chef at the Queen Elizabeth or Royal York. Leo Riviera, Second Cook, would come first in any culinary contest judged by me.

All these accolades may sound as if I'm being carried away by shipboard luxury. Well, consider this: deckhands are paid between $900 and $1,100 a month, and I don't think that they work very hard, daintily touching up rusted paint-work. For three months in the winter they collect unemployment insurance and drink beer. It occurs to me that I should have known about all this sooner, so that I too could have lived like Mary Pickford and that guy in the Boldt Castle, a middle-aged Croesus happily adding up the interest on my paycheques.

But it is not quite so simple. If not deprivation, there definitely is boredom on board a ship. Leo Riviera says, "You can't see your family for months on end. And what if you need a doctor or dentist in the middle of Lake Ontario? What happens then?"

(Of course, if there's something really wrong with you they can get a helicopter by radio-telephone.)

And George Rollier, who is French-French, says, "It's not like being on a deep-sea ship, there's not the same sense of brotherhood and good feeling."

And "Peewee," who is seventeen years old, has decided that after another two or three months, "I'm gone!" One youngster who signed on at Thorold jumped ship between locks at the Welland Canal, perhaps in a sudden frenzy of homesickness. Another deckhand, also from Thorold, demanded his pay in Baie Comeau at 4 a.m., but the Second Mate wouldn't wake Captain Freeman at that hour. Whereupon the discontented seaman jumped ship, stole a milk truck, and drove east until he was picked up by the Quebec Provincial Police at Forestville, seventy miles east.

The *Golden Hind* anchors in the St. Lawrence just below Montreal because of a labour slowdown at Baie Comeau. The stevedores' union there is deliberating about whether the men will go on strike or not. An electrician, nicknamed Freddy Kilowatt, has severe pains in his chest. He is sent to a hospital in the city. And Mike McNulty, one of the young deck hands, has love problems. It seems that there was this girl who liked him much, but he (the cad) brushed her off. She took him at his word and would have no more to do with him, despite prolonged pleading on Mike's part after he discerned the girl's true worth (because of her good judgment in males).

"Will you write me a letter to her?" Mike says, me not having made any secret of being a hack writer.

"Would that be honest?" I ask delicately. "Wouldn't it be love under false pretenses or something?"

"Never mind that. If the letter works, our first child will be named Al."

Okay.

> Dear Mary:
> I thought of you at the Welland locks, I thought of you anchored below Montreal, and I'll be thinking of you at Tadoussac and Baie Comeau if and when we ever get there. Right now there's a yellow cloud from a factory across the river reflecting itself on the water. It made me think of the yellow rose I gave you, before the ship sailed, to win you back . . .

"Mike, it's no good. Would any self-respecting, honest-to-goodness, red-blooded Canadian gal go for crap like that? She sounds too nice to con her, even if I could. I can't do it."

"Yes, you'll have to do better," Mike says judiciously.

"She won't believe it's you!"

"I'll tell her I had help, and besides, the first child will be named—"

"Yes, I know, after me. But the second and third and fourth, what about them?"

"By that time she'll be cussing you so bad you'll hear it in your grave." We stare at each other a moment, and I can see that it is the moment of truth.

"All right, okay," I say to a Mike. "I will, in my own inimitable manner and with all the one-syllable words at my command, flatter the hell outa her. What colour hair and eyes?"

After one day near Montreal the *Golden Hind* raised anchor for Ile du Bic, in the St. Lawrence near Rimouski, and there awaited further orders. It's some thirty degrees colder in this area, with still two feet of snow a few miles inland—and it's the beginning of June. Opposite the ship, several miles distant, a string of cottages on the shore looks like stranded icebergs. And just upriver the huge Saguenay River side-swipes the St. Lawrence, marking its passage into the greater river with a five-mile wavery track of foam. On our right—or I should say "starboard"—the freighter *Carol Lake* has been anchored since May nineteenth, also waiting orders for proceeding to Baie Comeau.

Everyone feels very pessimistic about the stoppage. Captain Freeman says it's just for a few days. First Mate Jean Perusse says a week. Glen Smith, the Third Mate, thinks longer than that. Glynn Perry, the First Cook, says gloomily, "We may never leave." I say hell, or even stronger words.

There's lots of time to talk, and Leo Riviera tells me about this friend of his, a deckhand on another ship, who died near Rimouski a few weeks ago. The remains of Tom Beckles were flown back to Barbados via Air Canada, his wife going with him on what was apparently his last journey. But the Canadian authorities hadn't filled in the cause of his death on the death certificate, so back came the body to Canada again. After which, armed with the proper information this time, Beckles and his widow again returned to Barbados.

But there's a prior episode which makes Beckles' death even more poignant for Leo Riviera. "Tom Beckles saved my life. It was in 1941, and I was working on the old Canadian National Steamship, *Lady Hawkins*, as a bellboy. The ship was torpedoed by a German sub off Cape Hatteras, and went down very quickly. There were a lot of people, crewmen and passengers, in the sea before lifeboats could be launched. I was one of them. The water was so cold that it must've weakened me, and I couldn't climb into the boat. I hung onto the gunwale and yelled: 'Tom, help me, help me!' Tom Beckles reached down and hauled me into that life-boat. There were seventy people in the lifeboat, including my two brothers. One of my brothers died of exposure before we were rescued. That's why I remember Tom Beckles."

And the morning and the afternoon were the second day of boredom, anchored near Ile du Bic in the St. Lawrence. Therefore I called a Royal Commission to investigate the Ontario Paper Company—with myself the only sitting member. (I'd brought along some relevant books for just this purpose.) It seems that Ontario Paper Company owns the Quebec and Ontario Transportation Company, which owns the *Golden Hind*, among other ships, and is itself a subsidiary of many-tentacled American interests, which also include the New York *News* and Chicago *Tribune*. The *Tribune* leads directly to Colonel Robert McCormick. The colonel, who died in 1955, controlled wide stretches of Canadian pulpwood territory at Baie Comeau and Heron Bay, in order to supply raw material for his paper mills, which in turn fed newsprint to the Chicago and New York dailies. And the spoon that fed paper to the US mouth was Ontario Paper Company.

Colonel McCormick is said to be a legendary character. He is credited with being the founding father of the North Shore towns of Shelter Bay (now Port Cartier) and Baie Comeau, and probably deserves it. But with the credit for providing employment must go some small opprobrium, since the country around both settlements, as well as around Heron Bay, is stripped of forest, and nothing meets the eye but rather unlovely underbrush. On the outskirts of Baie Comeau (population some 30,000) is a large canoe made of bronze, with the life-sized colonel sitting inside bolt upright, like a real *coureur du bois* instead of a newspaper tycoon—no doubt commissioned and paid for by Ontario Paper Company.

Colonel McCormick was not very popular in Canada During the last global conflict. An officer with General "Black Jack" Pershing in the First World War, he became an isolationist in the Second, apparently quite hostile to England, and *ipso facto* to Canada as well. Thunderous editorials against Britain in the Chicago *Tribune* reflected McCormick's anything-but-neutral views. As a result, a groundswell of public opinion in Canada rose up against his paper-making activities in this country, and newspaper editorials here became quite virulent against the colonel.

Perhaps Napoleon Comeau, for whom the town was named, is somewhat more deserving of transient immortal bronze. Before the century's turn Comeau was a fabulous hunter, trapper, naturalist, and author, who roamed the North Shore performing marvellous feats, rescuing people trapped on ice, and writing books. One of his rescue exploits is depicted on a crest for the new town of Baie Comeau; it is of course, somewhat less expensive than bronze.

One tid-bit of information about papermaking in the nine-teenth century, garnered from being the only sitting member on this RoyCom, is fascinating. Newsprint between 1850 and 1860 was made mostly from rags. Thus some newspapers, because of the expense, had to raise their prices to the then-exorbitant ten cents a copy. "Rags were so valuable that enterprising eastern mill operators (presumably in the US) imported shiploads of mummies from Egypt and used the linen wrappings to make paper." Well!—What would Anwar Sadat or Colonel Nasser say about that? or Moses, who led the Children of Israel out of Egypt? Some of that rag paper made a hundred years ago—could it have been recycled and used again and again? Are we in Canada, perhaps, reading McClelland and Stewart books printed on shiploads of Egyptian mummies?

And the morning and evening were the third day anchored at Ile du Bic. In dreams at night we sailed from boredom to ennui by way of tedium and monotony. The scotch was all gone, cigars had to be rationed, and "sleep it is a gentle thing, beloved from pole to pole"—but I couldn't court Morpheus without morphia for more that eight hours. And I'd read all my comic books. Lunch and dinner called for long walks aft to the dining room, but still I wasn't getting enough exercise. Pacing off the distance between cabin areas on the central deck of the 620-foot ship, it came to 325 paces for the full circuit, which ought to be around 975 feet if you're fairly tall like myself. Therefore a dozen circuits of the same deck ought to be at least two miles. So I walked two miles every evening. Observing my laudable attempts to keep in shape from deck chairs aft, the First Cook, the Second Cook, and assorted deckhands made inappropriate comments.

"That crummy writer is off his rocker," said Mike.

"He might be just crazy enough to jump overboard," Peewee remarked. Captain Freeman too looked at me slightly askance. I told him I was investigating the possibility that Canadians could walk faster anchored than Swedes could move on bicycles.

And morning and midnight were the seventh day, after which I rose from my bed and walked ashore at Baie Comeau. Orders had come from above to lift anchor aweigh; the stevedores were placated. The ship finally arrived at Napoleon Comeau's town on June eighth. Long steel-girder conveyors unfolded at the dock like praying mantises, sucking up corn and soy beans from the ship's hold amid a man-created storm of dust. A dozen crew members waited to go ashore at the gangplank, all dressed in good non-working clothes and looking strange to me, with a glow of anticipation on their faces. Anticipation for what?

Beer, and more beer, and more beer. The tables were loaded with it. But I couldn't keep up with them. The last I saw of Mike and Peewee was at the pub in Baie Comeau. They waved to me—on their way to more interesting establishments.

During the flight back to Montreal, I kept thinking of that immense river. The St. Lawrence, more than any other, is the river of Canada. You can't row a boat or swim a stroke there without crossing the paths of Jacques Cartier and Samuel de Champlain. Both are basic to what we were and what we have become.

After the long Atlantic journey, then the immigration station at Grosse Isle, newcomers were ferried with muscle and sweat by bateau and shank's mare to Lower and Upper Canada. Where there was no beer waiting for them. It is difficult not to think of those people on the river, the dispossessed from France, England, Scotland, and Ireland; difficult because we are their children, and their children's children.

*(1974)*

# Angus

A LONG TIME AGO—BEFORE MOST OF US were born: 1910. Seventeen-year-old Angus leaned on a fence during moments stolen from schoolwork, watching a fishing boat being built on a stretch of almost deserted beach—the sandy shores of Lake Ontario in Prince Edward County.

For the boy, that boat was a thing of beauty. He peddled his bicycle there and back home to Trenton every time there was time to watch the boat's water-bound shape afloat on land. The thing stirred young Angus, made his thoughts leap. It was built with hands, the big rough hands of Scott Hutcheson, a fisherman in his tough enduring sixties. It was built with the old manual tools, some having nearly forgotten names, like the adze known to pioneers. It was built with hands.

In the summer of 1968 Angus Mowat walked along that small Lake Ontario beach, as he sometimes did, for exercise and fresh air. Or just from feeling restless. Thinking his own thoughts, he almost stumbled over the derelict, its blurred shape sprouting weeds, and canvas rigging rotted into nowhere. An old fishing boat, washed up by the waves and left there, clothed in an overcoat of yellow sand.

Angus kicked sand away from the near-buried stern with idle curiosity. Derelicts were nothing new on this beach; dinghies and fishing boats drowned continually in paint-blistering sun on the jagged shoreline of Prince Edward County; sometimes he even saw the hundred-year-old timbers of a forgotten windjammer that sailed here, and then sailed by a little-known route into the long silence of sand and sun.

But this boat was different, touching Angus' own memory; a

fishing boat that he had seen emerging from someone's mind into physical existence, as he had been growing into being himself after leaving someone else's body.

Scott Hutcheson's boat was hauled from its sand grave to Angus' own backyard. He looked at it: a badly damaged boat. As Angus himself was a damaged human being—his right arm had been badly crippled by high explosive in World War I. Examining the boat brought a mixture of agony and love, a feeling that the past was being turned inside-out; with also the dangerous knowledge that he might be giving way to his own emotions, becoming a silly eccentric old man? For the dramatic thought was being born that the Scott Hutcheson should sail again. (Wow-ie, strike up the band, splice the main brace, sound a bugle or two!)

But it was also a sobering thought. For Angus was seventy-six years old, one arm nearly useless, and not a very big man, anyway, to take on all that back-breaking work rebuilding a twenty-nine-foot fishing sloop. Having been a soldier, librarian, and literary gent all his life, he'd never really worked with his hands. But apart from such categories that leave little room in a man's mind for being anything else, Angus was something else.

The old keel, rotting at one end, was removed; clamp after clamp cut with a hacksaw. A new oaken keel, twenty-six feet long, was hand-hewn with adze and sweat.

"That keel took 27,000 adze strokes," said Angus. "I counted 'em for five minutes, then multiplied that by the hours it took to make the keel, sometimes by guess or by God. But one of us had to be right." Perhaps both of them were, for the new keel fitted into place as if it had never been anywhere else.

The year 1968 became 1969. Summer became winter, and spring forged tiny green jewels on all the trees. Fifty-six narrow oaken ribs were removed from the boat, new ones cut to shape and steamed to proper curvature, then brass-screwed to the planking. The whole job took weeks, because it took all day for two ribs to be installed. Soon it was 1970 and summer again. The rotten planks were extracted, new white cedar planking tapered, steamed, and clamped into place. Elm and maple leaves turned red and fell, as the year turned a corner into autumn.

Boat-building books had to be consulted, of course: but what books say how to build a fishing boat that was born in 1910? Twenty-nine feet long, eight wide, with double-ended lap-strake planking? What authorities are there to measure thought and inches, to calculate stress and strain on a wooden boat whose parts all move in reaction to themselves and the water, each being both themselves and each part of the whole? Who knows that?

One building thought follows another, and the first has to be right or the second dependent thought can't be. An oaken board called a "clamp" runs along the top inside of the boat on both sides. Angus cut that clamp at the wrong angle.

"Maybe I was tired or something. I lived and breathed the boat for such a long time, morning and afternoon and even at night sometimes: maybe I thought it had its own feelings, and a voice would stop me from making mistakes. I was wrong. Weeks and months, and all wasted."

Angus went inside the house, arms tired, brain tired, so discouraged that he wondered if this silly dream was a nightmare, and whether the work of hands that he loved to watch in others was somehow impossible for him. It was early afternoon, the sun spattering the Bay of Quinte with spangles that danced tip-toe on blue waves. Angus had a drink and slept for a couple of hours. His wife, Barbara, made him a sandwich when he woke.

Outside in its canvas shelter, Scott Hutcheson's boat was still stubbornly imperfect, a wooden puzzle into which one of the parts refused to fit. Over Angus' shoulder in the late afternoon sun a voice said, "Awful isn't it?"—musingly, as if someone had been watching Angus work with sympathy, but no hint of condescension. Scott Hutcheson himself, of course. Angus knew that. Scott Hutcheson, who'd spent his life as a fisherman and then died. "Take that clamp out and do it again," Scott said.

"All right, then," Angus said, "I will."

How many of us living here and now hear voices from the past? "Dammit," said Angus, "I knew he was there! In my mind, in the earth, in the water, and all around me. Don't tell me I'm crazy, I know that already. But Scott knew I needed help, because after all he did have some small interest in the reconstruction of what had been something nearly perfect, the shape of a boat married to water. Or thought married to substance, if you want to call it that."

The Trenton of young Angus Mowat and old Scott Hutcheson at the century's turn was a town where everything moved slowly. Streets were dirt with farm wagons and buggies clopping down the road on market days, raising a smoky dust. Bells on horses' harnesses jingled in winter, and there was the crunch-crunch of your feet on dry snow like regular heartbeats. Loungers leaned against the Gilbert Hotel on the main street, chewing tobacco, watching things slowly happen with dispassionate and rather superior interest. There were no street lights. Buildings were lit with coal-oil lamps. When electricity first thrilled through the houses and blazed outside, the birds didn't know what to think.

Trenton was my town as well as Angus' town. I grew up there, too, twenty-five years after he did. Which is how I happen to know the way it was. What I didn't know then was that everything was about to change; the slow clop-clop of a small town's heart would soon speed up to a gallop, the horses mostly die and be replaced by tractors and motor cars. Maybe that's not bad. It had to happen. Just the same, it was a different morning then. On one of them I came down the stairs on tip-toe so I wouldn't wake my mother, closed the screen door softly, and crossed a dirt road to the river, my part airedale dog following like a dog-shadow behind. There's something uncanny in thinking about doing this so long afterwards.

Blacksmiths are, of course, necromancers and wizards. Angus knew this and so did I. We watched the cherry-red iron shoes glow and smelled the sweet-sickening odor of horses' hooves together and apart from our twenty-five-year interval of being there. The blacksmith's name was C.P. Yourex.

If you don't know how things are done, made, manufactured, it's a mysterious process to watch happening for the first time. The pumpmaker's shop was a dark dusty cave, full of strong scent of pine and cedar. Wheels turned and belts whirred. Enthralled boys crowded the doorway to watch—but timidly, for old MacLean's temper was an uncertain quantity. Sometimes he would grunt beneath his yellow beard, and chase Angus and me and the other boys off home with a terrifying yell. We never knew if it was real anger or only play-acting.

In winter with red scarves coiled around our cold noses we'd watch the sleighs coming upriver from the Bay of Quinte, each piled high with three-foot chunks of ice. The great horses' hooves beat on their ice road in heavy rhythm to match the zero-zero sound of bells. When the smoke-breathing teams stopped, we watched their crystal cargo conveyed along rollers to the sawdusty icehouse, horses doing the hauling and teamsters yelling "Giddyup" or "Whoa" in voices like thunder. Angus and I never knew exactly where that ice came from, until we snitched a ride on the sleighs one cold day, and watched the elemental stuff being sawed like lumber and magicked off to the housewives' town.

"Angus," I say, "was it like that for you as it was for me?"

"Until the war. Then everything changed. I was a kind of Victorian prig before that."

"What about the war?"

"I don't want to talk about the war."

"Look, I'm doing this piece about you. Don't be so damn difficult."

"Well (a little surlily), whaddaya wanta know?"

Angus dreams still of World War I. The Fourth Battalion marches and counter-marches in his head, all in vivid colour. One scrap of the rarely-talked-about reality: after being a private for fourteen months, Angus was commissioned in the field as a second looey. His Uncle Jack Mowat was a major in the Somme battle sector. At the same time there was this Sergeant Crouch who had a yen for souvenirs—always laden down with German turnip watches and helmets in the Regina Trench.

Comes attack and counter-attack by the enemy, and ground hard-won by Canadian troops is lost. Then with shells bursting and bullets whining, the Fourth Battalion retakes the Regina Trench. But Uncle Jack Mowat was wounded in one arm and is missing. Where is he now? Find him, says the CO. Sergeant Crouch and Second-Looey Angus go out to search: but there is nothing to find. Major Mowat had been blown apart, his body completely disintegrated. His soul? Maybe it screamed for a few seconds where his body had been hovering over a lost place in the Regina Trench on the Somme.

Angus was Major Angus in World War II, no longer a member of the Fourth Battalion, but the newly formed Hastings and Prince Edward Regiment—a staff officer this time.

"I was old," says Angus defensively. "And my right arm was nearly useless after the first war."

Long after the last of all our wars an echo of the Hasty P's regimental marching song is still heard sometimes at the armoury parade-ground in Belleville:

From the town of Napanee
Came a horse's ass—that's me,
Where my father shovelled horse shit on the street.
And one day late in the fall
He found me among the balls,
So he picked me up and called me
Hasty P—

After World War I Angus was a beekeeper, a fire ranger, and worked briefly in a sash and door factory. In 1924 he became librarian at Trenton. Says Angus: "It was known that I had once read a book." In the late thirties he wrote two of them himself, both novels: *Then I'll Look Up* (1939) and *Carrying Place* (1941). His son also writes.

Angus reorganized the libraries at Trenton, Belleville, Windsor, and Saskatoon before World War II. In 1937 he was appointed Director of Ontario Public Libraries. "I loved the work," he says. "People and books are the most important things in life."

"Angus, what is there about living in a small town at the turn of the nineteenth century?"

Angus has a full white beard, which he fondly imagines makes him look like a Highland Scot. He waved it at me thoughtfully. "Everyone was going to live forever, we all knew that. A boy could believe what older people told him, then. A man might be digging ditches, at the bottom of what you might call the social strata: but always in his mind he knew that he was a relative of the chief. No, not nobility, something more important—the feeling that you were known or even loved sometimes by everyone in that small town."

I mentioned dryly to Angus that my memory of Trenton held no such vision of inherent natural nobility. "You were a sonuvabitch even then," he said calmly. Of course, you have to be a bit cautious with Angus, flattery must be acid-coated and you get in another remark quickly before the bear waggles like a major or a library inspector or a literary gent. Angus is not exactly a gentleman of the old school, either, mannered and courtly. He bites.

We are sitting in Angus' living room under the high arched ceiling, drinking brandy slowly, and slowly words die down. Barbara and my wife are preparing dinner. The fireplace stirs, red coals and grey ash about to collapse on itself. It seems almost idyllic—a nice prettied-up picture of human existence. Hence I feel I've missed something, left something out.

Maybe after a long life that is crowded with shame and pride, adventure and monotony, what a man is becomes clear finally through where he is, how he talks, what goods and chattels he owns—all part of the total bundle of Angus. In my own worst moments many people seem to me to be only talking heads, pre-programmed to speak all the words inherited from the faraway grunts and moans of a million years of human ancestry. Speech is dubbed-in by fathers and mothers, the deliberate teaching of sound symbols and intuitive gestures of hand and body that we all inherit. And then the people who went before disappear at some point in our lives into empty space behind us. It must be done like that, of course, for there is no other way.

But then there's Scott Hutcheson's boat and its three years of rebuilding, with no power tools used; its subtle anachronistic design, in which the stern bolts are so arranged that no propeller can ever be installed—like a chastity belt against the machine age. For me that boat is a survival from the past, just as an unborn baby's swift progression through all the previous animal stages before the triumph of being born is such a survival. It speaks for all the Greek triremes and Roman galleys, dromonds and hollowed-out logs and Egyptian barges that rot and rot forever at the mouth of the Trent or some nameless river in the Mediterranean basin. It speaks for Angus.

Sipping the brandy slowly (Barbara frowns from the kitchen), Angus says, "The lines of that boat are as near perfection as a man or a boat can get. The only one of its kind left on the Bay of Quinte."

"Continuity and survival?" I say, unsubtly insistent. The beard waggles at me. He knows I know he knows.

But only yesterday Scott Hutcheson had the last word: "That deck beam is all wrong. It ain't worth a pinch of coon shit!"

*(1974)*

# Norma, Eunice, and Judy

"CANADA?" I'VE HEARD IT SAID, "Why, there's no such place!" A non-country, the only western so-called nation to have its 1936 Olympic athletes give Hitler the Nazi salute. A kind of vacuum between parentheses. The sort of place where anyone with the least vestige of ability leaves quickly to avoid contamination by their fellow nonentities. An outlying colony of imperial America, bought and paid for by the United States—if not yet signed, sealed, and delivered to them. A nation without culture, art, or literature; a 4,000-mile-wide chunk of Arctic desert; a Mobius strip facing the United States and turning away from itself uneasily because there is really no self to verify its own existence.

That's what many people think of Canada, including Canadians. It leaves the youngsters who are going to school here and just beginning to think for themselves in a terrible quandary. They ask themselves the old question "Who am I?"—then look around to discover that none of their schoolmates know, either; in fact, neither do many adult Canadians. And yet, incongruously, inside the vacuum a groundswell of nationalism is making itself felt. Nationalism as the knowledge that we are here, and reality begins here. For reality is what you can touch and feel in the areas immediately beyond your eyes, and in the space that surrounds your body. It is the consciousness of self as the last link in a long line of selves, a knowledge of what those others did in the past before the present self fades and rejoins the past.

But what if there is actually no knowledge—or very little—of our own reality in the present-past? Or none beyond a dead parade of events that recorded history does not bring to life—the record of occupied space and time without purpose or meaning? What does our young student in a Canadian secondary school feel then, in a country where the native literature is added to English Literature or American Literature like an afterthought? Where it is said to be not worth teaching? Who shall he turn to then? How shall he answer that question, "Who am I?" To whom can he turn for knowledge of Canadian literature?

There is really only one man: Jim Foley of Port Colborne, a high school teacher who has seen his own interest in Canadian writing balloon from personal enjoyment and spare time passion to lifelong, whole-hearted obsession. A mild-mannered, balding man in his early fifties, Foley says, "I guess I didn't know what was happening to me. I just got involved more or less gradually. But when I realized that Canada must be the only country in the world where high school kids aren't taught their own literature, then I had to tell them and their teachers about it. I had to tell them what they're missing!"

This spinning globe has a fair number of obsessed people walking around on it, even a few grinding their own axes in the interests of education. Jim Foley, with his wife and four children, his job teaching at the local high school—even with the recurrent coronaries that will probably kill him eventually—does not seem unusual. The way he walks and talks seems to say that high drama is for the athletes (although he was a football and hockey player during his own schooldays), drama is for Moses or Moishe Dayan or Richard Nixon: "I'm a teacher." And yet this is the man who, after an experimental CanLit course in Brantford in 1966, organized Port Colborne's Canada Day in 1971 and every year thereafter, which nearly every writer of any prominence in the country has attended, donating their services for free.

Canada Day in March, 1974, came off just after Jim Foley had his last heart attack; a mild one this time, no big deal, he says. But organizing the affair with its several dozen writers in attendance, along with visitors from outside, students of Port Colborne High School, Secretary of State Hugh Faulkner, and Mel Hurtig among the guests, and financing by the Canada Studies Foundation and the local mayor and chamber of commerce and Foley himself—all this calls for a driving man, maybe even a prophetic, vituperative Moses totally unlike the stricken image of Foley himself.

"It will come," he says in his non-Moses voice. "A few years from now, perhaps, but it will come. Margaret Laurence, Atwood, Layton, Garner, and all the others who talk about the place we live in, their voices will be heard and taught in our schools. Those writers are the people who dream for students, kind of like springboards from which the kids' own thoughts can leap somewhere else."

In the meantime Foley and his wife answer a thousand letters a month from all over Canada, mostly from teachers who want to teach CanLit, but don't know anything about it. In the meantime he fires off letters to Thomas Wells, Ontario Minister of Education, urging that CanLit be taught. In almost non-existent spare time he is compiling an Information Bank on Canadian books—7,000 of them—cross-indexing by topic: ethnic groups, cities, the Depression, women's rights, etc., etc.

He collects beer bottles with his students and shows movies to raise money for the annual Canada Day, as well as lecturing wherever anyone wants him to go, wheedling, coaxing, temporizing, and soliciting funds whenever anyone shows signs of interest. All this activity is a little like the mole that began moving a mountain mouthful by mouthful, then found that the mountain had a heart of stone.

Jim Foley was born in 1922. Both his parents died when he was four, so the youngster ended up in an orphanage, which he hated. He ran away from it at age nine, roaming the streets of Toronto's Cabbagetown, stealing apples and oranges from fruit stores, sleeping wherever he could find a warm place, running away from whoever was chasing him, whether cops or skid-row bums.

At 269 Carlton, just down the street from Maple Leaf Gardens, was a house that wasn't a home in 1932. Young Foley wandered into it looking for shelter, for food, looking for something. Three prostitutes who lived there adopted the boy unofficially. They fed and clothed him, sent him to school, wiped his nose, and made him do his homework. And gave him love: "No mother could have loved me more than those three," says Jim Foley. Their names were Norma, Eunice, and Judy. Hallowed be their names!

I don't know what to call 269 Carlton Street: was it a brothel, a house of ill fame, or a whore-house? At any rate, it was a home for Jim Foley from age nine onwards. He washed the floors and helped with the dishes. When he had a cold, Norma, Eunice, and Judy nursed him, tucked him into bed, told him bedtime stories. A few years later they paid his way to St. Michael's College, where he played football and hockey. Teammates at St. Mike's were Nick Metz, Pep Kelly, Art Jackson, and Roy Conacher; the first three played for the Toronto Leafs after junior hockey, always slightly in the shadow of the "Kid Line" of Busher Jackson, Joe Primeau, and Charlie Conacher during the Leafs' great days—the days of hockey heroes, the days when some of us are old enough now to have been young then. And in the gondola at Maple Leaf Gardens, down the street from 269 Carlton, Foster Hewitt shrieked into the radio microphone: "He shoots, he scores!"

But Jim Foley never scored. He was just too small, only 115 pounds soaking wet. But his days of wandering the streets of Cabbagetown, stealing fruit from Ciro's at the corner of Carlton and Parliament, swimming skinny in the Don River, being chased by conductors after pulling the trolley wires off street cars—those days were over. He went to Columbia University in New York instead, and became, he says, "a professional student" rather than a pro hockey players. Financed, of course, by Norma, Eunice, and Judy.

Twenty years later Jim Foley challenged Canadian writers, publishers, and educators during a Canada Day panel discussion on what he called "the apathy about Canadian Literature in this country." The little high school teacher, a mouse among the elephants, daring the Deputy Minister of Education for Ontario, George Waldrum, and other assorted big-wigs to contradict him, told about people being stopped on the streets of large cities two years ago and asked to name five Canadian writers. "Of the over one hundred people stopped, none could give five names." Which sounded like an accusation, and it was. "I looked through bookstores in Hamilton and Niagara Falls a while back," Foley added, then paused. "You know what I found, or rather what I did not find? On the shelves of those bookstores, zero to one per cent of the books were Canadian."

Somebody said "Harumphh"—maybe it was the Deputy Minister of Education—then, placatingly, that there was a need for a few more Port Colbornes in this country, in which case there would be no problem with apathy about Canadian literature. Publisher Jack Stoddart denied apathy entirely, mentioning as proof the 3,000 people in attendance at Canada Day. Novelist Hugh Garner said Canadian literature was just coming into its own. Poet Don Gutteridge felt likewise. Others too denied the charge.

If something is said vigorously, attacked vigorously, people will always be found to take the opposite viewpoint. The elephant's tail switches angrily at his tormentor, but the mouse is smiling. And no one could refute the charge that only zero to one per cent of the books in most of our bookstores were Canadian. And those one hundred people stopped on the street who couldn't name five authors—how many of some 23,000,000 Canadians could do any better? Or, reversing the question, could five authors contain in their writings the hopes and aspirations of 23,000,000 Canadians.

I asked Jim Foley, "What happened after you went to New York? What about those three surrogate mothers in Cabbagetown?"

"They wrote me a letter after I had spent two years at Columbia. They said that it's best we shouldn't see each other any more. They said: "It's better that way, now that you are at university and will amount to something, it's better that way."

"Did you ever see them again?"

"I went back to the house on Carlton Street, but couldn't find them."

"Everything else the way it was, exactly the same house?"

"Yes, but only strangers answered the door."

While at university, Foley worked as an orderly at a New York hospital and as a part-time janitor. He received athletic scholarships to play hockey and football, leaving Columbia with a PhD in Philosophy. After working in Japan during the Korean War, he taught high school in Rivers, Manitoba, in Sioux Lookout and then Brantford, and finally in Port Colborne; getting married in 1952, then the children.

In 1974 Foley is sitting in his office, cross-indexing 7,000 Canadian books, answering letters from teachers and kids, saying "Dear Mr. Suchandsuch: Yes, Hugh Garner writes about Cabbagetown in Toronto (I know it well). W.O. Mitchell writes about the Prairies, Jake and the Kid, and Crocus, Sask. Margaret Laurence about Manawaka. But don't let that fool you, Manawaka is really Neepawa, Manitoba. And there is Ernest Buckler in the Annapolis Valley, Hugh MacLennan in Nova Scotia, and Quebec with its 'Two Solitudes.' Yes, they are real places. Yes, they are home-country . . ."

*(1974)*

# Bon Jour?

ABOUT TEN YEARS AGO MY WIFE AND I were driving through Quebec, along the St. Lawrence River's south shore. We stopped at little villages, emitting oohs and ahs at the architecture of houses and churches, stopping when it felt comfortable to stop. We looked at the home craftsmanship in museums and local displays; crossed a river by ferry, connecting with a cable to the other shore; we met a cordial priest, who gave us a conducted tour of his old church, a place in which the whole interior felt touched and used by generations of people.

At one point we found ourselves driving over flat countryside, and had decided by then that we'd better speed up a little in order to reach our destination in the Maritimes before laziness overcame us entirely. Then another car appeared ahead of us, with Quebec license plates. It drove between fifteen and twenty miles per hour, and stayed directly in the road centre. My wife was patient for perhaps a quarter of an hour, then she beeped the horn. The car ahead stopped immediately, in the road's centre, and my wife braked our car. We looked at each other. Omigawd, I thought, and we both thought: the guy has seen our Ontario license plates in the rear view mirror, and now some racial unpleasantness is about to happen.

I got out of the car, walked around to the driver's side, got behind the wheel, and gunned it around the Quebec car, narrowly avoiding the ditch. The good feeling we had about being there was destroyed. And I've sometimes wondered since if I would have taken the same evasive action if the same incident had occurred in English-speaking Canada. It's doubtful; I am not notably meek in such situations.

But it's entirely unfair to base an opinion of Quebec on such an incident. I lived in Montreal a few years ago. Frank Scott, poet and ex-professor of law at McGill, provided a kind of meeting place for French and English. He was and still is the catalyst, enabling the two to join in an atmosphere of cordiality and liking. Among others, I met Jean Palardy, connoisseur and author of books on Quebec furniture, and Gilles Hénault, the poet, at Scott's place. And they were generous enough to speak English since my high school French is almost non-existent.

By any standards I can think of, the Quebec Premier, René Lévesque, is a man of good will. I don't happen to agree with his politics of Quebec separation, but no one could possibly deny that Lévesque is the most natural person and human politician it's possible to meet, whether on television or anywhere else. I met him six years ago in Montreal, when *Maclean's* magazine wanted me to write an article about him. The meeting has coloured all my thoughts about Quebec ever since.

*Arriving at Parti Québécois headquarters, I'm a little early for my appointment at 2:00 p.m. and walk around the Avenue Christophe Colomb area. It's commonplace and working-class, bakeries, garages, small apartment blocks, the CN railway tracks nearby—so humdrum ordinary you think nothing could ever happen here but babies. In six years I don't suppose it's changed much.*

*At the bright blue PQ building, with a fleur-de-lis flag waving, campaign workers dash around bearing dispatches and café au lait. A girl brings me a chair: Lévesque is late. Like a brisk small general he appears forty minutes later, carrying a briefcase, shakes my hand and says, "I'm sorry I kept you waiting. Be with you in five minutes."*

*Upstairs in his office Lévesque fiddles with papers, and nearly disappears behind a huge desk. I feel silly. I mean, me and twenty questions for a guy who's heard them all before. Not awe-struck—nobody could possibly feel that way with Lévesque. Hair brushed sideways from vanity across his bald head, puffing his millionth cigarette, tanned and healthy looking, not sallow and pale as on television. The exact opposite of bearded heroic Fidel Castro leading his rebels down a dirt road in Cuba's Oriente Province. And yet Lévesque is definitely a rebel, he says so himself.*

*But if he's heard all my twenty questions before, I've heard all his answers before—on television and in the newspapers. So what's the point of this interview? I guess it has to be impressionistic, its relevance tied to what I think of Lévesque personally. As well, the answer he gave to just one question of mine: "What do you think is your particular strength, the quality that makes you leader of the PQ? I mean, is it personality, vote-getting, decision-making or what?"*

*Lévesque says, "I represent the mainstream of change, the time that is nearly upon us."*

"The time that is nearly upon us" has arrived. Six years after that interview René Lévesque is Premier of his province. Within the next few months there will undoubtedly be a referendum in Quebec, at a time when Lévesque is reasonably certain that his people will vote for separation from the rest of Canada. The murder of Pierre Laporte by shadowy terrorists is long past; his killers are sweating out their exile in Cuba. And at this precise moment, Lévesque and his *confrères* are at the crest of an emotional high that would shame every LSD and speed addict in the world. Moses leads the Children of Israel out of Egypt; Simon Bolivar rides again; Leonidas is shaking his rusty sword at the Persians and cussing in joual, "Maudit Anglais," or something; Taras Shevchenko and Vladimir Lenin are tall in the saddle; the Boston tea-party is now equalization payments and the integrity of the French language in Quebec airspace. (I do think the part about airspace is a bit of a comedown.)

But get back to that statement of Lévesque's, that he is one of the most typical of the Québécois. Does everyone feel as he does, that separation is the only answer? The polls say no, only about 25 per cent feel that way. But the opinion polls aren't all-seeing and all-knowing. Time is actually on the side of the *Séparatistes*. And this latter twentieth century is a historic and fortunate time for the freedom-seekers, the age favours them: Vietnamese gutting invading Americans in their pestilent jungles; Basques in a small corner of Spain shrieking Freedom; Welsh and Scots in Britain murmuring discontentedly; African nations throwing off the shackles of their colonialist masters, etc., etc. And notice the terminology that seems impossible to escape: "freedom" (that old catchword), "throwing off the shackles," and so on.

What much of all this boils down to is an end-product of the old fierce blood-letting wars between England and France. When British Wolfe knocked off French Montcalm at Quebec in 1759, he set up a train of events the weak-chinned general could never possibly have anticipated. The defeated French have disliked and sometimes hated their conquerors ever since. Never mind all the polite talk from Ottawa and elsewhere, never mind the Quebec Prime Ministers like Wilfrid Laurier, Louis St. Laurent and now Pierre Trudeau. To many Québécois, these men of their own race were and are traitors and sell-outs. Never mind equalization payments. Pay no attention to any good that has come to Quebec as a result of being part of this loose (very loose) federation of Canadian provinces. Ignore goodwill, if you like, since it's apparently quite irrelevant in 1977. There's very little of it around.

In certain important respects, Quebec is quite right in disliking the English. (Of course we are no longer English, and they are no longer French.) As any self-respecting eighteenth century conqueror might be expected to do, the English took over all or most commercial, financial and military aspects of the new territory. Why not? It was the habit and tradition then to loot a conquered country. (It's still the custom, although methods used vary from one conqueror to another.) And if anyone doubts that this happened, take a fast look at the stately homes of Westmount in their stone splendour on the slopes of Mont Royal.

After 1759, the English dominated; then English Canadians took over that job; and now, rather ambiguously, it's Canadians. What many Québécois have lost sight of is the USA, omnipresent in both Quebec language and industry. Americans appear to escape Québécois dislike, despite their being originally English; the mouse does not dislike the elephant, but hates the sight of what looks like a cat.

What I'm saying is: if I'd been born in Quebec, then very likely I'd be a minor henchman or small plotter, too unimportant to be closer than six ranks away from Lévesque. Yes, a *Séparatiste*. Like that guy who stopped his car at the dead centre of the road in Quebec hinterlands ten years ago, hating the Ontario Anglais, hating me.

No Québécois fears that he personally will lose his language; he fears his children will. And when, a hundred years from now, the continent is completely anglicised, he fears that the people who lived in 1977, his people, will appear as oddities, not completely real, an aberration that history has corrected for the greater good of the human whole. At which date, Québécois children will not know their fathers, be ignorant of the struggles at Ville Marie on the island of Montreal, unaware of Adam Dollard and Madeleine de Verchères, the great French drum-roll of history and ma- and pa-ternity (oblivious of their father Pierre and mother Marie).

The children will not know, or knowing think it irrelevant and unimportant. And that fear is the fear we all have: that when we die and our bones rot, our unimportant lives forgotten, even our descendants will harbour no trace in themselves of what we were. The ongoing wave of time will not carry us with it: we will be what we are in our most spiritually depressed moments—nothing. (And of course, this passion for personal survival is a salient characteristic of the entire human race.) We would like to think that if we were able to send our misty astral self back after a thousand years, to explore that place in which we were born—we would like to believe that even after the lapse of millennia of time and distance, a child could be heard to whisper father and mother, or *mère* and *père*.

Is that gushy and sentimental? I hope not. And the words we speak, somehow only that, the Word, the thing we entered and which entered us, is all that can possibly survive of dying and being born and rising again as the grass springs green and the flesh is grass.

Reach back to 1960. In that year I worked for a mattress factory in Montreal East called Johnston's. Having spent some five years in Vancouver learning to operate the various machines used in the manufacture of mattresses (tape-edge, tufting, filler and roll-edge), it was inevitable that they would give me a job of which I was completely ignorant, making box springs; and Hymie Sloan was the prophet of those gods.

If ever there was a dog's breakfast of nationalities in one place, it was Johnston's on St. Germain. It included Giuseppe from somewhere around Naples, fat little Tony from Sicily who once tried to put a hex on me (and thought he'd succeeded when I came to work with a black eye one Monday), assorted Québécois, including Pierre (who thought Jewish bankers controlled the world), and pale Thérèse who was more beautiful than a straight seam. Top dog of this mongrel assemblage was Hymie Sloan, whose wisdom consisted of being Jewish, and thus in Pierre's mind kin to all the bankers who manipulate and control our spinning globe. Hymie was also foreman. The factory owners were English-speaking, but I never did find out if they were American, English or possibly even Canadian.

The language spoken in that factory was whatever you happened to be able to mumble with your mouth full of tacks, or remembered as your birthright; i.e., it was anything. Pierre, a journeyman upholsterer, worked next to me, and spoke perfect French and English, giving me valuable hints on box spring making in English between the tacks in his mouth, and I suspect cussing me in French for my slow-learning abilities.

Listening to Pierre talk about Jews controlling the financial world, I had a bright idea. At least it seemed bright at the time. I began to let slip tell-tale Jewish phrases, dropping them into the conversation as if by accident, then covering up by hurrying the conversation onto another subject. (I didn't know very many Jewish words at first, and had to ask Leslie Mayer and Henry Ballon for more ammunition while we were making home-made beer in my apartment—but that's another story.) Pierre forced me to admit eventually that lox, bagel and kosher fodder were my native diet, in short, that I was Jewish. His impression was that previously I had masqueraded as non-Jewish. Later, when he cornered me with questions about the Talmud, Torah and tough theologic conundrums, my imposture fell apart. But always after this episode, Pierre could never be absolutely sure that I wasn't an elderly child of Israel; and sometimes I caught him looking at me with wild surmise. It's the first time I was ever mistaken for a Jewish banker.

Anyway—downstairs in the foreign territory of French and Italian was Jacques. And Jacques could be called, on some very elemental level, the Bull of the Shop. He weighed only about 175 pounds compared to my 200, but was some fifteen years younger and in top physical shape. Jacques was very proud of his feats of physical strength, moving through the factory like a big cat with the hotfoot, everyone much aware that he was boss.

Eventually it came to the ears of the Bull of the Shop that a large Anglo newcomer on the floor above had delusions of physical grandeur. Jungle tom-toms wove their ominous music among the machines; grape vines whispered that denouement was inevitable. Tony, Pierre and Hymie Sloan knew it; and maybe even my beautiful Thérèse, whose eyes were dark pools in the moon-pallor of her face—maybe even she knew it. And they licked their lips in anticipation.

It started with a grin—from Jacques standing beside my work table. I knew what that grin meant. I grinned back; he knew what I meant. But since Jacques knew only a word or two of English and ditto me of French, it was somewhat like a jungle dialogue of "Me Tarzan, you Jane."

Arm-wrestling was the opening of hostilities. I insisted on using my left arm, my trusty left arm that had previously defeated pretenders to my non-existent title when I was in the RCAF years before. Besides, my right arm was lame, or so I conveyed to Jacques in pantomime. As things turned out, I won so quickly it was no contest, and discontent furrowed the manly brow of the Bull of the Shop. His prestige in the factory descended to the point where even little Tong dared to grin; and Thérèse, whom he loved with dumb passion, ignored him.

Battle was joined once more during noon-hour. Bull of the Shop and Anglo wrestled between the machines, kicking up clouds of dust and choking interested spectators. Jacques was very strong, his legs and arms toughened by toil. And Thérèse watched him admiringly in the front-row seats. We sweated, we rolled on the dusty wooden floor, first one and then the other having an advantage. But I knew he was too young and strong for me; if the contest continued for more than six rounds nothing could save me but the referee and we didn't have one.

Lunging and charging each other, we suddenly found ourselves in the men's john, and simultaneously had the idea of trying to duck the other in the toilet. Summoning reserves of endurance from a younger existence I wrestled the Bull to a standstill, and that was what it was, a standstill. We clasped each other unlovingly and sweatily above the porcelain bowl. Then one of us started to laugh. I don't remember which it was, but then we both laughed. We pointed to each other, grinning, as if to say, "Look at you, what a silly damn fool I am and we are." Then I became conscious of a strong odour—and it wasn't Chanel #5.

The battle was declared a draw. After that Jacques and I became, if not cordial, rather more wary of each other. I didn't intend to take another chance on getting my neck broken in that bastard's hands;

and perhaps he wasn't quite so eager to break it. His French and my English didn't mingle, but our sweat did. Thérèse again gazed on him, her moon-pallor tinged with attractive pink deriving from her innermost thoughts. And while I do not recommend the confrontation of elephant bulls as an aid to *détente* between French and English, it worked for Jacques and me. When I quit the factory a few months later Hymie Sloan shook hands; so did Pierre. Jacques, my necessary antagonist, also shook hands, and grinned slyly. (I think he knew he had me if our Roman games had continued). I don't know if we were friends, but we sure as hell weren't enemies.

It's hard to say whether such incidents have any real meaning; but in the wake of the Parti Québécois victory in Quebec, one re-examines them wondering what it is they signify. One thing I am sure of, and that is that the attitudes of English-speaking Canada towards Quebec have changed greatly. Oh, of course there are still some elements everywhere in Canada that say of the Québécois: "Let them go if they want to go so badly. They're more trouble than they're worth." At a time when simple justice is now possible for them, in the matters of language and economics, it seems they no longer want to be part of the larger federal union inside Canada.

And that is tragic to me, tragic that even after two hundred years our two races cannot settle their differences amicably. After two hundred years, race hatred is still strong; and that's what it is, race hatred. Of course they are somewhat paranoid, an easy thing to understand, isolated on their small Francophone island in a sea of English. The age-old phony catchwords of "freedom" and "masters in our own house" will probably destroy all bridges to the mainland. And make no mistake, everything outside Quebec is the mainland of this North American continent: no matter what emotional high Lévesque and his dedicated men are riding, isolation is neither attractive nor possible. Freedom, they say, and freedom they will have, come hell or heaven; and it will not be heaven. That desired haven is not available to any of us, no matter what our nationality may be.

Being alive in the twentieth century, it's never possible to get far away from such things as unemployment, strikes, economic exploitation, separatism, murder, corruption in high places, and so on. These are the constants of all our lives. But there are a few other worthwhile things besides in human existence: like trying to find purpose and meaning in your own day-to-day living, or exploring someone else's personality in relation to your own. And a country, any country, ought to be a kind of cocoon wrapped around each of us that permits such exploration, allows us to discover our own value, our own meaning as it relates to other people.

That is idealistic, and we have no time for it, because of our lives' outer turmoil. Strikes, political quarrels and constitutional squabbles must be settled first, to provide at least a personal clearing in the human jungle. But they are never settled, and there is never time. The sense of well-being when the sun shines is brief, the fixed instant of rapport with another person passes, and it seems we have imagined the memory.

And after a hundred years, if a Quebec car moving at fifteen miles per hour over the green countryside stops, blocking the passage of an Ontario car, what then? Will the drivers get out of their cars and shake hands? Of course not. But perhaps, hopefully, one might say, "Bon Jour"?

"Good morning,"—then.

*(1977)*

# Aklavik on the Mackenzie River

**T**HEY CAME OVER THE LAND BRIDGE connecting Asia with Alaska, those first men in the Western Hemisphere. The date was between 20,000 and 30,000 years ago. They were short and heavily built people with thick black hair, brown faces, and slightly slanted eyes. They were hunters, dressed in the skins of animals they hunted. Their weapons were stone-tipped spears. All this was long before Homer, before the dynasties of Egypt, before Sumer and the Land of the Two Rivers, and, of course, long before the Bible was written.

At that time the glaciers that had covered Canada and parts of the northeastern United States during the last ice age were melting. They melted first along river valleys, which turned into great misty, fog-haunted corridors between receding walls of ice. One of these river-valley corridors is known today as the Mackenzie River in the Northwest Territories.

The hunters roamed south along melting corridors of ice, pursuing animals for food and clothing. They died eventually, as all people do, and their children came after them in the long stammering repetition of humanity everywhere. The animals they hunted were principally caribou, bear, and mammoth—the latter long since extinct in North America. Camps of some of those early men have been discovered recently. They are the ghostly forbears of modern Indians and Eskimos.

"Coffee, sir?" the Pacific Western Airlines stewardess wants to know. She is black-haired and shapely, almost distracting me from my thoughts about those early people. I'm flying north from Edmonton to read poems at libraries of settlements in the Northwest Territories. I decline coffee politely and ask for beer. There is none.

Under me and under the big aeroplane is the Mackenzie River, concealed at this moment by cloud cover. The Mackenzie River drainage system is the biggest in Canada. It rises in the Rocky Mountains with the name of Athabaska, which flows east and then north to its namesake lake. The Slave River flows north from Lake Athabaska to empty into Great Slave Lake; and forty miles from Hay River on this lake, the true Mackenzie begins its thousand-mile journey north to the Beaufort Sea.

At 7:15 p.m. on May 23, we land at Inuvik Airport. Dick Hill, the quiet-mannered director of Inuvik Research Laboratories, drives me to town over a dirt road. High plumes of dust trail behind every car. I register at the Eskimo Inn which has seventy-nine rooms and colour TV via satellite. Taxis outside are coated with half-inch thick layers of dust. Taxis and colour TV! Can this be the Arctic of fierce husky dogs and bearded veterans of the north?

The temperature is about 40° F; population is about 5000 people, living and working in buildings resting on piles to make their uneasy peace with the permafrost, which under us is a thousand-foot-thick ice animal crouching. After falling asleep around 11 p.m., I awake briefly at four to find that the day still hasn't stopped or night begun. It is comforting to find that my childhood myths about the land of the midnight sun and its red-mouthed slavering polar bears were not entirely imaginary.

On Saturday, May 24, the sun is shining and the air outside is comfortable for me clad in tweed jacket and sweater. The big question now is how to get to Aklavik, "place of the barren ground grizzly bear," thirty-five miles across the Mackenzie delta. There are no roads. On weekdays, there are commercial flights for paying passengers. But it's Saturday, so I hope to share a charter with someone else.

Aklavik is still a mythic place for me, the big reason why I wanted so badly to come to the western Arctic. Built on sand and sediment thirty feet above the Mackenzie's Peel Channel, threatened by floods every spring (right now it's spring), inhabited by picturesque trappers and hunters, old codgers breathing history and fire from their own home-brew (I read that somewhere), its existence began in 1915. When the federal government in its wisdom decided in 1954 that

Aklavik was unfortunately situated, the town seemed doomed. The new modern Arctic settlement of Inuvik ("the place of man") began to rise on wooden piles in that year, complete with government buildings and schools, fresh water and sewage alike contained in above-ground metal utilidors. The native Indians and Eskimos were supposed to throng to the new town with cries of ecstasy, and some of them did. But it turned out they had to live in the old workers' construction shacks, whereas white workers moved into the newly built houses. Many natives thought they were better off in Aklavik, closer to their traplines, less dependent on white men, and perhaps also closer to their own kind of reality.

So Aklavik refused to lie down and die. Hemmed in by marshes and water, plagued with erosion and haunted by periodic river flooding, it was still a settlement that grew up naturally because of hunting, fishing, and trapping in the delta. There was nothing phony or artificial about it—quite the opposite of the oil-exploration and government town deliberately created at Inuvik; created scientifically and a little cold-bloodedly, a hovering outpost of southern man near the Arctic Sea. Aklavik's character is slightly raffish, a little off-colour—perhaps not quite so respectable. But it's much closer to my own romantic idea of the North, of Eskimos living comfortably amid ice and snow, of Arctic explorers and dog teams galloping across the tundra. The Canadian Arctic has changed greatly, and no longer are the old and admittedly romantic conceptions possible. Just the same, I cling to them; I like the idea of a town like Aklavik, rejecting the outside world—but, significantly, not its electricity and septic tanks.

I flew to Aklavik on Sunday in a Cessna 180. These tiny aeroplanes resemble an exceptionally large mosquito that climbs up the sky on a cobweb to an altitude of 3,000 feet. At that height you get a wide-angle view of the 10,000 square-mile Mackenzie delta, which is over a hundred miles long. The river splits into three channels at Point Separation farther south, then becomes an immense soggy blotting pad containing literally thousands of lakes—or perhaps thousands of islands, because land and water are so interwoven that you can't tell which is which. Seventy miles north of here is the Beaufort Sea, with oil exploration going on in both the delta and Arctic waters beyond. West is the Richardson Mountain chain; under us a dozen geese homing to their summer nesting grounds.

We land on a dirt runway and trundle to a bumpy stop. Beside the field is a small log structure, about ten feet by twelve, which is apparently the airport terminal: Aklavik International Airport? I say goodbye to the Cessna pilot, who is scheduled to return for me this evening at eight. It's now 9:15 a.m., so I have nearly eleven hours in which I can talk to people. But there is no one in sight, even though the Cessna landed close to the centre of Aklavik. Dick Hill had given me the name of the settlement-council chairman, Don McWatt, but I don't know where he lives. The whole community seems to be asleep, nothing moves. Only some formidable-looking husky dogs lift their heads as I walk past, and give me a sleepy evil eye: they don't like strangers.

At Aklavik, there are frame houses and trailers here and there, squatting in the mud; mounds of snow and ice, slowly melting in the 60 degree sun; tin cans and bottles along the boardwalk awaiting spring clean-up; and two graveyards in the town centre, with wooden crosses and markers surrounded by a white picket fence: "*Dearly Beloveds*" and "*RIPs*" cradled by water and mud. Mackie's General Store is locked and smokeless. The hotel-cum-restaurant has apparently never had a guest; the pool room is almost noisy with silence. There's a feeling of slight panic: I may walk these dirt streets all day long and never see a human face.

Two blocks away some native kids are walking. I hurry after them, but they disappear like smoke before I can catch up and ask directions to Don McWatt's house. It's like being born again into a world so different from the fat South that your mind works hard to adjust. I intrude past a sign that says "No Admittance" into the electric generating plant, where the man on duty tells me that Don McWatt lives in a white trailer, in a north-south-east-west direction from the river.

Don McWatt's place is completely silent, and I feel embarrassed at knocking and breaking into people's sleep. Some dogs in the willow brush behind make their displeasure known. But Don finally comes to the door sleepily.

Don is a Scotsman, a husky man in a T-shirt. He has a native wife and two children, works for the government, and does a little of everything to make a living. He thinks Aklavik is a great place to live, "At least I did until that thing happened a year ago. I thought this was the ideal place where you could settle down and feel at home."

And he told me about the murder: it seems that this Eskimo kid got liquored up last year and killed a priest. Why? There is no certain answer to that question, except that in Aklavik most native people are on social assistance, welfare, call it what you like. The people are split roughly into three divisions, Loucheaux Indians, Eskimos, and whites. Some members of these racial groups mix socially, but many do not. Native teenagers don't know what to do with their time; there is nothing that allows them to keep their self-respect, and most are handicapped by lack of training and education. Hunting, fishing, and trapping are the traditional occupations, but they don't provide a good living any more: not with the oil companies splashing money around lavishly and old native values disappearing quickly in this new world of the white man's north. So Don McWatt is worried over a possible explosion soon, one that will make his "ideal place to live" a battleground of racial warfare.

Neighbour Frank Rivet is sixty-eight, a veteran hunter and trapper with deep lines creasing both cheeks and a greying moustache. Frank won't allow me to use my cassette recorder, says his story is worth lots of money: "I can get thousands of dollars for it from a man in the States!" Well, then, can I make notes? It seems I can, yes. George Kuzzinie, an Indian friend of the family, comes calling. Both Frank and George agree that the Canadian Broadcasting Corporation is "the rottenest thing in the world. All the people here want to see murder, adventure, westerns. What do we get? Culture!" Their voices drip with disgust.

Frank says that 500 caribou were killed and left to rot in the Coppermine country east of here. "There won't be any caribou left if that sort of thing keeps on," he says. George Kuzzinie agrees. A few years ago 275,000 muskrats were taken in the delta: this year, only 40,000. Things are bad all over. "But I have this beautiful agate," Frank says. "My agate has pictures inside it, a lot of pictures, inside the stone itself. I want a million dollars for it."

Frank looks at me. Well, I don't have a million dollars in my pocket, at least not right at this moment. Frank seems to feel that I ought to have that money and it's hard to explain to him that I don't. So I asked about racial tension.

He says, "The country belongs to everybody." Which is a pretty good answer, except that some people generally want more of it than others.

Joe Carnagursky is something else again. He and his wife Dinah are both twenty-nine; their new house is the finest in Aklavik. Joe is of Czech extraction, has been here eight years. Dinah's great grandfather was John Firth, a Hudson's Bay Company factor called the "King of the North," ruling over a lively empire on the shores of the Arctic Sea before the century's turn. Dinah is part Loucheaux Indian, and her looks are somewhere between merely pretty and extremely beautiful. I kid her about entering a local beauty contest. She replies pertly that she'd never enter one—"then nobody else would have a chance." Joe and his brother operate Carn Construction, perhaps the biggest such outfit in the Territories.

I happened to have arrived here on the anniversary of Aklavik's murderous night a year ago. The circumstances of that night are still fresh in Joe's and Dinah's minds. One Peter Thrasher, an Alaska Eskimo now living in Aklavik, had received $805 in land settlement money on that date. He put most of it in the bank, bought some clothes and liquor at Inuvik, and gave his son twenty dollars. Whereupon the sixteen-year-old Eugene Lawrence Thrasher got very drunk, whether on his father's whisky or on local homebrew no one seems to know. He broke into the HBC store with an axe and stole a rifle, then made for the Catholic rectory. There he was overheard quarrelling loudly with Father Franche, a much-respected sixty-seven-year-old priest. Father Franche appears to have ejected Thrasher from the rectory. Once outside the young Eskimo fired a bullet through the closed door, wounding the old man seriously. Then he ran.

RCMP Constable Charles Bunting followed the crazed youngster toward some willows beside the river, fired three warning shorts over his head, then was shot himself. Frank Rivet, an expert marksman, heard the bombardment, and heard the wounded policeman call, "Shoot him. He shot the priest."

Frank Rivet fired one shot, intending to disable the boy. The slug hit young Thrasher in the chest, killing him. And later that night, another sixteen-year-old, Charles Koe, a friend of Lawrence Thrasher's, got drunk and sprayed bullets into the settlement in all directions. Another constable, rushed in to Aklavik after the earlier shooting, killed Koe. Three people died: Father Franche, Lawrence Thrasher, and Charles Koe.

Terror still haunts Aklavik from that night. Dinah Carnagursky thinks Frank Rivet should have brought down young Thrasher without killing him. Which, or course, is easy to say if you aren't on the scene yourself. Joe Carnagursky says Rivet could only see a small part of the boy's body, and had to bring him down the best way he could.

"And there's still a lot of racial tension here," Joe says. The Indian Brotherhood, the Métis Association, and COPE, the Eskimo organization, are all stirring up trouble. Native kids have nothing to do with themselves, no money or way to get it except by trapping muskrats.

After all this talk of hatred and murder, Dinah says, "I don't like whites!" And yet she is married to a wealthy white man, has many white friends, lives in the settlement's best house.

Peter Thrasher, father of the dead boy, is forty-seven, a man built along the lines of an Arctic Hercules run slightly to fat. He weighs 265 pounds, has a bad back, and is a diabetic. He works at Aklavik's fur garment shop. In Peter's kitchen kids scurry back and forth. Soon the whole Thrasher family is going into the bush on a picnic, to take advantage of the warm, sunny weather. I avoid mention of Peter's dead son, thinking that he must have talked about that more than he likes. I do ask him about racial tension. "There is none," he says flatly. More contradictions, a perfect maze of differing opinions.

Peter Thrasher went to mission school as a youngster, but his grandfather, Mingaksek, took him out of school at age fifteen to learn hunting, trapping, and wilderness survival. Mingaksek taught him everything. Once, when the boy nearly drowned in an Arctic river, his grandfather pulled him out and dosed him with homebrew to prevent pneumonia. Mingaksek was father and mother to Peter, since the boy's own mother died spitting blood when he was even younger. Peter followed the old man around everywhere, plainly worshipping him. Man and boy, the two could walk fifteen hours a day on their trapline and keep it up for weeks. As a man come to his full strength, Peter could take 800 pounds on his back and walk with it. Mingaksek died in 1964. Peter dug his grave above the permafrost.

Peter's son is dead, killed by Frank Rivet; Peter's daughter is in a mental hospital at Red Deer, Alberta, because she began to hate all white people after her brother's death; Peter himself is a diabetic with a bad back. Beyond my understanding, he seems to have adjusted to all this tragedy. In the northern world, where nearly everything has changed from the old days, in which roads and pipelines have altered migration patterns of game animals, with oil and gas exploration throughout the Arctic, Peter Thrasher has retained a humanity and warmth I could feel even as a complete stranger.

I walk along willows bordering the river, near the place where young Thrasher was killed. The banks are lined with steel plates against spring break-up, when ice chews at the soft land, sometimes breaking off fifty foot chunks of it, and carries the dissolving landscape north to the Beaufort Sea. Brown caribou skins rot among bottles and tin cans. Forty miles away the Richardson Mountains lift white peaks to the western horizon. It is a country of such mixed squalor and grandeur, of violence and peace, that one comes to terms with it only on *its* terms. But white men have never done that, and the day of the hunter is almost over.

As I fly back to Inuvik in early evening, a solid wall of cloud is rolling in from the Beaufort Sea. Soon everything—man, beast, and mountains—will be covered by that huge overcoat. Glancing down some three hundred feet I see the small Cessna reflected on water, apparently trapped inside a circle of mist in which a rainbow is also trapped. At this moment Peter Thrasher and his family must be gathering up knives and forks and tablecloth and picnic lunch to escape the threatening sky.

Peter is a descendant of those long ago hunters venturing along glacier-shadowed corridors of northern rivers, hunters of the mammoth and caribou, hunters of the bear. Those prehistoric Asian people moved eastward and the people of Europe moved westward during the long-past millennia, the two finally meeting just a few centuries ago on the eastern seaboard of North America. Westward explorations of Europeans, during the last 500 years, are known and mapped. Eastward migrations of Asians stopped long ago on this continent and turned south. But I have an unexplainable feeling—because of all these eastward and westward movements—that everyone may have been looking for everyone else on the face of the Earth. And that migrations and explorations might have deeper motives than the mere pursuit of food and profit: because humanity has always been searching for itself.

*(1976)*

# Harbour Deep

IT IS ANOTHER COUNTRY, THIS ROCK within the sea, Newfoundland. In remote outports the language is Elizabethan English, or a language as close to it as five hundred years past can echo into the twentieth century. A man like myself, used to the jargon of Americanized English in mid-Canada, listens to this speech with the despairing feeling that here is a land preserved out of time long past, and I am a foreigner. Not only in language, but also foreign to the life rhythms of fishermen and pulpwood cutters. Those are the bread-and-butter basics of this other country that joined Canada in 1949, but that still remains essentially different. Only the baby bonus, UIC benefits, the CBC, and similar federal encroachments into the great island reach the surface of awareness, but they scarcely touch the pride of people who live and die beside the sea.

Harbour Deep is an outport on the east coast of the Great Northern Peninsula. When my wife and I set out for that place, neither of us knew what we were getting into there, except that it would be hard to get out of, since ships called at Harbour Deep once a week only. And there were no roads.

I had been given the name of Ches Pittman, the storekeeper; he'd been asked to arrange accommodation for a few days. We met him on the Department of Transport dock after leaving the CN ship: a middle-aged man in a baseball cap, with the unmistakable look of a man in charge. A free enterpriser to end all free enterprisers, he once said to me, "Put me down any place on earth, and in a few hours I'll find a way to make money." I believe him.

Mountains and water surround Harbour Deep. Orange Bay sweeps in blue for several miles through a notch between green mountains, exploring half a dozen smaller coves and bays. The village itself is a necklace of houses strung along three miles of a single road and causeway between sea and mountains: road where there's room for houses, causeway where sheer cliffs crowd out the people. No police or fire department, no doctor. All is surrounded by a great quiet that finally, when your ears get used to it, breaks down into the small sounds of wind and waves, and of your own breathing body informing you that your life continues. Population a little over 400, with about six families predominating.

Over the 128 years that Harbour Deep has been in existence these original families have increased, and Ropsons, Cassells, Loders, Pittmans, Pollards, Elgars, and Randells outnumber all the others. In fact, the whole village has intermarried since its long-ago beginning, to the degree that just about everyone is liable to be the ninety-eighth cousin of just about everyone else, give or take a cousin and in-law or two. They are related in other ways as well, despite the psychological split between older generation and younger; the nineteenth century still lingers inside the shapes and forms of the twentieth. The teen-agers in "the theatre," playing pool near a pot-bellied stove, drinking beer, and necking, deafening rock music crowding every square inch of the building: these near-children clustering together for mutual dream-comfort are still the sons and daughters of fishermen whose working life is essentially an aloneness of water and distant sky.

We're sitting in a room at Ernie Cassell's house. "You'd better change those pants," my wife says. "Everybody will know you're from somewhere else, wearing those loud checked pants." She knows best almost always, but she's a little off-base this time.

"Of course I'm from somewhere else: everybody here knows that already."

We go to Pittman's store to buy some things, including a notebook and a package of cigarette tobacco.

"Oh, you roll your own, eh?" Ches Pittman says, I had antici-pated just such a reaction, and hoped my expression didn't change while building a beautiful roll-your-own in four seconds flat. Ches Pittman looked at me with new respect.

We walked onto Pittman's dock, away from the half-ton GMC pickup with three flat tires, used for hauling gravel on the road when its tires aren't flat. Boats are chugging in from the sea, for the salmon season is in full swing; from early June to about July 20 Pittmans, Pollards, Elgars, and all the rest bring in their catch. And for every week of salmon fishing Ches Pittman hands out one unemployment insurance stamp. Which is an interesting point, because you need twelve stamps to get UIC benefits during the long winter. Salmon fishing gives you six; for every 600 pounds of herring during the May season, one stamp; and 400 pounds of cod, one stamp. If you're good or lucky or both you can make this add up to twelve stamps without trouble.

However, only the merchant—and here that's Ches Pittman—can give you those UIC stamps. Therefore you can't sell your fish to anyone else, even at a much higher price: you're locked-in to the merchant, or else you and your family will not receive UIC benefits the following winter. The sign in front of Pittman's store and dock says: "With reference to salmon price: We are prepared to meet or best any competition provided in this area." But there is no competition this side of Englee, thirty miles distant. Last winter there was also Charlie Murcill, who'd been running a store and buying fish for forty years. But Murcill has cancer, and is now retired. The price for large salmon is a dollar a pound, and seventy-five cents for small. Some think the price would be higher if Ches Pittman had any competition.

Talking with Richard Ropson, a brown, middle-aged fisherman, on his landing stage, he mentions that occasionally a finback whale will break through the salmon nets: "It do happen," he says, "yiss, but not very often, sir." Richard caught eighty salmon in his nets that day, but another Ropson caught 110.

Ernest Walters, eighty, retired schoolmaster, came to Harbour Deep fifty years ago, and married a local girl. Bent, white-haired, and a little feeble, he runs a small store in South West Bottom, which is three miles away along the road and causeway from North West Bottom at the opposite end of the village. Walters is also Justice of the Peace. When I asked him about any local wrongdoing, he says that the crime wave hereabouts is pretty picayune: such things as young fellows getting drunk on beer, or infractions of the game laws. Walters leaves prosecutions to the magistrate from St. Anthony, who visits Harbour Deep twice a year.

Diane Elgar, in her mid-thirties, is the community nurse. She answered a Grenfell Mission advertisement in England and came here eight years ago. "I wanted adventure," she says. Adventure consists of pulling teeth, bandaging axe wounds, and attending to snowmobile accidents in winter. She is also educated as a midwife. In case of a really serious medical problem, she phones Dr. Tuton in St. Anthony, and he can get here within a few minutes by aeroplane. But the telephone itself came to Harbour Deep only last December; when accidents happened twenty ears ago, the only way a sick or injured person could reach St. Anthony was by dog team.

The yearly incomes of fishermen range all the way from $3,000 to $20,000. The disparity is explainable only in terms of the differences in people, equipment, and fishing know how. However, $3,000 in Harbour Deep would be equivalent to $8,000 or $10,000 a year in, say, Toronto. There is no property tax here; and even the poorest fisherman will have a refrigerator, a deep freeze, and television by satellite. Behind the village a mountain is wired for sound and pictures; sprouting television aerials arch among black spruce and tamarack.

The old men do not watch television much; they walk the long road between the two village Bottoms; they talk to each other, remembering the old days when there were no power boats, and you had to row fifteen miles to erect underwater fences in the sea to catch salmon; and sea-days of pulling at oars where the undersea currents were strong rivers crisscrossing under the waves. And then the salmon sold for only a few cents a pound. The hot summer sun preserves a pale memory of their once deep-mahogany faces.

They are playing pool at the theatre, the teenagers and sub-teenagers, when I visit the place. Beer is swigged, loud music plays, and I am three times the age of any teenager there. A few boys work for the hydro, a few help their fathers fish, but most leave the village, because Harbour Deep will not support more than its present forty fishing boats. Only a limited number of fishing areas is available, and each man draws his own by lot before the fishing season opens. And for girls there is nothing but school teaching or helping out at one of the stores. They must get married, or leave, and most do leave. But when people leave, something is lost out of themselves. This little beyond-the-end-of-anywhere outport has its own leisurely and fierce attraction. Some of them remember; some of them come back during holidays for a few hot weeks of summer.

Noah Pittman, now in his failing eighties, remembers the villages before this village. More than fifty years ago the people of Harbour Deep were scattered among the half-dozen coves around Orange Bay: Duggan's Cove, Jack's Cove, and several others. But came a voice from on high, which in this case was the M.J. Mooney Lumber Company, operating a mill at North East Bottom and employing many fishermen to cut pulpwood. The voice said: move yourselves and all your goods and chattels close to the mill, live there in a place most convenient to your employers. Lo and behold the people listened. They tore down their houses, laid each wall across two boats, and rowed them several miles to the present site of Harbour Deep.

The people came, all of them moved—except Noah Pittman's father. He refused—stubbornly, some of his neighbours thought—to obey the new masters. He kept on fishing as his father had done, while the rest abandoned the sea, allowing their nets and boats to rot beside the shore. But there came a day in the 1920s when the M.J. Mooney mill burned to a heap of ashes and closed down operations; and stubborn old Pittman was the only man still fishing. The villagers were forced to run again to the sea for a living, learn the old trade all over again, and mend damaged nets and caulk their sun-bleached boats along the shore. Perhaps it occurred to them at the time that some virtue may reside in stubbornness, some pride and perhaps some vision.

Surrounded by high green mountains, Harbour Deep's present location has much less level garden land than the old villages had; you could even escape the sun there, and sometimes wander off into cool green forests. But M.J. Mooney and all his works are gone now, save for a pair of rusty boilers squatting like sentinels near the water of North East Bottom. House foundations, lost children's toys, and even graveyards are impossible to find, overgrown with grass and underbrush; the old people who were ancestors of Ropsons, Cassells, Pittmans, Pollards, and Elgars remain there, like stubborn ghosts beside the sea.

During our stay at Harbour Deep we lived with Ernie and Bella Cassell: she vivid and bustling about her household tasks; he a small man in his mid-fifties, not taciturn exactly, but given to silences and periods of abstraction. Often after brewis (a Newfoundland dish of cod, boiled bread, beef, pork, and spices all mixed together) is served for lunch, with Bella talking to my wife over the teacups, I have seen Ernie build a cigarette and then slowly lean forward behind his wife's body, his mind disappearing altogether into a place where none of us can follow. I twist in my chair to watch him go, his face still having the semblance of being here, like a hostage left behind. It is both commonplace and mysterious, this disappearance.

Pleman Pollard, called "Ple" by his friends, is Ernie's fishing partner. Ple is also in his mid-fifties, eyes flashing behind bottle-bottom glasses—a volatile and sociable word-slinger in direct contrast to Ernie's silent departures. All fishermen have partners; work against wind and wave is too hard for one man alone.

On the fishing stage at five a.m., they prepare again and again for the continual expeditions outward that make up their lives. Between gateway mountains the sun is soon to appear in a narrow slot that designates the open sea. Ernie and Ple Pollard chug eastward to tend their nets and bring back salmon. Both are in character: Ernie is no doubt silent, Ple chattering. The round trip takes upwards of four hours, and is repeated twice a day. The two boats they operate were built by themselves, except for inboard diesel motors, also repaired by themselves if necessary. All their equipment, except the two-hundred-dollar, fifty-fathom nylon nets, is furnished by their own ingenuity. In fact, every fisherman in Harbour Deep builds his own boat.

We'd been at the village for three days when the first wedding in three years took place. Of course, other marriages of Harbour Deep people had occurred "outside," but this one was cause for local celebration. Melvin Cassell, twenty-six, and Drusilla Randell, nineteen, are the principals. Father Shepherd, from Jackson's Arm, is scheduled to arrive by boat to perform the nuptials in late afternoon at the Anglican Church. Afterwards everyone will jam the Orange Hall for a reception, complete with food and beer.

I heard someone say about Drusilla: "We're going to marry her up"—but time passed and Father Shepherd did not appear. It was 8 p.m. when he did arrive and the ceremony finally took place. Flashbulbs flashed as cameras recorded the moment when pale bride and slightly red-faced groom appeared at the church door. Several small boys and girls stood by with green switches cut from trees, which I thought at first represented some hangover from druidical rituals, until the flies attacked. Those flies divided into para-military squads of about forty, the better to concentrate separately on arms and legs and faces of wedding guests. Two friends of the groom lurked, fly-bitten, with shotguns in bushes outside the church. The guns boomed like a sudden God on Moses' mountain, and everyone jumped. The little black flies, locally called "skits," desisted not in their bloody work.

Back at Ernie's house, I am seeking refuge from the skits. Ple Pollard enters having partaken of at least one beer. Ple talks, my wife and I listen. Another man enters the kitchen, then a boy. All of us listen. Maybe it's Elizabethan English, maybe Newfoundlandese: but I understand about six words in ten, leaving me minus four, which I have my wife translate later.

"I loves fishing," Ple says, "but I hates working in the woods." That's the bare gist of it, but doesn't convey Ple's hypnotic outport bravura, which leaves me genuinely spellbound, and also slightly humiliated that I can't join this paean of thanksgiving to sun and sea and being alive.

Next morning at nine a.m., Ernie is still waiting patiently for his partner on the fishing stage; Ple has imbibed a little too much the night before. But then, a man who can so intoxicate with words should be forgiven a little alcohol.

One incident from forty years before overrides all others in the history of Harbour Deep. It concerns Joseph and Elijah Cassell, two brothers who were jigging for cod in Orange Bay. A giant finback whale surfaced near their small boat. Elijah screamed, either from fear or out of hope that he might scare off the beast. A huge tail smashed into the boat, crushing Elijah's neck and most of his ribs. He sank weighted down by his heavy seaboots. But Joseph clung to the ruined boat, yelling for help.

When other fishermen rescued him, the whale was long gone. They used cod jiggers to grapple for Elijah's body, with hooks scraping the bottom in forty fathoms of water; but without result. Finally Uncle Jim Randell noticed Elijah's jigger hanging from the wrecked boat.

"He'll know that jigger," said Uncle Jim, retrieving it and dropping the big hooks far down. And Elijah did know his own jigger, for Uncle Jim hooked something, the sleeve and hand of a dead man. Elijah emerged from the sea, dragged upward by one arm, his body twisting from side to side on the cod-jigging line, head waving slackly on its broken neck.

"He didn't look too good," Ernie Cassell remembers.

A shiver ran through the village forty years ago. Elijah was buried in the graveyard. Joseph, the survivor, now quite deaf and nearly eighty, still lives in Harbour Deep.

Around him the Pollards, Cassells, Pittmans, Ropsons, Garlands, Elgars—all of them—live non-fiction lives in their village, like other people in town and country and city; they are human, they are born and they die. And we are involved with all of them, in ways I can't explain. But perhaps when the cities die, one by one, drowned in their own garbage, and when fresh water lakes are choked with floating slime, men and women who can whittle survival from a piece of driftwood may still be living in villages beside the sea. Not idyllic lives, certainly; but they will survive as Joseph survived—close to the jaws of a monster whale.

*(1977)*

# Argus in Labrador

O N THE MORNING OF FEBRUARY 6, 1975, two hunters set out from the coastal Eskimo village of Nain in Labrador to trap foxes on Dog island, a few miles offshore. Their names were Jacko Onalik and Martin Senigak, ages twenty-four and fifty. They took no food along on their blue snowmobile, since they were intending to return to Nain that same night. By next morning they still hadn't shown up at Nain, and their families were alarmed. Friends went out to look for them, but found only the tracks of Jacko's and Martin's blue snowmobile. The tracks ended at an open lead in the water.

The RCMP detachment at Nain immediately radioed the Canadian Forces' Maritime Headquarters in Halifax, which sent a Buffalo Search and Rescue aircraft to look for the two lost hunters. Snowmobiles from that Eskimo village, 300 miles north of Newfoundland, also combed Labrador coastal waters; at this season the water was covered with ice for miles out into the North Atlantic. And a helicopter from Squadron 413 at Summerside, PEI, was dispatched to the scene. Without result. Jacko Onalik and Martin Senigak were still missing.

5 a.m., February 12. I'm at the Canadian Forces Base in Greenwood, Nova Scotia, with an Argus aircrew from Squadron 405, listening to coastal weather reports in the briefing room. And feeling rather bewildered at the rapid pace of events. Crew captain Major Ken Keir outlines the operation. He is a grey veteran with 9,000 hours flying time, who comes from Victoria, British Columbia. Today's flight would normally be a fisheries patrol, on which foreign trawlers operating outside or illegally inside the Canadian twelve-mile limit would be monitored and photographed. But Jacko and Martin were an

added factor. The village elders of Nain had asked that Search and Rescue try one more time. The two men might still be alive, floating on an ice-pan broken off from the shore ice. And they could have taken seal for food—might even be awaiting rescue at this very moment.

"But there's still another complication," Major Kier told the aircrew. An American DC7, flying from Prestwick, England, to Gander, Newfoundland, was now reported far off course—115 miles from Sable Island with only three hours' fuel left in its tanks. The DC7's navigation equipment must have gone completely haywire for the plane to have strayed so far south. There was now a strong possibility that it might be forced down in the sea.

A little later, Greenwood radio relayed the message that the American plane was 130 miles from Sydney, Nova Scotia. We scrub the DC7, and are free to search for Jacko and Martin. And afterwards, if there was time, we could prowl around the Strait of Belle Isle, overseeing foreign fishing trawlers.

The Argus aircraft itself is the principal character in this story, apart from the two Eskimos. When sixteen military crewmen and two civilians boarded it on a snow-covered field around 6 a.m., the thing looked enormous. And it is just that. One hundred and twenty-eight feet long, its wingspan wider that the tallest building in my hometown, it has an airframe by Canadair, with four prop-drive Pratt and Whitney engines. Unlike anonymous airline jets that all look the same to me, the Canadian Argus might be said to possess much the same character as that of its fellow countrymen. Slow and reliable, its cruising speed is only 180 to 220 miles an hour, but an Argus can stay in the air more than twenty-four hours if necessary. In service since 1958, and soon to be replaced by more modern aircraft, only one Argus has ever been lost: during Canadian-American exercises off Puerto Rico several years back. Ron Lasseter, today's tactical co-ordinator, says of that plane, "It may have been flying too low, looking for submarines, and caught one wing tip in the water." Fifteen Canadians died on that Argus, in the sea off Puerto Rico.

While the three pilots go through all the complicated rigmarole of getting the sky-buggy ready for 7 a.m. take-off, boyish-looking Capt. Lasseter shows me around the aircraft. I am slightly excited— well, maybe a little more than slightly. But all the military guys around me look calm and collected; it's nearly everyday stuff to them. The radio men check equipment; the navigators are about to navigate; the engineers see to their gauges and dials and things. And the three pilots, sitting in the big flight deck among so many gimmicks that no single Rube Goldberg brain could have conceived them all—the pilots look ordinary! And Ron Lasseter, from Huntsville, Ontario, is like a tour guide for me. He shows me everything but the secret stuff, which is canvas-covered. I don't know what it is, and don't want to know; but I harbour the hope that we have an electronic bug implanted in every foreign trawler's rear end.

On a more commonplace level, the Argus has all the household equipment normally found in a well-furnished apartment. Galley with an electric stove and fry pan, toaster and fridge; also radar, radio, and other communications gadgets not found in any home. And a chemical toilet, which is one step ahead of my own primitive rural outhouse. There are seats and bunks where you can flake out if flight-fatigue gets to you; also white paper bags, which Ron Lasseter says are for airsickness. The aircrew, if any of them do happen to get sick from too much aerobatics, just use the bags provided and go back to their jobs immediately; there's a pride involved in not having someone else take on the job you're supposed to do yourself. And among all the calm bustle around me, only the observers seem to be not quite so occupied as the rest. They've got nothing to observe yet, not until take-off. Which reminds me that Argus, in Greek mythology, had a hundred eyes, of which only two could sleep at one time. When we are air-borne, none of our human and electronic eyes will fall asleep.

7:20 a.m. Take-off time (and I feel very melodramatic about it)— 187,000 pounds of old-and-tired-from-years-of-service Argus lumber into the air above our planet. Unfastening my seatbelt, I stand behind Major Keir and Capt. Bob Fuller, noticing the worn condition of the Argus' padded instrument panel, noticing also with some surprise the American flag badge on Bob Fuller's shoulder. He's an American exchange officer from Glendale, California, on a two-year tour of duty in Canada. His counterpart is somewhere in the United States with the American military—a portable Canadian branch plant. Bob Fuller is a most likeable guy, and no doubt helps out with his abundant American know-how.

We are some 8,000 feet high, crossing over the Summerside Search and Rescue base, then above the Strait of Belle Isle between Newfoundland and Quebec. Under us ice and snow and more ice and snow. Paul Gelinas, a photographer, is dashing hither and yon making little rapturous noises and taking pictures. I circulate the hundred-foot cigar tube and talk to people. We are all dressed in bulky flying suits, and later rubberized orange Mae West lifejackets, each stuffed with a variety of survival equipment, in case of being forced down in the sea. I think of Jacko and Martin down there, for whom this mission of ours might mean life itself.

Breakfast is bacon and eggs, served on disposable plates to the accompaniment of four engines so noisy that you almost have to spit in someone's ear before your voice is audible. Grey dawn arrives without the prior announcement of a red sunrise: it's just here. Urgency and excitement subside, the dentist's drill of noise and vibration continues. I lie on the reclining seats, mulling over the general pattern of Canadian Forces' patrol operations. There are four main types of flights: Northern Patrols, Fisheries Patrols, Search and Rescue, plus the all-important Ocean Surveillance Patrols. Helicopters, Buffaloes, and the amphibious Albatross are employed for long-range Search and Rescue, and the general-purpose Argus for all four types of operations. Sovereignty is, of course, involved: the necessity of being on the spot and saying implicitly to foreign trawlers and the occasional ship traversing our North-West Passage: this is Canadian territory.

Anyway, I'm trying to get CanFor patrol operations straight and clear in my mind. It calls for tracing out a mental map of Canada, on which the long-range Argus flies north and west from the big Greenwood base to Frobisher Bay and Yellowknife in the central Arctic. And at the same time Maritime West planes from Comox, BC, fly north and east just inside the Canadian boundary from Alaska, also arriving at Yellowknife. They form a kind of giant pincers, covering the entire Canadian Arctic. The reasons for these flights involve much more than sovereignty: caribou herd counts, whale in the Beaufort Sea, movements of Indian and Eskimo peoples, possible military threat from across the polar regions, and much more.

In summer there are two Northern Patrols a month. In winter, eastern operations are limited to the area around Frobisher Bay on

Baffin Island, for a variety of reasons. The only hardtop airfields in the eastern Arctic are at Frobisher and Thule, Greenland (the latter an American base). Therefore, a suitable landing field in the central Arctic, perhaps at Resolute Bay, is an absolute necessity for both winter and summer operations. Another factor inhibiting all flights is the amount of fuel available: the Argus swills a great deal of its scarce and expensive 115 to 145 octane gasoline; big commercial jets and foreign military aircraft fly on a cheaper mixture. In addition, all "operational employment"—meaning the activities of both ships and aircraft—was reduced 30 percent in 1975, because of defence budget restrictions and a cutback in military personnel. Search and Rescue is still given first priority, but nevertheless this reduction in operational employment is spread over all the different types of operations. It means that the poverty-stricken Canadian Forces are crippled by lack of men and money. It's a curious paradox that we waste millions of dollars on such things as egg spoilage, the Hamilton Harbour corruption affair, and all our proliferating bureaucracy, but can't scrape up enough money to permit adequate Search and Rescue operations to save human lives, or sufficient Northern Patrols to preserve the national boundaries of Canada.

There's no way that you can get to know sixteen men in a sixteen-hour period of time, especially with those four Pratt and Whitneys yammering away like mad dogs. Climbing down into the Argus' plexiglas nose, my flesh feeling precarious and my bones very breakable, apparently surrounded by white sub-Arctic wasteland, I hear someone say on my radio headset, "Cover up that American flag, Bob. It's not that we don't love you, but . . . ."

And someone else says, "Doesn't matter, they've already photo-graphed it." I wonder if that dialogue was meant for me. Who's kidding who?

Aircrew hometowns range from one side of the country to the other. Capt. Bob Blouin, navigator from Quebec City, was in on the search and rescue of Marten Hartwell a few years back. So was Warrant Officer Rod Skanes, flight engineer from Bell Island, Newfoundland, with twenty-five years service in the Canadian Forces. (Marten Hart-well was the small-plane pilot who went down north of Yellowknife and survived until rescue by chewing on some of his dead passengers.) Corporal Glen Hooge, observer from Thompson, Manitoba, and now

Victoria, British Columbia, was originally in the army artillery before remustering to aircrew.

Captain Mike Gibbons, navigator from London, Ontario, was British-born. Gibbons is a greying veteran, now thirty-nine, previously stationed with Squadron 415 at Summerside. He's been involved in so many rescue flights that he can't remember them all: tankers breaking up in heavy seas, people floating in lifejackets, the pontooned Albatross landing in grey stucco waves to pick up survivors. He does remember Albert Muse, a fisherman in the Gulf of St. Lawrence. Muse's fishing trawler was awash in heavy seas in weather so rough that he tied himself to the mast in order not be swept overboard. All other crew members were already drowned. Sighting the rescue aircraft, he untied himself. Mike well remembers Albert's first words over the radio to his rescuers: "Well jeez, boy, I'll tell ya, it's some wet down here!"

Mike tells me about the MA-1 rescue kits, consisting of a long rope hung with survival items and a life raft at either end. One raft is dropped, then the other, after which wind and waves cause the two rafts to encircle floating survivors. In the old RCAF days at Summerside, it was much more difficult to rescue fishermen in distress. They would take long chances, fishing far out from shore, and in bad weather might be swept 300 miles into the Atlantic. They seldom had a radio, which made things difficult for Search and Rescue. Of course, radio now is standard equipment, unless you're competing in the Nanaimo Bathtub Derby.

10:30 a.m. We're roaring above Labrador, a mottled wasteland of granite and ice, so grim in aspect that it resembles "the bourne from which no traveller returns." Geologists say it's so old that it contains no fossil remnants of plants or animals. The Argus swoops low over Nain, an Eskimo village, surrounded by cliffs and mountains. Nain is composed of perhaps a hundred or so government prefab houses. The Argus radio is in touch with the RCMP down there.

East of the mainland village we begin our dog-leg sweeps, thirty miles in one direction, then back on an opposite course four miles distant from our previous swing but flying parallel to it. This allows two-mile visibility on either side of the aeroplane. Observers at side windows and in the nose scan the ice for anything unusual, anything that moves, anything alive. But there is nothing. Once, on a sweep over Dog Island, I catch sight of two wooden houses, no doubt gathered and painstakingly built from driftwood. Their chimneys are smokeless. They appear as deserted as the remains of stone houses built by Norsemen on this coast a thousand years ago.

Below is the unimaginable vastness of ice: ice in mosaic patterns of break-up and refreezing, ice in jagged pressure ridges, ice surrounding open black rapiers of cold water. The twenty Eskimo words for snow must be multiplied a dozen times to reach the sum total of names for different kinds of ice. And 300 feet up seems perilously close to the frozen Earth we came from, and to which we must not return too abruptly. Three times we sight small groups of caribou that have come over the ice to these stone islands searching for caribou moss and lichens. And of course there might be the occasional polar bear, white wanderers in their white world.

1:30 p.m. In the galley cooking steaks, I say to Ken Keir, "They must be goners; it's six days now since they went missing."

He stared at his paper plate a moment, than said quietly, "You know, I'd like to think that if I were down there, everyone would be doing their damndest."

At 2:15 it is evident that our damndest isn't enough. In three and a half hours we have criss-crossed, cross-examined, and in effect placed 2,000 square miles of the North Atlantic under our Argus microscope. All around stretches the vague misty horizon, blending white ice and sky of palest blue. Nothing moves there but a few caribou, bear, and seal; nothing else lives. There is nothing for us to do but radio the RCMP detachment at Nain. They will talk to the village elders, explain our failure. I hope that the village people understand: we tried our best.

Swinging around in a great circle, we head south toward fishing grounds near the Strait of Belle Isle. After the slow speed of low flying, acceleration is like hornets buzzing in my ears. On the flight deck, staring at hundreds of dials and gauges, I am fascinated by the engine monitor. There's an electronic stethoscope implanted in every spark plug, making green fluorescence twinkle under glass, remote from the plugs themselves. All medical devices for monitoring the human body must be parallelled here in a man-made aeroplane; qualified experts like these pilots can name them all. We are watching the plane's entire equipment with an electronic spy. And, watching everything, it makes you wonder: who is watching us?

A sudden radar blip from something fourteen miles away. Russian trawler or alien invaders from Mars? The Argus banks, my body weight appears to double and then triple, I weigh about 600 pounds and hold onto something that moves under my hand. It's Ron Lasseter, and he grins. Below us the towers and turrets of a great white castle are flashing past. "Radar can't tell the difference between icebergs and ships," Ron says.

Another iceberg. "Aha, did that thing ever fool you," I jibe at the radar absentmindedly, while Ron is talking. He's telling me about the Russian trawler caught inside our twelve-mile limit a few months ago, unhurriedly taking up lobster traps. I think: the nerve of those guys! If we ever did that in the Sea of Okhotsk, they'd demand Baffin Island for compensation.

"We photographed them," Ron says, "and let their government see the pictures. The Russians apologized."

I am mollified.

The plane swoops down again, with Ron acting as tour-guide of the ice floes. "These Russian factory ships run to 8,000 tons, their trawlers several times bigger than ours. We take their pictures, stare at them eyeball to eyeball, photographing them photographing us photographing them." I'm getting dizzy from this description, staring down at cameras and electronic spies and thinking, "Am I imagining myself imagining myself or is someone else doing it?" The giant Argus banks south, its hundred eyes shuttered, their work finished.

5:30 p.m. Bright weather has changed to grey mist outside. Somewhere west of us the sun seeds a thousand miles of cloud to orangey red, streaking the long horizon. We are homing to Greenwood Base. Monotony and tedium seep into the mind, which I didn't feel when outward bound. Three or four crew members flake out in bunks, others heat soup in the galley as Major Keir drives the big Argus steadily south. I am half-lying, feet braced against an aluminum partition, thinking about all this: this exclusively male world, because no women are aircrew, jobs that might be combat roles in future.

Although Greenwood does have many women in uniform, both commissioned and non-com(batant).

9 p.m. I am awakened by someone shouting in my ear that we may have a landing overshoot. We do not—and touch the runway like 187,000 pounds of feathers floating in no wind. And there is this deafening silence from engine stoppage, an absence of sound that rings in my head after being a day-long citizen of the sky-world. My ears are still adjusting during debriefing. But while we're in the mess, with yellow beer at table, the crew talking together casually, those four Pratt and Whitney engines recede to a silent snow-covered hangar elsewhere.

Beer begins to relax the tension, and I am aware after the fact that there has been tension. Major Chuck Smith, from another aircrew, talks about the need for more Northern Patrols and Search and Rescue capabilities. Military jargon again, but how else to refer to it? He tells me about the world air routes criss-crossing the Arctic; and how someday there's likely to be a godawful air disaster there, with 300 people crashed but alive, lost in those immense distances.

"And I've counted sixty-two Russian trawlers in one ten-mile area," he says. "During the season, several hundred foreign ships are trespassing on our continental shelf." I ask him if he thinks we should have a hundred-mile limit for Canadian waters. Chuck looks at me wryly.

"It's like this: you can have a village speed limit of twenty miles an hour, but that makes no difference at all if you don't have a village cop to enforce it." Cynical or not, the inference is unmistakable: if we don't control Canadian waters ourselves, the vacuum will be occupied by others.

Greenwood Base is slumbering toward midnight. Beyond snow-covered runways the hundred-eyed Argus sleeps in its hangar. Its crew straggles off to bed; the bar closes. And I am tired, the adventure almost over. Jacko Onalik's and Martin Senigak's life adventure is almost certainly ended, too. The only comfort for the living is to know that we did our best. And, hopefully, at the next report of sailors in lifejackets afloat in the North Atlantic, or of other Jackos or Martins lost from their northern settlements, the Argus or its successor may arrive at the scene on time.

*(1975)*

# "Her Gates Both East and West"

*O*N THE ROAD AGAIN: 1971. Sometimes it seems I've been wandering most of my life. Come to think of it, maybe wandering is my life: the last days at home in a fever to get away, the mind seeing places you want to go to superimposed on your own backyard. Of course, travelling is as much fun anticipating as doing—watching the distance shorten under blurred car wheels, or finally getting there and matching what you have in your head with the real thing. And when inward imaginings and outward reality rush together at sixty miles an hour, you gain something that can't be bought—except with the time of your life.

My wife and I hitched a five-year old trailer to our car that summer and drove through western Canada, hopping from one province to another whenever something interested us: riding around a Saskatchewan farm on a red, roaring combine; fantasizing over dinosaur fossils in Alberta. By the time we got back to Ontario it was getting cold, so I continued across the country alone by train and plane.

Thinking about the whole trip after I returned was like watching one of those jumpy old movies with the mind's eye. You know the kind: the picture jerks unexpectedly from scene to scene and place to place. For it was a journey of the mind as well as of miles, which means I can go back there any time . . .

## British Columbia

Maybe it's a flaw in my character, but I love Vancouver. I've been broke there, worked in factories there, picked blackberries on False Creek there, and been desperate there. The whole city is an adventure—the lush lotusland of the Fraser delta, where drunks pass out on evergreen lawns in winter and don't freeze: they just lie there until spring and peacefully mildew. And I have friends in Vancouver, some of them more or less level-headed, despite the Jaycee euphoria of the place. Reluctantly, they manage to forgive me for living somewhere else. So we park the trailer at a friend's house in suburban Burnaby for a few days.

A week later we're cutting across the waist of Vancouver Island, heading west toward Tofino and Ucluelet on a road so steep that the mountain goats all have psychiatrists. Mist hangs in upper reaches of stone; trees farther down visibly change colour to pale pea-green or dark grass-green as mist thins or thickens. It is, of course, magnificent. We stop at an unlevel place beside the road for lunch. A narrow mile-a-minute river has carved solid rock into a tortuous honeycombed maze. We eat sandwiches with bananas for dessert. I say, "Let's buy some land here and build a house!" (I have visions of merging my lesser nature into a larger Nature and being as creative as hell.)

The island's west coast between Ucluelet and Tofino is a marvellous thirty miles of level golden sand. Whales lollup, spouting a few miles out from our parking spot. I say, "Let's buy some land!"

Anything that's any good you always want to own yourself, to be able to have it and see it again and again. That is until you really think about it. It's taken me a long time to learn that anything marvellous—all those things that produce an emotion in your throat—why, I own those things already. The eyes take title and the mind possesses. That's not just writer's rhetoric. The act of appreciation doesn't constitute legal ownership, but nevertheless it embodies the knowledge that a human being is composed of all the things that he has seen and known and loved.

Just the same, when driving east later through high and wide Glacier National Park, I say, "Let's buy a goddamn mountain!"

# Alberta

From Brooks, Alberta (about 140 miles east of Calgary), we drive forty miles north to the dinosaur park. Fertile plains of wheat country give way to a moon landscape of grey skull-like hills in ghostly sunshine. Here, where ancient volcanoes spattered sky and earth with ashes long ago, the Red Deer River pushes its green wedge through nearly dead earth. Soon we're standing with other sightseers outside a large glass case containing a fossilized dinosaur skeleton, listening to the park warden's spiel.

Eighty million years ago a body of water 500 miles wide, called the "Bearpaw Sea" by geologists, split our whole continent from the Gulf of Mexico to the Arctic Ocean. That was in late afternoon of the day of the dinosaurs. Those overgrown lizards lived on the edge of that ancient sea when Alberta was semi-tropical. The carnivores among them—reptiles from five to forty feet long—roamed the land masses before the Rocky Mountains were born. The vegetarians, generally smaller in Alberta, were semi-aquatic beasts, feeding on plants and prehistoric green salad in the marshlands.

One particular dinosaur of that early era was a duckbilled vegetarian, some twenty-five feet long. I call him Albert, giving him a human handle to make the huge reptile less alien. Consider Albert. There he is, body half-submerged in water, eating greens and being completely at home in the sunlit landscape of ancient Earth. Albert probably had a personality—gentle, I think, and perhaps patient. Under a blue sky and bright white sun, chewing, chewing, chewing. No hint of danger from earth or water.

Then death appeared in the form of carnivorous Tyrannosaurus Rex, who was thirty-five feet long. He grabbed Albert's tail with teeth like ivory traps. Albert struggled, of course, and escaped eventually into deep water, mooing plaintively.

From that time on Albert's good disposition was ruined. His broken tail took a long time to heal, but it did, although aching continually. When he died much later, that tail was a primary reason. For Albert couldn't swim as well, and had to be cautious about shallow water; thus the more tender plants remained out of reach. His digestion and nervous system were also probably ruined; his love-life became a nightmare. And when he died, moon tides swept his body back to the edge of the Bearpaw Sea. It rotted there, and earth, a slow brown-green blanket, formed around Albert's skeleton.

I stand outside a glass case near Brooks, Alberta, in 1971, and there's Albert's skeleton, his tail still bearing marks of Tyrannosaurus' teeth after eighty million years. His bones are now completely fossilized, organic matter replaced with elements of earth. Only shape and form remain. But there's Albert still.

# Saskatchewan

Wilf McKenzie is a wheat farmer ("I'd rather go broke than do anything else!") near Moose Jaw, Saskatchewan—he's red-faced, forthright, and a consummate free enterpriser ("Don't like government handouts, never did!"): a man who thinks that the farmer's biggest problem is marketing.

"Look," he says, as the red, roaring combine grumbles around his 1,000 acres and I hold onto the railing, "we grow wheat for the world, food for the hungry, and there's something wrong when that food can't be sold."

For miles and miles in all directions the only thing you can see is bright yellow wheat. I bawl hoarsely into Wilf Mckenzie's ear, "Okay, it's the good life for you, but why?"

Spinning the big Massey-Ferguson around, he says, "Well, freedom for instance, close to nature and all that. My father homesteaded this section and a half, and now it's me. I've got no sons, but my daughter's husband will run the place after I'm gone."

"You mean tradition?"

"Yes, there's that. And what it says in the Bible, that man was made from dust, and from this same dust we take food for the world."

I look around at the sunlit miles of "dust," heavy clay soil laid down here on the edge of the Regina Plain when the last glaciers scrunched past nearly 20,000 years ago.

"But you're lucky," I say. "You inherited this place. So will your son-in-law. What about the kids who grow up today and in the future? They tell me it takes $100,000 worth of land and machinery to start a kingdom like this one. Say a young guy gets married and he and his wife want to be wheat farmers. How can they raise all that cash?"

Wilf replies so softly over the machine's roar that I have to bend close to his sunburned sixtyish face. "There isn't any way *that* kid can ever be a farmer," he says. "It's a kinda closed shop. If you're not born rich or a farmer's son, then farming a section of land is a great pipe dream.

"But I'm here, now," Wilf says. "Selling is the problem now. I don't care if the price is down, this year's crop oughta be sold. You know, I get thirty to thirty-five bushels of number two wheat here for every acre of God's dust. I take it to the elevator and the man says he's got bins for only number four wheat. What do I do? Take that wheat home? No, I give it to him for the same price he pays for number four."

"Aren't you getting cheated?"

"Sometimes, maybe; mostly not. But the thing is, that wheat is sold. I can go home and grow some more."

The combine roars steadily, sliding mile-long swathes of yellow down its busy gut. You can see almost forever in any direction except down. There's nothing small about anything here. Nothing defeatist. Sell the wheat and to hell with the price. Grow more, keep it coming, feed the world.

# Manitoba

A survivor of the Northwest Rebellion of 1885, now a very old man, was still living in Winnipeg in 1971. Duncan McLean was only eight years old when he was captured by Big Bear and Wandering Spirit. I went to see old Duncan at Gray's Travel Service, where I'd been told he was employed. The man at the travel agency desk said McLean wasn't in just then. I went back again later and was told the same thing. The third time I went back I had a flash of insight. I said to the man at the travel agency, "You're Duncan McLean, aren't you?"

He gave me an odd look and kind of bristled. Then he said, "If you think I'm going to admit that I was a prisoner of Big Bear during the Northwest Rebellion when I'm here selling jet air travel tickets to Rome and Paris, then you're much mistaken." He had a point.

Duncan McLean seemed only about seventy-five at most when I went to see him, but he was ninety-four. And he seemed to sense how I felt about him—living history and that sort of thing—perhaps with a slight resentment. I thought of him in connection with the French and English fur traders of those early days, wandering the prairie of Rupert's Land. But old Duncan fitted no stereotype. He was a snappy dresser, grey pinstripe suit and stylish satin tie making him an ancient man-about-town. Something inside me chortled about this, but I was half-reverent at the same time. It's silly, but I thought: touch the hand that touched the hand of Wandering Spirit and Louis Riel, even if this guy never did touch them.

We drank some coffee and McLean loosened up a little, but not much. What about fear? I said. But even as an eight year-old, his mother pregnant, his whole family prisoners of hostile Indians who had already murdered several whites, the small boy who became this formidable old man said he was never afraid.

"There was no time for that. You have to remember that the Indians were trying to keep ahead of the white men who were chasing them. And we had to keep up with the Indians, even as prisoners. If we hadn't it would have meant starvation in that wild bush country." He stopped to think back eighty-six years, then said reflectively, "Once I saw an old woman hanging from a tree by a rope. She'd killed herself."

"Why?"

"Couldn't keep up with her people, just too fat and old." McLean didn't say any more about that and didn't need to. But the story turned time around for me: a swift picture of the dead Indian woman formed in my mind, swaying slightly in the wind as she hung on a cottonwood tree. Old Duncan was still silent when I left.

# Ontario

Rural Ontario is a nice place to visit. It's also a nice place to live. My wife and I built a house on Roblin Lake near Ameliasburgh twenty years ago, and the "natives" still regard us as outsiders. People around there have voted Conservative since the last shot was fired in the American Revolution, which was when the United Empire Loyalists first started to arrive. And I have no doubt that those first arrivals looked snootily down their noses at the last johnny-come-latelies.

We built the house with a pile of used lumber bought in nearby Belleville, then went inside to wait out the winter. We had no electricity or plumbing. Three oil lamps were required to read a book, and I chopped through three- and four-foot-thick ice for water come February and March. An ancient iron cookstove was the only heat source. In really cold weather, I set the alarm clock for every two hours so that I could climb out of bed and stoke the stove. The neighbours, of course, thought I was plumb crazy and my wife even crazier to stay with me.

But while living there—trapped, if you like—I was forced to explore my own immediate surroundings. In 1957 the old Roblin grist-mill was still standing—an enormous ruined hulk four stories high, with three-foot thick stone walls. I poked into every corner of that mill, stepping gingerly over black holes in the floor that dropped forty feet straight down, marvelling at the twenty-four-inch-wide boards from vanished green forests. Old Owen Roblin built that grist-mill in 1842. Around 1960 they tore out its liver and lights, installing them in Black Creek Pioneer Village just outside Toronto for the edification of tourists.

Wandering the roads on foot or driving when we had money for gas, I got interested in old architecture—not as an expert, but with the idea that houses express the character of long-dead owners and builders. Gingerbread woodwork on a white frame house, for instance: the exact spot where nineteenth-century man worked an hour longer than he had to because he got interested and forgot about money. That lost nineteenth-century hour is still visible at one corner of the house.

I keep finding roads I never noticed before, even after all these years of being an outsider—as if some celestial roads department built them last night in the dark of the moon. Leafy and overgrown some of them, fading to a green dead end at run-down farmhouses, abandoned long since but still containing the map of people's lives. Roads like tunnels under trees so thick that the sun shatters into splinters among black branches. Country roads have this endearing quality of never going anywhere important, certainly not to a city; of being an end in themselves, as if at any place where you might care to stop the car you have already arrived.

# Quebec

Montreal always seems to me an overwhelmingly large metropolitan centre. But Quebec City is a step back in time; everything already happened and then stopped so that you can see the result. Even the tourists here are not quite so hell-bent for heaven.

In bright metallic fall sunshine, an elevator connecting the Lower Town and Upper Town grumbles and clanks between the two worlds. Above it's touristy; below, it's still touristy—but with a difference. Around the Chateau Frontenac Hotel, visitors are in their element; in the Lower Town they are on the outside of things, essentially sightseers on the lookout for something picturesque to remember when they get back home.

I am also a tourist, looking for handles for my memory to hold on to. Here on the waterfront—ships loading and unloading, lovers holding hands with their eyes, old stone buildings protruding from past to present, the quintessentially French feeling of the place— dates tick-tock through my mind like little tricolour flags.

Statues of Wolfe and Montcalm on Grande Allée, the Plains of Abraham surrounded by churches and hotels, French-Canadian his- tory, which joins and becomes my own history in 1759—you have to think of Quebec that way, with a whole net of capillaries and nerves stretching back to the past, woven into the body of Canada as well as into our own bodies, countless invisible threads binding us together in ways that we don't even know about. Which is a point I think the *séparatistes* pass over in silence—the point that the French-Canadian past and the English-Canadian past converge and join to exactly the degree that the spinal cord and pelvic arch of this country's creation belong to both of us.

# New Brunswick

In Saint John I intend to just wander the streets, being a ghostly observer of things. But a gale blows in from the sea at forty miles per hour, and even keeping to the sidewalk gets difficult. In the Loyalist Burying Ground I feel transient as thistledown in this wind; the dead are anchored permanently in the nineteenth century. Full summer brings office and factory workers here to eat their lunches in the green shade, for this is a cemetery without walls, right in the downtown area.

I remember Alden Nowlan, the Maritime poet, talking about the kind of vitality people down here have: "I grew up in Hartland, in midwestern New Brunswick, where they have that long covered bridge that's in tourist folders. The kind of place where everyone knows everything about everybody else. The basic kind of life. Farm- ers and fishermen and working in the woods. Most of them did a little of everything to scratch out a living. And never a very good living. Fights breaking out at dances. What the new schoolteacher was like. The kind of life stuff I try to get into my poems. That wild vitality you see here."

I wander through the Farmer's Market on Charlotte Street, where big orange lobsters stare menacingly at me from white porcelain, beside mobs of periwinkles and clams. I watch the people, trying to see them as Alden Nowlan does. In the harbour a few blocks away, freighters are loading and unloading. The sun sneaks out of shredded clouds, a bit afraid that it may be blown away by the gusting wind.

The Reversing Falls on the St. John River, Martello Tower, the 1810 Loyalist House and Saint John dry-dock—I've visited all these before and don't feel like retracing my steps. Instead, just by walking and looking at people, I get a feeling of this city by the sea, as if using tracing paper over something I wanted to remember. It's a slightly poorer area than central Canada, but one with its own vitality, its own sturdiness of character instilled by sea and land.

## Prince Edward Island

You can see all of Prince Edward Island in one glance from an aeroplane. Not a huge continent or a world, but something the eye and mind can grasp and hold onto. Potato counties and townships at the sea's edge. Dark red soil laid out in squares. Summer crops harvested now and the land nearly naked.

> Since I'm Island-born home's as precise
> as if a mumbly old carpenter,
> shoulder-straps crossed wrong,
> laid it out,
> refigured to the last three-eighths of a shingle.

That's what poet Milton Acorn wrote about his home island and, looking down from an aeroplane, it's like a big backyard, an outdoor living room, a calm place where nobody hurries.

I wander the streets of Charlottetown, past white frame mansions that potatoes built in the nineteenth century; the parliament buildings, where a war was raging about local schools being turned over to the provincial government, making people afraid that their taxes will go up. The province is like a miniature of the country as a whole. But things are slower here and not ashamed to be quaint. Jack McAndrew, the barrel-chested man who was then director of Charlottetown Festival, says: "A man is not depersonalized here; he can be involved and make his personality felt still." I think the whole island feels about the rest of Canada the way one PEI voter felt about the political candidate he didn't intend to vote for: "Good luck to you, anyway."

## Nova Scotia

From Sydney on Cape Breton Island, I drove thirty miles south to the fishing village of Gabarus. It's a scattered settlement of white frame houses strung out along the edge of a bay open directly to the sea, and it's more or less typical of the small villages on this stretch of Nova Scotia coast. When I got there, thirty-foot waves were leaping right out of the water like white animals and a gale of wind was blowing. Landing stages were empty and the village seemed deserted. But it turned out that everyone was at the general store, waiting for the mail from Sydney.

I spent the whole day talking to fishermen and drinking coffee. Any stereotypes that I had imagined them to fit disappeared as quickly as the coffee. You know the idea: identical fishermen dressed in oilskins selling cod-liver oil, as shown on some bottle label. The fishermen of Gabarus are mixed fishermen, like mixed farmers, harvesting lobster, cod, mackerel, or whatever there is. One thing they do have in common: all are over sixty, some well over seventy. Young men of the village all move away to cities to make a better living, and these aging men I talked to are probably the last of their kind.

So here's Trueman: dark brown face with deep lines, and something in his manner that says he'll always take a chance. In fact, Trueman is the only man left with nets still out. When the wind cuts down by five miles an hour, he'll be driving his Cape Island boat to sea again to retrieve the nets.

Albert is another sixty-year-old. But all these men look ten or fifteen years younger than their age. Albert fares pretty well with his life. He has a modern house, a new boat that cost some $5,000, and a walkie-talkie over which he talks to his wife ashore whenever they feel companionable. Once, when he ran out of gas, the walkie talkie may have saved his life. Such gadgets are not luxuries among men who fish the ice-cold Atlantic—merely necessities that not all of them are able to afford.

No, fishermen are not stereotypes in oilskins, but there is something common to all of them. I cudgel my brain to figure out what it is. Maybe a calm and quiet around them. Maybe a similarity to the sea itself. They are not animated and excitable men. They do not gesture much with their hands. Maybe you can say about fishermen that the flutter and excitement of verbal fireworks are for children. They are not children, and there is a dark constancy about them. It is for the long haul and has more to do with an essential quiet, as if life is more important than the words attempting to describe it.

Before driving back to Sydney, I had to sit down for a meal of breaded cods' tongues. They wouldn't allow me to leave the village without having eaten. Now, those cods' tongues imbued me with a certain amount of suspicion. Breaded, they look like any other food that's breaded, but an overactive imagination pictured myself talking to other codfish beneath the sea. I might burst out at table with a fishy remark and never know it except for the surprised laughter all around me. I ate them anyway, and they were tender and delicious. I had two helpings.

On the ferry slip at Sydney, NS, I watched the big ships leave for Port-aux-Basques in Newfoundland. Five years earlier my wife and I had driven a truck camper to Newfoundland. We had gone up the Great Northern Peninsula, stopping overnight in gravel quarries and clearings beside the road, buying cod for three-and-a-half cents a pound and halibut for ten cents from fishermen on the beach, eating raspberries from scarlet bushes, myself having an occasional libation of Newfie Screech to aid navigation. It tastes so bad that you can't feel any bumps on the road, unpaved on that particular alcoholic route.

The reason for our Newfoundland trip was Vikings. Ten centuries ago they landed at a point near L'Anse aux Meadows on the northern tip of the island, driving west through storm and ice from Greenland in oared longships to the Labrador coast. Maybe it was Leif the Lucky who landed in Newfoundland. Nobody really knows now. A thousand years of silence have intervened. But driving up the wooded, sea-lined coastal road, my thoughts were full of horned helmets, Vikings drinking mead and yelling "skoal!" at the Beothuk Indians, cutting down the local timber and generally making a helluva racket.

Helge Ingstad, a Norwegian archaeologist-explorer, had just finished excavating the site of what might have been Leif the Lucky's settlement. I had wanted to meet Ingstad. And now the trip remains in my mind as a mixture of raspberries and codfish, Ingstad (we had coffee with him) and Screech; also Vikings and the dark shadowy faces of Beothuk Indians vanished from earth in the nineteenth century.

In Newfoundland there are lakes surrounded by trees surrounded by water surrounded by clouds, places that seem to have been taken out of a peaceful territory in your own mind. But Sydney is the end of the line for me this time. There remains only the hippety-hop flight back to Montreal and the train rumbling west from there with the rhythm of bare bones on steel. At such times I never feel that there is a point-of-no-return. There is a kind of joy about both going and coming that stems from making the map of yourself on paper coincide with a 5,000-mile-wide country. Of course it never coincides: all you can do is hint at something much larger than yourself. But I feel lucky that I'm able to try.

*(1977)*

# Introduction to
# *Moths in the Iron Curtain*

I AM DOZING IN THE FRONT SEAT of the limousine, a big 300-horsepower Cheika. We are driving along a six-lane highway on the southern outskirts of Moscow, approaching a traffic light. When the light turns green our driver guns the car like a rocket; he cuts left of our line of traffic, then back again directly in front of the car nearest the intersection, narrowly missing oncoming traffic. Then, with a roar of power, he leaps ahead of everybody.

Riding with this mad Soviet cosmonaut, I gasp, completely awake but still semi-conscious, thinking I should have taken out life insurance before leaving Canada. I settle back again to snooze a little: again the driver guns our black Cheika, jamming my backbone against thick cushions. He's ruining my sleep. Here in Moscow it's later than it is by Toronto time. 9 a.m. here is 2 a.m. back home in Canada. Therefore, as far as I'm concerned, we are travelling in the middle of the night; and I've spent odd moments of the two days since arrival in falling asleep while standing. But it's hard to dream much at 130 kilometres an hour.

We are sailing past the birch forests outside Moscow while our interpreter, Victor Pogostin, explains about the Cheika: "Everybody knows what the car looks like. Only big-shot politicians, visiting foreign diplomats and newlyweds get to ride in Cheikas." We're passing an intersection while he's talking, and I notice a grey-clad cop standing at attention, saluting us for god's sake. "Did you see him, Victor? That cop?" The interpreter grins. "He thinks there's a foreign chief-of-state in the car. That's because he's a provincial cop. The Moscow cops aren't so fast with their salutes."

---

And that explains our speed-mad driver. He knows the police think he has bigwigs for passengers, therefore can get away with almost anything. And does, and does. And then some. A wake of harried and nerve-shattered minicars falls behind us, each with a cursing driver; ahead the black-topped road with flotillas of cars and trucks streaming toward us like blurred bugs, each of them awakening a mad gleam in our own driver's eye. They're a challenge to his manhood, potential rivals in worshipping the god of speed.

Despite imminent fear of death, I feel lucky to be here at all. The reason is an exchange-of-writers program with the Soviet Union. The Canadian Department of External Affairs pays the freight outward to Russia, then the host country is our nursemaid for three weeks in the USSR. Ralph Gustafson (he's the guy wearing glasses in the back seat) and myself are the first Canadian writers to benefit by the exchange. Later on, two Soviet writers will visit Canada, and be shown the sights from the Yonge Street sinstrip in Toronto to the Hastings Street drug scene in Vancouver. Our wives (Ralph's is Betty, mine is Eurithe), also come along as female chauvinist chaperones. Both are slightly dazed since the Writers' Union people at Moscow Airport presented them with roses—something their husbands rarely do.

It's about 250 kilometres to Yasnaya Polyana, Count Leo Tolstoy's country estate, which is our present objective. Tolstoy's place is now preserved as a national monument by the Soviet Union. And it occurs to me that the author of *War and Peace*, perhaps the greatest novel ever written, *should* be a national monument.

I doze again, and have a dialogue with Tolstoy in dream-sleep at a hundred kilometres plus. Victor Pogostin's voice keeps breaking into it. He is giving us a running description of the landmarks we pass. "That tangle of steel spokes by the road is a monument. It marks the point of farthest advance by the Germans toward Moscow in the Great Patriotic War." (World War II is always called the GPW by Russians, since their historic emphasis is that they fought a war of self defense with very little outside help.) And concerning the thick forests flashing by the car windows: "Wild pigs were brought in from somewhere else; the pigs prospered in their new environment. But now people are afraid to walk in the woods, because wild pigs attack them. A friend of mine had to climb a tree to escape. And then they tried to uproot the tree with their tusks. My friend sat up in a little birch tree, wondering if he was going to plunge down in the middle of a gang of wild pigs."

Victor's command of English is excellent. Short, broad and bearded, age thirty, he is a specialist in American Literature at Moscow University. He and other officials at the Writer's Union quickly dispelled one pre-impression I had of the Russian character, that it was solemn and rather self-important. Of course jokes at the expense of their political leaders are verboten, not to say dangerous. And visitors like Gus and myself are here in a semi-official capacity: in some minor way we represent Canada to the Soviets. Therefore one tactfully avoids particular subjects that might result in embarrassment. Besides, to disagree in conversation with the way in which the Soviet Union conducts its affairs would seem to me very bad manners toward our hosts. We are guests.

But Victor himself brought up the subject of the Russian warplane that recently landed in Japan. He said the Soviet Ambassador was only allowed to see the plane's pilot at a distance of twenty yards, and that the man appeared to be either drunk or on drugs. I mentioned that it seemed unlikely the Japanese or Americans would drug a willing defector. After which Victor and I agreed that we'd probably never know what really happened, since the stories from both sides conflicted so greatly.

And he asked me if I knew Arthur Miller, the American playwright who had visited the Soviet Union not long before. I said I didn't. "Miller moves in much more cultured literary circles than me, and I don't get to the US much anyway."

"Well, when Miller returned home he said some things to the American newspapers that made him very unpopular here. Which makes me sad, because I translated two of his short stories, and spent a lot of time doing it. Now I can't publish them because of what he said about the USSR. If you ever see him, ask him to go easier on us so I can publish those stories. And ask him to tell the truth about us, only the truth."

Yasnaya Polyana is about four hours of breakneck driving from Moscow. A state tourist attraction now, complete with walking tours and English-speaking guides. Tolstoy is a god, and gods are obviously attractive to worshippers. One index of the esteem in which he is held by the Soviets is their treatment of his house during the German invasion. They sacked it before the Germans could. Everything moveable was transported east of the Ural Mountains for safekeeping. The god's possessions were meticulously listed, numbered, coded and trucked away. And you know, I can't imagine a Canadian parallel to such loving care accorded writers, even politically popular writers. Just suppose the US Marines should invade Canada, as American troops have in past times. Would E.J. Pratt's possessions be removed forthwith from Toronto to the Northwest Territories for safety's sake? Not to compare Pratt with Tolstoy, but it seems unlikely.

The great man's grave is fifteen minutes walk along an avenue of tall birches, through park-like forest. Tolstoy wanted it to be anonymous, therefore the burial plot has no marker. Nevertheless, bright flowers cover the spot, an enclosure surrounded by a steel chain. And one has the sense that Tolstoy's life was a tremendous paradox: here he was a titled Russian aristocrat, who yet thought of himself as a peasant. But he couldn't give up the huge estate of Yasnaya and all the appurtenances of wealth. Corresponding with just about every prominent Russian writer of his day, there was one notable exception: Fyodor Dostoevsky. Why not? Did Dostoevsky, obsessive gambler in his youth, penetrate Count Leo's mask of self-deception and make the god uncomfortable?

There's one very attractive story about Tolstoy: it turns him into a very human god. Playing with grandchildren in his old age he said: "Tanechka, do not think of a white bear. Sasha, I will pay you and the others one kopeck each not to think of a white bear. Now tell me, have you succeeded? Have you been able to avoid it?"

And the children must have looked at him with mixed feelings. They knew something was being put over on them, but at that age didn't know exactly what. This bearded little gnome of a man in peasant shirt and knee-high boots, their grandfather, sun shining between birches on his balding head, why was he asking them such difficult things? And his favourite, Tanechka, did she say: "I can't help thinking of a white bear." Cunning old Tolstoy!—he knew that!

The Hotel Sovietski in Moscow is slightly old-fashioned, but provides solid bourgeois comfort for westerners. We had two rooms and bath, plus television and refrigerator. At a desk near the elevator and stairway on each floor was a duenna—or concierge or chaperone—: I never did find out the Russian name for this woman.

But just try to sneak some girl who wasn't your wife past her at midnight! Of course, I'd never do that anyway. Once there was a young girl fresh as apple blossoms at that desk. I smiled at her timidly. She returned a smile of professional cordiality, fairly close to the real thing. As I approached, I thought of all the other dazzled kindness-seeking tourists and fled.

Our first night in Moscow was taken up with Red Square sightseeing. Every visitor to the Soviet Union goes there, to see Lenin's tomb and that other place where so much ominous news comes from: the Kremlin. But I was more interested in St. Basil's Cathedral. Of a size not overwhelming, its colours are like a child's first discovery of magic in ordinary things. How can the supposedly dour Russian character ever have produced those flashing painted towers, so much like Disneyland without the vulgarity. I don't know, but stopped dazed for half a minute at first sight of the place. It's a visceral experience: a multiple sensation: you feel it thru eyes, ears, nose and tongue if you get close enough; and soul if you have one.

Ivan the Terrible, Tsar of all the Russias, commissioned St. Basil's from an architect named Barma in the 16th century. Then, looking at the place, he grew jealous of any other people besides himself who might see something just as beautiful in the future, something to match these Greek, Roman, Byzantine, Arab, Tartar and gothic silent towers of Babel. He blinded the architect. And Barma sat in darkness for the remainder of his life, with flashing light years of colour in his mind reduced to millimeters of greyness. I've seen no place in the man-created world like Barma's coloured toy, which sends my thoughts straight back to its creator, all creators.

No fruit at meals, which drove my wife straight to Vitamin C distraction. And we had great difficulty in making our starvation known in restaurants at all without the aid of Victor, the indispensable translator. On previous venturings to other countries, my wife had picked up Spanish on a week's notice, also a few words of German in the appropriate country, and even some traces of Greek. The last because her parents, no doubt frightened by Agamemnon and Homer, named her Eurithe. But the Russian Cyrillic alphabet reduced her linguistic aptitude to nil. "How do you say oranges and apples in Russian?" she would ask me at 2 a.m., knowing I didn't know either and moreover was asleep. "Huh?"

Both Gus—uh, I mean Ralph Gustafson—and myself wanted to see Samarkand in order to write great poems about the place. However, an Afro-Asian writers' conference was scheduled for Sept. 19 at Tashkent, in the Soviet Socialist Republic of Uzbekistan which contains Samarkand. Therefore airline and hotel space in Central Asia would be nonexistent after that date. Therefore we left Moscow for Tashkent Sept. 16, arriving after a five hour flight somewhat frazzled and flummoxed. Three hours in a crummy hotel made things worse. We rose, therefore, unrefreshed, around 11 a.m. I snarled at myself while brushing my teeth.

But Eleanor, the Tartar guide, extolling Uzbek-Soviet progress in Tashkent, helped a little. She had a good figure, also high cheekbones which I like in guides. Eleanor said cotton was the white gold of her country. Eleanor said the old caravan routes from India and China with their freight of spices, jewels and slaves now ended at the parking lot of the GUM department store. I was disabused of romantic notions by Eleanor. But she was beautiful. Her name was Eleanor.

We flew to Samarkand that evening, an hour's distance by air. I went to bed on arrival; the others went to look at tombs by moonlight. Early next morning I was watching from the hotel room balcony, as smoke rose from chimneys in the near distance and the city of 300,000 slowly shrugged itself awake. It was Sunday, and people weren't going to work, at least not many of them. I could see an old woman sweeping a factory yard with a twig broom half a mile away, and wondered what her life was like, knowing she is completely ignorant of me.

I got dressed and went outside, walking a mile or so from the hotel. Then kids, a dozen of them; they surrounded me, clamoring for chewing gum. Chewing gum in Samarkand? And I expected romance. Nearby a muezzin muttered something about Allah—at least I think it was Allah; the kids made so much noise my head felt like a loud bang inside a telephone booth.

In deserts beyond Tashkent and Samarkand day has moved silvery and silent, a desert laced and interlaced with irrigation canals blocking off the landscape into triangles and hexagons. Heat lifts from the city streets; you can feel it thru the soles of your shoes, something like 90 degrees Fahrenheit. Dark-skinned Uzbeks in silver-embroidered black skullcaps thronging the market to buy fresh fruit; open booths selling drinks and food, one of them making shishkabob on aluminum rods over a charcoal fire. Who could resist shishkabob in Samarkand? Certainly not me.

Another beautiful guide. Her name is Valentina, and she has blistered heels. Valentina explains that she attended a wedding the night before wearing tight shoes, and danced in them. She must have danced long into the night and then early morning, and must have been still dancing at the time I was besieged by mobs of kids in search of chewing gum.

Valentina gives us the grand tour of Tamerlane's city—or perhaps Alexander the Great's city, the conqueror having founded it in 329 BC and calling it Marakanda. The old town dates back nearly a thousand years before the new town of Samarkand; but older buildings have crumbled long since. It's a colour fantasy of glazed blue tile, round domes of mosques and mausoleums: the Gur Emir, tomb of Tamerlane whose all-conquering Golden Horde of desert horsemen terrorized Europe with their crossbows in the 14th century; also the mosque of Bibi Khanum the beautiful.

Bibi Khanum was a Chinese princess, beloved of Tamerlane, and apparently felt the same tender feelings toward the crippled conqueror. When he was away campaigning between 1399 and 1401 she decided to build a monument to her lover's magnificence, and employed a famous architect for the job. The architect predictably fell in love with Bibi. He threatened to leave his work unfinished unless she kissed him. The girl considered this presumption a little too much from one of the hired hands; just the same there was Tamerlane's soaring blue monument to consider. She compromised, allowing the architect to kiss her cheek, first placing her hands between the man's hot lips and her face.

No report survives as to either the girl's or man's reaction to the kiss. However, the guilty caress seared thru her hand, leaving an unmistakable brand of male osculatory equipment on her cheek. Tamerlane noticed it on returning, and had Bibi's architect executed. Thereafter, by the conqueror's decree, women were compelled to wear veils. Including Bibi. It all goes to show that even architects may lead dangerous lives. Altho Ivan the Terrible allowed his man to escape with his life, albeit blinded.

But Tamerlane in this century has suffered the same indignity graverobbers committed on Egyptians pharaohs. A Moscow professor dug up his bones a few years ago to make a plaster cast from the skull, and therefore get some idea of the conqueror's living face. The professor also confirmed that Tamerlane actually had been crippled. The architect sleeps on, undisturbed.

Samarkand is a city to remember, a Moslem town still despite Soviet replacement of religion with communism. Grave, bearded elders visit the mosques with reverent attitudes, each with his black skullcap, characteristic headgear of the Uzbeks. A city under the shadow of distant mountains:—south and east the Mountains of Heaven, or Tien Shans; also the Pamirs and Karakorum Range, some of the highest mountains on earth. China's Sinkiang Province is little more than a hundred miles south of Tashkent, separated by soaring stone. The Persians called those peaks "The Roof of the World." Armies marched and counter-marched beneath their shadows in time past, invading present day Russia many times. Finally Russia got the message, and did a little invading itself: in the 19th century many of those belligerent little eastern countries became subjects to the Tsar of Imperial Russia.

Three hundred miles west of Samarkand is the biggest lake in the world: so big it's called a sea, the Caspian. Once the central Asian Forest reached that sea; but climate changed over the centuries, and now there's only desert east of the Caspian. The red sands of Kizil Kum and black sands of Kara Kum are like another sea, in which cities and early races were completely submerged. Sometimes winds blow the sand apart to reveal the ruins of some ancient kingdom, "a rose-red city half as old as time." The remains of Merv, Queen of the World, now called Bayram Ali, lie slumbering near the Karakorum Canal. No signals reach us now from that time: only stone laid on stone under a blanket of sand, and dry wind whispering in many voices.

Back in Tashkent after a day in Samarkand, the local branch of the Writers' Union laid on a banquet and reception for us. But since rising at 4 a.m. on Monday was necessary to catch the plane for Kiev, none of us were especially anxious to celebrate our own undoubted presence in Uzbek SSR. But how does one resist cordiality and vodka, or vodka and cordiality, as the case might be? My character has always been weak at such times, A toast: Here's to Canada! (Hurray.) Here's to the Soviet Union! (Three Hurrays.) Here's to friendship! Here's to poetry!

It wasn't easy, but we always found another toast to which we must drink. And all the while, Victor Pogostin's interpreting eyes were deciding if we could drink later than midnight and still be capable of catching that early morning plane. And the flowery language: six adjectives marry one poor little male noun, which is semantic polygamy in any language. Next morning, roused in pitch darkness for the drive to the airport, I felt like a dead man walking. Perhaps only clichés describe a universal condition of blah.

Kiev is the Ukrainian capital city, with a population of a million and a half. We stayed four days, visiting Babii Yar and its memorial to the 100,000 dead buried there in the last war. We visited a complex of monasteries; the museum of Shevchenko, the Ukrainian national writer: and of course we visited the Writers' Union, standard watering hole for literary visitors. Mark Pinchevsky, writer and translator, presented me with a water glass full of brandy at a drinking spot downtown. My settled policy is never to refuse a drink. I downed it quickly. Later, more toasts at the Writers' Union: Here's to friendship! and Here's to poetry! I was getting a little tired of both of them at this point, but echoed all toasts in alcoholic obedience: Here's to friendship—damn your eyes!

Riga was more of the same. Cordiality haunted and pursued us. My own feeling of goodwill by this time included everything except the increasingly cold weather. But Riga is especially memorable to me because of the reception at the Writers' Union. Before we were even introduced, Lalla, wife of a Latvian writer, said to me: "John Colombo is a better writer than you, Purdy. He wrote a poem for me." I could not venture an opinion on Colombo's taste in this matter of writing a poem for Lalla, but was forced to admit (under such pressure) that Colombo might indeed be a better poet than Purdy.

After much black caviar and red caviar, vodka and Georgian wine, the Riga writers became musical. All of us ended up singing, in slightly drunken voices, every song we knew and some we obviously didn't. Peteris Peterson, a state director wearing glasses and looking rather effeminate, turned out to be quite the opposite, singing "Deutschland" with so much gusto that I stared awe-struck at his tonsils. ("Deutschland" is a German song, and I still wonder who the Latvians were aiming it at.) Even our solemn translator, Victor

Pogostin, got into the act. We were poured onto the overnight train for Leningrad, still mumbling "Lili Marlene" *sotto voce* and off-key.

Leningrad is enough to sober anyone, especially when you arrive on a railway platform glistening with white frost at 8 a.m. But after my wife had brewed coffee and tea with our electric coffee pot in a room at the Hotel Europe, we began to revive. (The coffee pot is worth a mention of itself. On travels in Japan, South Africa and especially in Peru and Mexico, I've used that electric dingus to kill bugs in water for years. In fact, I've blown hotel fuses all the way from Toronto to Cape Horn, Cape Town and Machu Picchu. "Who me? Must be somebody else. I never do any cooking in hotel rooms. I swear! By the rood! Well, then, on my honour?")

The Tsars of Imperial Russia must have tilted the whole country sideways and reduced the people to poverty so that all wealth might pour northward into the building of Leningrad. Peter the Great, the six-foot-seven-inch-tall-tsar built it (then called St. Petersburgh) in the early 18th century, living in a log cabin to supervise construction. His Winter Palace on the Neva River rivals the starry planets in magnificence. It was meant to outdo Versailles; and while I've never visited the French palace, it seems to me that the Sun King must have been a piker by comparison.

The main ballroom of the Winter Palace is about the size of a football field—and then some. It's about two-thirds lined and sheeted with gold, enough to give a blind man back his sight. Two million feet of floor space, 1,050 rooms, 117 staircases, the whole inlaid and decorated with lapis lazuli, porphyry, marble, green malachite, mother-of-pearl, amber, bronze, etc.; also many wood carvings from which the tree's life has long fled, but into which another life from the carver's mind has entered and still lives. Statistics of the joint still turn cartwheels in my head; I'm able to dream in gold instead of black and white.

However, mass graves on Leningrad's outskirts and the war memorial to the Russian dead—that's enough to take your mind far way from any long ago imperial tsar. Six hundred thousand bodies are interred here, mostly nameless dead; music plays continually from hidden loudspeakers. As if the dead had a voice. Seeing this outdoor mausoleum and talking to English-speaking Russians, knowing also the desolation brought to the Soviet Union by the "Great

Patriotic War"—then it becomes understandable why many Russians still hate the Germans violently.

There's something timeless about Leningrad, despite its scarcely more than two-and-a-half-centuries-old origins. Me, a country bumpkin in the Winter Palace, citizen of Ameliasburgh transported to the land of samovar and commissar, thinking of the 15,000 guests of Tsar Nicholas dancing thru the small hours of royalty during white nights on the Neva. The city's latitude is about the same as, say, northern Manitoba, and in late September line-ups waiting to buy fresh fruit from near-tropical Georgia are shivering a little. And me too at the Peterhof, summer residence of the tsars, graced by the biggest fountain in the world. I'm damn near frozen, watching gold statues of the Greek gods, twice life-size, standing negligently graceful in cold spray blown by a wind from the Baltic Sea. The sea itself only half a mile distant along a stone-bordered canal, that canal fed from the mouths of gilded lions' heads whose imperial aspect Peter the Great must have fancied.

Back in Moscow I stand in a three-kilometre-long line-up waiting to get inside Lenin's tomb. The great revolutionary is preserved and embalmed inside a squarish structure of dark red marble blocks, on top of which the Soviet political leaders harangue the people in Red Square on ceremonial occasions. As for Lenin, I've heard the embalmers have been called in once already to repair the bodily ravages of more than fifty years entombment.

Police motion me to remove hands from pockets as we approach the tomb; people are silent as we descend steps, turn right and glimpse the lighted glass coffin. A waxy-pale bald little man with sandy goatee, a man responsible for more simple adoration as well as deathly fear than any other since the world began. Whatever one thinks of Vladimir Lenin, it's indisputable that when Adolf Hitler is scarcely a fading nightmare, Lenin will still be the most potent symbol of revolution in existence. The long line of human beings shuffles slowly past his coffin.

Three weeks in the Soviet Union are nearly ended. My stereotype conception of Russian and Soviet solemnity is shattered. A story told in the Moscow Circus seems relevant in this regard. The actors involved play it straight. A bureaucrat is seen at his desk, large, self-important, a drinker of copious quantities of vodka, rather like his business counterpart in the capitalistic world. A rather shy citizen comes to apply for a job. The bureaucrat keeps him waiting, perhaps just from a sense of his own power over ordinary people. At last he fires questions like bullets at the shy little job seeker. Has he got his card of identification? Does he have a photograph of himself, his wife, parents and parents-in law, all their marriage and birth certificates, his own documents of national service, etc.?

With each request the little job-seeker slaps the relevant document on the desk, while the bureaucrat gets more and more disturbed that he might finally have no excuse for turning down the applicant. His final despairing question is: "Have you got your mother-in-law's fingerprints?" These too are produced in triumph. Whereupon the bureaucrat pulls a pistol from his desk and shoots himself.

I think that story has a universal moral, no matter what part of the solar system you find most congenial to life, love and the pursuit of happiness.

There are some physical facts about the Soviet Union that startled me, too many facts to mention here. However: the USSR is as large as the visible face of the full moon, several times the size of Europe. A land of both sub-tropic and arctic character, it is the largest producer of wheat in the world (despite possible Canadian illusions about that), produces more butter, cotton, milk and surprisingly for me, books, than any place in the world. Sabre-tooth tigers and red haired wolves roam the forests of far eastern Siberia. The wild Far East is not yet tamed, and has no counterpart in North America.

But the world is growing smaller it seems, and while not yet a global village as Marshall McLuhan asserts, it seems to me there is a value in such village contacts as we have made for the last three weeks with Soviet writers and ordinary people. They are passengers on the same spaceship on which we all travel. The French *détente* might be used to describe a reason for the trip, but I would rather use the English "friendship." The word is not yet outmoded.

*(1977)*

# Field Notes:
## *Birdwatching at the Equator*

ONE POEM IN THIS SMALL COLLECTION goes far to disprove W.H. Auden's thesis that "Poetry makes nothing happen." The poem, "Birdwatching at the Equator," instigated unarmed combat between myself and another *littérateur* and was read in the House of Commons by a Conservative MP who was trying to make the Liberals admit they supported such nonsense thru the agency of the Canada Council. But more of that later.

In March 1980, my wife and I flew from Miami to Guayaquil in Ecuador, and thence six hundred Pacific Ocean miles to the Galapagos Islands. Earlier I had flunked the biology course set by Charles Darwin in his *Origin of Species* and *The Descent of Man*, and couldn't finish them. But the islands themselves were a painless and non-didactic education in biology.

Santa Cruz Island, sparsely populated, is twenty-five miles wide. In the coastal lowlands it rarely rains in summer (March is summer in South America) and is so hot that no matter how much coffee or beer you drink a visit to the john isn't necessary: you just sweat it out. But the highlands do have fairly plentiful moisture and dense rain forests. The single village on Santa Cruz is like an old-time western movie set, except for its location on the sea's edge. People clop around on burros and horses, wear spurs and cowboy hats, look kinda macho. I'd seen similar places before in the silent movies of childhood with Tom Mix and Hoot Gibson.

Our lodgings in Santa Cruz village had a concrete apron fronting on a small arm of the sea. Black marine iguanas lazed in the sun there, scuttling around your feet if you seemed about to step on them. Otherwise they ignored you. Pelicans settled on the canvas awning above, when they got tired of plunking into the sea like living torpedos in search of fish. And scarlet crabs dashed sideways among the beach rocks, the only shy creatures I noticed.

Darwin Research station, a mile distant from our living quarters, swarmed with thousands of land tortoises of all sizes and ages, from new-born infants to seven-hundred-pound monsters up to 160 years old. Those big ones moved with such slow deliberation that it seemed you were witnessing the end result of a movement begun the day before.

Unlike some Galapagos visitors, we didn't join one of the expensive tours, whose benefits include hotel, meals, guides, and boat trips. We booked our own accommodations on arrival, boat trips on the yacht *Delfin* when we felt like going, and bought our own meals. An electric coffee pot made sure the water was drinkable; fresh fruit was easily obtainable in the village. It was actually much more fun that way, without having everything mapped out in advance. And while still costly, was not as ruinously expensive as the posh tours.

We visited several of the islands in the course of a week-long stay, one of them especially memorable. It was jammed with blue-footed boobys every few feet, their nests interspersed with yellowy-gold land iguanas. And a few prehistoric-looking frigate birds lurked ominously in desiccated shrubbery.

Before visiting the island and seeing the birds, I had read a poem called "The Blue Booby," by James Tate. This poem says the boobys collect everything blue, incorporating it aesthetically into their nests. I saw no evidence of this collecting mania among the boobys. I think Tate must have read about them in some natural history manual, and decided it would make a poem. If I'd read the same book first, I might have written his poem before he did. As it is, I claim my poem is more accurate, as well as being responsible for fisticuffs and mention in the Canadian government's *Hansard*.

Some of the boobys were doing their mating dance when tourists arrived, flapping their wings like helicopters to lift themselves a few feet in the air, then just hovering for the edification of female boobys. Since the booby is quite a large bird with wide wingspan, this per-formance stirred up a small hurricane of dust and dead leaves. Other boobys flapped their wings and pranced, parading back and forth in heroic poses, tilting their feet upward, expecting their females to admire the brilliant colours. And they whistled, not the human male streetcorner kind of whistle, but like a small boy just learning how. It was the only sound in the still island on the edge of nowhere, except for tourists jabbering. The booby antics made me think how ridiculous I must have looked myself at high school, sticking out my chest, walking tall, playing football, writing poems—all to attract female attention. It didn't work.

The land iguanas, like tarnished costume jewellery, were a foot to three feet long. They ignored us. And chewed on cactus buds, being fierce-looking but harmless vegetarians. One that my wife photographed had the look of a favorite uncle of mine. One isn't supposed to compare animals to people, anthropomorphize, that is, but they did look benevolent. Even kindly.

These volcanic islands take you back mentally and almost physically to an earlier time. Beyond Darwin and even beyond man. One feels like a temporal recidivist, with technology and philosophy forgotten. And even agree with Rousseau about a nature in precise adjustment, the world a harmony of balanced life and blending disparate forms. The niches permitting existence all filled; wildlife tame and vegetarian, except for frigate birds and fish-eating seals.

If one is theologically inclined, a good case could be made for divine order and plan on these populous atolls (one of which is a hundred miles long) under a great blue emptiness. Or if an unbeliever, the values you can abstract from this place also seem valid. I mean the values of adjustment in nature, the conservation of something that was triggered by unknown causes a billion years ago and which will continue indefinitely, hermetically sealed by distance.

They are values of which the inhabitants of these island zoos are ignorant, but booby, iguana, pelican, and the rest live by them. You can even, by an act of the imagination, see their bodily forms changing from what they were to what they are to what they might become. And shall we human beings still be hanging around to watch these metamorphoses?

That bit about unarmed combat? My wife and I spent a month in Victoria, BC, at the beginning of 1981. When the Super Bowl football game was scheduled on television, I went to my brother-in-law's to watch and drink some beer. The Oakland Raiders and Philly Eagles were deciding the American Championship of the world at a game that was invented in Montreal or Kingston. Or so an old linebacker tells me.

There were six or seven people at this apartment, including a guy named Gary, who is introduced to me as the manager of a dry cleaning establishment. He is 30 to 35 years old, not bad looking, something over 160 pounds. He wears casual clothes, shirt open at the neck, has an appearance of some prosperity. I sit next to him on a high stool at the bar. We sip our beer delicately, me anticipating companionship, good-natured badinage, an enjoyable football game.

But Gary, it seems, has read a piece about me in the Victoria newspaper, to the effect that a lousy poem I wrote about the blue-footed booby has been subsidized by the Canada Council, hence also the Canadian taxpayer. Meaning him personally.

Gary compliments me in uncomplimentary terms for "ripping off" the taxpayers, saying that he would like to get away with such ripoffs himself if he could. There is quite a barrage of these remarks from Gary, to which I make mild rejoinder as is my wont, hoping to keep the peace. Finally it gets on my nerves a little. I wonder, audibly, what it is he wants from me, an apology or a refund? "Why are you being so insulting, Gary?" I ask. "We're all of us here with a good feeling, me at my bro-in-law's and among friends, just trying to get along."

"I'm not your friend," Gary says.

I'm beginning to feel a little alarmed. Just in case, I take a fast assessment of the physical capabilities of dry cleaning managers. He's much younger than me, but lighter, and doesn't look in bad shape. But it's too fantastic that anyone should dislike a poem of mine enough to—enough to what? I didn't know, and didn't want to know.

Insults continued for two hours. Oakland was far ahead of Philly for the Canadian championship. I'd consumed maybe three or four beers. Then a period of interregnum, during which Gary told a youngster present that his older brother (not present) was double-crossing him, and there was a small argument over that. I was relieved, since my advanced age of over sixty ought to preclude the sort of juvenile violence that had appeared to be impending. Besides, my arthritic knees wouldn't hold up if I had to move quickly or rise from a prone position and forthwith flee to a safe place. Besides, I felt, some respect was due my grey hairs.

Anyway, I felt safe in commenting on something another person had said. It was a mistake. Gary said my opinion was worthless, coming from "a piece of shit like you!"

I hit him. No delay, no thought, bugger all. As hard as I could. And was about to leap atop his prone body on the floor, perhaps whomp his head a few times on the soft carpet. But my bro-in-law jumped in front before I could accomplish this fell design. (On later reflection, bro-in-laws are good people to have around if your knees are arthritic.)

Gary is taken to the washroom to have the blood washed from his face. I feel quite emotionally disturbed. The pinball game is ruined for me (and just about over anyway), and I say so. Ask someone to drive me home. Gary emerges from the bathroom, a little pale. We are invited to shake hands. I agree (kind and forgiving as always), but he refuses. (The clot!)

I'm still all a-twitter when I get back home. Ask my wife to walk around the block with me a few times until I calm down. She says, "No, I have to get supper. There isn't time." That's my sweet understanding wife, ministering to all my needs.

About Gary, I hear later that at the time of our love-match his girlfriend had left him for another. Also that he had previously gotten into a disagreement with my bro-in-law, but backed off. His retiring action on that occasion is understandable, since my bro-in-law weighs 240 and is six feet five. And now I feel rather sorry for Gary. But all this does go to prove that Auden was wrong.

In May of this year (these stories never end), Ron Everson, a Montreal poet friend, tells me about the blue booby poem being read aloud in the House of Commons by a Conservative member. This was done, of course, to embarass the Liberal government with the mediocrity of the literature it subsidizes thru the Canada Council. Gary had apparently seen a write-up of the same incident when he assaulted me (verbally) and I assaulted him back (physically) at the Canadian parcheesi championships held in Victoria. And for all this I blame the Conservative Party.

Do I need to say that in even rather light-hearted poems there are serious aspects? Are cost analysis and symbolic meaning necessary to point out for the benefit of Conservative understanding?

I will admit that now, a few months after these events, they don't seem at all funny to me. And I thought they would when I started to write about them. Now, everyone concerned seems merely stupid, including myself.

But an iguana I called Uncle Wilfred, a 160-year-old tortoise I dubbed Moses—these are more pleasant people. And the blue-footed boobys doing their mating dance, these were truly and seriously funny. The poems, well, I hope they are both slightly funny and serious, and that no member of the Conservative caucus will ever read them.

*(1983)*

# Northern Reflections

IT WAS THE SUMMER OF 1965, and I was flying to Baffin Island. During the night of July 10, I watched southern darkness change into northern light. I'd read about this 24-hours-of-daylight business before, but to be there at the geographical point where darkness is left behind and there's nothing but light in the sky ahead—that's a different thing from having it described on paper. A strange feeling.

The aircraft was a bellowing old DC4 that sounded as if it couldn't make it over a goldfish bowl. In fact, two nights before, when we'd first started out for Baffin Island, the plane had begun to leak fuel, which forced a return to Montreal's Dorval Airport. And now, repairs completed, I was embarking on my great adventure, a summer in the Canadian Arctic.

The other passengers were, apparently, old northern hands. They all went to sleep half an hour after takeoff. Only an extroverted former sailor and I remained awake. He was employed in the meteorological division of the Department of Transport at Frobisher Bay and chattered away to me about how he was going to "make time" with the attractive flight attendant, Suzanne. Then he suddenly got airsick and had to take refuge in the aircraft's washroom. In his absence, Suzanne and I discussed French Canadian *joie de vivre*, folk singer Gilles Vigneault, religion and just about everything else. Suzanne surprised me a little at one point. She told me she was an agnostic and then, motioning outside where the moon touched our wings with silver, said, "But I see angels out there sometimes."

At around 4:00 a.m. I could see snow-streaked hills below us, where our tiny shadow kept pace with the aircraft. It was a land of dark hills, ice rimming every shoreline, from bathtub-sized lakes to the wide expanse of Frobisher Bay itself.

In a kind of exaltation, I rushed from one side of the plane to the other in order to see all there was to see. The worst of this kind of euphoric feeling is that it always wears off, but the down side is never a complete reversal of the enchantment in your enthralled mind.

At 5:00 a.m. we stumbled from the aircraft with smudged grouchy faces averted from the smudged grouchy sky. Among us were the former sailor, now subdued and silent, not even bidding goodbye to Suzanne; a brown and leathery Yorkshire engineer bound for a construction job; a couple of civilian weathermen; and a young Swedish writer-photographer team, Tore and Jan, who both had hair so blond it actually glowed. They planned to write a book about the Northwest Passage and always had a bottle of good Scotch in their pack. (I had brought along my own bottle of good Canadian rye). In all there were thirteen passengers.

Baffin Island is a huge chunk of territory, about four times the size of England. In 1965 the administrative centre, Frobisher Bay, was a kind of frontier town of 1,800 people. Most visitors and government personnel bunked at the Federal Building, a sprawling complex of offices, warehouses, workshops and living quarters owned by the Canadian government.

After 10 days of wandering around Frobisher Bay, I hitched a ride on a mining company charter bound for Pangnirtung, a village of 200 or so near the Arctic Circle. Everybody met the plane at Pang: Inuit residents, Mounties and Northern Affairs people, including Wayne Morrison, the regional administrator. Wayne was fresh-faced, around thirty and very tall. Married, he had his own house, to which I was invited for meals a couple of times.

Staying at the hostel where Inuit kids lived during the school year, I wandered all over the settlement, climbed a small mountain nearby, talked to the Inuit hunters and old people—in fact talked to nearly everyone. And one grey day I went for a long walk with a public works man from Ottawa. His job involved finding the proper variety of gravel at Pang to mix into concrete.

During our search we passed a small graveyard, where a dead body was lying above ground wrapped in blankets. "When the permafrost has melted some, they can bury the lady," explained my companion. He shoved at the ground with the tip of his spade; it was still iron-hard, the temperature around freezing in mid-July, a few snowflakes coming down. "You often find good gravel near a graveyard, where the digging is easier," he said.

I intended to take some gifts for friends when I returned home and got permission to open some cases of Inuit carvings returned from Frobisher Bay because the authorities there said they weren't good enough. And I guess those people were right. I rummaged through three wooden crates, top to bottom getting itchy packing inside my shirt, searching for:

. . . one good carving
one piece that says "I AM"
to keep a southern promise
One 6-inch walrus (tusk broken)
cribbage board (ivory inlay gone)
dog that has to be labelled dog
polar bear (badly crippled)
what might be a seal (minus flipper)
and I'm getting tired of this . . .
there must be something
one piece that glows
one slap-happy idiot seal
alien to the whole seal-nation
one anthropomorphic walrus
singing Hallelujah I'm a Bum
in a whiskey baritone
But they're all flawed
broken
   bent
     misshapen
failed animals
with vital parts missing—
("The Sculptors")

I had a vision of the carvers themselves at that moment: TB outpatients, failed hunters, losers always. And here I was, intruding into their lives and work , seeing them for what they were and were not, as if I knew them personally. And perhaps I did.

But Pangnirtung didn't seem like my eventual destination either. It was a bit too civilized for my purpose, despite the polar bear furs and sealskins at the Hudson's Bay Company store. I arranged through Wayne Morrison to accompany an Inuit hunter and his family to their summer home on the Kikastan Islands in Cumberland Sound.

Our heavily loaded Peterborough boat left the dock in late afternoon the next day. The passengers were Jonesee, the hunter, his wife, Leah, and their three children, one a baby on Leah's back. They carried supplies meant to last an indefinite period. I took along groceries for two weeks, a Coleman stove, a portable typewriter and plenty of warm clothing.

Jonesee was a very good hunter, Wayne had told me: "Or else he couldn't afford all that expensive equipment." Jonesee was a medium-sized man of about thirty, pleasant looking with a small scar in the middle of his cheek. When he smiled the scar on his cheek disappeared into a dimple. But neither Jonesee nor his wife spoke very much English. Leah was seriously pleasant to me. And the two kids, well, they were like any other kids. I forgot to mention four other passengers—a blind husky bitch with white milky eyes, apparently a family pet, and her three pups.

We followed thirty-metre-high cliffs to the mouth of Pangnirtung Fjord, which opened on Cumberland Sound, an arm of the sea some 300 kilometres long. On the way we passed a small island infested with at least fifty dogs. They rushed howling and whining down to the shore as we went by. I was told later that it was an Inuit habit to leave dogs on an island to fend for themselves during the summer, when there was no sled-hauling work to be done. You'd think they'd starve to death on those barren little islands but apparently not.

At 8:00 p.m. the Jonesee expedition landed on another small rocky island. And since I'd been informed that the Kikastan group of islands we were bound for contained a tiny Inuit village, I knew this island was definitely not our destination, even though the place did seem to be inhabited. There were a dozen or so people in residence, plus dogs (not all of them are left alone on islands). But their dwellings were only transient tents. I didn't know where we were, and nobody spoke enough English for me to ask them.

At our landing place I lifted the blind husky and her pups onto shore, a job I inherited thereafter. The dog seemed to trust herself at my hands, and I had to trust her not to bite.

It was an island of hunters. They gathered atop a small mountain, firing rifles at seals in the water below. Then came a period of stillness, while other hunters dashed out from shore to pick up bodies. Rifles boomed and echoes crashed from other islands all around us.

Inuit children scampered around playing hunting games and games with secret rules. Dogs sidled away from me, suspicious and savage if I approached them placatingly. A weird "ouw-ouw-ouw" sound drifted though the night-long twilight, a sound so empty of meaning or previous association that it dragged my spirits down like lead. Unlike any other bird cry I have ever heard, it was the call of old squaw ducks, and birds with names like that can't be very terrifying.

Huddled in my sleeping bag later, a windup phonograph nearby grinding out "You Are My Sunshine," I thought what a strange experience this was for me: trying to sleep on a nameless Arctic island in Cumberland Sound, my guide and mentor a native hunter who couldn't speak English and tell me what was going on, all the euphoria I'd felt on arriving at Baffin spent—like counterfeit money. It was midnight by my wristwatch, the light a sort of amber that was neither day nor night, those ducks rehearsing their mournful dirge all around me.

> Here I'm alone as I've ever been in my life
> a windup gramophone scratching out "You Are
> My Sunshine"
>> in the next tent
> the sea crowded with invisible animals
> the horizon full of vague white shapes
> of icebergs in whispering lagoons where
> Old Squaw Ducks are going
>> "ouw-ouw-ouw"
> And I think to the other side of that sound
> I have to
>> because it gathers everything
> all the self-deception and phoniness
> of my lifetime into an empty place
> and the RUNNER IN THE SKIES
> I invented
>> as symbol of the human spirit
>> crashes like a housefly

my only strength is blind will
                    to go on
I think to the other side of that sound
("Metrics")

I thought of those lines while listening to the ducks, then fell asleep. Next morning I wrote them down.

After two days we embarked again for the Kikastan Islands, which I estimated to be thirty or forty kilometres from Pangnirtung. As our voyage drew to a close, Jonesee's island rose out of the water like an ancient ruined kingdom in a blue desert, its jumbled lion-coloured rocks glowing in the sun.

There were only two Inuit families on this particular island—just two families, but several abandoned winter houses. And I wouldn't have been surprised to wake up one morning and find them occupied again, the people having just returned from founding a colony in Carthage or Antarctica.

I set up my tent in a cleared area near the beach, my portable typewriter on a cardboard grocery box, the Coleman stove in one corner, a clutter of groceries and clothing in another. A well among the rocks supplied water. But the toilet was a problem. I decided an outdoor one some distance from camp must be the answer. But there were a dozen or so dogs prowling around, great multi-coloured brutes who growled at me suspiciously every time I approached. They were impossible to avoid. With no summer work they just hung around the little settlement. When I started across the island, they followed me. Threatening to throw stones had no effect whatsoever. The dogs were right at my heels.

Finally one of the kids noticed my predicament and stood guard against the dogs. But they hovered a short distance away, and the Inuit youngster laughed at at my discomfort. With some horror, it occurred to me this same scene might be frequently repeated and I rewarded my escort suitably, with a dime.

The wind blew hard all that first night on the island, and twice I heard a loud crash close to the tent. I didn't stir from my sleeping bag. Around 7:00 a.m., after a breakfast of beans and bread, I went down to the beach. A great fairy castle of shining minarets and fantastic towers of silver and pale blue-green was grounded close to shore. Wind had driven an iceberg onto the beach, and it was much more beautiful than castles in Spain or on the Rhine.

I edged as close to it as I could, water dripping from the ice almost at my feet. Then I felt myself grabbed from behind and pulled back from the berg. It was Jonesee, his brown face smiling but reproving. "Bad, bad!" he said, one of the few English words he knew. As if at a signal, a large chunk of rotten grey ice crashed from the berg and splashed us with watery crystals. I grinned weakly at Jonesee and shrugged my shoulders. "Thank you," I said. "Thank you very much."

Jonesee and his friend Simonie—alike as twins except that Simonie was slightly older—went hunting before I was awake every day. I went with them once and nearly froze to death, thereafter remaining in my sleeping bag, immune to Jonesee's coaxing at the tent entrance.

One bright day Leah was doing her washing, absorbed in scrubbing, rinsing and wringing in a galvanized tub. I stood nearby like an alien shadow. She paid no attention to me. So I joined her, rinsing and wringing her clothes myself. She thought that was strange; I could see my presence enter her face and mind, disturbing her private thoughts, pushing in among them. Then she smiled, the dimples forming in her cheeks.

Every morning Leah and her baby and Leah's friend Regally (Simonie's wife) came over to my tent for tea. The two women, actually little more than teenage girls, sat opposite me on the air mattress while the Coleman stove boiled water and I made tea. It became a ritual that began each day. Leah would breast-feed her baby while I talked in English, which of course they didn't understand. And they would giggle, turn to each other and smile. Sometimes we'd sing songs together, including the detestable "You Are My Sunshine," the words of which they had memorized. I think we became good friends.

Once the two hunters were away for three days, returning with a boatload of seal and arctic char. On the beach they stripped the skins off the seals, throwing the bodies into the water. When the bodies struck the surface, all the dozen or so dogs jumped in after them. The dogs fought one another for meat. They splashed and threatened and grinned with bloody jaws. It seemed almost prehistoric.

While this was going on the two wives stood some distance away from their husbands. Small things had happened during the hunters' absence; the separate streams of living had to be joined and flow together again. One could feel a slight strangeness between the husbands and wives, then the beginning of a moulding and joining.

> On the beach dogs are still fighting
> over the bones and shreds of seal meat
> a red pool 10 feet across in the water
> is a death-area of widening crimson
> then slowly turning blue again
> and beyond these islands
> other adjustments are being made—

("Two Hunters")

It seemed to me that the life I lived on that island was about as basic as you could get. The big icebergs sailed by like ships every blue or grey day. I picked yellow and blue flowers from among the scanty vegetation. The wind blew continually. Twice an aeroplane passed high overhead, and I felt like waving my arms at it and screaming, "My name is Robinson Crusoe—please rescue me!"

After nearly two weeks on the island I picked up a fever. My forehead felt very hot. I got into all the clothes I had with me, climbed into my sleeping bag and dosed myself with quinine pills. It wasn't a cold exactly, at least it didn't feel like one. I swallowed a lot of pills and drank hot tea.

By the second day the fever was still high. I felt a bit scared, there being no doctor on the island—there wasn't one, I'd been told, nearer than Pangnirtung. I drank the last of my rye. When Leah and Regally came over that morning for the ritual tea, I shrugged at them helplessly and mimed illness. They looked sympathetic and went away. I felt sorry for myself and depressed. But my moods fluctuated with the fever, which left me sweating or else cold and unable to get myself warm.

> Here I am again . . .
> lying in bed with fever
> and I'm so glad to be here
> no matter what happens
> —riding the wind to Pang
> or being bored at Frobisher
> (waiting for clearing weather)
> I'm so glad to be here

with the chance that comes but once
to any man in his lifetime
to travel deep in himself
to meet himself as a stranger
at the northern end of the world
Now the bullying wind blows faster
the yellow flags rush seaward
the stones cry out like people
as my fever suddenly goes
and the huskies bark like hell
the huskies bark like hell

In a cave hollowed out in the rain
near a pile of ghostly groceries
and some books
—morning soon

("Still Life in a Tent")

Obviously, a signal had been sent and received; it was time to leave the island. I talked to Jonesee and mimed returning to Pang in the Peterborough boat. As I left, Leah and Regally stood on the beach among rotting seal flippers and bones waving goodbye.

That was nearly thirty years ago, almost another age and era in the Arctic. But if I were to fly over Baffin Island today, viewing the landscape from above, it would seem that little had changed: the mountains, rivers and glaciers of this immense island would look as if they had never been seen by human eyes.

But on the land below, the town of Frobisher Bay is not Frobisher Bay any longer: its name has been changed to Iqaluit, and its growing population now stands at more than 3,000. Tourist hotels have mushroomed there and at several other settlements. In 1987 the Hudson's Bay Company sold its northern stores to the Winnipeg-based North West Company. And Baffin Island is now part of the one-fifth of Canada's land mass that will soon be called Nunavut (Our Land), which is scheduled to be governed by the Nunavut legislative assembly, to be elected in 1999. The Inuit have taken charge of their own destiny.

Ever since my summer there in 1965 I've had a vested interest in Baffin Island, apart from but related to my being a Canadian. A ghostly citizenship in my blood awakens every time I see a good photograph of Baffin Island, and I want to return. Leaving there in 1965 I had the feeling that my life had been turned around: I was moving into a different future, in which the multiple choices of youth were again possible.

*(1993)*

# Jackovich and the Salmon Princess

*It is a tale they told long ago among the Haida villages of the Queen Charlotte Islands and the Tsimshian villages on the mainland.*

IN HIS UNDERSEA PALACE SOMEWHERE west of the Skeena River's mouth lives the King Salmon, sovereign of all the salmon nations, Coho, Sockeye, Humpback and the lordly Tyee. His palace has many rooms, all of them suffused with dim green light on the other side of reality. There, in one of the connected suites, lives the Salmon Princess—so beautiful that the sea all around her body is kept warm by her beauty. The Princess resembles, in all respects but one, a young human girl, her eyes dancing for love of living in the faint green light beneath the water. But she is not human.

It is also said that a young man from the above-water-world may seek her out, swimming down to the undersea palace, searching through the countless rooms and crying out, "Princess, Princess, I have come for you!" If she truly loves him the Princess will accompany her new husband to his home in the Haida or Tsimshian village on this side of reality. And there they will live together forever, or for as long as he remains faithful to her. Of course, for the young man this is a very dangerous quest, and if he fails he will die.

In 1975 when my friend Jack Jackovich, a fishing guide at Campbell River, invited me west to fish for salmon and drink some beer with him, I wondered if the Salmon Princess would appeal to Jackovich. Knowing his lecherous nature, I was almost sure she would.

Jack Jackovich's history goes back a few years to Hamilton, Ontario, where he played pro football for the Hamilton Tiger Cats in 1959-60. Built more or less like a tanker truck at 265 pounds, hairy as a mountain goat with black eyebrows nearly meeting above a rather menacing face, Jack had artistic leanings. He painted—not houses but landscapes in oils. A great bruising middle linebacker pounding triumphantly into the enemy team's backfield to flatten the quarterback and yelling in his ear, "GOTCHA"! Then to be told you're not good enough and released by the Hamilton coach, it was humiliating. Then the woman you love saying, "Jack, I don't love you any more." It's enough to make you lose faith in your own invulnerability, and say to yourself softly, "Boo-hoo."

But Jack pulled himself together manfully; his spirits revived. He travelled west to Campbell River on Vancouver Island, got a job teaching at the local high school, became a fishing guide, started painting again, branched out into making pottery on the side, and 24 hours a day left him a little short of time. Then, once more, he got married—to Patty of the blonde hair, Patty of the slow warm smile.

Which is where I come in. Jack and I sit in a Campbell River pub drinking beer companionably and talking about the meaning of life. About being a fishing guide for rich tourists: "Some of the bastards use money to cover up what they ain't got, but some are nice guys." About teaching: "I get along with the kids. They look at me as if they can't believe I'm who I am, and when they decide I am I tell them I'm not. Then we laugh."

Watching that black-browed face so much in love with life, I envied him a little. The sort of face that overcomes obstacles, gets discouraged sometimes but then works its way past and over that feeling. Then I wondered: am I making all this up, transferring some of my own feelings to him and pleased with myself and not knowing I'm doing it?

While I was looking again at that strong dark face with the beard waiting to spring out just below the surface, there was a sudden twitch of movement in the light around us. None of the other beer-drinkers seemed to notice, but the light in that pub had changed to a dim underwater-green colour. And Jack—I was startled to see him in full football uniform, helmet and all, sweater peeling off his back slightly and waving in the water, number 69 plainly discernible. There was a yearning expression on his face, searching for the palace of the Salmon Princess to make her wife number three along with Patty of the slow smile . . .

I became aware of shouting and minor tumult. Jack was standing over me shaking my shoulder. "You okay, kid? Thought you'd passed out for a minute. The beer ain't that bad, is it?"

"I'm all right. It's just that I was thinking of something so hard I forgot everything else."

"If that's how it gets you, maybe I won't be a writer after all. I was thinking of trying my hand."

"Don't do it," I said, shuddering a little.

"Want to tell me what was going on in your head?" Jack said, looking concerned. "Your eyes kinda didn't focus for a minute, and it was like you weren't breathing . . . "

For a moment I thought of telling Jack I'd seen him swimming beneath the sea, searching for the Salmon Princess in full football uniform, number 69 on his sweater. Then realized I didn't know Jack all that well, he might be really annoyed. And shrugged my shoulders hard, as if shaking off a monetary queasiness. "I'm fine," I told him. "Writers just get like this sometimes. All you can do is pity them."

For the next couple of days I stayed at Strathcona Park on Buttle Lake, while Jack was finishing off a teaching session there. The Park is a kinda "wilderness survival" outfit, thirty miles from town, deep in the spiny ridge of mountains which is the backbone of Vancouver Island. Jim Boulding, who runs the place, built it by taking a small portable sawmill into the bush to cut his own fir and cedar lumber. Jim says he thinks of the lodge as "a small year-round rural village, with a lifestyle in keeping with the ecological challenge of today's world."

A bit pretentious perhaps, but Jim is a passionate idealist, built on the same moose-like lines as Jack Jackovich. With a voice like an insane foghorn, he expounds the theory and practise of what Strathcona Park is now and what it should be in future. "Don't confuse it with a commune or some island retreat that shuts off reality. It's a working village. Everybody does something. And people's responsibility is to appreciate the country, instead of littering it with glass and tin cans, preserve instead of destroy." He paused for breath. I watched him with sympathy.

In the evening of my first full day at Strathcona, Jim Boulding and Jack show up with a bottle of cognac. I'm glad to note that, despite Jim's rigid ecological standards, he is slightly corrupted by alcoholic and other civilized amenities. So we drink and conversation ranges all the way from women to Roderick Haig-Brown, to the skiing rights on nearby Elk Mountain, which have to be applied for in the office of an American executive (the mountain is US owned).

Somewhere among these mountains, or else farther north among the tangled islands of the inland passage, it seems there is a 60-foot Haida war canoe rotting among the towering fir trees. "Canoes of that size were made from a single tree by the entire village," Jim says. "But in this case the village was wiped out completely by white men's diseases, before the canoe could be launched. Of course it was very long ago."

And I have a vision of the house-sized war canoe in full-coloured Haida regalia, waiting forever somewhere beyond the dark. Waiting for the people to return. But I notice Jack watching me in some alarm, and grin at him.

"It's the cognac."

Two hours before nightfall Jim gives us a lesson in fly-fishing on Buttle Lake. He wades right out into the snow-fed water in old dungarees, with impressive disregard for comfort, then shouts bull-moose instructions to Jack and me. Expert *aficionado* things like "12 o'clock" and "9 o'clock," which have to do with the angle at which you hold the fly rod.

And then Karl Klein, Jack's fellow instructor, comes down from 6000-foot Crown Mountain where he has spent the day, treading lightly among high snow ridges in case sudden movement might trigger an avalanche. Karl is able to find his way back from the mountain by tying bits of yellow ribbon to trees on the outward journey, like Theseus in the maze. And the cognac is gone.

Next day it's back to Campbell River for our fishing expedition. The town is jammed with people, from all over Canada and the US. Hotels and motels are filled. Two trailer camps, each called "Little America" for obvious reasons, are crowded with campers and mobile homes. Tents and pavilions balloon on the main street. There is a $500 prize for the biggest fish caught in the local salmon derby. Which is a nice contrast to the British Columbia Salmon Festival at Vancouver, where the prize is $25,000. "But their biggest fish last year was 33 pounds, and that might not be among the first 20 at Campbell River," Jack tells me.

On the trophy-wall at Painter's Lodge the record catch with

hook and line, apart from net fishing, is 77 pounds. Also hanging here are photographs of celebrities come in pursuit of tyee salmon: Archie Moore, the ex-light heavyweight champion; Bob Hope and Vincent Price from Hollywood; John Diefenbaker and Wacky Bennett from our own political zoo; Johnny Bucyk of the Boston Bruins—all posing proudly with a giant fish held straight out in front of them so the camera will make it appear even larger. (I'm told that in case any famous person fails to catch a fish, a big rubber phony salmon is available for photographic purposes.)

"Young Joe" Painter, fishing guide and schoolteacher, whose family once owned Painter's Lodge, shows us the fibreglass boat copied from his father's boats built years ago. These are now collector's items. Not being much of a fisherman myself, I am trying to find out about this mystique which surrounds the big fish, even to the point of there being a "Campbell River Tyee Club," whose membership includes only those whose catch has exceeded thirty pounds.

Joe Painter says the big thrill is when the fish strikes when you're using only a light line and small boat and the personal struggle is uppermost. "You kinda put your brain on the end of a fishing line?" I say. "I mean with all these lures and plugs and things?"

Joe doesn't like this idea. "It's when the fish strikes," he insists.

"The time a man spends fishing," Jack says portentously, "will not be deducted from his life span." Which gives me the uncanny feeling that we are living on borrowed time, and I'm not sure I know what he means. But it sounds good anyway.

Thousands of small boats jam the marina at Campbell River. Don Van Humbeck (Jack's brother-in-law) joins us in an 18-foot fibreglass runabout with an 80-horse motor for the fishing expedition. After all the prelude and talk, the actual going forth seems a bit anticlimactic. I thought we needed a flourish of trumpets to suit the occasion. All we had were six bottles of warm beer for possible libations and toasts.

Ten miles north of us across the dark evening water is Ripple Rock in Seymour Narrows, long a navigational hazard. An undersea mountain, its peak was blasted off in 1958 by the biggest dynamite explosion ever until that year. But the place is still very dangerous. Currents and whirlpools can seize a 40-foot log, and drag it into the depths below. "Then, unexpectedly," Jack says, "the log will zoom up from hundreds of feet like a spear, and maybe crash through the bottom of a boat if the boat happens to be in the wrong place." And this is the same sea passage through which the United States is sending giant oil tankers.

We cruise back and forth in Forestry Hole, trailing three lines behind the boat—one of them with a "No. 3 Wonder Spoon," whatever that is. There are also such spoons and lugs as the "Hootchie-Kootchie" (it looks like an agitated squid), "Deadly Dick," "Buzz Bomb" and "No. 1 Flasher." There's a jargon attached to the paraphernalia of every trade and sport, like a "thieves' jargon" in crime and war.

The fish are being courted by countless stuttering small boats, each with its personal assortment of fishing lures, each boat fishing at a different depth, everyone trying to outguess the mood of monster salmon, courted, in a sense, as movie queens are courted by millions of moviegoers. And the courtship includes suitors like Jack and myself: the burly gridiron dropout and—come to think of it—another ex-football player, name of Purdy. Years ago I stayed in school an extra year, despite mediocre marks, just to play football. And here we both are, a little chastened by time, and certainly less self-important, wondering how the transition to oil on canvas and ballpoint was accomplished.

"Jack, how does a football player get to be a painter?"

"Well, he's gotta be a small kid before he's a football player. My mother sent me to a famous guy named Adrian Dingle in Toronto. When I was twelve years old, he looked kinda fat and old. But when I saw him again last year he was slim and young. How do you explain that?"

I don't try to explain it and ask, "What about the pottery—stuff like that vase sitting on your table with the hand coming out of its mouth?"

"I don't know. I'm a painter—it seemed natural to do pottery as well."

"And football? Didn't the other players in a tough steel town like Hamilton kid you a little about sissy painting?"

"Not many people knew I was painting in Hamilton; I didn't stay there long enough. I wasn't a very good football player."

"Okay, you were dropped from the Hamilton Ti-Cats, then you

were an IBM programmer in Victoria, BC, in 1961. Your marriage broke up, you lost your job, and presto right after that you're a fishing guide-school teacher-painter. What happened? I mean, did rainbows explode in your head?"

"I guess I took a look at myself, what I was doing and had been doing, and how much I liked it—which wasn't all that much—and started to think about where I was at, and what I wanted to be and do for the rest of my life."

The sea around us is gently rocking the boat, other fishermen some distance away, a quiet moment. It seemed a good time to tell Jack about my picture of him swimming down into the watery depths in search of the Salmon Princess. Jackovich with the brilliant Ti-Cat logo on his helmet, bubbles trailing behind him like confetti, searching for love under the sea. Should I tell him? Those black brows and menacing face—despite the sensitive recital of his childhood, he'd be liable to throw me overboard. Save it for when he's more vulnerable, or just before I'm leaving.

We are sauntering at slow speed in Discovery Pass, travelling two miles south and then ten miles north, feeling half-asleep. Quadra Island and Row-and-Be-Damned Point to the east, an 8 p.m. sun dipping low over Campbell River. Don opens a beer for each of us. And we talk about tyee salmon in their five-to seven-year life span: before they spawn and die in their birthplace river, the great fish may reach a weight of 120 pounds at maturity, but 92 pounds is the largest ever taken with light tackle. The main item in their diet is herring. They make a rush through a school of herring, cripple many of them, then turn back and swallow the meal at their leisure. Not a particularly attractive carnivore in that respect.

When the smaller coho and sockeye salmon strike and know some godlike force holds them prisoner, they run away sideways or backwards, then stop like they'd been shot, and you try to reel them in before they make another run. The same goes for spring and tyee, except the big fish dive instead of swimming sideways, moving so fast they can't lift their gill covers to breathe. Therefore: they have to make a rest stop, and that's when you take up the slack in the line, before they rush frantically away from pain and fear. And I don't much like the idea of causing such pain and fear.

My own first strike wasn't even noticed by me, not until Jack grabbed my rod from its holder and yelled "Reel it in!" A hundred feet behind the boat you could see it, a small whirlpool in the water that might drag down a toothpick. I am thinking about pain and fear when Jack yells at me again, exasperatedly: "Look—I promised you a salmon. You're gonna lose it if you don't wake up and haul it back into the boat!"

So I wake up, standing in the stern with the butt end of the fishing rod digging into my gut every time I twirl the reel frantically. Poor Jack, I think. He'll lose face or something, if I lose this salmon. And you're gonna lose it if you don't learn how to be a fisherman in three seconds flat. On the other hand, all the technological forces of mankind arrayed against one helpless little fish; all the plastic, steel, cork, fibreglass, nylon, plus human cunning and know-how and know-little pitted against coho and tyee. But having me on the other end of the line makes the contest more or less even.

"Hold that rod up!" Jack yells again. If salmon sells for two bucks a pound to the fisherman, I'm sure that damn fish reads my mind and says I'll make you pay more than two bucks a pound for me in sweat alone. The butt on the rod digs hard into my belly; the fish whips first one way then another, also in a sideways direction unknown to cartographers, which means he must be a coho. With manual dexterity I never knew I possessed and still don't, the fish is dragged close to the boat, fighting all the way in silver spray. And yep, it's a coho, six or seven pounds. So beautiful that for three or four seconds it wipes out the entire landscape of sea and shore from my mind.

Again we parade back and forth between Quadra Island and Campbell River. Once we caught a dogfish. Don was very careful not to get nipped by the nasty teeth before throwing it back in the water. Then another strike, but this time I refused to take the rod, and Don reeled in a big spring salmon. Before we packed it in, four salmon were flopping in the boat, including a 16-inch spring, another smaller one, and two coho.

Patty of the blonde hair is waiting for us at home, having prepared something to eat for the hungry fishermen. Afterwards, all the incidents of this westward trip begin to separate themselves in my mind. My own coho salmon which will very likely be the only fish I will catch in a lifetime. Jack himself and his multiple talents. The paintings whose style he calls a combination of hard-edge with free brush strokes for contrast, although he employs several other styles as well: in one of them a forest grows inside a man's body. In another, everything is so faintly and whisperingly depicted that the world before your eyes seems to partake of the painting, growing vague and insubstantial.

Before leaving I think again of mentioning to Jack my fantasy of him swimming down into Discovery Pass or Hecate Strait to marry the Salmon Princess. Again the burly football player dives into the dim enchanted water, with one small detail changed from before: there's a ragged hole in Jack's football jersey. But that's only natural. It's wornout from the many years since Jack burst into the Calgary Stampeder backfield to bury Doug Flutie, or whoever it was, with a thunderous tackle.

But I decided not to mention it.

It will always be three hours earlier in the British Columbia rain forest than in the grey East, and pearl-strung rivers looped around the throat of the land remain in the mind as talismans long after your own departure. Mountains are folded on mountains, so that a few square miles of marvellous verticals seem capable of being flattened out into a thousand miles of the mundane horizontal. Maybe our minds can do the same.

On sea-pounded beaches there, small life scurries and sidles and skitters under the stones. The great tyee continue their long life-journey into the Pacific, then return home to inland rivers where they were born. And I am childishly pleased with the results of our fishing expedition: for I didn't really want to catch one of those 100-pound giants on hook and line anyway. It would have been too much like catching my Skeena Salmon Princess—and I wouldn't know what to say to her.

*(1975)*

# Part Two:
# The Writing Life

# Autobiographical Introduction

I STARTED TO WRITE "POEMS" at the age of 13 in grade school. At the time I thought I wasn't getting enough attention from playing football, and, having failed to excel at fullback, being the school poet might ensure my natural modesty due recognition. One of the first things I wrote got printed in the school magazine and paid me a buck, which seemed an easy way to raise money for pot. On the other hand I might have started to write because I was in love with Bliss Carman's "Peony," thus acquiring the monotonous Carman iambic habit which took twenty years to kick. In either case, as egotistic show-off or from messy puppy-love of Carman, the result has been that I'm not able to stop.

During adolescence I wrote book-length sagas about Robin Hood and the Norse myths, gathered rhyming clichés and inversions from every bad poet rampant in school texts of the Victorian 1930s in Canada. As a kid of 16–17 I rode freight trains across the country during the Great Depression, continuing to write—absolute Crap! Realizing that has now engendered a spatial insecurity of the enfibulated psyche that may drive me to drink or from sex.

I suppose the above is facetious, but not entirely so. I was still writing crap while serving as a sullen pimpled aircraftsman in the RCAF, getting promoted up to sergeant in the war years when military competence was scarce, then demoted back to much less than civilian. During my wartime stint (migawd, six years!) I published (and paid for) a book of my own verse (called *The Enchanted Echo*) which I thought at the time was genius. In fact, I think this naive ability to think one is a genius is a necessary and valuable quality. It enables a great many bad poets to go on writing until they either get better, or else abandon Great Literature in favour of Machine Tools and Advertising.

During the war and afterwards my taste in poetry changed somewhat. I exchanged the earlier romantics for later ones, traded Tennyson and Carman for Chesterton and W. J. Turner, started reading Virginia Woolf, Hemingway and Dostoevsky on the advice of a drunken Vancouver bookseller. These poets and novelists named do not bear much relation to each other, but I respected the taste of my bookseller friend (though I suspected his motives), and plowed doggedly through the novelists but read Chesterton, Turner and James Elroy Flecker for pleasure. It reminds me of reading the entire works of Charles Dickens as a small child, because my mother paid me a nickel for reading each novel. (Imagine reading the 800 or so pages of David Copperfield for 5¢.)

Around that time—when I was 11 or 12—a neighbour moved to another town, gifting me with a complete paperback set of the adventures of Frank Merriwell by Burt L. Standish. This would be some 200 books. I was enthralled by Frank Merriwell, who always won at whatever games he played, whether football, baseball or hockey, or dominos with his girl friend, Inza Burriage. I therefore pretended to be sick, went to bed for two months, reading the Merriwell collected works in one long eye-bending marathon. My worried mother fed me ice cream and called the local doctor, who was unable to diagnose my literary illness but admitted it was serious. My mother eventually recovered.

I had always been afflicted with stupidity, although not consciously aware of the root cause of this inexplicable happiness. In the post-Merriwell period, during the early 1950s, I fell in with a group of science fiction lovers in Vancouver, one of whom was a child genius (about fifteen) named Curt Lang. I was over thirty at the time, and began to feel more and more inadequate in this company, and made a conscious effort to change my own tastes and appreciations. Working in a Vancouver mattress factory I read Dylan Thomas on the interurban going to and from work, T.S. Eliot at the bootleggers, and Irving Layton while drinking home brew.

As a result of all this self-improvement, the style of crap I was writing began to change. I used off-rhyme and assonance in poems. I used multisyllabic words whose meanings I kept forgetting after I wrote the poems. I used line breaks about that time. I used home brew. A friend and myself got a union started in the mattress factory, with resulting personal unpopularity with the management. Sitting on the house roof in Vancouver with my wife fixing a leak, we decided that her love for me and my love for her was indeed dead as a roofing nail. I moved all my books out that afternoon and wrote a poem. I moved all my books back that evening and wrote another poem, as we decided morosely that love might still be beautiful.

I know all this sounds like making jokes, but it isn't, not entirely. It wasn't a joke to quit the job I'd been working at for five years and go to Europe with some of the friends I met in Vancouver. The decision to go was agonizing: Yes I will! No I won't! If there are big decisions in a person's life, that was mine. As well, the factory manager had peeked over the toilet door to find me smoking a cigarette instead of crapping, and it was made clear that my continued employment at Vancouver Bedding Ltd. depended on stopping smoking. My wife also made it clear that if she couldn't go to Europe and share all my hardships, then I needn't bother coming back to her. So I stopped smoking.

All this was in 1955. I had just written a verse play idealizing childhood (my childhood was actually paranoiac hell), which CBC accepted and produced. Among Canadian poets, I was reading Earle Birney, Louis Dudek and Irving Layton, being one of many hypnotized by Layton. It's rather like falling in love to have this personal spell of another poet envelop you with a metrical womb. I slept on Layton's living room floor in Montreal on my way to Europe; and I'm still recovering from the effect of his poems.

Back from Europe (alone), my wife and I decided to go to Montreal so that she could enjoy working in an office and I could claim the well-merited renown awaiting my genius. I was damn sick of working, the nobility of which is continually exaggerated by those who don't know any better. Besides, I loathed that factory manager's gleaming white shirt and toothy grin as he urged the serfs to greater depths of production.

In Montreal I worked like hell writing poems and plays. CBC rejected my next dozen or so plays after accepting the first one. Ryerson Press published a chapbook of poems in 1955, and the University of New Brunswick another in 1956. A CBC editor named

Alice Frick, seeing that Purdy unchecked meant the end of drama as she knew it, gave me writing hints that permitted the acceptance of two more plays. I met Milton Acorn, who slept on the floor of my apartment and Layton's while recruiting me for the Marxist millennium. I met a fictional gal named Annette who tutored me in Montreal Yiddish already. We ran out of money.

My wife and I had a family conference at this time, one of those serious affairs in which decisions are arrived at which affect the future. Her decision was: if I could get away without working for a living she could too. Therefore we moved to Ameliasburgh in rural Ontario, building, or rather half-building, a cottage with the proceeds of the two CBC play sales, and a pile of second-hand lumber. Then we went inside the house, each keeping a close watch on the other. Either I would give in and go to work, or she would leave me as her family urged her to do. We settled for twin beds.

*(1976)*

# Charles Bukowski
## *It Catches My Heart in Its Hands*

RECEIVING THIS BOOK THRU THE MAILS is a bit like having a tribe of Indians in full war paint dropped into your mail-box. It's a Christmas tree of a book—dressed up with a varicoloured paper, and skilfully and lovingly put together. From the value point of view alone, it's worth any man's five bucks. An ugly-beautiful lavish anomaly of a book judged by the usual standards of contemporary pinch-penny publishing.

Having said that, what about the important thing: the poems themselves? From my highly personal viewpoint Bukowski is the best American poet to come down the non-existent pike in several years. Layton's *Red Carpet for the Sun* is the only other book of comparable vigour and freshness that I've seen.

Despite having published three previous books in extreme secrecy, and having been around a long time if you judge by the deliberately tough and fortyish phiz in the photograph on the book cover, Bukowski is a new poet. The only other place I've seen his poems is in Jon Webb's magazine *The Outsider*, tho undoubtedly he did publish elsewhere. I am quite sure he was writing good poems when *The New American Poetry 1945–1960* came out a few years back. Bukowski was not included in that supposedly classical anthology. Which is something of a puzzle to me. It would seem Bukowski belongs to no school or group, bears little relation to the snug coteries of Olson-Duncan-Creeley and even less to such academic pilchards as Richard Wilbur and Robert Lowell. The only relation I can dig up for Bukowski stems from the title, which is a quote from Robinson Jeffers.

---

Now Jeffers was a magnificent nihilist, believing in no human value or permanence. He maintained that the raw naked beautiful power of nature was more admirably suited to survive over the centuries than anything man could accomplish ("I'd sooner, except the penalties, kill a man than a hawk"). And into his long, heavily booming lines, he packed enough images (to Jeffers the eagle's wings were "folded storms at his shoulders") to sustain his vision of a savage unreasoning nature projected far into the future after the last bomb falls.

At first glance it appears that Bukowski is a similar nihilist, the smiler with a knife for contemporary pseudo values. A roaring hedonist, believing in momentary enjoyment only, but with a despairing note crouching in his laughter. However, Bukowski gets off the nihilistic hook by a perhaps unreasonable belief in Art with a capital A. And Art certainly presupposes man: you can't have one without the other—or so the monkies tell me. Therefore, a longer, harder look must show that Bukowski does indeed believe in man, however much he may dislike individual examples of the species.

And speaking of Art as counterpoint to Life: "The Life of Borodin" is a superb example of Bukowski's wry twisted casual understatement. It achieves its effect by the simple device of listing a symphony title in full; and this contrasts so strongly with the composer's detailed personal misery that it knocks you for a loop. It hits hard, and what else can you ask from a poem? It's one of those pieces impossible to quote from, which are nothing except in entirety.

I am also pleased the Bukowski book has one of those clever built-in introductions at the front, with which I find it quite pleasurable to disagree. In this introduction John William Corrington says that "critics at the end of our century may well claim that Charles Bukowski's work was the watershed that divided 20th Century American poetry between the Pound-Eliot/Auden period and the new time in which the human voice speaking came into its own." Well—that's nice.

As a follow-up Corrington goes on to say it's Bukowski's "voice" and "idiom" that make him remarkable. Here I agree. But I dislike the strong implication that to employ natural speech idioms is the best or only way to write poetry. There seem to me to be a million ways to write a poem. To exclude any of them is to make academic strictures on what poems are and should be.

But I must admit that I like the Bukowski idiom very much. Even if I don't agree with Corrington that this poet has done for the "American" language (are Canadians included under this semantic nationalism?) what Rimbaud did in French and W.C. Williams claimed to have done in the "American" language. It seems to be enough that Bukowski is a tremendous poet without making such absurd and grandiose academic claims. In fact I disagree with Corrington on nearly every point of his handy laudatory predigested opinion included with the book for the benefit of non-literary types like myself.

However, the important thing is Bukowski. At least Corrington likes some of the same poems I do, but says of the following excerpt that it sounds like Lorca ("more than a little of Lorca"):

I have heard Domenico Theotocopoulos
on nights of frost, cough in his grave,
and God, no taller than a landlady,
hair dyed red, has asked me the time:

I think it sounds like Bukowski, and it's pretty damn good. The man who has the sexual aplomb to write

positively grieve no more, ultimo ultimo
par chevii par grassi hold still bitch

ought to be saying it to Jacqueline Kennedy or Elizabeth of all the Elizabeths.

Charles Bukowski has painted a picture of what he thinks himself to be in these pages. Portrait of a semi-con-man, racetrack tout with cigarette dangling from lower lip, a Bogartish, tough boy with the ladies and whores under the grandstand. He sees himself grown old, physical prowess lessening (only once a night now?), waist thickening. He doesn't like it. Nobody does. And he talks tough and lives tough in the poems.

I would wish there to be no doubt that I think these are fine poems. However, isn't all this toughness and machine-gun language, even in its cumulative effect—isn't that only part of a man? Is there no other angle and aspect to Charles Bukowski? I certainly wouldn't go into the business of naming the parts of which a man of many parts should be composed. (I dislike even my own strictures.) But certainly the sum-total impression of the portrait painted in these poems is that of a living stance, a leaning attitude. The tough face with pockmarks he presents to the reader on book covers always looks the same. Tough, wise-cracking, enigmatic except in poems. The psychological attitude is predictable, always the same. Well, that's nonsense. No man always looks the same. We are as many and various in mood and manner as there are days to a life, hours of sunshine or hours of rain.

I'd like to quote "The Japanese Wife," a poem that makes me a liar because it has elements of tenderness in spite of the husband being chased under the bed and kept there for two days by his Japanese wife with a bread-knife in her hand. However, Bukowski's absolutely fiendish humour demands I quote "the state of world affairs from a 3rd floor window." I've showed this piece to several friends and acquaintances. It broke them up. Even my wife (who once really did threaten me with a bread-knife when we were young) betrayed feelings of humour; her eyes produced tears in an iron trickle as a result of the de-icer poems, the moisture descending to tile floor where it froze once more.

> O lord, he said, Japanese women,
> real women, they have not forgotten,
> bowing and smiling
> closing the wounds men have made;
> tear a lampshade,
> American women care less than a dime,
> they've gotten derailed,
> they're too nervous to make good:
> always scowling, belly-aching,
> disillusioned, overwrought;
> but oh lord, say, the Japanese women:
> there was this one,
> I came home and the door was locked
> and when I broke in she broke out the bread knife
> and chased me under the bed
> and her sister came
> and they kept me under that bed for two days,
> and when I came out, at last,
> she didn't mention attorneys,
> just said, you will never wrong me again,
> and I didn't; but she died on me,
> and dying, said, you can wrong me now,
> and I did,

but you know, I felt worse then
than when she was living;
there was no voice, no knife,
nothing but little Japanese prints on the wall,
all those tiny people sitting by red rivers
with flying green birds,
and I took them down and put them face down
in a drawer with my shirts,
and it was the first time I realized
that she was dead, even though I buried her;
and some day I'll take them all out again,
all the tan-faced little people
sitting happily by their bridges and huts
and mountains—
but not right now,
not just yet.

("The Japanese Wife")

By no means let anything I've said prevent you from getting this book. I think it's a fine book, and I've read it about ten times. Maybe even "critics at the end of our century may well claim that Charles Bukowski's work . . ." Ugahh! I'm glad the poet himself sounds better than that. And he does.

*(1964)*

# Leonard Cohen:
## A Personal Look

WHEN LEONARD COHEN PUBLISHED *Let Us Compare Mytholo-gies* in 1956, his book was of such merit as to invite comparison with Earle Birney's *David* and Irving Layton's first book, published in 1945. Now, a little more than eight years later, he has a fairly substantial body of work behind him: two more books of poetry and a first novel. An assessment of his work is long overdue, and with the publication of *Flowers for Hitler* (1964) it becomes possible to take a look at the contemporary writer in relation to the past.

Cohen's first two books of poetry were, I think, absolutely conventional in metre and form. They gained distinction from other people's poems through a heavy sensuality, sometimes almost cloy-ing, integral to nearly everything he wrote. As the title of his first book implies, comparative mythology, coeval social habits and mores were also included. Most avant-garde work south of the border seemed to have escaped his attention; or if it didn't, then he paid little heed. And English poetry in this day and age apparently has nothing to teach anyone.

For the last few years in this country there has been strong emphasis placed on such things as mythology and "archetypal myths," and whether it was Humpty-Dumpty who fell first or Adam. All of which seems rather a literary game to anyone who has to live in the world of now, go to work on a streetcar, say, and eat jam sandwiches for lunch in a quiet factory corner away from the machines.

But Cohen makes use of the Bible and fairy tales in his myths, suburban neighbours, his own grandparents, Jewish popular cus-toms, almost anything that will make a poem. Insecurity is a prime factor, and much of his work conveys a strong feeling that the world as presently constituted is liable to fly apart any moment:

If your neighbour disappears
O if your neighbour disappears
The quiet man who raked his lawn
The girl who always took the sun

Never mention it to your wife
Never say at dinner time
Whatever happened to that man
Who used to rake his lawn

Never say to your daughter
As you're walking home from church
Funny thing about that girl
I haven't seen her for a month

("Warning")

Which is perhaps modern archetypal. Of course husbands have always disappeared occasionally, and wives too have taken it on the lam for the quiet boredom of a lover in another town or street. Cohen means something a good deal more mysterious than that. By leaving it unnamed he manages to suggest the secret police, subterranean monsters and the lemmings' baptist instinct. All with a regular metric beat that blends casual after-dinner talk with the happenchance of human fatality.

As well, Cohen writes about sex; not the adolescent fumbling with a girl's bra-strap behind the closet door type either. Cohen's is a knowledgeable sex which explores the gamey musky-smelling post-coital bedroom world. No clinical nonsense either. Nor pregnancies. Romance rules supreme, and one measure of his success is that both Cohen's first two books sold out fairly quickly. But they are also good poems.

You could say that many of them expound the philosophy of meaninglessness very convincingly: i.e., they have an initial concrete incident or feeling, which is expressed so well that its magic drives any question of such things as meaning right out of your head. Take this passage:

My lover Peterson
He named me Goldenmouth

I changed him to a bird
And he migrated south

My lover Frederick
Wrote sonnets to my breast
I changed him to a horse
And he galloped west

My lover Levite
He named me Bitterfeast
I changed him to a serpent
And he wriggled east

("Song")

It's rather Sitwellish. "The King of China's Daughter," or something like that. In other words it's an attitude and way of writing a good craftsman can easily employ, though perhaps not quite at will. You adopt, for a poem's purposes, a particular way of thinking or feeling, then write the poem. And if you believe this suspension of personal identity and belief is possible and desirable, then the poet is in large degree an actor who plays many parts; but an actor so skilful you can't always tell the difference between acting and fakery. For instance, "My lover Peterson." What does it mean? Nothing. But it's magic.

Think of all the young poets who burst suddenly on the not-so-astonished world. Rimbaud, Chatterton, even the young Dylan Thomas. Is Cohen at the age of 30 one of these? I think not. Though very definitely one could compare poems in this first book with the youthful Yeatsian romanticism of "I will arise and go now, and go to Innisfree." Or the redolent Swinburne who wrote:

There lived a singer in France of old,
By the tideless dolorous midland sea.
In a land of sand and ruin and gold
There shone one woman, and none but she.

("The Triumph of Time")

Which is almost Cohen plus punctuation.

But Cohen has other facets too. In one of them he creates his mythology from the Auschwitz furnaces, imbuing it with a peculiar and grotesquely modern sensitivity:

And at the hot ovens they
Cunningly managed a brief
Kiss before the soldier came
To knock out her golden teeth.

And in the furnace itself
As the flames flamed higher,
He tried to kiss her burning breasts
As she burned in the fire.

("Lovers")

At this point I am aware of something common to much modern verse in Cohen. Not just disillusion and gamey decadence, but the present fact that all good things in life are done and past. A longing for what was, the sense of inadequacy in what is. One would think the ten-year-old yearned for his mother's breast, the adolescent for puberty, the stripling for renewed puppy love, and the only common denominator we all have is return to the womb fixations. The "fall" in other words. Once we were happy, now we are not. Rather ridiculous. Also completely ruinous for any possible present content.

Well, what does the reader want from a poem? Rather, what do I think he wants? Primarily, I suppose, to be entertained. And that involves tuning in on some emotions or feeling or discovery that is larger and more permanent that he is. Some flashing insight that adds a new perspective to living. Values also. And that is a great deal. Most of the time it's asking far too much.

Will you find any of these things in Cohen? Realities shoved from the periphery of your mind to forefront by the author. Not copy-book maxims, just real things and feelings.

Perhaps in Cohen's world the things he writes about exist, but only rarely do they touch on my personal existence. I admire the poems tremendously; they are the work of a master craftsman, who must simply be living in another time dimension than my own. I admire many of them as works of art I don't believe in. His figures swim dreamily through bedrooms, move out of Eden in slow motion, loll languorously on beaches of time. Slowly one of the inhabitants of this world lifts up, and says without much emotion: "Return to the past. Return to the past." Then he sinks back without a human grunt from the effort required to speak.

But that is one-sided, which I did not intend. There are also Cohen's magnificent incantatory effects. You can read many of his poems in your mind, and have the same bravura feeling as in Chesterton's "Lepanto." Some descriptions of unreal things are so vivid they can make you breathless with delight.

With *The Spice-Box of Earth* in 1961 Cohen brought to near perfection the techniques and rhythms of his first book. The "tone" seems a mixture of the Old Testament and, probably, other Jewish religious writings.

But I think this "tone" is important. Cohen rarely overstates or exaggerates. His emphasis is secured by underemphasis, never finding it necessary to raise his voice. There is always a casual offhand prosody, which lends even his rewrite job on the Bible the authority of someone present on the scene, and probably making notes behind his fig leaf.

> O Solomon, call away your spies.
> You remember the angels in that garden,
> After the man and woman had been expelled,
> Lying under the holy trees while their swords burnt out,
> And Eve was in some distant branches,
> Calling for her lover, and doubled up with pain.

("The Adulterous Wives of Solomon")

There is little intensity in this passage, or in any of Cohen for that matter. The effect is achieved by a kind of remote sadness, the knowledge we all have that being human has pain for continuing counterpoint. Despite the instructions to Solomon, no positive note or clear meaning comes out of the poem. Of course you can ring in "The Fall" *ad nauseam.* Lost innocence, lost happiness, exhausted vitality. In fact this decadent feeling the poem generates in a reader is one of its attractions. And for Cohen to raise his voice in a shout, or to possess carefree feelings of more than momentary happiness would be the complete *non sequitur.*

However, what seem to be shortcomings in the poems are turned into positive virtues. Using the same tone and metre Cohen writes love poems which are probably the best ever written in this country. Image succeeds image in a flow natural as birdsong:

> Now
> I know why many men have stopped and wept

Half-way between the loves they leave and seek,
And wondered if travel leads them anywhere—
Horizons keep the soft line of your cheek,
The windy sky's a locket for your hair.

("Travel")

I think those last two lines are demonstrably perfect and inimitable. There are many others almost as good. Cohen subdues everything to his touch. Even the zest and exuberance of, "Layton, when we dance our freilach" becomes something other than exuberance. The poem ends not unexpectedly on a quite different note: "we who dance so beautifully / though we know that freilachs end."

In another poem there is this wonderful passage:

Is it the king
who lies beside you listening?
Is it Solomon or David
or stuttering Charlemagne?
Is that his crown
in the suitcase beside your bed?

("You All in White")

When anyone can write like that, it seems unjust to complain about anything.

*The Favourite Game,* a novel, appeared in 1963. As first novels go (and most of them don't stay around long), it was a decided success. This one tells the story of Laurence Breavman, Montreal poet, child voyeur, adolescent in a world without fixed values. Breavman is a child when the novel opens, and a child still when it closes—though by this time he is presumably permitted to vote. The book traces his sexual initiation all the way from Montreal to New York. At the end Breavman is still being initiated into something or other. If not, then sexual retardation lasts quite a long time.

In any formal sense the novel has no plot. Time passes, of course. Breavman becomes older, his experiment with being alive more complicated. He is passed like a basketball from girl friend to girl friend (euphemisms for bedmates), arrives finally at his great Love, and predictably forsakes her in the end. For permanence in anything is anathema to our boy. Remember please, he is a writer.

If the above seems to indicate I disliked Cohen's novel, then appearances are misleading. I read it first last year, and again for the purposes of this review. Without a plot, without any "message" or insight into what it's like to be an ordinary human being and not Laurence Breavman, the book held me interested, if not spellbound, on both readings. The reason: reality seeps through somehow, with convincing detail and dialogue.

What Cohen's poetry lacks is found here in large measure. *The Favourite Game* is rich in humour, zest for living, the sort of febrile intensity a moth who lives less than 24 hours might have; also, the continual sense of Breavman watching himself watching himself, which is, I think, a characteristic of most writers. From every corner of the room, ceiling and floor, Breavman watches himself, because he wants to write it all down later. He wants to say what it was like to be uniquely himself, and yet to be Everyman as well.

Coitus interruptus and a handy night light. In the case of women writers, a ball-point pen that writes upside down. Sex for the sake of love, but it turns out to be just sex. (And what's wrong with that?) Living as an experiment, an adventure, as many separate adventures without permanence. Breavman as the iconoclast, searching for a Colossus of Rhodes he can't destroy. For if he can destroy the thing or the emotion, then it wasn't real—it never happened. Well, what did happen? As it turns out, only what was written down on paper.

Cohen has, in this book, developed the technique which will enable him to write other and better novels. This one is not a failure, but is badly flawed in that it seems to tail off at the end without saying anything very convincingly. Not that I mean a moral should be pointed or a tale adorned. But no one will care very much that Breavman will never return to his Great Love. He becomes suddenly rather a cardboard figure. He was created in the author's mind, and in some important way seems to be there still not working very hard at getting out and being Laurence Breavman.

But *The Favourite Game* is an interesting novel, up to this point. What it says about being alive is its own parable, never stated explicitly. Much of the dialogue sounds like tape recorder stuff. On this evidence, it can hardly be doubted that Cohen is a novelist possessing much more than mere "promise."

If Dylan Thomas had lived longer than his 39 years he would have found it necessary to change. He was at a dead end, with exaggeration piled on exaggeration. But Jeffers, with his nihilistic view of mankind, lived long into his seventies and didn't change. Neither did A.E. Housman and his hopeless view of human life.

With *Flowers for Hitler* Cohen recognizes the necessity to get away from his sensuous unrealistic parables and flesh fantasies. Cohen does change. But the change has puzzled me somewhat. I've asked everyone I know who's interested in poetry what they think of *Flowers for Hitler*, and why. Some shared my own small puzzlements. The answers I got boiled down to equal approval and dislike. None thought the book outstanding, and some thought it pretty undistinguished.

Cohen quotes Primo Levi before the poems begin: "If from the inside of the Lager, a message could have seeped out to free men, it would have been this: Take care not to suffer in your own homes what is inflicted on us here." This presages the communal guilt theme of the book.

But there are other motifs. Personal dissatisfaction with the world Cohen never made. Guilt plus erotica. Obsession with drugs. Two Cuban poems, one of which suggests the future death of Fidel Castro in chilling fashion.

Several themes. But none come through as overriding strengths that make the book a consistent whole, as Cohen undoubtedly wished. Not that they should necessarily; for life is a pot-pourri, a grab bag of seemingly unrelated things. But lacking thematic consistency, the poems do not accurately portray reality either. They seem playful exercises, poems for the sake of poems. Hitler and the communal guilt ploy seem to me like the talk of a good conversationalist who had to say something, whether it was real or not.

Here's what Cohen says of his poems on the cover: "This book moves me from the work of the golden-boy poet into the dungpile of the front-line writer. I didn't plan it this way. I loved the tender notices *Spice-Box* got but they embarrassed me a little. *Hitler* won't get the same hospitality from the papers. My sounds are too new, therefore people will say: this is derivative, this is slight, his power has failed. Well, I say there has never been a book like this, prose or poetry, written in Canada. All I ask is that you put it in the hands of my generation and it will be recognized."

Let's assume that the claims Cohen makes for his new book are sincere, dubious as that may seem. The bit about the "golden-boy poet" and "dung pile of the front-line writer" I choose to ignore, for it seems gratuitous ego and sales come-on. But are Cohen's sounds new? (By sounds I take it he means his idioms, tone, and contemporary speech rhythms.) In other words, has Cohen effected a revolution in prosody, written something so startling that time is required before his innovations are recognized? Has he done that?

No.

I agree there has never been a book like *Flowers for Hitler* published in Canada. Cohen is an individual poet, possessing his own strong merit and equally indubitable weaknesses. But even so there are traces of other people's influence. Laurence Hope's *Indian Love Lyrics*, surprisingly enough. Some of the Elizabethans. Donne's "Sweetest love I do not go"—cf. *The Favourite Game*. Waller's "On a Girdle." Swinburne with arthritis. Dowson's "Cynara" even.

But I'm not very fond of that favourite game. Cohen has come swimming out of all such traces of other poets, emerges as himself. As for the dust jacket blurb, I don't want to fall into the trap of treating an author's ad agency gabblings as important. Only poems are. And pretentiousness aside, there are a few things in *Hitler* which I value:

> I once believed a single line
> in a Chinese poem could change
> forever how blossoms fell
> and that the moon itself climbed on
> the grief of concise weeping men
> to journey over cups of wine
>
> ("For E.J.P")

Of course that is the "old" Cohen. Here is the guilty "new" Cohen:

> I do not know if the world has lied
> I have lied
> I do not know if the world has conspired against love
> I have conspired against love
> The atmosphere of torture is no comfort
> I have tortured
> Even without the mushroom cloud
> still I would have hated
>
> ("What I'm Doing Here")

And so on. He ends the poem: "I wait/for each one of you to confess." Well, he's gonna have to wait a long time. Liars, torturers and conspirators don't confess by reason of such poems as this one. And the life Cohen portrays in his poems has to be unreal by my personal standards.

Sure, I've done all the things he says he's done. But I'm not personally preoccupied with guilt, and I think few people are or should be. Life being lived now, and personal change being more important than morbid preoccupation with past imperfections, I feel no particular urge to confess anything; though in a sense I suppose I have, in the first sentence of this paragraph. What then IS important in poetry and life?

Well, much of the time being alive at all has puzzled me. What am I going to do with my awareness, the mixed curse and blessing of sentience? Yes, life—it includes things I haven't even thought of yet. It also includes the various dictionary emotions, including a negligible amount of guilt. What then is important?

Perhaps to take a new and searching look at people, redefining what they are as against what they were previously thought to be. Man himself is the unknown animal. We know more about nuclear physics, crop rotation and fertilizers than we do about our own nature and potentialities. As well, we might look for a new road on which mankind can travel. The one he's on now appears to be heading straight for The Bomb. Science, politics, philosophy and something like religion are all mixed in with the new poetry.

Those are grandiose things of course. Has Cohen discovered any new roads, or should I expect him to discover them? That question too is theatric, perhaps ill-considered. Well then, is he living now, asking the questions we all ask ourselves, making discoveries about himself, explaining the scope and nature of what a human being might be? Sometimes he is.

But I'm no longer puzzled about Cohen. He has changed, veered at a sharp angle from his previous work, struck off in another direction entirely. For the "now" poet is an exploding self, whom critics cannot predict, nor can the poet himself. Where he is going he does not know exactly, and where he has been he can only remember imperfectly. He inhabits language as well as the world, infuses words with something of his own questioning stance, his own black depression and joyous life.

One can only guess where Cohen is going now. But when I see

the human confusion and uncertainty of his last book, I have hope it may be *terra incognita* where he is going. With a ball-point pen. And may survive there and map the territory.

*(1965)*

∞

## *Beautiful Losers*

THE PRINCIPAL CHARACTER in Leonard Cohen's *Beautiful Losers* is Nameless (my own cognomen for him), an old scholar whose wife, Edith, has been killed at the bottom of an elevator shaft. I suppose this is meant to symbolize that she went about as far as she could go. Anyhow, Nameless is much interested in the "A—s," an extinct Indian tribe, of which his wife was a member. Nameless is in love with Catherine Tekakwitha, a dead Indian saint of the Mohawk tribe. F. is a nameless friend of Nameless, and died of syphilis five years before the novel begins.

Nameless, Edith and F. shared in a sexual round-robin when all were alive, and in sexual fantasies when two are dead. The old scholar, Nameless, is searching for a method of sexual union with the afore-mentioned Tekakwitha, who died of self-inflicted mortifications of the flesh in 1680. Nameless is understandably feeling rather frus-trated, but bridges the gulf of time with imagination.

Those are the bare bones of a plot whose complexity and changes of narrative perspective make the Minotaur's maze look like a baseball field in the Sahara Desert by comparison. Of course Cohen has much more on his mind than merely telling a story. His characters get themselves into every kind of sexual orgy possible, including assault by a fucking machine called a Danish Vibrator, which proceeds to drown itself in the Atlantic Ocean afterwards. Everything is here but incest.

My own impression is that Cohen intends to break any and all barriers of language, so-called morality and contortionist possibility, in order that his "hero" may achieve "a state of grace" plus positive physical and mental identification with the Iroquois saint, and so partake of Catherine Tekakwitha's own absolutes.

Salvation thru degradation is becoming more literarily popular as the minutes fly by. Scott Symons' *Place D' Armes* is most recent in this respectable genre.

William Burroughs is also an obvious influence, probably de Sade and Huysmans—the latter two being more concerned with sex and pain as pleasure and sensation etc.

*Beautiful Losers*, therefore, is in a valid literary tradition. It tries to do something attempted several times (at least) before. But in jumping his characters thru their sexual hoopla and triple-header saturnalias, Cohen sacrifices whatever reality his people may ever have had. It simply isn't possible to suspend disbelief—not because the people are abnormal, but because Cohen doesn't make their abnormality and quest for "vital truth" real. His characters are just coat hangers for his "message" and virtuoso language.

Therefore one may be mildly entertained by language pyrotechnics, or else keep one's eye firmly fixed on the philosophic ball, "salvation thru degradation" or "identification with absolutes," or whatever one thinks Cohen is getting at. He is getting at something, without doubt, but to me novels must include among their several levels the ground floor basic of being interesting.

*Beautiful Losers* loses with me, too, falls flat as week-old beer, not because it's pornographically repetitive, but because it's boring as hell. I can't think of a worse condemnation, but fortunately for Cohen few other reviewers agree with me. I'd be happy to believe in Nameless, Edith and F. as real people and not an author's cardboard characters, and also their search for "vital truth" of which the world seems to have little. But I want help from Cohen as a writer, something he isn't disposed to give.

*(1967)*

# Irving Layton
## *Balls for a One-Armed Juggler*

QUESTION: IS IT POSSIBLE TO SITUATE IRVING LAYTON anywhere in the general "tradition" of Canadian poetry?

ANSWER: I don't think so, in spite of the fact that he's here. There has never been anyone quite like Layton—for good or bad—in Canadian poetry. He's the sport and anomaly of tradition

Q: Layton has been called an innovator and a meticulous craftsman. Is this true?

A: He is not an innovator—unless you consider that his subject matter and language are innovation. Which in a sense I do. But given the tradition of preaching Christ-like sensualists and moralists such as Nietzsche, Lawrence and Shaw—then Layton is a fine craftsman. And this is relevant in an odd way. It allows Layton to swing expertly and acrobatically around the fixed trapeze of his own and other men's certainties.

Q.: To what poets or group of present day writers has he most affinity?

A: Leaving out the dead men for whom Layton professes admiration, one has to point to the Americans whom Layton affects to despise, such as Ginsberg, Kerouac, etc.—the Beats. But Layton has a singing magnificence in his earlier work which I find absent from theirs.

Q: There is preoccupation with physical violence and cruelty in many Layton poems. What does this indicate?

A: That he is a moralist. The reader may generally draw a conclusion or point a moral with Layton's poems of animal death and human violence.

---

Q: How good is he?

A: The best in the country.

There is much to be said for the idea that Layton is his own mythology. He stalks through most of the poems in *Balls for a One-Armed Juggler* much larger than life-size, far more angry than it's possible to sustain in the living flesh and bone of the human mind. So that his poems are frozen anger, solidified passion—set rigidly into forms which do not allow this anger to dissipate away into sleep or lessen into human anti-climax.

Of course there are modulations and degrees of printed emotion. There are also rare flashes of the characteristic early lyricism, which now seems to be fading away in the poet's impassioned middle age. Label this excerpt pity:

> for I loved you from the first
> who know what they do not know,
> seeing in your death a tragic portent
> for all of us who crawl and die
> under the wheeling disappearing stars;
> ("Elegy for Marilyn Monroe")

Humour in Layton is liable to be savage as an executioner laughing at his victims. The philosophic moments are hardly ever calm, but generally vital:

> Yet vitality proves nothing except that
> something is alive
> So is a pole-cat; so is a water-rat
> ("On Rereading the Beats")

I don't think I've ever met a human being with such impressive qualities of being right all the time as Irving Layton. And in this regard man and poems are inseparable. In a sense that's admirable. I admire the passion and bluster and candour it gives to the poems. In another sense I don't like anybody to be so right all the time. For it is not a very human quality; it withdraws its possessor from participation in the storms and passions of the actual world, makes him a mere angry supreme court spectator. It turns a man into a megalomaniac god. I think some readers share this dislike of the absolute, and certainly the tendency of a few is to rebel against it.

However, that is ungrateful. God pities the dead little fox in "Predator." God explains "Why I Can't Sleep Nights" in the poem of that title. God condemns and castigates the sinful individual in "Epigram for Roy Daniells." And God has written parables for his worshippers—"Butterfly on Rock" and "A Tall Man Executes a Jig" (of which Irving said to me once, "Al, in ten years you'll be able to understand this poem. In twenty you might be able to write one as good." I was moved to a great humbleness by this statement.)

But I'm not one of Layton's detractors. Balls is an excellent book of poems. It deserves to be read by all—especially those to whom Layton addresses the poems specifically. And I notice that even those who dislike Layton always read him—if only to rush indignantly to their typewriters. For perhaps I'm wrong about this god-idea, and the anger of some of Layton's critics is the only indication they are alive.

*(1963)*

∾
## *The Collected Poems of Irving Layton*

T*HE COLLECTED POEMS OF IRVING LAYTON* is a large block-buster of a book. It takes in most of Layton's published work for the last twenty years, replaces the earlier *Red Carpet for the Sun* from the standpoint of quantity, and allows the reader to indulge in some wide generalizations.

For instance, some people believe that Layton has been slipping badly as a poet, perhaps ever since about 1960 when he was receiving greatest recognition. In fact I shared this belief myself and mentioned it to Milton Wilson. But Wilson said he saw no change one way or the other in Layton's work (this is only an approximate quote), and that very likely it was the poetry reader who had changed—not Layton.

Looking at the present *Collected Poems* I now think Milton Wilson was right. Since reading Layton for the first time I've changed, at least my own attitudes have; and other readers too have retreated some-what from an earlier enthusiasm.

I find that curious. One might suppose that a work of art endures unchanged in one's own mind forever, or the personal equivalent of forever. Not so. And it does chill me a little to think that perhaps one day I may tire of Peter Breughel, W.B. Yeats, the French Impressionists etc.

The question is: why has my own attitude (as well as that of some other people) changed regarding Layton's poems? For he is in many obvious ways, the great trail-blazer in Canadian poetry. He antedated and outdid the blessedly unborn American Beats as long ago as 1950. He broke the sound barrier of taboo and prudery thru his use of words relating to the sexual act, at a time when many young poets now using his methods and perhaps believing themselves excessively daring were yet unborn. (In Vancouver during the early fifties the poems of this then unknown poet of Montreal affected me like a personal revelation, thru which I thought life had been stripped down to its basics of delight and honesty.)

The trouble is that Layton is still doing the same things today. He has not changed. And on closer inspection what looked daring then seems commonplace now. The sexual words turn out to be those found in textbooks, phallus, penis, and the like. And I have been inoculated to some degree against Layton by repeated and massive doses of Layton. Whereas the younger generation has not been so inoculated. He is fresh and new to them: which is perhaps as it should be, for he is a poet of youth and the flesh, the quick and easy judgment, immediate praise or condemnation whatever the grounds for either.

Layton's critics select specific objectives at which to aim their criticism. For instance, Robin Skelton says he rants, brags and boasts tiresomely. This is true, and can be substantiated by quoting particular poems. Louis Dudek says, among other things, that Layton's awkward juxtapositions of words in order to make them conform to a metric scheme result in Layton being a species of literary troglodyte. Again, this is true, and could be demonstrated by means of quoting Layton's poems. But the verdict that follows such logic is not necessarily true, for it is as one-sided and unjust as the immediate magisterial verdicts Layton himself hands down in his poems.

For these knowledgeable critics have selected Layton's worst and most awkward poems in order to make their point effectively. Skelton and Dudek have been largely correct with their specific complaints. However, there is a great deal more to be said of Layton than these comparatively minor points, true as the particular criticism may be.

As I look at 350 odd pages of *Collected Poems*, beginning with verse published in Layton's first book (*Here and Now*, 1945), I find a most curious homogenized texture from first to last. The early themes—sex, Jewishness, love of life, bitter complaints about philistinism, and many others—are there now and still in the same abundance. Of course the poet became a bit more technically expert in handling his themes, but the themes themselves are the same. And for that matter, I don't see why they shouldn't be.

And during Layton's mid-period, say around the early 1950s, he produced his finest poems, things like "The Birth of Tragedy," which he affects to dislike as academic thesis fodder, but which I am sure delight him in reality.

In attempting to explain this "homogeneity" previously mentioned I'm forced to settle for the word "tone." And I don't mean idiom. The best way I can explain what I mean by "tone" is to give a precariously related example. Suppose a man yells aloud every day for 20 years, and each time a scientific device registers his volume as, say, 467 decibels. The exact number doesn't matter, and besides I don't know how many decibels amount to a whisper. Anyhow, transfer this metaphor to Layton's poems, and say he's been giving vent to a stentorian yowl of exactly 467 decibels every day for the last 20 years.

I'd like to be as metaphorically exact as I can. Therefore: the 467 decibels (of course) comprise other things beside volume. Included also are cocksureness, conceit, delicacy, a modicum of wisdom, and occasional magnificence. (This last being very rare in any poet.) And all thru those 20 years, the "tone," the decibels, yowl of stance and attitude have been largely the same.

Take the following two lines: "Here private lust is public gain and shame;" "When evil has become our normal climate." The first is from a poem in *Here and Now*, Layton's first book; the second is from "On the Assassination of President Kennedy." The "tone," the "decibels," the voltage, call it what you like, seem to me the same.

Of course I'm doing here exactly the same thing I say Skelton and Dudek are doing—selecting appropriate passages to prove my particular point. But I don't maintain there are not slight variations in the overall tone. "A Tall Man Executes a Jig" is certainly one of those variations. Here Layton lowers his tone and intensity about 200 decibels with corresponding benefit to the poem. But these poems are exceptions. And while it might seem that a poet ought to have an "unmistakable voice," as Layton does, the actual possession of one makes for monotony over 20 years.

Another thing that has always troubled me about Layton's poems, after the early euphoric sensation wore thin, is that I am seldom able to share his personal feeling and emotion, when attempting to relate my own feelings to the circumstance of the poem. (Of course I wasn't there.) Just once in a while, when Layton is joyously "lord of all the marquees" and "the traffic cop moving his lips/Like a poet composing/Whistles a discovery of sparrows." Such moments are the "happy time," that I think all members of the human race must share, at least once in a while. And for tribute to the man who puts it into words all I can say is: Wow!

But generally speaking, I admire the rhetoric from outside, as if watching a very good actor perform, tho not quite good enough. What Layton says is much too frequently a little off to one side of the way I think things actually are, not quite my truth, tho I suppose Layton's' truth.

As an example of this feeling of mine, take the last line in "The Bull Calf"—a much admired Layton poem: "I turned away and wept." Now I'm as sentimental a person as the next, but can't conceive myself weeping in these circumstances of death. Tho some can. I can only conclude there may have been other things, other feelings in Layton himself, which he has failed to communicate to me. Or perhaps I'm just insensitive. And the reference to the late President Kennedy as "our noble prince" strikes me as maudlin and a little embarrassing.

Nor do I subscribe to the trivia of "In Memory of Stephen Ward" or the "Earth Goddess" poem for Marilyn Monroe (tho I wrote one myself and regret it). But they and others are by-products of Layton's poetic renderings. Against trivia you can balance and overbalance occasional genuine magnificence.

Another commonly held theory about Layton is that he is a marvellous craftsman (this is true in some degree) and a technical innovator. The last is sheer nonsense. Layton picked up and developed his form and tone from fairly obvious sources, perhaps Horace Gregory's translations of Catullus being most easily apparent. The enjambments and juxtapositions of much modern poetry are, in Layton, conspicuous by their absence. To me he is a traditionalist, with a good ear for the modern idiom.

As in most of the poets, iambs throng in his work like veteran marching armies who have conquered before and certainly will again. Nor is this reprehensible in any way. A poet would have to be insane to discard entirely the arts and technical craft that have taken a thousand years to develop, but yet continue to change and move forward.

With Layton a soliloquy generally amounts to a harangue. On page 308 begins a short sequence of poems concerning, presumably, marital infidelity. And I'm amused to note that in these poems Layton condemns the woman as vociferously as he does modern culture in general. The woman is "evil"; the man, it is taken for granted, is virtuous and blameless. Apart from ye olde double standard, such judgments are predictable, and after a while very monotonous.

It makes you wonder if there is no possibility of the man being wrong. Is everything one-sided, simple and transparent to this angry all-wise sage? Yes it is.

But it's unfair to carp and cavil all thru Layton's *Collected Poems*. I hope I haven't seemed entirely too one-sided in my criticism, as Layton sometimes is in his poems. Despite obvious faults, these poems are the most substantial body of good work published in the country. You have to accept the bad with the good, and be thankful for both, for they're interrelated and mutually dependent.

But decide for yourself which is which. Don't let Layton overpower you, either with rhetoric or personality, or the dogmatism that makes him a prize example of his own pet theory about the despised academics.

Layton is a fine poet, and if I disbelieve his genius-assessment of himself, there's enough justice and/or truth in what he says to make me think about the possibility seriously before I make up my own mind. Which is my 10 (minor) decibels' worth.

*(1966)*

# Dylan Thomas

## Constantine Fitzgibbon: *The Life of Dylan Thomas*

THIS BIOGRAPHY OF DYLAN THOMAS turns out very much like an autopsy, and not the story of a once-living man. While reading it I thought also of reading Dylan's *Collected Poems* riding the bus in Vancouver on my way to a job I didn't like during the early 1950s. Despite accompaniment of stepped-on feet and hastily averted eyes from glum going-to-work faces, I managed to read through the book several times with iron self-discipline and only once or twice went past my stop.

I was puzzled and delighted by the poems then. I am puzzled and slightly dismayed by this "official autopsy" now, which is yet an absolute must for anyone who admires the poems of a man who ranked himself literarily as "captain of the second eleven."

The book's pace is slowed to a crawl by such qualificatory sentences as: "I think I should suggest very tentatively what in my view his earliest years portend." (If Thomas has known they were going to portend that frightening twaddle, he would have jumped off the dock at Laugharne before reaching twenty-one.) Or: "Nevertheless I must give it as my opinion . . . " It makes me want to bite the nearest PhD (Lit.).

Let's get back to Dylan himself. I think there's no doubt he was partly taken in by the myth he helped create. And finally his reputation as a boozer and wencher made him decide that was exactly what he was, and what a poet should be. Being self-conscious, his life must have been a continual comparison of his own legend versus reality, mind swivelling back and forth between the two, alternating glimpses of myth and reality like a spectator at a tennis match. But Dylan was sadly more than a spectator of his own life and death.

The best thing about this book is the liberal Thomas quotes, stories, anecdotes and snippets. They almost depict his joyous and terrible pub-crawl through the world. They almost, though not quite, bring it to life.

Such things as Dylan eating a bowl of chrysanthemums at a party.

Or the lovely malicious remarks he used to make about people. Here's a Dylan pseudo-quote of Charles Morgan: "I spent twenty years perfecting the use of the colon: then the war came."

And the time he was scheduled to be guest of honour at the annual banquet of the Swansea Branch of the British Medical Association—but predictably didn't show up. In a letter of apology to the medicos, he tells of being in Swansea later, becoming ill but afraid to go to the hospital, and says: "I felt sudden and excruciating pains, and when I whimpered about them to a friend he said 'Whatever you do, don't get ill in Swansea, it's more than your life is worth. Go in with a cough and they'll circumcise you!'"

Or the early dog days when he was in love with Caitlin Macnamara, who was also painter Augustus John's beloved. Afflicted with a dose of clap picked up during a London drunk, Dylan made necessarily platonic love to Caitlin in John's car on a motor trip near Laugharne. The old painter was thoroughly annoyed by this public lovemaking, and the two men came to blows in a car-park. John had no trouble knocking Dylan flat on his back, even though forty years older than the poet. Then he and Caitlin got in the car and drove away, leaving Dylan to trudge back to Swansea on foot.

It's a lovely picaresque situation, and let's not bring morals into it. Imagine belligerent old Augustus John "protecting" Caitlin, long beard blowing and quivering with indignation, standing over the recumbent undoubtedly drunken Dylan like Zeus in a Welsh car-park long ago. And the physically futile almost comically afflicted poet walking the long road back to Swansea, feeling like the last apple left in a winter orchard, and that one wormy.

Fitzgibbon describes this last episode as if he were colour-blind. He leaves out the laughter. And yet the official biographer has done an awesome amount of research on Dylan's life. Even the most trivial facts and personal habits are brought to light. For instance, the name "Dylan" comes from the Welsh Mabinogion. It means "Son of the Sea Wave."

The myth of instant Dylan is still with us twelve years after his death. He continues to be the immortal sponger and boozer, woman-chaser and catcher, sneak-thief of other men's shirts and perhaps a genius. I think he was, and don't agree with that "second eleven" stuff at all.

Among things that appear certain is Dylan's enormous talent for self-destruction. But that was part of the self which also included the great poet. As much lament Kit Marlowe's liking for low-life friends that led to his murder with a threepenny knife and was also part of the condition of Marlowe's being a poet.

I suppose that's a fatalistic attitude. But I prefer not to lament Thomas or mourn the disordered life he lived. I'm thankful he lived at all. One needs only to read the sadly magnificent lines of "In the White Giant's Thigh" to know that mourning is unnecessary. Or "Fern Hill," perhaps the best poem about childhood ever written. Or "Lament," that gusty, breathing canticle of lechery and comic frustration.

As time passes the legend of boyo Dylan begins to merge with and become his poems. As for stealing shirts, being drunk much of the time, etc. etc., who would really hold it against him? Who cares? As Louis MacNeice said while reviewing Brinnin's somewhat unflattering book, *Dylan Thomas in America*: "What vomit had John Keats?"

The faeces of extraordinary men hold fascination for the newspaper-reading public. And perhaps the mythical "common man" says as he reads of Dylan's mammoth foolishness: "Why he was just like me!" But he wasn't.

In any final judgment of Dylan (for we all judge), it must be said that essentially he did what he wanted with his life, apart from all mistakes and errors of commission. And I'm sure he thought it was important. Which can be said of few of us, before or after our own deaths.

I think of Dylan's friends in London searching for him through pub after pub, only to find he had always left just before them; and the multi-faced barkeep's continual reply to queries: "E woz ere but he gorn."

*(1966)*

# Farley Mowat
## *Westviking*

# Helge Ingstad
## *Land Under the Pole Star*

IN GREY EARLY MORNING, with fog hanging over the sea, a broad-beamed high-bowed ship some 70–80 feet long dropped anchor in a small bay whose shores humped above the mist to form a vague country of green spruce and marshy bog land. Cattle bawled on the ship, hungry for fresh forage not far away. Armed men peered through the mist, wondering if the forest concealed savage human or super-human enemies. Women crouched behind the men—also wondering. And then the settlers splashed ashore with weapons ready, and stood for the first time on the outside rim of the New Country.

The time of all this was a few years less than a thousand years ago. The place was Epaves Bay (L'Anse aux Meadows), at the tip of the Great Northern Peninsula of Newfoundland—Canada. Combined archaeological, cartographic and written evidence has confirmed this Viking landing to the point where no unprejudiced person would now doubt its validity—confirmed it to the absurd modern culmination of Italo-American supporters of C. Columbus parading public loyalty to the "firstness" of their own undoubted hero.

In Farley Mowat's book the whole business has been reduced to a further absurdity—Did Leif Eriksson turn left or right at the first stop sign?—while the Vikings cogitate over wind and ocean currents like a bunch of company directors deciding on a corporate merger.

Probably I'm being unfair to Mowat. That the Vikings discovered America first seems indisputable. What their mental processes were while doing so is thus bound to be important, though not necessarily interesting (depending on the writer), and certainly speculative at this late date. But Mowat's "author-hubris" in this book (a disease some of us are familiar with in poets) interferes with and spoils the story for me at least to some extent.

The stated object of *Westviking* is to resolve "the degree of Celtic participation in the westward thrust; the real scope of Erik the Red's explorations . . . the identities of the several native peoples encountered; the detailed tracks followed by all the voyagers; the identity and location of the landfalls, havens and settlements; the major factors which prompted, shaped, and sometimes doomed the efforts of westward venturers; and many lesser matters."

For its factual structure and basis *Westviking* draws on three sagas: *Erik the Red's Saga*, *The Karlsefni Saga* and *The Short Saga*, these being Icelandic literary sources written in the twelfth and thirteenth centuries. The book also draws on several historical (as apart from "literary") sources, such as the *Islendingabok* by Ari the Learned, written in Iceland during the twelfth century; and only mentions Adam of Bremen's writings which date less than a century after the actual westward voyages of Leif Eriksson and Karlsefni.

Mowat excerpts and arranges his quotations from both sagas and historical sources, jerking many quotes out of their original context in order to compile a single coherent story which, naturally enough, agrees with and supports his own conclusions. After quoting his composite story, Mowat goes ahead to elaborate and explain how, why, and in what way things actually happened. Thus we have the sagas plus quotes from Icelandic histories mixed together, followed by modern commentary. This for 300 pages. At the end of the book there is a series of long appendices, on everything from Norse sailing vessels (they were exceptionally seaworthy) to the recent excavations by Helge Ingstad at L'Anse aux Meadows (Mowat thinks the Ingstad site was a Basque whale fishery, then reverses himself to declare it a Norse site.)

In a long introduction to their Penguin translation of the Vinland *Sagas*, Magnus Magnussen and Herman Palsson comment on the free and easy treatment other writers besides Mowat have given the sagas: "Too often they have been served up to the public in filleted versions, with their texts emended or cut or adapted or even conflated into a single uneasy narrative in an attempt to gloss over their inconsistencies. The sagas themselves have become obscured rather than illuminated by editors who arbitrarily selected textual variants to suit their own theories." I'd go along with Magnussen and Palsson in this, for it scares me to think what Mowat might do to *Elder Edda*, not to mention the Dead Sea Scrolls.

But there are several good things about *Westviking*. In the first place it's a commendable thing that a popular writer like Mowat should examine the sagas (however wildly), and thus draw them to the attention of the general public. For there is a whole fascinating range of Icelandic literature, quite apart from the sagas themselves. *The Floamanna Saga*, for instance, was quite new to me. It tells of Thorgisl Orrabeinfostri, a friend of Erik the Red, whose ship was wrecked on the way to Greenland to join his friend. Thorgisl had just been converted to Christianity, and his dreams were troubled by visits from a red-headed pagan god called Thor. Indeed, when one considers the factual Skraelings (Dorset Eskimos) and human giants like Thorgisl Orrabeinfostri, one need only jog over a slight mental bump, and there we are back at *The Elder Edda* with the Fenris Wolf and Midgard Serpent.

One passage in the sagas makes long-dead Erik the Red similar to a modern hen-pecked husband and very human. When his wife, Thorhild, was converted to Christianity, she refused to sleep with Erik because he was still a heathen. That was certainly one reason why Erik decided to go along with his son on another voyage to Vinland. He fell off his horse on the way to the ship. Erik went anyway, aching shoulder and all, but stormy weather drove him back to Greenland. He died a year later, still unrepentant and presumably unconverted.

But does Mowat accomplish his stated goals in writing his book? Concerning the degree of Celtic participation in the Viking westward thrust (he believes the Celts were in Greenland before the Norse): the only possible evidence for this is that Norse house foundations in Greenland were underlaid by ruins of a slightly different nature. Of course it is pretty well established now that Celtic anchorites were in Iceland before the Norse, which is not very good ground for assuming they were also in Greenland.

As to the identities of native peoples encountered in the area, there were only Beothuk Indians and Dorset Eskimos. Mowat mentions no others. And the possibility that Thule Eskimos (the Dorsets' successors), who moved eastward from Alaska around 900 AD might have arrived on the eastern Atlantic seaboard a hundred years later is somewhat remote. In Newfoundland itself only Dorset and Beothuk remains have been found.

Mowat also identifies, at least to his own satisfaction, "—the detailed tracks, identity and location of landfalls etc." The general area of Norse exploration (the east coast of Canada and the United States, including Newfoundland) can be taken for granted, since it is documented and fairly well substantiated. That Cape Porcupine on the Labrador coast is the Norse "Marvel-Strands" and L'Anse aux Meadows (Epaves Bay) an early settlement seems to me beyond question. But that Vinland is Tickle Cove on Trinity Bay, Nfld. (as Mowat maintains) is decidedly unproven. However, it's an interesting speculation.

No doubt Mowat does possess more types of specialized knowledge, such as navigation and familiarity with ocean currents, etc., than any ordinary person. I respect this knowledge, but doubt if it enables its possessor to do more than probe and prod this 1,000-year-old detective story, raise the puzzling questions themselves. And this is much. Mowat may certainly have stumbled on to some of the correct answers, but how are we to know this? His case is decidedly unproven.

In his Epaves Bay appendix Mowat discusses Helge Ingstad's discovery of an early Norse settlement at L'Anse aux Meadows (which I visited this summer). Ingstad has unearthed the remains of several buildings, a smithy where bog iron had been smelted, a spindle whorl of early Norse design. Carbon-14 tests on charcoal found at the site established the dates of 860 plus or minus 90 years. These dates are to be found in Ingstad's *National Geographic* article for Nov. 1964; the dates in Mowat's appendix run from 680 to 1060. (It would seem that Mowat's first date is a mistake, and that he simply turned Ingstad's figure backwards.) All of this adds up to fairly satisfactory proof of a Norse settlement at that time in question. Mowat admits this reluctantly. Despite the scarcity of artifacts (only a Norse spindle whorl), the authenticity of the site seems beyond doubt. But is it also the original Vinland of Leif Eriksson? That's something else altogether.

For some unknown reason Mowat seems to have formed a dislike for Ingstad, and suggests the Norse writer and his archaeologist-wife found the site under false pretenses. Mowat says that George Decker, on whose farm the site was located, thought Ingstad an associate of Danish archaeologist Jorgen Meldgaard, and guided him to the spot under that impression. In his *National Geographic* article Ingstad says a fisherman told him there were ruins on Decker's farm. There seems no reason to doubt Ingstad's word in this matter. And Decker, a friend of Ingstad, is now dead. As a mere reviewer here I would venture the opinion that Mowat is less than generous to a man who had made an important discovery: the only early Norse settlement in North America. The discovery had been authenticated by Canadian, American and British archaeologists who helped unearth the site, which is now a Newfoundland museum.

To put forward all the questions Mowat has raised in *Westviking* is a fine and wonderful accomplishment. That he has not answered the questions satisfactorily detracts little from the book. (Only Ingstad has made a single step towards their solution.) *The Floamanna Saga* alone is sufficient reason for reading the whole book. And the Viking ships coming into Epaves Bay 1,000 years ago, on a grey morning with cattle bawling and women crouching behind armed men—all this now seems a little more real to me. Those early Norse discoverers were fascinating literary characters: I'm pleased they were also real, though they lived and died 1,000 years ago.

*Land Under the Pole Star*, Ingstad's own book, deals with the Norse in Greenland—the jumping-off point for Leif the Lucky and Thorfinn Karlsefni to the New World. It does little more than mention the discoveries at L'Anse aux Meadows, which are reserved for another book. But this one amounts to a companion volume for *Westviking*, in that it deals intensively with Greenland circumstances, with exploration, settlement, and the 500-year-old question: why did the Norse in Greenland disappear so completely, with only ruins and graves left behind? Ingstad presents his own answer, as well as portraying a people somewhat different from the conventional view of hard-drinking, quarrelsome Norse sea-raiders who were the world's scourge for a period of more than 200 years.

But again the claims made on the dust jacket for the book seem a little excessive, though not as exuberant as those for *Westviking*.

Many sagas are quoted, most of them unknown to me, that of the "Foster-Brothers" being especially interesting. It is a guided tour of the ancient eastern and western settlements of Greenland, and occasionally becomes much too discursive. Detail is piled on detail, as if Ingstad had bodily removed all the intervening years, one by one, from Viking graves in the permafrost. Even some of their clothing has been preserved by cold. And magical runes of the period, carved on wood and stone, persist into the twentieth century.

As for Vinland, I would like to think Ingstad's site at Epaves Bay near the village of L'Anse aux Meadows in Newfoundland was the land of grapes and wheat. But I doubt if any modern archaeologist can establish that. The ancient Norse language is relatively as remote as Greek Linear B, and subject to many interpretations. The Atlantic coastal area where the Vikings ranged is vast, and while there are Norse church ruins in Greenland, none have been found in the New World. And it is interesting to speculate that Vinland was discovered by pagans, and that the last leap across the sea from Greenland was too much for a Christian god to accomplish before the square-pooped sailing ships of Columbus.

*(1967)*

## ∞
# Sea of Slaughter

WHEN THE ANCESTORS OF HOMO SAPIENS first came skittering nervously down from the trees they were—presumably—vegetarians. They were also equipped with opposable thumbs, or developed them shortly thereafter; and started in on terrestrial life on the right foot, picking off grubs and worms for the quick energy provided by protein food. Later on they became tool-makers, and used throwing sticks, arrows, spears, and volleys of stones to kill lovable wild creatures of the forest and plain, feasting enormously on the delicious protein these beasts reluctantly provided.

At least that's the way I understand what happened—up to five million years ago, according to anthropologists-geologists Louis and Mary Leakey and their successors in South Africa's Olduvai Gorge. Australopithecus, and latterly Homo sapiens, developed a strong appetite for red meat and on occasion, fowl. And as their tool-making abilities increased, especially in this last century—guns, bombs and the like added to their arsenal—beasts and birds had little chance against them. Sometimes they also killed for love of killing, as well as for food and various by-products of their victims' bodies. They also justified what had become, in many cases, animal genocide with such casuistries as: "the death of any animal or species which contributes thereby to the satisfaction of human desires is not only justifiable but somehow tinged with a kind of nobility."

Which is what this Farley Mowat book is about: the depredations of man on animal species of the world, but principally those on the northeast coast of North America. It is, of course, a "viewing with alarm" book, an indignant recapitulation of animal murder that has been going on for many centuries, and may result in man himself (both genders) becoming the only remaining animal in God's universe.

Returning from the last war in 1945 on a Liberty ship, Mowat and the captain delighted in spotting sea life on the voyage west. It became a game between them, a small triumph to be first to spot and identify whales, porpoises, swordfish, eider ducks, etc. They were there in astonishing numbers. The world was blossoming with its creatures after the great slaughter in Europe, and there was a paradisiacal feeling about it for the future writer.

(My own equivalent of this natural ocean paradise was a visit to the Galapagos Islands in 1980, where the protected wildlife very nearly ate out of your hand. You were intruders in their kingdom, but not unwelcome; these creatures, who spoke a different language, lived a different life in different and more interesting bodies)

Over the last two hundred years the killing has increased to such a tempo that some animal species are gravely depleted, and some are disappearing altogether. The great auk or spearbill is the classic example of extinctions in which disappearing species (as the great auks became scarce they also became much more valuable) are hunted down remorselessly for museums and institutions. The last two alive were killed on a lonely Icelandic island in 1844.

Nascopie Indians of Ungava named a bird we know as the Eskimo curlew the *swiftwing*. When these birds migrated from northeastern Canada to the tip of South America, Patagonians called them *cloud of wonder*. The curlew weighed "no more than a pound," and was a foot high. In Patagonia sheer numbers of them darkened the sky at century's turn. At Bathurst Inlet in the Canadian Arctic, its whistle sounded like *pi-pi-piuk*, and it was called that by the Eskimos. Their numbers were like a moving cloud by day, and clouds of bullets killed them: there are no more *swiftwings*. They were citizens of the world.

Polar bears have been killed off by hunters and sportsmen for many years. Mowat says the number of "kills" probably reached 2,000 in 1968, out of a total world population of somewhat more than 15,000. And since the female polar bear gives birth only every third year, there is real danger of extinction. The bear's magnificent white overcoat is the trophy and prize: Mowat says a good polar bear skin fetched $1,000 in 1964. By contrast, I was offered one for $100 by Jim Cumming of the Hudson's Bay Company at Pangnirtung on Baffin Island in that same year. (However, it was a small skin: I didn't buy it.) The price has now reached as much as $5,000 "for an especially good one." Poor citizen of the Arctic!

It is a ghastly parade, blood, slaughter, stink, and the deaths of entire populations. Victims include whales, walrus, seals, and dozens of bird species, in such numbers that human slaughter of humans seems minuscule by comparison. Mowat documents it all in a mixture of legend, hearsay, speculation and definite recorded fact, one sometimes indistinguishable from the other. His quotations of historical sources range from George Cartwright in eighteenth-century Labrador to the contemporary Smithsonian Institution.

Presumably the book took five years to write, since the date of Mowat's last book was 1979. Its more than 400 pages certainly demonstrate such long-term labour. Mowat calls it his "most important book." "Important" is an interesting distinction from "best," which term I think belongs to his moving and completely unpretentious evocation of World War Two, *And No Birds Sang*. But I agree, the book is important.

I am troubled by other considerations, however. Mowat has undertaken and accomplished an enormous and valuable task in this book. I admire his extensive personal knowledge and research, the gut feeling he has woven into his narrative that such horrible slaughter should cease. And his good flexible prose learned by matching the word to the thing itself, the primitive excelling the so-called civilized, as in *swiftwing* and *cloud of wonder*.

However, wading through more than 400 pages of slaughter grows tiresome and monotonous, despite Mowat's undoubted abilities. His thesis, I agree with completely: save the animals. I also think motherhood is a very good thing, no matter what the species. Therefore I can read this book in sections, half an hour or so at a time, with great interest; whereas longer than that is tiresome.

It seems to me that the only thing that can save the animal species of the world from animal humans is human emotion. Not statistics, not body count and numbers, but a feeling that they too are with us as part of the crews of this stone ship sailing through nowhere into the void. And I think emotion is best evoked in fiction; and if so, what a paradox that the non-real best portrays reality? I mean, go back to Thornton Burgess and the Brer Rabbit people even, go back to Thompson Seton and Charles G.D. Roberts, and the child following his eyes and sinking past the printed word into the fictional-real-world where our bodies loved and our minds made magic.

But that's unjust to Mowat: this is a worthy and "important" book. It documents and describes the very real danger that we shall soon have exterminated every species but ourselves, and shall be living alone in the universe without God. And He will be next, since we're responsible for his birth in the first place.

*(1985)*

# Milton Acorn
## Introduction to *I've Tasted My Blood*

"**I**RVINGLAYTONSENTME," the big red-faced man said, shuffling his feet at the apartment door. "He told me you wrote plays for CBC and could give me some tips—"

That was the first time I met Milton Acorn, a hot summer evening in Montreal in 1956, hot inside and out. We talked poems until early morning, disagreeing violently about almost everything, but seemed to get along well anyway. Drama was scarcely mentioned in that discussion: besides I wasn't really much of a playwright: I had to write a dozen plays before I got one accepted by CBC.

For the next few years I saw quite a bit of Milton Acorn. He was a carpenter by trade, but had decided to give it up and be a writer, just like that. I went along when he sold his expensive-looking tools at a shop on St. Antoine St. Talk about burning your bridges! But Milton had made up his mind to sell those tools, and couldn't be convinced to wait until he made some money writing. And as it turns out, I think he was right.

Montreal at that time was a nest of poets—including Louis Dudek, Irving Layton, Frank Scott, Miriam Waddington, Alan Pearson, Bryan McCarthy, Eldon Grier, Ron Everson, and several others. I was there myself because I'd sold in Vancouver the first play I ever wrote and decided that I was a writer of genius and all I had to do was turn out the stuff like sausage, Montreal being a good place to make sausages and drink beer. Acorn was from Prince Edward Island, thirty-four years old, and had been in the army during the early years of the war.

During that winter of 1956–57 Acorn and I wrote poems and plays, did a great deal of talking, and went to the occasional party at

225

Irving Layton's or Louis Dudek's. Milton had published a small book of poems at his own expense the year before I met him, called *In Love and Anger*. I was not impressed with this book, for the poems were highly metrical and, I thought, pretty sentimental. I felt I was an authority on sentimentality, something I may never escape.

But in 1957 Milton was writing excellent short lyrics, in fact much better poems than mine, which I didn't realize then. He had a room on St. Antoine St., a place where you had to wade knee-deep thru poems, waste paper and books. The only free space in the room was above your waist.

In 1957 I used the proceeds from two play sales to CBC to buy a pile of used lumber and make the down payment on a lot at Roblin Lake, near Ameliasburgh, Ont. My wife and I built a cottage there, and settled down to a life of rural discomfort where you had to cluster five coal-oil lamps to read a book at night. I still pretended to be a writer, and my wife had made up her mind that if I could get away without working she could too. We watched each other for months to see who would weaken first. In 1959 both of us gave way at once, and we went back to Montreal to get jobs rather than endure further starvation.

Milton was still there, living on Sanguinet and later on St. Urbain St. I don't know what he was doing for money; most of the time he didn't have any. After I got a job at a mattress factory on St. Germain in Montreal East he came and stayed at our apartment, sometimes for a day or two and sometimes for a couple of weeks. We started a "little" magazine, *Moment*, around that time. Milt liberated a used mimeograph machine from somewhere (I think it belonged to the CP), and we turned out the magazine on the floor of our Maplewood apartment.

As I've said, Acorn and I used to disagree on practically everything. I'm not sure how such disagreement was possible between two people who remained friends. But Milton took advantage of me: he read all my books for ammunition, and fired the arguments back at me faster than I could read them myself. Once he read a four-volume set of Sigmund Freud (free gift from a book club) from cover to cover before I had even opened it, and was full of psychological information to confound me with when I came home from work. I had to read at frantic speed to catch up and protect myself in the semantic clinches.

In 1960 I quit my job making box springs for other men's playgrounds, and went back to the cottage at Roblin Lake. Milton came with me, my wife remaining in Montreal to keep the away fires burning. It was early March at Roblin Lake and cold. There was no fuel for the wood stove, but plenty of scrap lumber I'd scrounged from the CPR. Milt and I cut it up with a handsaw and frozen hands. And continued our long argument. Later I wrote a poem about that time, one that seems to tell more than I can say in prose. It's the closest we'll come to publishing the book we wanted to do together, this poem of mine in his book.

For two months we quarrelled over socialism   poetry   how to
     boil water
doing the dishes   carpentry   Russian steel production figures
     and whether
you could believe them and whether Toronto Maple Leafs would
     take it all
that year and maybe hockey was rather like a good jazz combo
never knowing what came next
Listening
how the new house made with salvaged old lumber
bent a little in the wind and dreamt of the trees it came from
the time it was travelling thru
and the world of snow moving all night in its blowing sleep
while we discussed ultimate responsibility for a pile of dirty dishes
Jews in the Negev   the Bible as mythic literature   Peking Man
and in early morning looking outside to see the pink shapes of wind
printed on snow and a red sun tumbling upward almost touching
     the house
and fretwork tracks of rabbits outside where the window light had
     lain
last night an audience
watching in wonderment the odd human argument
that uses words instead of teeth
and got bored and went away

Of course there was wild grape wine and a stove full of Douglas fir
(railway salvage) and lake ice cracking its knuckles in hard Ontario
     weather
and working with saw and hammer at the house all winter afternoon
disagreeing about how to pound nails
arguing vehemently over how to make good coffee

Marcus Aurelius   Spartacus   Plato and François Villon
And it used to frustrate him terribly
that even when I was wrong he couldn't prove it
and when I agreed with him he was always suspicious
and thought he must be wrong because I said he was right
Every night the house shook from his snoring
a great motor driving us on into daylight
and the vibration was terrible
Every morning I'd get up and say "Look at the nails—
you snored them out half an inch in the night—"
He'd believe me at first and look and get mad and glare
and stare angrily out the window while I watched 10 minutes of
    irritation
drain from his eyes onto fields and farms and miles and miles of
    snow

We quarrelled over how dour I was in early morning
and how cheerful he was for counterpoint
and I argued that a million years of evolution
from snarling apeman had to be traversed before noon
and the desirability of murder in a case like his
and whether the Etruscans were really Semites
the Celtic invasion of Britain   European languages   Roman law
we argued about white being white (prove it dammit) &
    cockroaches
bedbugs in Montreal   separatism   Nietzsche   Iroquois
    horsebreakers on the prairies
death of the individual and the ultimate destiny of man
and one night we quarrelled over how to cook eggs
In the morning driving to town we hardly spoke
and water poured downhill all day at the lake for it was spring
when we were gone with frogs mentioning lyrically
Russian steel production figures on Roblin Lake which were almost
    nil
I left him hitch hiking on #2 Highway to Montreal
and I guess I was wrong about those eggs

("House Guest")

In Montreal Milton went back to his room on St. Urbain St. I
went to British Columbia shortly after. When I rejoined my wife in
Montreal he was in Toronto, and later went to Vancouver. Our ways

have separated, tho not completely. We meet every now and then, accidentally or intentionally, and remain friends.

These hewn poems have the queer bite and abrasiveness of reality. Among the mass of public relations poetry breaking out in North America today—verse with little use except as down payment on a Guggenheim—they stand out with an odd antediluvian air. They're like artifacts of a nobler, more durable age.

In appearance, Milton Acorn himself is vividly antediluvian: heavy brown ridges, a face carved out of red rock, and a build that suggests the cave rather than the drawing-room. I can't imagine anyone less like a PR man, a TV producer or any other kind of slickie. I remember seeing him once, standing half way up a cliff in pouring Laurentian rain. It was a startling apparition—like the materialization of some local rock-god.

(Bryan McCarthy in *The Canadian Forum*)

That's a pretty good picture of Milton Acorn, and it isn't really much exaggerated. But the most important fact about him—and this he would tell you without being asked—is that he is a Marxist poet, a Communist. ( In fact he's the only Communist poet in Canada. Others, such as Joe Wallace, have been mere jingling versifiers by comparison.)

But it is a paradox that Acorn has quarrelled violently with every socialist organization he ever had anything to do with, and is a member in good standing of none. In short, Milton Acorn is a red-necked maverick, both in politics and poetry.

In Montreal about ten years ago Acorn and I visited Leonard Cohen in the latter's apartment. If ever two men were the antithesis of each other it's Cohen and Acorn. The first elegant, even in morning disarray, self-possessed and entirely aware, moving within a slight but perceptible aura of decadence—decadence not in the sense of decline, but of standing aside and apart, not being intimately involved. And Acorn: a red fire hydrant wearing blue denims, genuine, haltingly articulate, recently emerged from the noble servitude of labour, completely out of his element in that distinguished apartment which bore all the marks of Leonard Cohen's own personality.

After coffee (the thick stuff they brew in Paris—I forget its name) the conversation got around to politics. (It always does if Acorn is involved.) Cohen said, "Milton, if communism is ever outlawed in Canada, and the Mounties round up all subversives, you'd be among the first arrested." I don't remember what Milt said to that, but I think he denied it. Of course it's true: Acorn stands out from whatever background like a neon sign on the dark side of the moon. He doesn't sneak around corners distributing leaflets, he'd be more likely to walk into Jean Drapeau's office and present him with a copy of *The Collected Works of V.I. Lenin.* Or send a singing telegram of the "Internationale" to John D.'s grandson, Nelson.

Of course Milton would be arrested immediately in a round-up of Communists. But they'd be wrong, as Cohen was wrong in his assessment, not in the fact of arrest but in not taking him seriously.

Milton Acorn is a dedicated Communist, in the same way that some of the best Christians are not formal members of the church. But with him communism is more idealism than Marxist philosophy.

He probably knows the *Manifesto* by heart, but I doubt that he would label the Russian invasion of Czechoslovakia (going on as I write this) as anything other than a crime against humanity. (As is the Vietnam war, for that matter.)

What I want to convey about Acorn is paradox. If simplistic labels were feasible then Cohen would be a decadent public relations man of genius, an aging Ronald Firbank tuned in to the young on a middle-aged wavelength. Acorn would be more of a passionate and tender-hearted anarchist than Communist (and I would be a cynical Canadian nationalist, a lyrical Farley Mowat maybe).

I'd better talk about the poems. Here's what George Bowering says about "Jawbreakers":

> Milton Acorn has a persistence to let nothing rest, to abide no defense or acceptance of the social status quo. It is at the elemental social level that I would like to describe him as a political poet. Further I would say that it is only at this level that poetry should have anything to do with politics, because as with so many other things, language can be emasculated at the so-called higher level of political philosophy or political "science."
>
> So Acorn is topical, somewhat romantic in the best sense, and public. In his voice he is confident, even-paced and active. Nothing is more noticeable in his poetry than its directness and an unfaltering certainty of opinion.

That "elemental social level" Bowering mentions irritates me. Aren't all the best political poems elemental? Isn't Pablo Neruda elemental, passionate and romantic? Bad poems depend on the poet for badness, not on the subject of the poems.

Acorn's poems for me are marked by idealism and compassion for people. In some of them it's possible to discern the shadowy figures of, say, Bertolt Brecht and Mayakovsky; but I don't think there's any influence from other poets except in the matter of techniques. I think only Brecht and Mayakovsky have any direct bearing on Acorn. (Tho I know he would add the unlikely figure of Hugh McDiarmid.)

But politics is only one side of Milton Acorn. He also writes lyrics of nature, sensitive love poems, pieces that see inside the human character like a cardiogram of the intellect. As well, some beautiful evocations of his native Prince Edward Island.

> Since I'm Island-born home's as precise
> as if a mumbly old carpenter,
> shoulder-straps crossed wrong,
> laid it out, refigured
> to the last three-eighths of a shingle.

("The Island")

For those who may not know, carpenters once used the taper of shingles for everything from wedges to exact measurement of intangibles. "Mumbly old carpenters" probably still use them in some localities. There's a warm and human touch in such poems, especially in "Sky's Poem for Christmas."

> Christmas I became that ho-ho-ho of a saint
> to wind on a piebald disbelieving burro
> along the wisemen's trail thru a desert of grown-up people—

At his best Acorn has a feeling of humanity, in general and particular—their laughter and their tragedies—that I think is the high point of his work. In "Callum" he talks about a novice miner killed in a pit accident that may not have been quite an accident. After the boy was killed Acorn says:

> Look anywhere:
> at buildings bumping on clouds,
> at spider-grill bridges:
> you'll see no plaque or stone for men killed there:

but on the late shift
the drill I'm bucking bangs his name in code—

Poems written from 1964 to 1968 have changed in style and somewhat in content from the earlier poems. The subject matter is sometimes more "public." Acorn is now more liable than ever to write about people such as Che Guevara, General Ridgway and Muhammad Ali, rather than, say, Red, the waitress. In a way I regret these stylistic and thematic differences; but all poets build on the past, and it would be against the laws of nature if acorns didn't change into oaks.

The stylistic changes particularly are very marked. Acorn has become in many poems—and I hesitate to use the word—more "diffuse." During the years prior to 1964 his poems were hard, muscular, chiseled out of verbal rock and very much to the point. Now some of them—not all—read as if the writer had infinite time to describe every detail and mused on all of them lovingly. I would instance "Tears the Dew of Beauty's Mourning." This is a difficult poem to read, because you wonder if there's any single point to be made, any real conclusion to be reached. It wanders from one concept to another with scarcely any sequence, or so it seems. And yet this poem, dated 1967, is a penetrating soliloquy on death, pain and evil. That's all I want to say without robbing the poem, for it says everything and makes me reluctant to describe it further.

I mention "Tears" as an example of Acorn's "diffuseness," generally taken to be an unflattering word, but not in his case. "Poem Written in a One-Tree Forest" is another of this genre. Somehow these poems do give the impression of infinite time, the fading detail on the underside of a leaf, verisimilitude to life—no longer punched out of rock: such a tracery of tangential thoughts that one very nearly experiences small cardiac and cerebral shocks while the poem unfolds, unpretentiously and certainly unpredictably.

It's a style that accommodates the leisure soliloquy, thought probing slowly for an opening, which relegates impatience to a corner of the mind, and may find its point in a small phrase or subordinate clause in the middle of the poem rather than a brassy clang of symbols at the end. After we have become accustomed to Acorn's early style we do not quite know what to make of the later one. And yet, I've come to believe, the last two poems I've mentioned, as well as certain others, have an effect on the mentality comparable to flickering northern lights spreading across half a continent, much too large an area for the very familiar regional thunderstorms in the nerves and cortex.

Most litcrits would say the two short stories included in this book are "poet's short stories," by which is meant dreamy and otherworldly, as of course these two are. In most cases where the term is used it is meant to be both flattering and denigrating at the same time. It certainly shoves them into much too easy a category, for the stories are not ones that could be written by any other poet in Canada. They are a complete surprise, especially coming from a word-buster like Acorn.

It's possible to analyze them, of course, to say that "Legend of the Winged Dingus" is a parable against war, and asserts with tongue-in-cheek that the natural human instincts and functions are beautiful and should not be artificially restrained. "The Red and Green Pony" implies that a free world of the imagination is possible if we'd only stop nattering to each other; and the story also has a definite psychological basis (did he get it out of my four volume Freud set?).

However, I'd rather call both stories simple magic, for each is a long-term spell cast on the reader. I'm a pretty factual person myself, and yet no matter how many times I read these stories or type them—they get to me. And I start to wonder: could there be a world like that? Well, if there can't be, the next best thing is Acorn's stories. My belief amounts to a naive certainty that both are masterpieces.

George Bowering speaks of directness in Acorn's poems. It's certainly there, especially in the early work. He doesn't mince words for anyone's digestion, tho never uses invective for its own sake, i.e. for shock value. In fact, if one reads Acorn's work carefully it will be found that he is a highly moral poet. I don't mean that in just the political sense, and certainly not that he stands for magisterial law and order, good housekeeping and conventional marriage.

Acorn speaks from a personal conception of utopian order, as full citizen of a world that never was and perhaps never will be. All his poems are written from this viewpoint, poems of absolutes, black and white poems: evil is evil and good is good, and never shall the painter's palette or the politician's double tongue turn either to a wishy-washy grey. It's a stance that sometimes appears naive, occasionally mistaken; but never insincere, always with a voice of power and conviction.

Acorn believes in the perfectibility of people, the infinite capacities and hidden potentials within the individual man—these qualities being inherent and standard equipment with the ordinary person; but not there at all in those who are politically or commercially corrupted.

As I said, it's a black and white universe that Acorn inhabits. Most of the time—in fact nearly always—these absolutes lend a power to his work that is foreign to contemporary poets. Acorn himself would say that these other poets don't care enough to take stands, try to change the world, rear up on their hind legs and speak their minds in loud, vulgar and must-be-heard noises.

Milton Wilson has commented that these qualities in Acorn make him appear to be an exotic among the current voices in poetry (so much the worse for the current voices in poetry). Well, an "exotic" is something brought in from outside, imported from foreign parts, and that Acorn is not. I suppose Marxism is imported in the strictest sense, but idealism and the "brotherhood of man" have been with us for a long time, may even spread to the US State Department or the Kremlin someday.

The truth is that most litcrits think like George Bowering: they don't really want poets to express political opinions or write nasty polemics about injustice that name names and label phonies: but to do Bowering justice, I believe he has since changed his mind about this. The guild of poets is also against it. Well, Acorn doesn't belong to the guild of poets, or any other guild, including the communist one. They wouldn't tolerate him, and he couldn't tolerate them.

The Acorn-picture I want to convey is of a maverick and outsider, a man who speaks out at the wrong time, asks embarrassing questions of human society, and will not be satisfied by evasions. The fact that the man who asks the questions is humanly fallible and often angrily impulsive makes some kind of answers to his questions no less urgent.

It's a melodramatic portrait of Acorn, perhaps—a man replete with contradiction and paradox—but I think it gives an impression of the man that is essentially accurate. A man who, in a handful of poems, comes somewhere close to greatness. Ideally he lives in the child's dream country of the two short stories in this book, and wakes up every morning in the real world that inspires him with such savage discontent.

It might be noted that several of Acorn's poems mention Purdy. Despite the extreme danger of the reader thinking this is a mutual admiration society of egotists, I believe these are good poems and include them. At one time Acorn and myself were about as close to blood brothers as you can get outside an Indian village. We exchanged ideas, techniques and shirts, arguing ferociously. And while it's a certainty that we influenced each other, it may be a good thing that "there needs to be no losers."

*(1969)*

# Margaret Atwood
## *The Animals in That Country*

I READ A REVIEW OF THIS BOOK a short time ago which ended with: "Being a woman can't be that awful": meaning, I suppose, menopause and purgatorio, or *mea culpa*, sansculotte, etc.

But these are not "women's poems," not in the way that term is generally applied anyhow. Certainly not about babies, kitchen sinks and ding-dong husbands. But they are pretty black, yes. The writer seems besieged from without by her own inner perceptions.

In connection with these poems I think of those old western movie mellerdrammers: the ones where all the defenders of the frontier fort are messily killed by anti-WASP Indians, except one. This lone survivor runs around like mad on the log stockade, reloading and firing the rifles of his dead comrades one after the other, giving an illusion to the Indians that the fort is fully manned and bristling with defenders. In the real world this lone survivor dies like a dog: in movies the US Cavalry (Vietnam Regiment) rescues him with appropriate ta-ra-boom-de-ay, and the lights come up.

Well, in Atwood's poems the lights stay down and will finally go out altogether, as they should and must for both Indians and ephemeral settlers. And the writer is besieged from both within and without:

The idea of an animal
patters across the roof.

In the darkness the fields
defend themselves with fences
in vain:

everything
is getting in.

("Progressive Insanities of a Pioneer")

But the animals in "that country" are obviously at home in this country, though their name-tags are missing. Simplistically, all you have to do is fit the poems over ordinary situations with people, but stereotyped labels on the real-life situations won't help identify the poem-situations: and we have not been here before.

Did Margaret Atwood once say to me that in my poems I made simple things complicated, whereas she made complicated things simple in hers? Or did I say that to her? I guess it hardly matters who said what to whom, but the idea has relevance. In a poem about the tourist centre in Boston, Atwood talks about the model of Canada under glass there, and speculates that there's more to her country than this indicates, suggests that the simple model is really complicated. Which is a switch (and if you're getting dizzy, so am I).

I suggest that most of Atwood's poems really do make complicated things simple, and people being animals do have the same simple motivations of animals—except that the Atwood-animal is pretty damn self-conscious about the whole business. In "What Happened" the Atwood-animal says to others in the menagerie that they (read we) are just that, and our communications don't amount to more than a grunt on a row of beans, a delayed reaction grunt, probably misinterpreted first and last. As animals we are unaware of the possible results of our actions in "It is Dangerous to Read Newspapers." And in "Arctic Syndrome: dream fox," the Peggy-animal metamorphosis is complete as she attacks the man-animal, tearing at his throat with her teeth (as I suspect she wanted to do all along).

"Backdrop Addresses Cowboy" might be about the animal territorial idea, naturalists affirming that birds and animals occupy and defend a particular territory: the unsapient man-animal also defends his territory, but attacks and destroys that of others as well. Or the poem might be about the US Marines, or technology. Take your pick.

There isn't a belly-laugh or even a sly chuckle in any of these poems. I think Atwood has not yet really fired off all the muskets in the stockade she defends. Perhaps she is too terrified of the Indians (animals, dammit!) on the outside of her stockade (skin). Perhaps sooner or later she'll begin to laugh helplessly as the seventh or seventeenth musket misfires, and the Indian will all run away, scared to death by the silence.

The imagery in the poems amounts to the poems themselves, and no vivid distortions of reality are undertaken in brief—only in the total poems. No complicated rhetoric either, if you take rhetoric as a series of piled-on exaggerations. Almost any prose writer uses more. But these are poems, and very good ones—: tremendous, soul-stirring, awesomely analytical, penetrating, complicated—uh, simplicities?

*(1969)*

## ∽
## *The Journals of Susanna Moodie*

SUSANNA MOODIE WAS AN ENGLISH emigrant to Canada in 1832. She settled with her husband in Douro Township, near Peterborough, and her book, *Roughing It in the Bush*, is one of the basic pioneer documents of Canada.

Margaret Atwood says in the Afterword to her own book that "These poems were generated by a dream. I dreamt that I was watching an opera I had written about Susanna Moodie. I was alone in the theatre: on the empty white stage, a single figure was singing." And later, about her poems: "I suppose many of these were suggested by Mrs. Moodie's books, though it was not her conscious voice, but the other voice running like a counterpoint through her work that made the most impression on me."

Well, that "other voice" is also the one that makes the poems impressive. Perhaps it is Atwood's own voice, or perhaps it is Susanna Moodie herself singing Atwood's opera. The duality is there. But I think Margaret Atwood has always had this duality in herself, a quality that she suggests is Canadian, a kind of "paranoid schizophrenia" which enables her to be a ghostly observer peering over the ghostly shoulder of Susanna Moodie. In spite of hard physical details (fire and plague, dead children, trees, emigrant, etc.),these poems make a strange slightly-off-from-reality impression on the reader: and browsing through *Roughing It in the Bush*, I don't think Moodie's 19th century prose has this ingredient. The poems' impact is in this strangeness: as if Atwood were from Mars and Moodie an English-woman of "gentle" birth. And Atwood is not talking to a possible reader; she is an entirely subjective Martian.

*The Journals of Susanna Moodie* has many of the qualities of fictional biography: the reader knows very well (the Canadian reader, anyhow) that Moodie was a real person, and reading the poems both the Moodie and Atwood personae are inescapable. John Berryman did something similar in *Homage to Mistress Bradstreet*, assuming the persona of a long-dead American woman of pioneer days. A similar authoritative and undeniably once-actual personage takes over in both books: Moodie and Bradstreet, with Atwood and Berryman as shadow manipulators coming to life in the publishers' blurbs. The puppets steal the show (but not the royalties): and this to me, is fiction.

Another advantage of using a once-living protagonist is the cohesive and intensive quality that a single viewpoint—or time or geographic area—gives a book of poems. (Bowering's *Rocky Mountain Foot* is another example of the latter.) But there is a sub-basic quality in the poet's self that cannot be conveyed by speaking in another person's voice. Because, in its finest expression, the poet's voice is for every man, not just a single person. And I think it's a very debatable point whether a poet can occupy another body and mind and still retain the sub-basic qualities of himself or herself. That is, Atwood as Atwood strikes me as authentic, but Atwood as Moodie is a very fine tour de force. But the latter is entirely legitimate, valuable and, in this case, rather marvellous fiction.

Peggy Atwood said to me about three weeks ago that a reviewer (that's me) should seek to fathom the author's (that's her) intent, implying that marks should be given, according to how close the author came to achieving that intent. This I disagree with, in Atwood's absence, almost completely—unless the reviewer, knowing the intent, feels it was achieved and is, in addition, impressive as hell.

Re intent, I prefer Earle Birney's opinion (also verbal, though maybe he's written it somewhere too): that whatever meaning or levels of meaning the reader "extracts" from the work, this meaning is legitimate and valid. Because (my own comment as well as Birney's) there is something in a writer's head which causes him or her to incorporate meanings and possible interpretations he (or she) doesn't even know are there. Writers are generally a bit stupid—and I cite my own case particularly—feeling that too much knowledge and accumulation of literary debris in their heads can be a handicap: this apart from straight intelligence. Of course that's an alibi on my part, as I'm aware.

What I'm getting at: I'm not really interested in what Atwood is trying to do in her opinion: I'm interested in what she succeeds in doing—in my opinion. The two may be identical. I think they probably are in this book, but I'm far too cautious to say what I think she's trying to do, even though she more or less says what that is in the book's Afterword. And I guess that sounds pretty convoluted and involved.

Well, I've held certain opinions about writing poems for a long time, but these opinions have changed recently. For instance: consistency of tone and metre. I've thought previously that inconsistency was the best way to write poems, in fact the only way for myself. Part of the reason for that opinion has been that critics seemed to demand consistency. Well—well, I still hold to the view that consistency of tone and metre would be a bad thing for me, for me —but not necessarily for others. Particularly in a book like this one where a related and integrated outlook on the author-persona's part appears to make the poems more believable. In fact, I think Atwood's book has caused me to change my mind on this point. And I do think the Moodie poems are that impressive.

But looking at Atwood's books, I believe they all have this consistent and distinctive tone. And that's okay for her: what's sauce for the goose is not for the gander, and the difference in gender is not unintentional. For I believe that my personal outlook on life is markedly inconsistent: I may be temperamentally up one hour and down the next; I may be happy, I may be sad; I may be in love with life and all women, I may not. I want to convey these human inconsistencies in poems, and I try. But of course, I say all this after I look at my own poems and know (think) that they do reflect these attitudes.

In Atwood's poems I see no humour other than satire, very little love for anything (except possibly the Atwood-Moodie dead children in "Death of a Young Son by Drowning"; I do see subjective navel-watching and analysis, a hard cold look at the human condition. In the past I've said these shortcomings were a bad thing in any writer. But now I cannot transplant my own hang-ups into Atwood. If she lacks these things (and I think she does), it does not in any way lessen her poems. I would say they were just short of magnificent—except, that's another quality I don't think she has. One can cite a mixed bag of poets—say Yeats, Eliot, Layton and Birney: Yeats has magnificence, satire and no humour: Eliot, satire, magnificence and no humour: Layton the same: only Birney has genuine self-conscious humour as well. But I should add joy to this catalogue, for Layton does have that.

In John Glassco's *Memoirs of Montparnasse*, here's what Ford Madox Ford said about joy:

> All modern effusions of joy are definitely unbalanced. Very well. Now, if poetry expresses the reality of existence—as I believe, along with Willie Yeats, it does, and as I hope you will too, my young friend—it follows that the experience of joy is in the nature of a fever, of hysteria, and not a well-founded natural human experience or condition. Therefore we can say: joy itself is hysteria, a drunkenness, an unnatural state.

It doesn't follow at all: joy isn't an unnatural state, even in the human-animal. And add that drunkenness (of the spirit, not artificially induced) is natural. Joy is part of the *condition humaine*, which isn't all terror and foreboding, can't be that or we'd all collapse damn quick under the psychic weight. Three of the people mentioned above whom I know (Layton, Birney and Atwood) all have joy personally, but Atwood has not communicated the feeling in poems and probably has not wanted to. Again, I must not read my own preoccupations re how to write poems into Atwood. For I think she is a marvellous poet, perhaps the only one right now in Canada whose poems I look forward to reading with tremendous anticipation each time a book of hers appears. And she is what she is, without what I say to be shortcomings or weaknesses being shortcomings or weaknesses. Therefore, I say I have been wrong in my opinions that certain human life-qualities are necessary poem-qualities. (They were pretty naive opinions anyway.) At least, not for her, as not for Yeats and Eliot.

Having said what Atwood does not have, it devolves on me to

say what she does. And, sticking to the Moodie book, I believe in Atwood-Moodie. I think the Moodie conveyed by Atwood is scared to death of life, but is nevertheless a real person. Moodie is also afraid of the rough and tough pioneer forest of early Canada, but what nice sweet well-bred and bedded English gentlewoman wouldn't be?

In "The Wereman":

My husband walks in the frosted field
an X, a concept
defined against a blank;
he swerves, enters the forest
and is blotted out.

Why, that Moodie bitch! I say. There isn't a scintilla, not a jot or milligram of affection for anyone but herself (Moodie) in the poem (in *Roughing It in the Bush* she calls her husband "Moodie"!). This I say, knowing Atwood meant to convey something quite different. I think she meant to say that humans are undefined as such, that they waver into hate and love like ghosts and things of mist in other people's minds. She meant (perhaps) to convey human inconsistency, as I have said her writing did not. Whereas I, becoming a vicarious female while reading the poem, growl soprano-bass that Moodie should have rushed after her husband into the dark forest, at least she should have if she gave a single damn. But she didn't, and that's one reason why Moodie is not quite human, was only worried about herself in the poem, was absolutely solipsistic. (Which is one of Atwood's strengths.)

On the other hand, I guess most Victorian women felt themselves to be only sexual objects (or so books tell me, and also certain Victorian Female survivals), individuals only privately and partly, in their fears and hates but not their loves.

However, the Atwood-Moodie persona crosses me up in "Death of a Young Son," about whom she/they say:

I planted him in this country
like a flag.

The line has multiple meanings, none of which I intend to mention. Unless to say that sons were loved but husbands were not, which interpretation should come from the whole book, not this one poem.

Here's an example of Atwood's verbal virtuosity:

After we had crossed the long illness
that was the ocean . . .

("Further Arrivals")

No ordinary pioneer woman would say that, and neither would Victorian-literary Moodie: but Atwood-Moodie might and did. Here I believe both. And briefly I see hundreds of miles of ocean vomit. I see sickness of the spirit and endurance. I believe. (Hallelujah!)

For the first few years in Canada the historical Susanna Moodie hated the new country (Canada), hated it like hell and the devil; but in later years she came up with phony-sounding eulogies for the country that don't ring true. Along those lines, Atwood makes Moodie come to love the country as well. But I don't think Moodie ever really did. But Atwood does, and that's probably the most love lifting out of these pages of print. For the Moodie-Atwood persona becomes some kind of primitive corn-mother-spirit that sits in a modern bus along St. Clair Ave. in Toronto, embodying the ghostly citified barbarism of this country. I don't believe that double-love, only Atwood's.

Well, I could go on and on with these poems, tearing them apart, figuring them out, the radar echoes between them and me bouncing back and forth, back and forth, hypnotically boring. But if I'm talking to anyone here, I hope they carry this review farther than I am energetic enough to take it.

I disagree with most of Atwood's viewpoints wholeheartedly, and the circumstances will never arrive when I can say the rest of this review to her personally because she wouldn't listen to such confused and partly intuitive arguments. I've said here that she lacks many things in her poems which I think desirable (and I retract nothing), such as magnificence which she has not got in single poems. Taking the whole book, though, she mysteriously does have that quality. Also clarity of intellect (if the reader will read hard, and give the poems at least the attention of a personal monetary transaction). The country itself is the Atwood-Moodie children (hail, corn-mother!) who never had a chance to grow to adulthood and be what the actual country may never become.

What I'm saying is that this book will stand in any company, despite what I call shortcomings that are not shortcomings in Atwood. I can think of no comparisons for the book. Which seems to me a high compliment. Atwood may even deserve it.

*(1971)*

# Malcolm Lowry

A N UNKNOWN WRITER NAMED MALCOLM LOWRY, living in a beach shack on Burrard Inlet near Vancouver, published a novel called *Under the Volcano* in 1947. What happened afterwards was what every writer secretly dreams of: the critics responded like trained seals—Lowry was superior to Hemingway, compared to Joyce and Thomas Wolfe; and better still, his symbolic tale about a compulsive drunk was said to be unique. Somewhat appalled by all the hoopla, Lowry reacted with a poem:

> Success is like some horrible disaster
> Worse than your house burning, the sounds of ruination
> As the roof tree falls following each other faster
> While you stand, the helpless witness of your damnation.

("After Publication of *Under the Volcano*")

He needn't have worried. A few years later and Lowry was again a nearly unknown drunk. Ten years after the novel was published, he died under mysterious circumstances in England, almost forgotten at age forty-eight. And then came the great turnaround when his posthumous reputation increased year by year. Books and magazine articles were written about him; his unfinished manuscripts were edited and published, to the accompaniment of rapturous cries of critical ecstasy. Full circle.

Considered as a human being rather than a literary genius—the way those people in close contact had to—Lowry was a failure on almost every level: a suicidal life-long alcoholic. He tried to kill himself in Acapulco by swimming farther out to sea than he had strength to return from, was attacked by a barracuda and escaped the marine assassin by taking refuge on a nearby island. In 1946 he slashed his wrists with a razor, and spent a few days in hospital recovering. He finally made it to "easeful death" in 1957 while living in the village of Ripe, in Sussex, England. Margerie, Lowry's wife, "tried to stop him from starting on the gin." She smashed the bottle, and he hit her. Margerie fled next door, afraid to return. Next morning she found him on the floor beside the smashed gin bottle. A bottle of sleeping tablets was missing. Lowry was, of course, dead.

*In early summer of 1954 the dead man sat beside me in my little Ford Prefect driving from Dollarton to Vancouver to buy booze. Myself and two friends, along with Lowry and his wife, had managed to consume all there was in the beach shack. At the night liquor store near Main and Hastings, Lowry bought six bottles of Bols gin. Then he turned to me with red face and pale blue eyes and said, "There's a church near here with beautiful windows."*

*There actually was a church. But a man of God dressed in black was standing guard at the door. He explained to us that a wedding was about to take place and pointed out that we were not invited guests. I think he decided on first glance that we were waterfront bums, perhaps because Lowry wore an old pair of corduroy pants and black sweater. I was dressed much the same.*

*I explained to the priest that my friend thought the windows of his church were very beautiful and wanted to see them again. Lowry stood by silently while I talked. I tried to convey an impression of respectability and perfect sobriety, but it was difficult. We were both frankly stoned. And I had the virtuous feeling that I'd better do all the talking myself: for if Lowry spoke just once, a bottle of Bols gin was liable to pop out of his mouth and float high-away over Vancouver's skid row before the horrified eyes of the man of God.*

Malcolm Lowry, born in 1909, was the youngest of four brothers. He was the son of Arthur O. Lowry, a Liverpool cottonbroker, and Evelyn Boden. Backward and shy at home, Lowry blossomed into a seeming extrovert at Cambridge University, became a champion weightlifter, golfer, swimmer, and tennis player. He also fell romantically in love with the idea of being a writer. And he was in rebellion always against authority, embodied first in the shape of father Arthur O., who had a seven-inch chest expansion and was England's best-developed man in 1904; in rebellion against uniforms, especially police uniforms; in rebellion against his wife, who came to symbolize all his own shortcomings; in rebellion, finally, against everything, including himself.

The young Lowry was first influenced by the wild tales of Jack

London and Eugene O'Neill's early sea plays. In 1927 the eighteen-year-old apprentice writer went to sea himself, having pressured Arthur O. into allowing his son to accept such plebeian employment and thus becoming a man. Poppa even chose the ship on which his son should sail as a deckhand, the *Pyrrhus*.

If a writer can ever be said to be reticent about a segment of his life used freely in his writing, Lowry was closemouthed about that voyage on the *Pyrrhus*. It did result in a youthful novel, *Ultramarine*, in 1933: and years later the same sea waves rolled through the pages of *Under the Volcano*. His writing was often nearly a direct transcript from his own life; the young sailor who early in the voyage lost most of his illusions is the same man who referred to the sea later as that "nauseous overrated expanse."

At Cambridge, Malcolm (his first name was actually Clarence, and he tried to escape it all his life) played the ukulele, read many books, attended few lectures, and established the firm foundation for his later career of alcoholic consumption on a heroic scale. A member of one Charlotte Haldane's literary salon, he was an attractive male tidbit to her, and she pursued him hill-and-dale all over the salon.

An American poet and novelist, Conrad Aiken, then living in England, appeared on the scene in 1928. Lowry worshipped the older man's writing. Deciding that he preferred this surrogate father to his own, he prevailed on Arthur O. to allow him to join Aiken when the latter returned home to the Land of the Free—in return for a weekly stipend to Aiken of five or six guineas, of course.

In Boston the aspiring young writer and the older poet hit it off perfectly. Aiken has often said of the relationship, "We were natural father and son." But that first evening together doesn't sound like a living *pater* and dutiful sibling. They threw a wild party, in which the finale was a wrestling match between Lowry and Aiken for possession of a porcelain toilet seat. Weightlifter Malcolm tossed his surrogate father into the stone fireplace and fractured his skull. "That," says Aiken, "was the beginning of a beautiful friendship."

*So I talked. The dead man and the priest listened. A car drew up at the curb during my unpersuasive discourse, disgorging some wedding guests. The man of God hurried to greet them. While he did so, I was suddenly shocked to realize that Lowry had disappeared as my harangue continued, and had simply walked into the church. I'd been the unflattering red herring for his entrance, as now the wedding guests were for mine.*

*Lowry knelt on the floor inside the church, praying to some God or other, with six bottles of Bols gin in a brown paper grocery bag on the seat behind him. I thought of Coleridge's Ancient Mariner. And Lowry dressed in a strange medieval seaman's costume: hung around his neck, instead of a dead albatross, six bottles of Bols gin in a brown grocery bag. Then, with burning eyes, he began collaring the wedding guests at the curb outside, whisking one of them away from the officious priest. "Listen," he would say to the wedding guest, "once, in a Mexican town called Quauhnahuac, there was a consul.—"*

After sitting at Aiken's feet, picking his brains for clues to genius, drinking and carousing with him, Lowry returned to England and Cambridge University. And more drinking, drinking, drinking. Arthur O. gave him an allowance of seven pounds a week, but on condition that he appear personally to collect it at the company's London office. Malcolm refused to go—he was too dirty, and had no shoes, and didn't want to shave.

What kind of writer-genius, as apart from an ordinary human being, does all this signify? Self-indulgent, spoiled, drunken, prey to wild fantasies, archetype of all the self-destructive people with time bombs ticking in their heads since time began. But one fact emerges over all others: Lowry thought that life was hell, and he was delineating the map of hell in all he lived and wrote.

If Lowry had been just an ivory tower aesthete, concerned only with his navel (which he was, among other things), we humans could all dismiss him with the customary shrug we reserve for boring TV programs. But pain, embarrassment, horror, shame, and all those words streaming out of our guts are common to all of us; if one is in a depressed state, their sum total might actually be called "hell." Lowry contains all our hells—and did even when he was twenty-two years old.

*On our second visit to the beach shack, the dead man went swimming in Burrard Inlet, his red face and barrel chest bobbing around in the cold water like pieces of coloured driftwood. Later, it seemed completely natural that my friend and I, Lowry and his wife, drank Bols gin, which sometimes replaced coffee and tea in that household.*

*It grew darker then. Across black water silver candles of the oil refinery lit the early evening, the same ones Lowry called, ironically, "the loveliest of oil refineries." He and my friend sang songs outside, while I sat at Lowry's typewriter and copied his poems by lamplight, feeling very literary and virtuous.*

*They were odd, doom-laden poems, very regular and formal, maybe even Elizabethan-sounding, death implicit in all of them. But in each poem, generally at the end, a line or two would silently go "boom": a phrase incandescent—*

*No Kraken shall depart till bade by name,*
*No peace but that must pay full toll to hell.*

*Then the rough-tender voices of my friends, the literary drunks, floated through the window to join in my mind the many-tentacled Kraken: "Away, away, away you rolling river."*

In 1933 Lowry lived in Paris for a time with Julian Trevelyan, the painter. Then he accompanied Conrad Aiken and the latter's second wife to Spain, where Lowry drank heavily, grew fat, and became known as *el borracho ingles*, known also to the Spanish Civil Guard. While there he met an attractive American girl, Jan Gabrial. Lowry sobered immediately, and fell in love.

Leaving Spain, the Aikens and Lowry sailed for England, and Malcolm shared a cabin with "three Somerset Maugham colonels who were dying of the hiccups." The floating circus then played a few months of one-night stands in Mexico. By this time Lowry had caught up with the luscious Jan Gabrial, and married her. The relationship made progress: he drunk in Cuernavaca; she living somewhere else. Aiken observed all this with pity and horrified love; both of them writing, writing, writing . . .

"He's drinking the alarm clock," cried Jan at Cuernavaca after the Aikens were gone. "I just don't care about him, but I can't buy another alarm clock." Apparently Lowry had abducted the timepiece to pawn it and buy booze. But if Lowry was no more valuable than an alarm clock to Jan, then apparently the end of their marriage could be predicted. It was. Jan soon departed for other ports of call.

Lowry stayed on in Mexico, through more alcoholic misadventures: went to jail in Oaxaca ("where they cure syphilis with Sloans liniment/And clap with another dose"); and wandered the bone-dry hills of central Mexico with a friend. Expelled from Mexico, he ended up in Los Angeles, where Arthur O. came to the rescue of his prodigal son (Arthur O. used that very phrase to describe him). In the American film capital Lowry met Margerie, whom he loved—and hated—and married.

*The dead man was cheerful, dreadfully potted and sounding very English, but still alive. During the long evening of Bols gin and talk, Lowry recited his poem, "Sestina in a Cantina," his thick voice bearing the full weight of archaic fear and horror: how the world is a giant prison ruled by tossing mooseheads and witch-doctors in business suits. And Lowry talked about the weird sorcerers of Central America, their seeming imperviousness to the pain of red-hot coals, how sailors all seem to be part mystic and . . .*

*Falling silent, he stared at nothing in front of him, as if the room were completely empty. Perhaps thinking of tossing mooseheads that ruled the world? or the match-like spurt of distant flame on its lone steel swan's neck at the oil refinery across the inlet? Of ships that sailed forever, revisiting old ports over and over again, bells clanging out of time:*

> *In sleep all night he grapples with a sail!*
> *But words beyond the life of ships dream on.*

("Joseph Conrad")

That first meeting of Margerie Bonner and Lowry at the corner of Hollywood Boulevard and Western was a passionate embrace. Margerie, a former movie starlet and radio writer, was general factotum to actress Penny Singleton. Married to her drunken literary genius, she emerged as a woman of character and strength, and probably discovered more drama in her life with Lowry than existed in the entire dream city of Hollywood.

The Lowrys moved to Vancouver in 1939, and fell almost immediately into the clutches of one Maurice Carey, a retired sergeant-major from the Canadian army. Lowry's monthly allowance from Arthur O. was nonsensically signed over to Carey. In return Carey gave the Lowrys an unheated attic room for lodgings and two dollars a week for spending money. From this unhappy haven Lowry disappeared on one cold and rainy October night. Margerie found him in a Vancouver whore-house, where he had sold his clothes to buy a bottle of gin. She threatened the madam into giving her man's clothes back to him and they went out into the rain, he doubled over with shame and a hangover.

In 1940 the Lowrys found their shack on Burrard Inlet. It was one of some fifteen such jerry-built structures, with low rent because the land was owned by Vancouver's Harbour Board. This was Lowry's Eden, his Walden Pond, and it supplied material and experience for *The Forest Path to the Spring*, as fine a work as he ever wrote. When the shack burned down, the Lowrys scrounged enough money to build another. Here also much of the final draft of *Under the Volcano* was transferred to paper from Lowry's head. Often he would hand his wife a page he had just written and say, "Margie, kindly tell me what the hell I'm talking about here." Which is to say that Margerie herself deserved much credit for the novel that some say is the greatest written in the twentieth century.

The fourteen years at Dollarton (until 1954) were interspersed with trips to other parts of the world, including Mexico, from which Lowry was again expelled for non-payment of a small fine that he had been assessed years before. Also interspersed with frequent gargantuan benders, of which he once said that "he was pitting, like Paracelsus, the effects of alcohol against the effects of increased physical exercise . . . to drink through and out the other side of a nervous breakdown, or worse." A strange reason for keeping the distilleries working at full capacity. But much of Lowry's lifetime was spent either drinking or taking treatment for drinking, the latter sometimes in hospitals or similar institutions. And the pure horror he experienced in not being cured seems far worse than the horror of drinking itself.

Many people would consider Malcolm Lowry a failure, but if so, surely he was an immortal failure. He had many qualities of those other historic drunks, Brendan Behan and Dylan Thomas: people loved him, for instance. They arranged things for him, smoothed his way if they could, and came when he called to them in desperation. And much of his life was desperation! In some ways Lowry was not a weak man: witness the fierce and continual devotion to writing. Which itself is a reflection of himself and his conviction that living life is experiencing a nether hell.

To be alive is to have the skin prickle, the genitals cringe at what happens to all of us: and what happens to all of us also happened in intensified form to Lowry. He was a feeler and experiencer—of the lower depths. And sometimes out of this evil human world suddenly appeared human-created good.

The reasons why Lowry wrote—both loving and hating writing—might be summed up in that couplet about the Kraken who must not be named, and the peace that has to be paid for by a preceding hell. Hell must be mapped and named, the beasts of our minds exorcised with words of knowledge. Therefore Malcolm Lowry wrote about his own personal predicament, which is also the human predicament and no other species can make that statement.

*For several months after the Lowrys went to Europe in 1954, I was involved with introducing a union into the mattress factory on Clarke Drive, where I worked. Then I returned to the beach shack near Dollarton with my friend and a beautiful girl. We brought along a bottle of wine to drink, pouring the heel of it into the sea at the end of Lowry's dock. A self-conscious gesture, a libation to Bacchus and Lowry, an act whose meaninglessness somehow stands out in my mind.*

*Drinking coffee with Irving Layton at Murray's Restaurant in Montreal in 1957, Layton told me that Lowry was dead in England. I felt suddenly desolate.*

*But Lowry surfaced again in 1962, when I read his posthumous book of stories,* Hear Us O Lord from Heaven Thy Dwelling Place, *with its recurring song of a ship's engines. And freighters are still moving outward from Burrard Inlet toward the Lions Gate through the fog, past the razed shack at the sea's edge, throb of engines whispering among the trees near an overgrown path through the forest:*

*Frère Jacques*
*Frère Jacques*
*Dormez-vous?*
*Dormez-vous?*

*(1974)*

# George Woodcock
## Introduction to *Notes on Visitations: Poems 1936-75*

G EORGE WOODCOCK HAS WRITTEN some dozens of books; I don't know how many. I have twenty of them, signed by him, in my bookcase. He's an authority on nearly everything: Bakunin, anarchism, Gabriel Dumont (you don't know who Dumont is?), Doukhobors, India, Gandhi, Orwell, Peru and McCleery Street in Vancouver. He writes books like other people breathe, and is a wise man, somewhat shy.

Woodcock is also the editor of *Canadian Literature*, a sort of house organ for the stuff. In fact, in some not obscure sense, he *is* CanLit—to the degree that a few universities in this country are now including it on their curriculum. Woodcock the all-rounder, a literary and human person seemingly interested in and knowledgeable about everything. I don't mean that I think him infallible or any such silly quality: but if all this sounds like exaggeration, take a look at what the man has written.

I've wondered occasionally how he does it, has the sheer vitality to write all those books. One big reason is Inge, his wife. She drives the Volks and he doesn't. She also cooks and writes, so that they make a pair whose total is more than the parts. And wondering when I was travelling recently in Peru (on which Woodcock wrote twenty years ago) how he does it, I had a few thoughts.

The place is Transylvania or wherever. The Woodcocks arrive by plane or train or car or afoot. They book into their hotel, and Inge calls all the people George wants to meet and talk with. They arrive all at once, and of course it's a little crowded: prime ministers, business execs, peasants and dirt farmers sit on the edge of the bathtub, waiting their turn to talk to George. But there is no confusion. Inge gives them all number cards as at the butcher store. While this is going on, wives, mistresses and secretaries jam the hotel switchboard. The resulting definitive and much-praised book by George Woodcock is published one week later.

Of course that is fantasy, which ignores all the hard-slogging footwork armchair readers don't see. But there does seem some quality of magic in the way Woodcock produces books. He is a calm even-tempered person generally; therefore you wouldn't suspect him of being fevered and frenetic inside.

My acquaintance dates from fifteen years ago when I was encamped in northern BC near Woodcock (of all places), with a transistor radio, and heard George Woodcock's verse play "Maskerman" on CBC. I've forgotten most of that play, except its essential quality, which was a decadent sadness, a quite deliberate over-ripeness, as he has mentioned since. Homer without heroics, if you like. I wrote him an admiring note, as I have to a few other writers I liked. The acquaintance grew into something more than that, and there are times when I think I know him slightly well.

Woodcock's *Selected Poems*, appearing in 1967, were surprising to me. They seemed a strong contrast to his easy-flowing, crystal clear and admirable prose. They bore a strong relation to Auden-Mac-Neice-Spender-Eliot, etc. My own opinions of English poetry in the 1930s were formed mostly from those people, and I admire them principally for what they said rather than how they said it. It took me a very long time to break away from using conventional metrics myself. After I had done so it took me another long period before I could go back and admire such usage uncritically. I was too stupid then to realize there's an umbilical cord between form and content. Sometime before 1965 I had realized this vital fact.

Anyway, Woodcock grew up in the English Auden-Spender literary milieu, and wrote in the manner of that slightly earlier day when political philosophy was, perhaps, more literarily important than it is now. Those poets apparently wrote in a form and mood which seemed to debar some areas of the human personality—or so it seemed to me years ago. I now feel that those earlier methods may actually reveal a more fully-rounded persona behind the poems—one not nearly as obvious and blatant as that shown in the work of some addicts of the reality-drug today.

Woodcock's development is incredibly similar to my own: that is, his early poems are metrical and contained inside the forms he chose for them. But in the last few years he has achieved an ability to go in all prosodic directions, both metric and free forms. You can see that whole development in this book. Whereas I discarded nearly everything I wrote prior to about 1958, because I thought and still think it was junk. I felt I could not say anything of value within rigid forms; whereas Woodcock could. Inside those disciplined early metrics, with understatement being the parallel to present-day throwaway lines, you can find surprising things, every adjective and verb chosen for its absolute employability.

But I won't continue the parallel between George and myself, except to add that we are both similar and dissimilar, his conciseness the opposite of my verbosity. And yet a thousand years of poetry resides in Woodcock much more than it does in me. The implications of his work plunge below the surface of history and philosophy; many times his lightest lines will have anvil-weight. His poems, as he has said elsewhere, have turned around from their earlier forms to become freer; and everything he says now seems inevitably right as to form and content, approaching some more classic definition of what poetry ought to be.

And there is such terror in some of these poems!—stemming from what Woodcock calls "a naturally pessimistic side to my mind" which considers "that man may be an evolutionary failure and on his way to join the dinosaurs . . . " A terror that is prophetic of course. But beside this you must place the onrushing joy he describes when writing poems, which is caught up in his own life. There is a particular vision of life in some of these pieces. Perhaps it's as well that the excerpted last verse of "Memorandum from Arcadia" doesn't convey the complete vision:

> I shall do the thing the neatest and cleanest way.
> Cord rots soon. I shall drop to the floor.
> I shall be found behind the kitchen door
> Sprawling untidily on the trodden clay.

That is not Auden or Spender or MacNeice, but Woodcock. As is "Poem for Garcia Lorca" which ends: "Remember Lorca, who died only being Lorca."

After the manner of Auden's "As I Walked Out One Evening" is "Ballad for W.H. Auden" which includes this verse:

I walked down Granville with Spender
In a different golden year,
And Spender said: "God and Auden,
They call each other Dear!"

I burst out laughing when I read that passage, because George sorta snuck up on me unexpectedly. But the verse comes from a serious poem, and connects with a later one:

If your Anglican God had received you
As Auden or Wystan or Dear,
I know that all is accepted
With irony, without fear . . .

It's an invocation and tribute to W.H. Auden, as Auden himself paid his own masterful tribute to Yeats.

I would have liked this short Intro to be my own tribute to George Woodcock, but it is not. That would take someone who understood his complexity better than myself. All I understand is that Woodcock is a great human being, protean and in some understated way, magnificent. He is largely responsible for the regeneration of a country's literature; he is a writer and poet like none presently existing here, nor I suppose, anywhere else. He is also a friend.

*(1975)*

## ∾ George Woodcock 1912-1995

A COUNTRY MUST BE AWARE OF ITSELF. Quite apart from the regional and national news that flies outward to various media-distributing points, artists need to communicate with other artists, composers and musicians with their opposite numbers elsewhere, and writers need to know what other writers are up to, what new ideas are being born in Halifax, Regina, St. John's and Vancouver.

Novels are being written among the giant trees of Vancouver Island; poems are dreaming in the mountains. Articles and short stories are born in Nova Scotia and Newfoundland. And thinking about it: when a word is attached to a thing, that thing becomes different, it changes and joins the human mind and consciousness. There is a passion about the naming of things. Without the word, what do we know?

Well, among writers I think George Woodcock is largely responsible for creating a new sense of self-awareness in Canada. We say and the Bible says: "In the beginning was the word." In 1959 G.W. was the leading spirit behind the founding in Vancouver of *Canadian Literature*, the first journal devoted entirely to a critical view of this country's writing. And he began to write letters from Vancouver to everywhere. To everywhere in Canada he wrote letters asking for contributions to the new magazine.

And they were personal letters, despite G.W. being an editor. The letters seemed to know their recipients, and were knowledgeable about what they had written previously. They sought them out. They addressed him or her as an equal, requesting articles and reviews. CanLit went into libraries and bookstores, sprang to life in the minds of writers, from the outports of Newfoundland, prairie villages, small towns in Ontario and the Maritimes: *In the beginning was the word.*

In 1960, a year after the inception of *CanLit*, I was camped in the northern wilderness near Hazelton, BC. (The Canada Council had amazingly given me a thousand dollars to write poems). I'd bought a 1948 Pontiac for a hundred bucks, driven north from Vancouver, camped on a side road near a burbling little creek, and set up shop with a portable typewriter. One day in the Hazelton pub I interviewed an Indian youngster for over an hour: when I finished asking questions about his aboriginal background, he shyly informed me that he was the Chinese-Canadian hotel proprietor's son.

And I listened to CBC Radio in early evening. A new play called "Maskerman," by George Woodcock, a writer unknown to me, was featured. I thought the play pretty good, slightly decadent but good. I wrote Woodcock a letter expressing admiration, something I've done several times with other writers who pleased me. After I'd returned East—coasting most of the way half asleep at 40 mph in my elderly Pontiac with throttle pulled out—Woodcock replied. Very probably he asked me to review some book or other. Which I did.

Over the years I learned quite a bit about George Woodcock, some of it from pieces written about him, most of it from himself in letters. G.W. was born in Winnipeg in 1912. The family had emigrated to Canada shortly before that event, but couldn't make a go of it in "the colonies" and skipped back to England after a couple of cold Manitoba winters. Samuel Woodcock, George's father, had Bright's Disease, which meant that the family always floated not far above the poverty line. At school back in England, the young G.W., an excellent student, was offered a partial scholarship at Oxford University. He decided to go to work for an electrical company instead, and later became a railway clerk. And started writing.

In London the Woodcock literary career began to blossom in a small way. He met all the bigwigs of the 1930s, Herbert Read, George Orwell, Julian Symons, T.S. Eliot and the rest. In that little world with big ideas George started magazines, wrote books, embraced the anarchist political philosophy, and became an intellectual in that word's truest sense. No one taught him, although he learned from others, and it would be more accurate to say he taught himself.

G.W.'s literary career led him into leftist politics. Through Herbert Read, and later the daughter of Italian anarchist Camillo Berneri, he became deeply involved in anarchism, and later wrote the definitive book on that subject. In England his first full-length book was *Aphra Behn: The English Sappho* (1948). And of course, he wrote poetry.

During World War II, G.W. did farmwork, receiving an exemption from the army after addressing an examining tribunal: "I cannot believe it is right to use violence against other violence. What is intrinsically wrong is always wrong, and to counter one evil by another only produces greater eventual evil."

In the aftermath of war, with England at her lowest spiritual and economic level, it must have seemed to George and his new wife, Ingeborg (whom he married in Germany), that even a bare living had become impossible for a writer. They emigrated to Canada in 1949, settled near Sooke, 40 kilometres northwest of Victoria on Vancouver Island. George was in his late thirties, Inge five years younger. The venturesome pair bought land and cleared it, planning to live off their own home-grown produce. It's indicative of their financial condition that one of George's first jobs in Canada was spreading manure at 75 cents an hour.

However, soil on the Woodcock land had already been "worked-out," and was useless for anything except perhaps grazing cattle. At this point Earle Birney, poet and UBC prof, came to their assistance with literary work. The painter Jack Shadbolt, and his wife, Doris, were also among G.W.'s benefactors. Publisher Allan Wingate in London and the CBC in Toronto commissioned a travel narrative that took the Woodcocks and two friends north in BC by auto, to the Indian country of Hazelton and Kispiox.

The resulting book, *Ravens and Prophets*, (1952) was the first of G.W.'s travel books. (In the RCAF during the war, I had been stationed near Hazelton myself, at a tiny dot on the map called Woodcock—not named for G.W.) George and Inge moved to Vancouver in 1953. The English expatriate—who was really a full citizen of Canada—was beginning to find life easier. He wrote more travel books: *To the City of the Dead*, about Mexico; *Incas and Other Men*, which describes an extended trip to Peru.

I have a small connection with that Peruvian book. I went there in 1975, with G.W. providing me with some travel info. He said the plane he and Inge took for the flight to Macchu Picchu 15 years before was not pressurized. And that the pilot had informed passengers about this omission right after take-off, when they couldn't jump out of the plane in mid-air. The pilot also told them that everyone would lose consciousness except him, since he was used to the scarcity of oxygen. However, by 1975 when my wife and I flew to Cuzco near Macchu Picchu, technology had triumphed: blessed oxygen was plentiful.

The Woodcock move to Vancouver was signal for a period of "frenzied" literary activity. Estimates of the number of books G.W. published during his lifetime range from 100 to 200. Probably even George doesn't know the correct figure. Articles and monographs poured from the old Olympia typewriter he had used all his life. Gifted with a style that made extensive revisions unnecessary, the stuff literally flooded from his brain and hands. Gifted also with a talent for friendship, G.W. knew and corresponded with writers and artists of all genres in every part of the country, writing many thousands of letters.

In 1966 Woodcock published *The Crystal Spirit*, a biography of his friend, George Orwell. His title derived from a short verse by Orwell that ends: "No bomb that ever burst/Shatters the crystal spirit." I think those lines could also describe George Woodcock himself.

That same year, 1966, G.W. had a very serious heart attack. I visited him while he was still recovering at his home in Vancouver. I thought he was indomitable in a quiet way. George's wife, Inge, ministered to him, as she has always done. His face against the white bedsheets looked just as pale. But I had the sense that new projects were being planned during this convalescence. What's the Keats line about gleaning his teeming brain? I didn't stay long on that occasion. Much later George admitted to me that his voluminous writing was in some sense an attempt to cheat death before death inevitably returned.

From being nearly penniless on first arriving at Sooke in 1949, George and Inge became the moving spirits behind a dozen schemes to raise money for such projects as the Canada India Village Aid Society and the Tibetan Aid Society. My wife and I were sitting with the Woodcocks at Harbourfront in Toronto when they outlined plans that their lifetime savings should become an emergency fund to help Canadian writers in distress. Since they had no children, the writers of Canada became, in effect, their surrogate children.

Having dinner at the Woodcock house a few years ago still stands out in my mind. This was during my heavy beer-drinking days, and I'd spent all afternoon with a friend trying to exhaust the supply of suds in Vancouver breweries. The friend (who shall remain nameless) was one of the best storytellers I've ever encountered; a mere twist of his mouth could elicit paroxysms and seizures. And later you'd wonder what he'd said to start it all off.

Anyway, my friend told me about buying a couple of Egyptian mummies which had been on display in Woodward's store window. And the mind boggles here: Egyptian mummies in Woodward's display windows? But that's what he told me: and raffled them off at a buck a throw. Now whether that story was true or not didn't matter. And I can't remember the details, only that it was hilarious. (I guess you had to be there.)

When the drinking paused briefly in late afternoon, it was nearly time for me to take a taxi to the Woodcock place. I'd previously conveyed, as delicately as possible, that my friend wasn't invited and I had to leave now, tout de suite or whatever they say on the Left Bank.

"Oh," he said, "I'm not good enough to meet your friends, huh? You're ashamed of me."

That one stopped me. I looked at him for a moment or so, brain a bit numb. "Okay, come on."

George and Inge were both slightly startled at the unexpected extra guest. But they made him welcome, sat both of us down among the other guests. Those were William New, who had succeeded George as editor of *CanLit* in 1977, and Robert Fulford, editor of *Saturday Night* magazine. (It was almost a plague of editors.)

George and Inge were gracious hosts; in fact I've never seen them any other way. My friend told his stories (they really were funny), was duly applauded, and everything seemed to go well. But I was uncomfortable, having the sense I'd pulled a boner and everyone knew it. I didn't feel very good about myself when we left.

I was with the Woodcocks for dinner again some time later. Another guest was a young but fairly well-known theatre director, also G.W.'s friend. The conversation after dinner got into some fairly esoteric areas, and to my slight surprise I couldn't follow where the ideas were going. This shocked and surprised me. To put it bluntly: I was too stupid to understand what was being discussed. So I kept my mouth shut and listened. But I add ruefully, this doesn't happen very often, that I declare myself brain-dead.

In October of last year I visited George and Inge again. The taxi dropped me off at the wrong house at about 8:30 p.m., and I had to walk for kilometres that seemed like miles. George McWhirter, a UBC prof, and his wife were guests as well. G.W. was using one of those metal walker contraptions, and seemed very subdued. When I asked how he was, he mentioned congestive heart failure.

I'd been having much trouble with feet and lower legs myself, which an Ontario medic in Kingston said was caused by excessive beer-drinking. G.W. and Inge wanted me to go to their Vancouver neurologist, presumably superior to the eastern variety. I pleaded weariness of all medics except Galen and Hippocrates; but those two weren't in the Vancouver phone book.

"How about Robin Skelton then?" G.W. said. "He's a witch, and I think might be able to help." I must have raised my eyebrows at the idea of Robin Skelton, a Victoria poet, as a purveyor of magic healing. "He made a pass over me," George went on, "and cured me of something else."

"Why don't you try him for your heart then?"

"That's too serious for even a good witch."

After which there was slight gloom, and then the conversation flowed around us while we were finishing off some of Inge's pastries. When we left, George was sitting behind his walker, pale and smiling. It was the last time I saw him.

Ingeborg and George—they roamed the world together. At home in Canada, she was hostess, wife, companion, and sometimes critic of George's writing as well. She chauffeured him around everywhere (he never did learn to drive) in their little Volkswagen bug; I am quite sure G.W.'s writing output would have been halved without Inge. (I can say this with some certainly, since my own wife occupies the same important place in my life.) I think such women flatter their husbands immensely though they would probably never admit it to anyone except themselves.

George Woodcock's books range from history to biography, travel, drama, poetry and fiction, with some unclassifiable side excursions. But such a bare listing doesn't do his variety justice, although all his books partake of each other, if only through writing excellence. His mind will fly off on tangents, even with the most ordinary subject. And over a long lifetime of assiduous reading, G.W. qualifies as an autodidact, an awkward word like a flightless heron. I think he was a person on whom a university education would have been wasted: he could have taught professors their business long before he became one himself.

Over the years in Canada, G.W. became a Canadian nationalist in almost every sense of the word except an aggressive one. It was a nationalism rooted in the local and regional. He never did lose that English-sounding accent, and when he was taunted in print about being English, I've seen resentment not far beneath the surface. And this strong feeling about Canada permeates all his writing.

It seems to me impossible to trace G.W.'s prose ancestors and influences. They were too many and various. But in poetry Auden is undoubtedly the principal mentor.

One couldn't write as many books as George Woodcock did, and maintain invariable high quality. A very few of his books were not as good as others, but most were excellent. I would cite his award-winning Orwell biography, *The Crystal Spirit*, as top level.

G.W. had an extremely logical and even-toned mind that

precluded stylistic and emotional excesses. He was a "civilized" man in that word's best sense. He was not a perfect writer—and there is no such beast (you never stop learning). But he was an endlessly fascinating individual, something close to greatness in his character, a man so fully himself and so human in every aspect that he had my entire admiration.

The principal heritage George Woodcock has left Canada is an alive and vital literary community, which it was not in 1959 at the inception of *CanLit*. He made writers aware both of themselves and each other, and knew nearly every one of them through correspondence. When he died at 1:30 a.m. on January 29, 1995 at age 82, the country lost a man who saw from the beginning that excellence was possible, and was instrumental in bringing it about.

It was the letters that did it, those and the feeling they gave their recipients that they too were part of the literary network, and their views and opinions of high importance. You send a little piece of yourself outward in letters, the human part, your opinions and personality and warmth distributed across the country from Newfoundland to Vancouver Island. That's what George did: he made his first name known among writers everywhere in Canada, and added his last name like a hyphenated addition to the country itself.

G.W. once wrote, "Canadians do not like heroes, and so they do not have them. They do not even have great men in the accepted sense of the word." George Galt in a *Globe and Mail* piece said, "You were wrong about that, George." Yes, you were wrong about that.

*(1995)*

# Literary History of Canada:
## Canadian Literature in English

B EFORE I READ THIS *LITERARY HISTORY*, a novelist I know
told me it was dull. I think most practising writers—novelists
and poets, that is—would tend to feel the same way, perhaps from
scorn of dusty encyclopaedias, or else being forced by their mothers
to read a dozen volumes of the *Book of Knowledge* as a child. Such
massive tomes have a tendency to scare off any but "serious" or
"scholarly" readers.

That would be a great pity. These books are, quite literally, a
history of Canada, the country's life and thought since its beginning.
Every country in the world sooner or later comes up with such an
historic record, some countries with many of them. There's no reason
why Canada should be any exception to this rule. And in fact the
books are sometimes dull, but then in turn fascinating, depending on
who's writing about what. In other words, the *History* should be judged
primarily on its merits as a collection of writings about Canadian
literature; only secondarily as a necessary and valuable reference
book, which it certainly is.

The *History* was first published in 1965 in one volume. Now it is
reissued, the earlier sections largely revised, and with an additional
volume included to cover the years 1960 to 1974. This added book,
dealing with an explosion of writing in Canada during that 14-year
period, is the main reason for this enlarged second edition being
published.

However, all three volumes are integral to an understanding of
writing in Canada—English writing only, I hasten to add—since
Wolfe and Montcalm. The first volume deals with actual military and

political history, explorers and voyagers West; also stirrings of literary activity in the Maritimes during the 19th century, the Upper and Lower Canadas, Haliburton and Howe, D'Arcy McGee, the Moodies, Stricklands and Traills, transplanted Englishmen, writers suddenly or gradually aware that they were Canadians—such as Roberts, Carmen, and Lampman. It also deals with "forces," "growth," and many varieties of writing.

The second volume adds the sciences, drama, essays, literary scholarship, religion, autobiography, travel, history, as well as the novel and poetry. There are a few more chapter-headings, but I don't want to make this a catalogue of a catalogue of a catalogue. The new third volume repeats the second one's subjects with some new writers added. And as binder twine to tie things together, we have such chapters as "The Writer and his Public, Politics and Literature in the 1960s," with a conclusion by Northrop Frye, for both the original edition in 1965 and its 1976 successor.

In fact, Northrop Frye is omnipresent throughout the entire *History*: being quoted by the other writers; given credit or discredit for a critical climate of thinking (the mythopoeic); and sometimes answering his own critics to explain what he really meant. I'm not complaining about this, since like many other people I find Frye's analytical writing interesting; although sometimes I wonder if the striking images he uses (likening the Gulf of St. Lawrence to "an inconceivably large whale" for instance) don't occasionally detract from more intensive examination of the actual thesis his image embellishes. I find him so interesting that I feel rather suspicious (a reaction I'm sure he would call typically Canadian), even while agreeing when he says: "Canada has always been a cool climate for heroes." (Trudeau was an obvious exception eight years ago.) In some ways Frye himself has been a cultural hero for other scholars, and this *History* demonstrates to just what extent.

The dullest part of the book—and that is obviously what my novelist friend meant—is the critical listings of writers. But one of the most interesting chapters is the treatment of Canadian history writing in Volume II by William Kilbourn. Here we have an account of scholarly disagreements between environmentalists (proponents of the importance of landscape in history) and the advocates of cities (who maintain that large metropolitan centres now supersede landscape). We encounter the Laurentians, Harold Innis and Donald Creighton, who believed that "Canada existed not in spite of geography, but because of it." And Kilbourn explicating Creighton, refers to explorers like Cartier and Champlain on the St. Lawrence River. "In the hero's act of penetration and possession of the land of the St. Lawrence there lay the central secret of Canadian history." It sounds like a vivid adventure story, with later literary detectives adding motives and making obviously erotic parallels. Of course, much more is added by Michael Cross in Volume III.

Jay Macpherson, in her chapter on autobiographies, says they "generally offer more of historical or social than literary interest." But she mentions Frederick Philip Grove as having committed the most deliberate attempt to portray the artist as such, the hero of *In Search of Myself* playing out Grove's favourite drama, "that of the strong man with a wound that will take his whole lifetime to kill him." Since Douglas Spettigue's admirable detective work in Europe of tracing down pseudo-Grove's real identity as Felix Paul Greve, an obscure German novelist, the Greve-Grove persona has acquired a relation to the Canadian identity trauma that hasn't been adequately touched, let alone explored.

The late Desmond Pacey's chapter on Canadian criticism in Volume III pays due respect to Northrop Frye and others, such as A.J.M. Smith and E.K. Brown. But he disagrees with Frye's "theoretical views that criticism is not and should not be concerned with evaluation, and that literature owes more to other works of literature than to the writer's own life and times." (I happen to agree with that disagreement—with trepidation, to be sure.) And Pacey comes up with an interesting quote from A.J.M. Smith for young writers: "Send your work to the best English and American magazines. Until you are sure that your work is acceptable there, leave the Canadian magazines alone." Would Smith also advise Canadian writers to pay attention only to English and American critics, and leave Canadian critics alone? Since he has himself long been an American citizen, perhaps his advice should be heeded. In any case, as Pacey points out. "The influence of criticism upon creative writers is at best indirect, at worst quite irrelevant." And yet, paradoxically, I think writers have much to learn from people like Frye and Smith, even if indirectly.

Malcolm Ross, in his chapter on critical theory, discusses some of the same things as Pacey, but carries it a few steps further. He gets to the basic questions: "Do we have a recognizable cultural identity? Do we indeed have culture, a literature, our own moment or place in the larger imaginative order?" Regarding any of these questions, one can only point to the literary and artistic works that exist in this country as evidence for or against. And that's all that can be done in any country. However, Ross's outline of critical theory is one of the most interesting in this massive history.

There isn't space here to deal with other chapters on different sub-species of literature, therefore I'll go direct to fiction in Volume III (discussed by William New) and poetry (whose overseer is George Woodcock). During the period between 1960 and 1973, "some 1,125 books of verse, not counting anthologies," had been published, Woodcock says. A slightly lesser explosion occurred in fiction, during the same period. However, "nowadays poetry is not merely—in numbers of titles—the most published of all genres in Canada: it sells more reliably than fiction . . . " (Woodcock). That being the case, one wonders why fiction receives so much more space in newspaper and magazine reviews, and also more space in this literary history (50 pages in Volume III for fiction as compared to 33 for poetry)?

It's also a matter for some amazement, even among foreign literary critics such as England's William Walsh, that poetry should be so dominant in Canada and maintain its generally high level of quality—something that doesn't happen in other Commonwealth countries. In a letter to Claude Bissell, Walsh said: "I must say I did find this question fascinating, infinitely more so than agitation about identities and images in Canada. The question, that is, first why Canadians should be such good poets, or more precisely that there should be so many good Canadian poets." (Quoted from the Toronto *Star*, Oct. 16, 1976.)

The chapters on fiction and poetry both discuss individual writers briefly; the better-known novelists such as Laurence, Richler, MacLennan, and so on receive slightly more space than others from New. He also mentions that, during this time, "vital fiction became the accomplishment of many writers and remained no longer the preserve of a select few." If fiction actually was "the preserve of a select few," then I suppose the recent proliferation of small publishers offered them a wider outlet. But conversely, these small publishers have generally concentrated on poetry, leaving fiction to larger commercial giants such as McGraw-Hill Ryerson and others. In any case, the novel and short story did gain increasing national momentum during the past dozen years.

George Woodcock, in the limited space allotted him, prefaces his poetry essay with a general outline of what has happened inside his time period. Poetry magazines sprout like mushrooms; phonograph records of verse are out; cross-country readings; listening audiences of up to 500 (this reviewer had one of 500 when a folk singer was advertised, but didn't show); many small publishers, a few spending their own money when they can't get a grant from the Canada Council. A time of long-shot gamblers in literature, showdown at the OK poetry corral; an ominous Black Mountain appears on the Vancouver skyline. Unheard of poets are heard of: the miracle of Atwood; MacEwen astounds; Wayman exhibits; Layton shouts; Cohen might be said to sing; Birney falls from a tree in Toronto, and publishes three books since the fall. In short, fiesta and CanLit carnival, a situation of poem popularity certain Montreal academics view with considerable suspicion.

As mentioned, Frye permeates all three volumes, and it is rare that anyone disagrees with his major premises. Desmond Pacey has done so on two of those premises; but Pacey is safe in so doing for obvious reasons. And I can't help agreeing when Frye ends all three sections of the history with this sentence: "This book is about what has been created, in words and in Canada, during the present age, and the whole body of that creation will be the main reason for whatever interest posterity may take in us." My only comment would be that we are our own future: that is, Canadian writers now are mapping the country, both psychologically and physically. It has not been done before, despite the evidence of this History, and I am bound to think the job important.

Among more percipient utterances of the Frye-oracle is this one: "It seems to me that a very curious and significant exchange of identities between Canada and the United States has taken place since then [1967]. The latter, traditionally so buoyant, extroverted, and forward-looking, appears to be entering a prolonged period of self-examination." Whereas Canada, always in the past a narcissistic navel-watcher, has gained something remarkably like a certainty of its own existence, even if for no obvious purpose other than survival.

Frye also says: "It seems to me that the decisive cultural event in English Canada during the past fifteen years has been the impact of French Canada and its new sense of identity." I think he's right again, and that both French and English are, in some odd way, necessary antagonists to each other. Each would miss the other badly if an Ontario-Quebec wall were erected on the boundary and would feel like a man with an amputated leg that still aches in cold weather.

What this History fails to indicate, and which is not entirely in its field, is that the existence of Canada as a unified country has never been so precarious. The provinces are fighting against Ottawa; Quebec, as I write this, may be about to separate; the weight of American investment finally threatens to tip the country southward so that whatever wealth is left automatically streams willy-nilly into the vaults of the Chase-Manhattan Bank; and finally, foreign landlords control 80 per cent of so-called Canadian publishing (Toronto *Star*, Oct. 19, 1976).

All of the foregoing is a lead-in to the repeated question: Why the outburst of Canadian literary works over the past dozen years—in fact in all the creative arts? Seemingly, culture has never been more healthy; although the same can't be said economically. The present Literary History does not satisfactorily provide an answer. (Why more babies during a war?) What it does do is provide a valuable critical literary record over the fairly brief period of Canada's existence as a nation, which will be of decided historical interest in times to come.

*(1977)*

# Peter Trower
## Introduction to *Ragged Horizons*

Peter Trower is a poet of mean streets, logging camps, pubs, and the immense blue and green sprawl of British Columbia. I met him first in a pub, several years ago, perhaps the Marble Arch, certainly one of those drinking holes where a fight seems just on the point of breaking out. Trower seemed to belong in such a place, a natural habitué (although he lives now in a green village called Gibsons): the sort of guy who personifies my own description of the "west coat lotusland, lush Fraser delta country where drunks don't freeze in winter: they just lie there peacefully on evergreen lawns and mildew."

Not that Trower is a drunk. But when I met him a second time it was also at some hotel pub. And the third and the fourth. From which encounters it might be reasonably deduced that I too am an habitué of mean streets, low joints, sin strips, and crummy hotels? Sure, why not.

Anyway, every time I saw the guy he had a sheaf of poems in his hip pocket. They were good poems too; in fact, I believe I first heard "The Last Spar-Tree" at the Marble Arch. All the beer-drinkers stood up and applauded; the waiters served our table free beer; then the manager came around and shook hands respectfully. Can you imagine: "Dream on in peace old tree/perhaps you're a truer monument to man/than any rocktop crucifix in Rio de Janeiro?" Can you imagine the surprise of that ending, Rio de Janeiro in a Vancouver pub at the end of a logging poem that isn't exactly a logging poem?

I've been a booster of Trower from that time on—along with John Newlove and a few others also aware that here is a poet worth knowing. Of course, Trower himself is his own best booster, a man with some fierce drive for excellence and success that he has harnessed to writing.

For antecedents look to Robert Swanson, who once wrote unending doggerel about logging camps in the manner of Service and Kipling. His books sold, literally, in the hundreds of thousands because of their subject matter, and because the west coast of Canada is almost entirely preoccupied with its own navel—scarcely aware that the rest of Canada exists. But despite some reiterated stresses that you become aware of when you read his poems, Trower does not resemble Swanson except in the logging parallel. The man who wrote "slugs move like severed yellow fingers" could even have been Earle Birney, but was actually Peter Trower.

I am reminded, too, of Kipling, poet of the now-gone-bad reputation in once-imperial England. (In point of fact, Trower departed that sinking island at the age of ten during World War Two.) Both Trower and Kipling are preoccupied with the world's work, the sweat and slugging grind, the blue-collar terminology of bull-block, jerkwire punks, gas-rigs, and chokers. And make no mistake: Kipling was an excellent poet, not a bad writer at all from whom to derive a ghost-resemblance. But there are many other antecedents, because Trower has read widely, distilling this present amalgam; you have to be a literary detective to find them, which must mean that I have become that.

Later on, Trower, myself, and a couple of other friends were drinking beer at the Marble Arch. I had a bright idea. Why not buy some steaks, expand the yellow evening by cooking them, and continue to stretch this woozy moment into eternity? I was staying at Earle Birney's apartment then; but he was away somewhere, delivering an address on Chaucer and the relation of Middle English to pub-jargon in Shaughnessy Heights. Then why not surprise Esther Birney with our pseudo-intellectual talk and ten pounds of prime sirloin?

The idea was received with acclaim. We took a cab to Safeway's; I bought the steaks; we rang the doorbell of the Birney apartment. I began to have a few qualms at this point, in fact wondered if this was an entirely wise and judicious move from the Marble Arch. Besides, I had forgotten to buy roses for Esther. And had I zipped my pants after the last visit to the john? Yes.

Anyway, Esther received us with surprise and the greatest possible cordiality, under the circumstances. She cooked the steaks. Peter read his poems, and all of us trembled in the excess of his genius. And "there was much comradeship and laughter—/great yarns beside noon donkeys, hillhumour between turns—/excellent shits behind stumps with the wind fanning the stink away" in Esther Birney's drawing room.

Peter Trower was born at St. Leonard's-On-Sea, England, in 1930. His test-pilot father was killed in a Belgium plane crash when Trower was four. The family emigrated to Canada in 1940.

In Canada the Trower family lived for a time in Vancouver, then moved up-coast to Port Mellon where Peter's mother married Trygg Iversen, a pulp mill superintendent. Iversen was drowned in 1944; it seems Mrs. Trower was a little unlucky in her choice of life-long mates.

At school, Peter was a cartoonist and wrote doggerel verse. But money was short. He quit school and went to work in the logging camps, this and related jobs being his main occupations for the next twenty-two years. It sounds like a hand-to-mouth existence the way he describes it: a course at Vancouver's Art School, jobs as millwright's helper and cartoonist for the Steelworkers' Union, living in one scruffy room after another (and Vancouver skid-road hotels and rooming houses are about as scruffy as you can get). In fact Trower's life bears some resemblance to my own, with the difference that I was married and this provided some stability.

Among "unknown poets" Peter Trower ranks with Milton Acorn, who managed to remain relatively unknown despite winning the Governor General's Award a couple of years ago. Trower has published three books, but his name is known only on the west coast, a kind of latter-day Robert Swanson despite the virtuosity of his poems. Their subject matter encompasses a much wider area than did Swanson's poems, nevertheless this identification remains.

But Trower would not wish to escape the lyrical umbilical cord connecting him with the landscape, for his mini-poems range back to a previous logging era, almost in tune with Roderick Haig-Brown of a slightly earlier day. Haig-Brown is a prose parallel, to some degree at least, of Trower:

They have stoical Swenska faces
white-stubbled
cured to creased red leather
by a many-weathered craft.

They have crinkled Swenska voices
like wind in the branches
of the countless killed trees
who have given them their tongues . . .

They have returned to the resinous hills
like ancestral gunslingers
for one final showdown
with the reluctant trees.

But the voice inside the voice of "The Last Handfallers" is entirely
Trower's own.

*(1978)*

# R.G. Everson

## Introduction to *Everson at Eighty*

$A$ FTER READING AND COGITATING about the work of a lifetime, you begin to have an overview of a person's poems. About
ten years ago Ron Everson's syntax straightened out and untangled
(not that it ever was really indecipherable), became very nearly a
model of how to write a good poem-sentence in English, while still
retaining all its implications and levels of meaning.

And more important, the poems themselves got better and
better. And that's not just the enthusiasm of an editor. How do I
explain it, even to myself? People who think poems should rhyme to
be poems won't like Everson. The audience for Rod McKuen, Edgar
Guest and Edna Jacques will never hear his name. None of which
matters a damn.

Two things: Everson has become unique. There is no one writing
in Canada, or anywhere else that I know of, who resembles him in the
least. And second, those people who kept saying that he was neglected
ten years ago were dead wrong. At that time I think he deserved
approximately the amount of recognition he received. But now I
regard him as among the very few excellent poets writing in Canada.

It all sounds very familiar, I suppose. The editor blatting about
his latest phony enthusiasm; the blurb-writer blurbering. Well—let
me try to describe what I think the reader will find if he reads several
Everson poems. That aforementioned pellucid syntax. (Please,
please, Ron, make it so!) A circularity of writing that leads inevitably
to a sometimes thumping, sometimes quiet climax. I mean, the
poem-circumstance often leads inevitably to that kind of ending.
Also, morality. (That horrid word!) The white, WASP liberal sort of

stuff—in fact damn near archetypal. Everson is almost a guideline to a never-never ideal world of the future.

He seems to have one foot in the nineteenth century and the other in the twentieth. Two worlds. For instance, language. Everson would use the word *rake* instead of womanizer for someone who sleeps around. (All such terms somehow euphemisms.) You won't find *rake* in any of these poems, but it's still there in his mind. You won't find hip or junkie jargon from the fifties and sixties either. Conversely, Everson's language is right now.

I don't know how he does this, unless it's from talking to the janitor of his apartment (who's French Canadian anyway), motel desk-clerks, pelicans and spider-crabs on the beach in Florida. The working jargon of coal miners, construction workers, etc. was never there anyway. Moreover, the language he does use is peculiarly natural, it *fits*, it adheres to the bones of his poems.

All this is froth anyway! The reader wants to be moved, emotionally, intellectually, sexually (but keep it clean) and, if possible, to lose himself/herself in a believable magnificence. And above all, that's what Everson is, believable.

We were sailing north off the Labrador coast on a CNR coastal boat, the *William Carson*, five or six years ago. Everson and his wife, Lorna; my wife, Eurithe and her husband. None of us could escape each other. Icebergs kept butting us and we butted them. A leathery Newfoundlander called Jonas or Jonah kept saying to me meaningfully, "The left hand is the evil hand." It has only occurred to me since that I should have asked him, "Is the evil hand the masturbating hand?" And, "Jonah, are you right-handed?"

My reason for being on the *William Carson* was that I had to write a magazine article about life in the Newfoundland outports. But that came later. First we journeyed north to Nain, Labrador, with Ron and me writing poems continually. I said, "How many poems have you written?" he said, "Fourteen." That stopped me, I only had a dozen. "Are they any good?" I said. He showed me, and they were good. Much better than mine.

We parted company on another ship at Harbour Deep, a hundred miles or so south of St. Anthony's, Newfoundland. Since there was no guaranteed accommodation at the outport, Ron and Lorna headed for the nearest airport. My wife Eurithe and her husband were rowed ashore, he brooding about the excellence of his friend's poems. (The *William Carson* sank in subarctic waters a year or so after our luxury cruise, as reported on CBC.)

There have been other jaunts and expeditions, to establish my credentials as having some slight acquaintance with the man. Much later, when I took on the job of editing his poems, he gave me reviews of his books to read, stretching back some 25 years. (They were all flattering; I presume he burned the nasty ones. I do that myself.) Reading these reviews, I wonder over and over again just who it is they are talking about. That Ron Everson is not the man I know; how could they be so wrong?

In any case, it's interesting to see how critics and reviewers have received a man's work over 25 years.

Reviewing *A Lattice for Momos* in 1958, Northrop Frye said that Everson's theme is that of the "innocent vision," the "original sin of childhood rapture, which in adult life operates as love." Given the tone and content of Everson's poems, it's difficult to include innocence as part of his prosodic and philosophic armoury. He was, of course, present at Genesis, which experience instilled conservatism and a traditional morality.

The reviews march forward in time until now, many of them betraying a slightly surprised air at Everson's excellence. James Dickey, also reviewing *Momos*, called him "almost greatly gifted" in the *Sewanne Review*. And adds that he has "just enough of the amateur about him to make his work interesting." Since Dickey is a professional poet if there ever was one, does that make his own work uninteresting? The same critic also says nice things about *Blind Man's Holiday*, 1963.

The reviewer of *Wrestle with an Angel* in the *U of T Quarterly*, 1966, says, "The strength of his best poems lies in their reticence, their refusal to indulge in peripheral emotion or secondary implications, an intense concentration on a single theme." I would think just the opposite, that Everson's mind jumps in many directions in the manner of free scientific research, looking for anything interesting.

Reviewers are also surprised at Everson's advanced age, or perhaps by his maturity. My own theory is that writers have some ten years at most to be at their best (Yeats notwithstanding); therefore Everson's excellence at 80 might indeed be thought a little surprising.

Robert Weaver, reviewing the *Selected Poems* (*Globe & Mail*, 1970), thinks of him as being "still a back-concession puritan from Southern Ontario"—an opinion I agree with. Dorothy Livesay in 1976 describes Everson as a "latecomer into print," a mistake other reviewers have made, and that it is "the low profile he seeks." Many of Everson's poems are objective, excluding the personal, but it's difficult to believe that he seeks anonymity. Else why publish at all? And Louis Dudek says, in his review of the 1976 *Indian Summer*, that Everson "is himself the typical representative of much Canadian humour, the humble self-effacing little man who wins out somehow in his own way." That may or may not be typical of Canadian humour, but certainly not of Mr. Ronald G. Everson. Humble? Self-effacing? Anyone who has either read his poems with insight or listened to him dominate a conversation would think such an opinion ludicrous.

The most recent Oberon books get the best treatment by reviewers. But it is obvious that many reviewers still do not know what to make of him. Both Everson's age and his ability seem to surprise them. But generally it is a pleasant surprise, sometimes with a slight condescension about it: "Hey, look at the good poet I've discovered, who's so old that no one else noticed him." I find many of their comments amusing, saying to myself complacently that I've known the same thing for at least ten years.

Which brings me to the potted biography.

Ron Everson was born in Oshawa, Ontario, in 1903, of Norse, Scottish and English ancestry. The family—parents and seven children—lived on a small farm at the west end of town. There was a trout stream, a barn, horses, a cow, chickens and homing pigeons—fields and woods to the west and north and the Kingston Road to the south.

Until the age of fourteen, Ron delivered newspapers in that earlier and smaller Oshawa. He worked summers and holidays on the General Motors assembly line.

At University of Toronto Schools, Everson won a poem prize of $10. At the University of Toronto, E.J. Pratt was the poetry guru, friendship between the two surviving this experience. At the U of T Everson was editor of *Acta Victoriana*. He paid his fees at the Upper Canada Law School by writing detective stories and westerns for Street & Smith, a US pulp-magazine publisher.

In 1930, *Poetry Chicago* bought three poems. The editor, Harriet

Monro, asked the new contributor to send her all the poems he produced. Everson replied that he couldn't afford to write poetry, since it had taken him several months to write the poems for which she had paid him $15, even less than the fraction-of-a-cent rate Street & Smith paid its pulp writers.

Ron was 26 at that time, and says his poetry career has been going downhill ever since. In the same year Witter Bynner wrote personally that one of Everson's poems was "the best he had seen in ten years, by an unknown." And the *Story-Teller*, an English mag, featured in large type on its cover: G.K. CHESTERTON, and, in much smaller type, T.S. Eliot and R.G. Everson.

1930 was an eventful year. Everson received his law degree (he has never practised), acquired a wife and dog and moved to a log cabin in the Muskoka woods. Living in rural solitude, he wrote poems four days a week and western-detective-and-mystery stories the other three days. One of his verbal anecdotes about that period concerns soaking a worn-out typewriter ribbon with 3-in-1 gun oil, festooning it from tree to forest tree, rejuvenating it enough to pound out another thousand words of prose or a poem.

During that six-year Muskoka period, there were poems in *Willison's Monthly* and the *Canadian Forum*. Macmillan rejected a book manuscript but suggested that Everson keep on writing. He did. But in 1936 the pulp market was declining, partly because soft cover books were enjoying greater popularity. After living on 80 cents a day in the woods, a sudden and serious family illness resulted in hospital bills that ran to $12,000 a year.

In Montreal, Everson was offered two law partnerships, but needed more money. He took a job with a PR firm instead. By 1938 he was president. It sounds a bit like Horatio Alger, if there's anyone still left alive who remembers the old Alger "strive and succeed" books. If he'd joined the army, I expect he'd have become a field marshal by the age of 34.

It should be mentioned that PR in Everson's case meant something different from the usual public relations of industry. Everson's firm advised various industries as to corporate conduct, management, philosophy and efficiency, ranging all the way to the sexual conduct of senior directors.

During the last war, Everson worked for William Stephenson,

the Canadian spymaster, who was also a preceptor of the US Central Intelligence Agency. Not cloak-and-dagger stuff, but discreet intelligence gathering in Everson's own familiar industrial areas.

The poet-lawyer-PR man retired in 1963 at the age of 59, selling his own shares in Johnston, Everson and Charlesworth. "I continued," he says, "to have an office address as chairman of another firm until 1966. That was partly in order to have someone to type my poems." Surely one of the oddest reasons ever for remaining a company chairman.

In 1970 the *Selected Poems*, published by Delta, was nominated for the Montreal Prize. It didn't win. The same book was also nominated for the American Book Award. However, the author was eliminated when he refused to apply for US citizenship. No doubt that information, coming from Everson, is somewhat tongue-in-cheek, though accurate. It reminds me of Bliss Carman and C.G.D. Roberts, passing for American citizens despite the northern colour of their skins.

On a more personal note, Everson has been married for over 52 years to the same wife. He lives about half the year in Montreal, the other half due south of the last snowbank.

I could end by listing the things that Everson is not: shy and retiring, humble and unassuming, latecomer into print, etc. I'd rather emphasize what he actually is: someone who has written most of his life, and has changed himself, transformed himself from being merely a good writer to being one of high excellence.

He's still an odd combination of qualities, a back-concession puritan living in a big city, formal and at the same time pretty comfortable with language, his mind shifting easily back and forth between past and present like a time machine. In some ways the eternal amateur, he is a wide-ranging reader of books, much given to moral judgments, insatiably curious about this world and the larger universe.

Everson's memory is enormous, capacious as a Pentagon computer. Sitting in the back seat of his car, listening to a flood of information, echoes shuttling madly around the tin box, helpless to interrupt and not really wanting to—that is an unforgettable experience. I have heard, for instance, a minute and detailed recital of Admiral John Byng's behaviour prior to being executed in 1757 for backwardness in battle. It occurs to me that the Québécois slogan, *Je me souviens*, which reminds them of their own lost battle on the Plains of Abraham—that slogan is even more appropriate to Ron Everson.

The work has dignity. It is exemplified for me, especially, in certain favourite poems. "Over the Orkneys" is still as humanly magnificent as when I read it first, feeling wave after wave of stubborn Orkneymen climbing through my own blood. "The Throwback Voice," by contrast, is impossible to read without both inner and outer selves grinning aloud. And in "Haycocks" I have fallen asleep among new-mown hay, waking to feel an emotion "mystical and unexplained as Asia."

Proteus? Certainly not Everson. The most important thing about him: he is singular and he is original, a poet of high excellence.

*(1983)*

# Earle Birney

## *The Creative Writer*

NINETEEN SIXTY-SIX HAS BEEN a good year for Earle Birney. His *Selected Poems* appeared in the spring, focusing the full panorama of a lifetime's work between the covers of one book. In July a musical play, based on the novel, *Turvey*, was produced at the Charlottetown Summer Festival. And now seven of Birney's radio "talks" have been published by CBC, entitled *The Creative Writer* .

The book is a compendium of the author's attitudes towards everything from the creative process itself to the education of a writer. The chapters are not literary essays in a conventional sense, each with a point to hammer home (although they do have points), and there is nothing of preaching or forcible imposition of the writer's own opinions. And the book's origin as radio talks for the "listening pleasure" of the general public is plainly visible in its simplicity and "openness" to anyone who wants to let Birney's speaking voice flow into his mind.

And yet the book's simplicity is partly an illusion. The subjects discussed are not simple or easily resolved, in fact are frequently controversial, which means that the writing is an object lesson in good prose—interesting, easily understood, and presenting ideas whose depths require further mental sounding on the part of the reader (or listener).

Well, what does Earle Birney think about creative writing courses, for instance? As might be expected, since he headed such a department for several years at UBC, Birney approves—with reservations. But: "he [the creative writer] should not stay around after graduation, however many of his fellow artists are there in academic chains around him."

Of course the writer of those words has stayed around universities himself, though one is inclined to let him off this self-created hook because he has somehow escaped or transcended the "academic chains" of his own warnings. And one cannot imagine Earle Birney shackled or gagged in any sense.

In his first chapter Birney deals with "Reasons and Unreasons for Poetry"—both the objective value of having poetry at all, and personal reasons for writing the stuff. Since poetry seems to me its own objective justification, Birney's thoughts on the poet's compulsions seem more interesting. Among them, the habit, like a drug habit or collecting postage stamps and match folders. And there is the additional reason of not knowing what your thoughts are, about almost anything, until you get them down on paper.

Birney himself, he tells us in Chapter II, writes as a form of exorcism for some experience or thought in his own past. He describes the genesis and reasons for writing three of his poems: "The Bear on the Delhi Road" (partly guilt); "Aluroid" (he was haunted by the drama of a living cliché); and most fascinating of all to myself, "Bushed." Once I wrote a 1,500-word analysis of "Bushed," describing it as primarily a poem of personal change, internal metamorphosis from the outside. Now Birney tells us it is a simple description of the mental processes of an old trapper who went bush-crazy from too much solitude. All my complicated explication gone down the drain! I am double-crossed and literarily betrayed!

But elsewhere in the book Birney says something to the effect that the mental processes of a poet work in such a way as to make the reader aware of all sorts of allusions, symbols, inferences, and interpretations that he (the poet) may not have been thinking about when he wrote the poem: i.e., if you see something different in the poem than I put into it, then your vision is still valid 20-20. Or, if you saw only my vision, that's all right too. Therefore, I (the reviewer) may still insist that "Bushed" is about personal change. "Only among other things!"—I hear Birney interject in his most magisterial voice.

"A poem, a painting, always requires all, more than all, the maker has—." In other words, the ordinary self of the poet couldn't have written the poem. But for a little while, during composition, the writer is somewhat more than himself; brief flashing thoughts occur to him, that must be committed to paper immediately; he is stretched to his limits, has become very different from his ordinary self, which may be a university prof., a social worker, or a bank clerk. And this is no sooner consciously realized than the experience is gone.

Birney also discusses experimentalism (including the Black Mountain boys and "found poems"), the feasibility of a writer having his wife support him (temporarily), and the vicissitudes of writing his novel, *Turvey*. It seems that a real "Mr. Turvey" turned up to paint Birney's house, a man who possessed some of the fictional Turvey's background. And then the publisher nearly went crazy, wanting to get "Mr. Turvey" to sign legal waivers precluding a future lawsuit.

Fortunately I disagree with Earle Birney on one or two factual points. If I didn't this review might sound like a Hollywood eulogy for the genius of the great dead Sam Goldwyn. Birney says: "—nobody reads the lyrics of the Hittities and the Sumerians, because they are crumbled into non-existence." Well, *The Epic of Gilgamesh* is admittedly narrative, but I think it also includes lyricism. And so do the god-myths of Sumer, in Henri Frankfort's *Before Philosophy*.

And re prose-writers being only that, and poets narrowly poets: "—the tradition is that Callaghan, Gabrielle Roy, MacLennan, Richler, and so on, write what is called prose, while Souster, Anne Hébert, Acorn, Purdy, etc., write what is called verse, and never does one species whistle in the other's territory." While the generality may be true, the specific instances, apart from Souster, are not. Anne Hébert has written short stories, among them being "The House on the Esplanade"; Acorn has written many short stories, and I myself perhaps a hundred plays, among them being a dramatization of Birney's own poem, "David." But in general I suppose the point is true.

And the general thesis of this book certainly holds true: that in a continuing age of war, radicalism, abuse of individual freedom, increasing conformity, the writer and artist can hold up a mirror to humanity and advocate sanity by portraying insanity. And yet, Birney insists, the writer is not a preacher or a man with a mission. He serves his own peculiar gods, iconoclast though he may be in other respects.

Towards the end of his book Birney says: "Personally, I want to be a creative man, not a bee nor a rat nor a grizzly nor a mouse. Which means that I strive, in this herding age, to remain a cayuse, an unbroken horse, who will have to be dragged, or ridden and broken to arrive at the roundup or the horse butcher's. I'll even settle for the role of the coyote, that lonely yapping ornery stinking enduring snooty creature, that wild-to-hell-with-conformity dog, that prototype of the damn-you-general critter we call a writer—howling alone, yet hoping to hear one other yip-yip start up over the next hill." Which is pretty dramatic, but I don't think he overstates his case.

And beyond all this, past such personal credos, on the other side of talk, remains the puzzling paradoxical as-yet-unwritten-down Birney, perhaps a cipher even to himself, still working on his ideas and still examining and re-examining his own entrails; from the perspective of both floor and ceiling, trying to decide what everything means, if it means anything. And with the death of any of us unlikely to be more than fifty or sixty years away, the question still seems important.

*(1967)*

∞
# Afterword to *Turvey*

WHEN I WAS TWENTY-ONE AND TWENTY-TWO years old, I'd reluctantly wake up early every morning and hear—"DAH-DAH—DAH–DAH–DAH . . ." It was the Royal Canadian Air Force band at Trenton Air Base playing "Colonel Bogey" on the parade square. It was the same tune to which many thousands of servicemen marched over dirt roads and highways during the Second World War. And many survivors of that war can probably hear it in their minds still.

I loved that sound, the quick staccato "DAH-DAH." It seeped into your blood and guts like overproof whiskey. "DAH-DAH," and winter was over, spring arrived. I loved the music, but hated the military.

R52768, that was me, Aircraftsman 2nd class, A. Purdy, from January 10, 1940 until July 1945; nearly six years. During those years I changed from a boy to more-or-less a man. Many things happened to me, a lot of them funny. But I didn't appreciate their humour until much later.

And what has all this to do with Private Thomas Leadbeater Turvey, Earle Birney's literary creation? Well, quite a lot, actually. You see, I am Turvey.

I know, I know—my name is different; and Birney didn't model his accident-prone hero on me. But my age would be about the same if T.L. Turvey had survived into 1989. My character and temperament, however, are very different from Turvey's. Nevertheless, I insist that I am Turvey.

In writing his novel, Earle Birney included a few of his own adventures: Birney was a personnel officer during the war, like those he described administering torture tests to his novel's hero. He read recruits' dossiers; looked into their heads; and knew what happened to them before and during, although not after, their military service.

Birney was there; he knew what he was talking about.

When I first read *Turvey* years ago, I thought yeah, it's kinda funny, things that happened to Turvey. And I thought: when all those similar things happened to me, they weren't a damn bit funny. In fact, I thought they were downright solemn, almost tragic. This wasn't some cardboard recreation of a comic hero, this was me, this was real life, this was earnest.

But reading *Turvey* now, Aircraftsman 2nd class A. Purdy wears that old uniform again, the fancy blue one with brass buttons instead of Turvey's shit-brown battle dress. And Colonel Bogey is loud in my ears; my toes wriggle with it.

Somebody out of time yells, "Prisoner and escort, 'Foh-wahd mah!'" I march, laif-rye-laif-rye into the OC's office, a hatless prisoner. And scared.

"Prisoner and escort, 'Ha-h-h'!" (That means halt.)

It was not a damn bit funny. The Officer Commanding said, "Will you accept my punishment?" (For whatever it was.)

(That non-flying flight loony's tone was dolorous as an undertaker burying his best friend without charge. I had visions of being locked away from the light for years.)

"Yessir," I said.

"You are hereby reduced in rank to corporal," the OC said. (I had been acting sergeant.)

Lo and behold it was so.

Somewhat later, another OC said the same thing, and I was

reduced in rank farther down; then successively into the depths, to LAC, AC1, AC2, and lower still. After I had expiated my sins, somewhat depressed in spirit after these swift descents, I was permitted outside the military base. On the streets of Trenton, encountering a drunken civilian, I saluted him.

Turvey was faced with a very similar Officer Commanding when his rank was acting corporal. And at one time he almost became an officer. I too was almost an officer. I took the air crew medical, thinking, "Gee whiz, I'm gonna be an officer"—amid visions of the sexy girls my wings insignia would doubtless attract. The prosodic strains of "The Flying Instructor's Lament,"

> What did you do in the war, daddy,
> How did you help us to win?
> Circuits and bumps and turns, laddie,
> And how to get out of a spin . . .

rang in my head along with Colonel Bogey. Alas, Turvey's, I mean Purdy's, blood pressure shot sky-high at the thought of leaving the surly bonds of earth. The excitement aroused by my prospective adventures had been too much for me. Later, I took the air crew medical again, with the same result. Afterwards, my blood pressure went back to normal.

On guard duty late at night, Turvey shoots a German paratrooper with his Sten gun. But it turns out that the German Turvey shot was his own greatcoat he'd hung on a fence and forgotten about. The greatcoat was, of course, ruined by the bullet holes.

I had a similar experience. And it's true, not Earle Birney's fiction. I swear it's true. Here's the scene. I'm on guard duty at #2 Equipment Depot in Vancouver, the Burrard Viaduct looming overhead, wartime traffic scanty late at night. Below the Burrard bridge another much smaller one, for streetcars crossing False Creek. I march back and forth on the RCAF dock, now less than a civilian, and bored out of my skin.

In oily water below the dock, a gaggle of ducks were quacking about how nice it was to be a duck and not to be shot at. On sudden impulse, I lifted my Sten gun and it went "rat-a-tat-tat" as Sten guns do. Water splattered. Bridge traffic continued. The ducks just sat there, didn't fly away, trying to decide if there was any danger. Of course they were in no danger. The marksmanship of R52768, AC2 Purdy was lamentable, as instructors had often pointed out.

Reading *Turvey* again, I am mesmerized by the account of how Turvey went AW. Loose in Buffalo—where, through diligent application of the requisite equipment, he kept two female employees of the Earthquake Aircraft Company busily happy on the swing shift. Punishment, two days confined to barracks. Very mild punishment, I think. Since I did not have a kindly author in charge of me, my own awards were never less than a week's CB.

Turvey searches for his friend Mac, a member of the Kootenay Highlanders and eventually finds him. Turvey urinates on an army major's head, having taken a wrong turn in the barracks at midnight. Turvey imbibes a little too freely at an English pub, then finds himself trapped in the middle of a minefield late at night. Turvey is quarantined for diptheria. The guy is accident-prone, but survives all mishaps, always swims and never sinks. Me, I sank.

There was the time I was posted from #9 Construction and Maintenance Unit, Vancouver, to Woodcock in northern British Columbia. I had been married not long before, and being extremely uxorious in the early days of nuptials, yearned for my absent wife.

At Woodcock, we were building an airfield in expectation of imminent Japanese invasion. My sergeant there was one Jackson, an ex-typewriter mechanic. (That's his real name.) He was a miserable s.o.b. I made friends with another guy, Leo LeBlanc (that's his real name too), and pulled every string I could think of to get back to Vancouver with my wife.

I wrote letters to a flight sergeant in the #9 CMU orderly room, requesting return posting to Vancouver on compassionate grounds. I wrote my wife, asking her to apply for a travel warrant, a free RCAF ticket, enabling her to take a train from Vancouver to Woodcock in order to soothe my subcutaneous wifeless membranes.

In the meantime, Leo LeBlanc and I rode the freights to Hazelton on the Skeena River, to drink beer in the frontier town. And the great mountains loomed overhead, surrounding us like picture postcards propped vertically in circular splendour. Eagles surveyed their kingdom; only man was vile; and I do mean Sergeant Jackson.

Requests to my flight sergeant friend for return posting to Vancouver, my injunctions to spouse to get a travel warrant and fly to my arms in Woodcock—both bore fruit simultaneously. She and I passed each other going in opposite directions, about halfway between Woodcock and Vancouver. And she liked it at Woodcock, got a job as a waitress in the airmen's mess, and refused to return despite my womanless detumescent condition.

I have, I hope, made my point. *I am Turvey.* Not exactly the cheerful and rather naive character in Birney's book but nevertheless a completely authentic version of Turvey's reverse image. Yet I wasn't always sweet-natured and cheerful. Oh, no! Over those nearly six years of military servitude I became a dour and depressed loser, the guy on the sidewalk with his chin scraping the gutter. I saluted civilians. I was less than the least. As I remember that time, only Colonel Bogey remains sweet and nostalgic.

When I say I'm Turvey, it's as another dimension of that grinning creation of Earle Birney's. For how could you write a novel about Turvey or Schweik as depressive characters? Even James Jones and Norman Mailer didn't do that in their supposedly realistic war novels. Nevertheless, Turvey is real; except for the small cavil that he didn't change a bit through all his adventures, the timeless episodes of war.

Those six years of Armageddon are now seen from a distance; events are fixed and unchanging. They involve all of us, soldiers, sailors, and airmen, who went through the war. And our laughter at Turvey is reminiscent laughter at ourselves. Those ex-servicemen— except for Sergeant Jackson—they are all Turveys too.

George Woodcock has observed that *Turvey* is a "poet's novel." I guess he meant one of those strange books that hover on the far edge of reality, a dream in words. Along with *Turvey*, he mentioned Herbert Read's *The Green Child* and Alain Fournier's *Le Grand Meaulnes*. I don't agree. Despite the laughter, there is nothing of childhood and dreams in *Turvey*, as there was in those other two books. One does not fail to see men dying in World War II and all the wars since then, in Afghanistan and Nicaragua and Vietnam. Reality supersedes the image.

But Colonel Bogey sounds in my ears. What an irony for me to have all my blood stir with music as I read the book. Now birds build their nests in springtime. The world renews itself annually. And "DAH-DAH" goes that music, as it will again and again, as Birney and Turvey knew it would.

*(1989)*

## ∾
# Introduction to *Last Makings*

I'VE KNOWN EARLE BIRNEY since the early 1950s. A young genius named Curt Lang and I scraped acquaintance by writing provocative letters to him; and also to Edmund Wilson and Roy Campbell. I'd been reading Wilson's masterly criticism and mentioned my feelings about it. I received a card back, a printed form signed by Wilson that said Mr. Wilson does not do this and does not do that, leaving me wondering what he actually did do. Later, reading his memoirs of the twenties and thirties, I realize he kept pretty busy, getting married three times (I think it was three), and of course writing many books.

The letter sent to Roy Campbell was to the effect that now he was getting older he wouldn't be able to continue all the adventurous things he'd done in the past. Curt and I got a letter back listing everything he'd accomplished in the past year. It was truly incredible. I guess we'd touched some kind of nerve in Campbell's ego.

I can't remember what I said to Birney, but he too replied, inviting both Curt and me for lunch at UBC where he was teaching. Of course we went, and were rather tongue-tied facing Birney's tremendous vitality and a flow of energy strong enough to gag Mount St. Helens.

Both of us knew his poems well. But it was "Bushed," "Vancouver Lights," and "David" that made the most impression on me. "David" has received and merited a great deal of attention since. A few years ago I dramatized it into a half-hour radio play. And I believe Dorothy Livesay in her criticism as much as accused Birney of pushing his friend off that mountain. (The implication was very annoying to him.) The other two poems mentioned—well, I actually felt a bit reverent about them, sometimes repeating several lines to myself from "Vancouver Lights": can even remember the last part now without looking it up: "O stranger/Plutonian, beast in the crouching night/there was light." But I'd better look it up anyway. Okay, add "descendant" and make it "stretching night." Well, I was close.

Birney was always careful and solicitous about the welfare and encouragement of his students. (This attitude contrasted somewhat with my own feelings when I was writer-in-rez at various halls of learning. I thought few of the students really wanted criticism: all wanted to be called geniuses!) But this solicitude of Birney's was an active concern of his, a thing he practised.

One occasion sticks in my mind. I was in Vancouver, sleeping at a friend's apartment while the friend was off somewhere skiing. And in the morning heard a steady, persistent knocking at the door. It was Earle, and he wanted me to go with him down the street to his student's apartment. It seems this student in his creative writing class, a foreign exchange student at UBC, had not shown up that morning. And from various things she had told him about her husband, Earle thought he might be keeping her prisoner at their apartment, not allowing her to escape him on that bright autumn day.

I wasn't sure why my own presence was necessary in this possibly harmless domestic dispute, but Earle seemed to think so. Anyway, I was rushed into clothes and off we went—"just down the street."

A few minutes later, Birney knocked on their apartment door several times. No answer. Then we called on the superintendent, Earle explaining that he felt responsible for this student of his. She was a foreigner, and very young; there was a fatherly, avuncular, and trustworthy note in Birney's voice as he spoke. And I'm sure the super, facing this imposing professor of English, felt something close to awe, was almost flattered that his help was being sought.

The superintendent unlocked the apartment door with his master key. It was chainlocked from the inside. Birney talked through the narrow opening, calling softly to his student inside. Both she and her husband emerged. The girl, very tall, was wearing a housecoat. She and Birney talked in low tones, while I stood with her husband off to one side.

The husband was quite large and husky, wearing those white pyjamas ju-jitsu practitioners affect. He looked at me; I looked at him. He shrugged; I shrugged; we kept our faces expressionless. But I felt slightly embarrassed by this time, wondering what I'd gotten into. And Birney? He'd achieved his purpose, making sure his student was free to come to his classes.

What does all this have to do with Earle Birney's poetry? Well, I think it indicates strongly that he takes responsibility in both life and literature. Social responsibility, you could call it, and exemplified by his friendship and admiration for Leon Trotsky, the fugitive Russian revolutionary, before the last war. And by his personal sacrifices in that same war, from which he emerged with the rank of major.

The really wondrous thing about Birney—leaving his personality aside—is craft. And I know that sounds a bit mundane. But I mean CRAFT. He can take the most ordinary subject-thing and make it into a verse of nearly passionate interest. How? Through juxtapositions, word play, enjambments, images, and endings that circle back to something said at the beginning, and thereby often make the whole poem meaningful. But that attempt to analyze his methods says very little, because, in the end, I don't know how he does it.

"Still Life Near Bangalore" ends with a question. I'm not sure what the answer to that question is and am not very interested anyway. From my view the real point to the poem is the completely fascinating "Still Life" itself. Sure, there are a lot more questions scattered through the poem; and I think the two-line question at the beginning has been added since I first read the poem several years ago. But what interests me are descriptions like: "Behind each slatey team an almost naked/human beast, bareheaded, breached with rags" describing a ploughman near Bangalore.

Other readers will, of course, find those questions of more interest than I do. To me, the poem is transport provided by Birney into Bangalore itself, the smells, the workmen, the talking women, the geography of an almost dream. And despite the exoticism of a far eastern country, mere description is often mundane: Birney makes it fascinating.

I should probably talk about only the poems included in this collection, at least that seems to me to be the general idea of writing an intro or preface for someone's book. But this is Birney's last book of poems. And he has been a very large presence in Canada, one that extends backward in time, and into the future, for I'm sure that his work will remain alive for a long time to come. My admiration for him also reaches out in many directions.

Acting as a critic (which I am certainly not), I believe his judgment of other people's work has been both relentless and kind. He went out of his way to help younger writers. I believe, in fact, that the creative writing course he established at UBC was the first one in Canada. There was also that aforementioned responsibility to his students, and kindness to young writers. Earle has always been a man with passionate feelings for his own country, and at the same time his is a world view that encompasses all creation.

Does that seem to be saying a great deal—far too much? Am I being carried away on behalf of a friend? If it appears that way, then let me say also that he was both curmudgeonly and magnificent, close with money and wildly generous at the same time. A human being, that is. I have to explain that occasional past tense by mentioning that Birney suffered a serious illness four years ago, one that left him severely incapacitated.

Years ago, when I was struggling with machines in a Vancouver mattress factory, there were Birney poems that stiffened my spine. The previously mentioned "Vancouver Lights." The strange world of "Mappemounde" with medieval sailors sailing off the world's edge. The same poem's "That sea is hight Time/it hems hearts' landtrace"— over which, much later, I disagreed with his addition of "*all* hearts' landtrace," which served to touch every emotional base. I claimed the extra word wasn't needed. And "Bushed," that most Canadian of poems, in which the forest imprints itself on a man's brain as a country itself lives in human genes.

And now, in these "last makings," we traverse with Birney the long climb from childhood to young man and maturity and middle age to—quite old (although Earle was such a *bounding* man that decrepitude always seemed foreign to him). And travel by limey freighter to Grimsby, England, in a sequence of poems that has the later Birney's scrambled-egg-words exemplifying his never-leave-em-alone work habits. And we linger over the sky and sea and mountain landscapes that spell British Columbia. As I look again at "Buoy off Juan de Fuca," I notice that I scribbled *WOW!* on first reading it in my copy of the book. His love poems, and one about a girl's toes. Toes? Yes, toes. One

    so clean and succulent
    so tiny
    it's no toe at all
    but a spare nipple    ummmm
    ("i should have begun with your toes")

Well?

Three versions of "Ellesmereland" and another three of "Canada: Case History," the last trio also demonstrating something of the Birney method and movement from then to now.

There are many poems to Wailan:

being twenty-seven she believes
I can keep the sap alive
even at seventy-two

after three days
the blossoms wreathe our floor

("Fall in Spring")

These Wailan poems are enchanting. They don't *seem* to be that way, they are. In some sense the whole book is Wailan, for Wailan, and of Wailan. Poems for her birthday, poems any day and all days. For her. The love of one being for another: and what else is there?—to paraphrase a certain blue-footed booby I once knew. Wailan on her 26th, 27th, 29th, and if you know Earle, you count them off until

& never tell me it's time
that i'm to die
or she's to leave me

("My Love is Young")

but we do, dammit, we all do!

And this piece becomes my own farewell to Birney. I remember him best when he was at his best; striding the streets of Charlottetown when his picaresque novel, *Turvey*, was adapted into a musical play by Don Harron and Norman Campbell. You'd have thought he was twenty years younger than I instead of nearly twenty years older, the way he had to stop and encourage my wife and me to keep going. (Our tongues were hanging out at the pace he set.) And one time, disagreeing over whether to take a cab or streetcar from Church Street to Spadina Avenue in Toronto: "For chrissake, Earle, I'll pay for the cab!" "That's not the point, Al. You're liable to want a beer later and need the money you spent on the cab."

Something quite magnificent about him at times; not phony, not the sort of guy who prepared "a face to meet the faces that you meet." A man joined to the texture of what he wrote about, Wailan, his country, the world.

*(1991)*

# F.R. Scott
## *The Dance is One*

FRANK SCOTT IS HIS OWN MAN AND, as Milton Wilson said in the *University of Toronto Quarterly*: "He's one of the few poets I could sit down and read at any time and at any place." I agree. It's a pleasure to read him, and superlatives of praise or blame are unnecessary.

The essence of Scott's literary credo is that he wants to be understood. At least that's an important point in his own mind. Years ago he asked me how I understood one of his poems called, "For Brian Priestman." I didn't understand his intent, therefore he intended to change the poem's subtitle. Which surprised me—that a poet should pay any attention at all to somebody else's interpretation of his poems. But more than that, I learned something: it isn't shameful to be understood nor is there necessarily a loss of literary integrity. Before that incident I had been writing private poems. Two weeks after their composition I had difficulty understanding them myself; 15 years later I can't.

Just below the top rank of poets are a great number not recognized as being in these upper echelons. They're all over the place, in any country you want to name: England has Larkin and Hughes, the US Bly and Lowell. In some ways I'd rather read Larkin, Hughes, Bly, Lowell and Scott than those with big literary reputations. Such poets, and Scott particularly, are not continually straining, as some certainly are, with war-club adjectives, to knock your reading glasses off and make you murmur in tense soliloquy, "Eternal truths have been revisited to me through this man."

Among Scott's equipment is sardonic humour (the cutting

chuckle-kind, not the jokesmith clown's); and while not a confession poet, he does not shrink from opening some aspects of his personal life. As others have remarked about him so many times, he has a keen sense of social criticism. And urbanity, which is perhaps rare these days. As well, technique and craft, an interesting mind, aspects of a poet who is rarely monotonous.

Of course I can't prove any of these things without quoting the whole book, in all its variety. And that's impossible. But I will make a positive statement about one of the poems, "On Saying Goodbye to My Room in Chancellor Day Hall." It's a good, good poem, and I'd love to have written it. I quote the first verse, which absolutely doesn't prove my point about Scott:

> Rude and rough men are invading my sanctuary.
> They are carting away all my books and papers.
> My pictures are stacked in an ugly pile in the corner.
> There is murder in my cathedral.

I think: dear, dear; the poor boy, those rude and rough men, it really is dreadful of them! The sheer desecration; I should live to see the day! And that litref to Eliot! And worse, the whole thing sounds like an echo of John Glassco's "The Burden of Junk."

But there are ten verses. Few images, but some good metaphors, if one can separate the two. And you know, the damn thing adds up, makes a poem, in fact makes one of the best poems I've read since the last time I was too scornful of anybody. What I thought was a bad beginning (and I swear it is a bad beginning) is typical Scott, part of his stately idiosyncrasy, method, skill and subtlety. I might even think he anticipated a reader like me, who would say exactly what I've said. And then double-crossed me.

The Dance has a lot of variety, including a sentimental love poem ("Question") that one hardly forgives in such a cynical worldly-wise public man as Scott. (What's that bit from Yeats: "A sixty-year-old smiling public man?" Well Scott was 94 last birthday.) The point is, he can change gears and surprise you, and the surprise is like a douche of good rye whiskey.

Also included is the poem sequence, "Letters from the Macken-zie River." Oh migawd, I think not another paean to our glorious US exploited North. Well, it is—and it isn't. A kind of travel diary, without the abiding curse of dullness connected to that term. And here again, it's difficult to quote. It's the whole, not the parts. But a man with a sense of history wrote it, a man with fine command of stripped-down language. The poem says "It's a lonely life for me now/ I tried to get along with the missus/ But she made my life a hell . . . " If you thought Scott was speaking with his own voice you might say shit; but he's quoting. After the quote Scott himself says, "Outside the Slave rolled on/ Farther and farther from home." No hell, but a good contrast. The poem-sequence ends with a line about the big river: "In a land so bleak and bare/ a single plume of smoke/ is a scroll of history."

And a bunch of translations. Some I like, some I don't. But in either case, I would bet my like or dislike is because of the original author, not Scott's translation.

I suppose that—like George Woodcock—I dislike and distrust politicians. In many ways Scott has always been one of those. Others have written poem after poem about him. I've never understood their reasons, nor felt the least inclination to rhapsodize the man. Because what he writes himself is far better than anything written about him. Sure, along with his admiring poem-writers, I admire him too, applaud things he has done. (Among them: being at least partially responsible for breaking Duplessis' padlock law; his writing and social philosophy strongly influencing the original CCF credo, the Regina Manifesto...) He is the 98-year-old smiling public man, and seems to have been here forever.

But I don't mean to make the guy sound perfect, or even close to it—a strong danger in writing about a poet you admire. Scott won't "shake the reader with storms of uncontrollable emotion or intellectual insanity," or anything like that. What he will do is that rare thing, make you feel like he did when he wrote the poems. Not a politician's craft or sullen art. Not really. But the poems of a man who has lived a long and full life; and communicated it admirably. Ruminating jealously, I say: What couldn't I have written if I'd lived a life like that? But it's his.

*(1973)*

∞

# Sandra Djwa's *The Politics of the Imagination, A Life of F.R. Scott*

H
E WAS A TALL MAN, ABOUT SIX FEET THREE INCHES. And he had stature, not just height. His self-composure settled a cloak of calm over everything. It was almost impossible to be excited around him for very long. And when I say "self-composure," I mean the same sort of ambience that Doug Harvey, the old Montreal Canadiens' defenceman, used to have. Harvey would dominate a hockey game, in the sense that he forced it into the speed and pace he wanted it to take. Frank Scott had the same sort of ambience, a calm in which he was at the centre, affable, humorous and gracious: a presence I found fascinating, and questioned in my own mind as to why this should be so.

He was a Canadian aristocrat, of course, the son of Canon Frederick George Scott, a Canadian hero in World War I. Leaving out the aristocracy of money, Scott was a member of the aristocracy in which you *feel* that quality about the other person, which is no more explainable than giving reasons why you like someone else, or why you fell in love. You just feel it, and it's so.

He dressed like the generation just before mine. That means grey flannels and generally darker apparel. He always wore a tie, and there was always a touch of formality about him. But once or twice, I am sure, I've seen him in a smoking jacket. Of course he smoked a pipe. It was sort of like that long cigarette holder Franklin Roosevelt affected in newsreels. It gave Scott the Rhodes Scholar look, which was accurate but nevertheless a bit misleading.

There were gatherings—you couldn't call them parties exactly—at the Clarke Avenue residence. There were reasons for them. They generally celebrated something, including friendship. Frank and Marian Scott as host and hostess are at least partly responsible for my definition of that word. In their sixties and seventies, Frank with a somewhat uncanny gaze seen from the wrong angle (he had an artificial eye, the legacy of a boyhood accident); Marian just as imperturbable as Frank, and gracious in a way that made you feel at ease. And you said to yourself, am I living in another era than my own? Uncanny as Frank's glass eye, the good manners, the graciousness, the friendship of these dwellers in another world.

But they weren't from another world! Migawd, Frank Scott wrote poems! Marian painted pictures! But I felt privileged to know them. Along with Irving and Betty Layton and Louis Dudek, the Scotts were my own introduction to how interesting life can be, my transition from one level of existence to another. Something in the back of my mind whispered: throw away all your preconceptions? No, not all, but a lot of them. And at the time I met the Scotts, I was changing myself, into and being someone I can't keep track of, who sometimes blurted out uncomfortable things or thoughts. They saw me in one of those incarnations and said Hello.

Frank's father, the Reverend F.G. Scott, was rector of St. Matthew's Anglican Church in Quebec City at century's turn. Tall and athletic, he had rescued a man from drowning, preached to Canadian troops on their way to the Boer War, and later, in his mid-fifties, he was chaplain in the Canadian Army during World War I. And Canon Scott wrote poetry, sometimes stopping acquaintances on the street in Quebec City to hand them little cards with copies of his latest poem. There were seven children, only one girl. Frank was the second youngest, born in 1899, one of the last Victorians. The family was dominated by religion, strong patriotism and poetry. One of Frank's earliest memories: "Father would come rushing out of the study calling to the family, 'I have written a new poem! Amy! Amy! Children! Come and hear!'" It's a matter of some wonder to me that Frank didn't grow up to hate the stuff!

However, there's little doubt that this family upbringing, containing unequal parts of religion, poetry, duty and patriotism, instilled in Frank Scott the desire to excel. At age 20 he wrote, "So far I have done nothing to justify my existence." At 21 he applied for a Rhodes Scholarship, and was successful. At Oxford, away from a dominating father and older brother William, Frank began to come out of his shell socially; and he read omnivorously, including H.G. Wells, Thomas à Kempis and Rupert Brooke, and was even more obsessed with "doing something great."

After Oxford, Scott was involved with A.J.M. Smith, Leon Edel and two others, all students at McGill. They published the *McGill*

*Fortnightly Review*, a literary magazine funded principally by its editors. And the editors enjoyed themselves, satirizing McGill stodginess in poems and editorials, raising university hackles in the process. Smith, who had a fairly intimate knowledge of modern poetry, told Scott to throw away his own stuff and write some more. Scott did. And along with the poems of Abraham Klein, also in Montreal, this era in the early 1920s may be regarded as the beginning of modern poetry in Canada.

In 1924 Scott joined the law faculty at McGill. He remained there forty years. At McGill his interest grew in social problems and the intricacies of municipal and national politics. Climbing Mount Greylock in Massachusetts during an academic conference there in 1931, Scott, Frank Underhill and Percy Corbett laid the foundations of the "League For Social Reconstruction." Ann Moreau, in the Scott issue of *Brick* Magazine (1987), says that "Scott and Harry Cassidy went around to all the little towns and villages of Quebec, including Ste. Rose, and he discovered that in the clothing industry women were earning wages of about four cents an hour at that time, which he found upsetting." (I suppose the understatement is deliberate.) Scott and Cassidy published a report on this situation.

He had met J.S. Woodsworth, the social activist, earlier, and was impressed. When the Regina Manifesto of the CCF was written in 1935, Scott, Frank Underhill and several others joined in its writing. And here also I am rather puzzled. Eugene Forsey (also an early socialist) says in *Brick* that the Regina Manifesto "was written I think largely by Frank Scott and Frank Underhill." And while Sandra Djwa does mention Scott's involvement, that involvement is not nearly to the extent implied by Forsey.

In 1936 Scott and Arthur Smith (the latter then teaching in the US) edited *New Provinces*, an anthology meant to sweep away the old romanticism and sentimentality of the Carman-Roberts-Campbell school of poetry. But all sorts of hassles grew out of this book. E.J. Pratt, a staunch traditionalist himself, objected to Smith's introduction. Scott hurriedly wrote another one, in order not to offend Pratt, on whose sales popularity their own anthology depended. When dust settled and the book was published, very few copies were sold anyway. Nevertheless, *New Provinces* remains, rather more than a milestone on the way to a distinctive Canadian literature.

In 1942 a young Englishman, Patrick Anderson, emigrated to Canada to avoid the wartime draft in his home country. Anderson was a student of W.H. Auden, Spencer and Day-Lewis, and brought the Dylan Thomas rhythms to Montreal. Anderson and his wife, Scott, Neufville Shaw, Bruce Ruddick, P.K. Page and A.M. Klein united to start another little magazine, *Preview*.

Irving Layton, Louis Dudek, Audrey Aikman and John Sutherland were stimulated enough to set up a rival magazine, *First Statement*. The *Preview* group of poets was thought to be cultured and cosmopolitan, and admired British poetry; the *First Statement* people were crude by comparison, somewhat visceral, and admired US poetry. When *Preview* seemed to lose energy at war's end, the two older magazines merged into a new one, *Northern Review*. And trouble began at once. As Djwa describes it, during a literary get-together at Scott's place the old *First Statement* people were ushered into the kitchen for food, and the ex-*Preview* group into the more posh dining room. Earle Birney, who had been a teetotaler, took his first drink of Scotch in six months and became very ill. Irving Layton then claimed that Birney was a drunkard. It must have been a great party. Marian Scott writes, "How could you call us 'gracious' if we were capable of such outrageous behaviour!! As I remember it, everyone met in the living room for discussion—refreshments were on the table in the 'posh'! dining room so that people could wander back and forth; as there was some disagreement between the two groups, probably some or all of the *First Statement* members may have gone into the kitchen to discuss things—and that was maybe how the myth was born??" (Personal letter, June 1988).

On his way to becoming an establishment figure himself, long before the end of his life, Frank Scott managed to offend and/or antagonize many of the entrenched and privileged stuffed shirts he encountered along the way. He spoke out loud and clear on literally dozens of issues, municipal, provincial and national. Sir Arthur Currie, McGill principal and Canadian commanding general in World War I, was extremely worried at the very idea of his university being involved in politics. As a result of this sinful interest on Scott's part, he was denied the job of Dean of Law at McGill for many years.

Premier Duplessis of Quebec was also a Scott antagonist. Duplessis objected to Montreal restaurant owner Frank Roncarelli supplying bail for Jehovah's Witnesses in their occasional brushes with the law. He also objected strongly to the religious sect itself. Duplessis had Roncarelli's liquor license cancelled, which meant sure death for the eating place. A.L. Stein, the Roncarelli lawyer, enlisted Frank Scott to fight Duplessis in the Quebec courtrooms. Criminal law was not Scott's special legal field (that was constitutional law). But he took the case anyway, and after years of talk-talk-talk the team of Stein and Scott defeated Premier Duplessis in his own courtrooms. And loud cheers were heard across Quebec, except in the Montreal *Star*'s editorial offices where they believed socialists were communists under another name.

In the early 1970s, Mavor Moore wrote a television play about Scott and the Roncarelli case. My wife and I were at Scott's place in Montreal when the play was first produced. In some aspects it was like a Hollywood premiere, with searchlights criss-crossing the sky. A.L. Stein was there. Roncarelli was there. So was Frank Scott. All the principals except Duplessis (he was dead) were there. I had the weird feeling that history was being made; and what was I doing right in the middle of it, a bemused spectator? Well, at least a repetition of legal history. And Frank Scott was the principal actor in Mavor Moore's play, loving every minute of it. How could one ever say in those circumstances that the play was bad or even mediocre? Have another drink and admire the man, and feel fortunate to meet these people at this re-enactment of a turning point in their lives.

Frank Scott reminds me in many ways of a citizen of the ancient Greek *polis*, Athens particularly. He was not a politician *per se*, but everything that happened (or so it seemed) in Canada was in his realm of thought and action. He understood the problems of Quebec in a largely Anglophone nation, problems like conscription in World War II, and a constitution drawn up in England. He was a member of the Royal Commission on Bilingualism and Biculturalism in 1963. He spoke out strongly in 1946 against the displacement of Japanese Canadians during the war. "The real problem we have in Canada has nothing to do with the Japanese at all: it is the problem of racial intolerance." In other words, it's our problem here and now as Canadians in 1989.

The "October Crisis" in 1970 seemed like a terrorist revolution to some Canadians, among them Frank Scott. Bombs were exploding in Montreal mail boxes. James Cross, British trade commissioner in Montreal, was kidnapped by the Front de Libération du Quebec (the FLQ). They demanded Quebec separation from English Canada. Pierre Laporte, a cabinet minister in Quebec's Liberal government, was kidnapped and murdered. Prime Minister Pierre Trudeau proclaimed the War Measures Act, conferring emergency power on the government. It was a time of turbulence and fear in Canada. The political right and left were polarized: socialists condemned the War Measures Act, conservatives were for it. But surprise, that staunch old socialist Frank Scott supported the government. On the evidence of terrorism at the time, I myself agreed with the government's action. And what can one say years later? The aftermath demonstrated that there had been no genuine revolution planned by the FLQ, just some isolated but alarming crimes of terrorism and murder.

One looks back at that time with mixed feelings. I think the socialist left were against the War Measures Act on general principles of freedom, no matter the seeming danger at the time. Their feelings were not based on the evidence at hand. But as it turned out, they were right; Frank Scott and many others, including myself, were wrong. For whatever reason, Pierre Trudeau decided that a show of force was needed: but this was not justified despite the terrorist acts, and has not been justified by any evidence since produced. It was a sad time for Canada, with a legacy that protrudes into relations between Quebec and English Canada, to this day.

Even among his friends, Frank Scott was thought of as a "public person." Nearly everything he said and did was known and talked about in Montreal and wider circles. Very little of his life was private; even a couple of love affairs were known and discussed. Sandra Djwa doesn't say much about them in this biography for obvious reasons. It's the penalty for being a public man. (Did Pericles have a girl friend—was Caesar's wife a lesbian?)

George Woodcock has an essay in his *Northern Spring* comparing Scott to the ancient Greek dramatist, Aeschylus. Composing his own epitaph, Aeschylus ignored all the plays he'd written, mentioning only that he'd fought for Athens against the Persians at Marathon, in the ranks of ordinary spearmen. In a sense, that was Aeschylus's prideful identity, long before historians decided the fate of Western civilization had depended on that battle. (Personally, I think Western civilization was a lot tougher than that.) The Greek playwright was obviously not an "ivory tower" sort of writer. Woodcock places Scott in the same category. He also mentions Milton, Hugo and Zola among the artists who took sides politically, espoused causes, fought the battles of words and principle, were men of good conscience, men of honour. There are not many artists who do this. It is a small but distinguished company, those who commit themselves to civil action, who can look forward and backward, citizens of the *polis*.

One thinks of his friends, Frank Scott's friends. They were multitudinous. Who knows how close and warm they were. One simply can't tell at this point. But I'm sure dead Arthur Smith was a friend, with accompanying feeling as well as shared interest. And a passion for social reform was shared by Scott with many others, that dream-passion similar to friendship and even love. And I think of myself, not really close to him at all, a dweller on the periphery, a kind of hero-worshipping admirer.

But search back into the past. Was there someone it was possible to admire and look up to then, someone wiser than yourself—that eternal adolescent, yourself? All of us, we supposed adults, are still adolescents in one part of our minds. In a cynical and corrupt world, we need someone like Scott. He/she needn't be perfect, but someone, maybe an Arthur Koestler (and I scrabble for other names), well, Archbishop Tutu . . . Someone.

Frank Scott did a great deal of writing in his long lifetime. Much of it was of the social kind, books, tracts and manifestos, taking the temperature and pulse of the country, that sort of thing. I've seen no bibliography of it, although perhaps one exists somewhere. The rest is poetry. Scott always thought of himself as a poet, and many of his friends were poets. One must discuss the quality of his poems, and not wish to sound overly ambiguous. Because his poetry was not exactly top-drawer, although something much better than a mediocre average. But I wish he'd been better than he actually was, in that medium he cherished.

Many of the poems were political, but the best-known one is undoubtedly "The Canadian Authors Meet," a satire on the Canadian Authors Association, of which the following is the last verse:

Shall we go round the mulberry bush, or shall
We gather at the river, or shall we

Appoint a Poet Laureate this fall,
Or shall we have another cup of tea?

First published in 1945, and satirizing bad poets, I still find the poem extremely funny. To be fair about it, the CAA has changed a great deal from that fuddy-duddy image. But its executive still feels sensitive about the poem: in fact I had a proposal last winter that I write a poem myself, refuting the Scott one. I pleaded lack of inspiration, which was true: I couldn't possibly write a poem that good anyway.

Some of Scott's most amusing work focuses on the difference between French and English usage: "DEEP APPLE PIE/TART AUX POMMES PROFONDES."

"Lakeshore" is often the poem that takes a critical laurel wreath. I'm not sure I agree. "For Bryan Priestman" and "Eden" are my own favourites. The Priestman poem, about a professor of chemistry who drowned trying to save a child, has a surface simplicity. Scott saw Priestman as testing himself, in perhaps the Hemingway manner, the attempted rescue as an experiment that risked his own life. However, one might say that Priestman should have focused more on the child rather than on an experiment with himself. But poems like that one, which can set the mind at work, burrowing and tunnelling into the deeply buried self, these are better poems than I have thought they were. And that is my fault. Because I'd like to be as generous as Frank Scott was, and still be accurately honest about it.

And how good a biography is this one? I'd say better than average, but not up to the best of its genre. It isn't easy to write about a man like Scott, since his was largely an inner life. And errors—one that pertains to myself: I've never "received support" from the Canada Foundation (as distinct from the Canada Council) to my certain knowledge. But this was not an error by the biographer, just inaccurate information.

Sometimes, when my wife practises her silence on me, I can hear Frank Scott's voice in memory . . . It's one of those literary-cum-political gatherings at his place on Clarke Avenue in Montreal. The bartenders—who are Frank and Marian—are busy. Doug Jones, Arthur Smith and Leon Edel are discussing Henry James and Eliot's *Waste Land*. Dudek is trying to get a word in edgeways, or any other way. Layton claims his new poem is an immortal masterpiece. Pierre

Trudeau is condemning Meech Lake and Free Trade with Scott, Frank Underhill and Eugene Forsey. Lou Stein and Frank Roncarelli are wondering if they should bring another suit against Premier Duplessis for damages; but that's impossible: Duplessis is dead. Phyllis Webb and Pat Page are discussing the syntax of comparative prosody in French and English with Anne Hébert and Gilles Hénault. Leonard Cohen is trying plaintively to get somebody, "anybody, please, please—listen to Bob Dylan rocking with Ben Jonson with 'Drink to Me Only With Thine Eyes.'" And Suzanne, sitting disconsolate in the room's corner, wants to go back to her place by the river . . .

It's an exercise in sentimentality to think these things. But when you review the life of someone you liked and admired, such lapses in taste may perhaps be permitted. Would I be permitted also to end with the last verse of a poem I wrote about Frank Scott?

At least a dozen Scotts exist
—each a prosecuting attorney somewhere
fighting intolerance anti-Semitism such
blood sports of racists
by which we mark ourselves
as inescapably human
—each a defense witness as well:
include mention of that mysterious
        phrase "What's right"
all ambiguous crap removed
what's fair and equitable for everyone
What's right?
       Frank Scott knew

*(1989)*

# E.J. Pratt

## *The Master Years,* by David G. Pitt

**D**URING MOST OF THE YEARS mentioned in the book's title, Edwin John Pratt, an ex-preacher from Newfoundland, was generally regarded as the foremost poet in Canada. Pratt's bibliography lists seventeen books of poetry, including three Governor General's Award winners. Many other honours, medals, honorary degrees from universities, memberships in learned societies, etc., were showered on him. Despite the contemporary presence of A.J.M. Smith, F.R. Scott, A.M. Klein, and Wilson MacDonald, Pratt was considered to be the poet, a monolithic presence, a dominating figure—and was scarcely known at all outside Canada.

Pratt's poetry deals with "society in a state of emergency," according to Northrop Frye. Others have called it epic and heroic in conception. Men and the sea are major motifs; verse forms are traditional and nearly always metrical; Canadian history is a large theme. Nevertheless, Pratt was something of an anomaly, partly because of the largeness of his themes and his muscular treatment of them. Nothing even resembling him had ever occurred in CanLit. The short lyric had always been most prominent despite oddballs like Heavysege—in this country. I doubt that Pratt ever wrote a poem in the first person, or dealt with a personal theme except in the abstract.

I had previously conceived of Pratt as something like his poems, monolithic and stern, unapproachable and given over completely to duty and literature. Pitt's biography changes that picture somewhat. Teaching at the University of Toronto for most of his adult years, Pratt was a gregarious man with many friends (quite a number of whom just happened to be critics and book reviewers), hosting "stag parties" and hoisting the convivial glass fairly often. A family man with one daughter (whose long-term illnesses were always in his mind), perennially short of money, he worked summer and winter, teaching and writing, with few holidays. Pratt was a conservative, in both philosophy and literature; some of his friends called him "Cautious Ned" for his refusal to espouse causes.

The Pitt biography deals with Pratt's life in minute detail, describing a milieu of readings, teaching, stag parties, friends, feuds, talk, and even a minor extramarital love affair. There are some interesting incidents: Pratt was a spiritualist, attended seances, and believed he communicated with his dead mother at one of them. Ellen Elliott, a publisher's secretary, was one of his occasional "mediums." In 1942 she held a seance for Mackenzie King, at which the spirits present included Queen Victoria, Florence Nightingale, Anne Boleyn, Sir Frederick Banting, and others.

Pratt's tongue could be sharp on occasion. He described Audrey Alexandra Brown as "a stuck-up little thing, [who] spoke about Nanaimo as claiming her and not Victoria. Yes siree she belonged to Nanaimo." Pratt's contemporary, Wilson MacDonald, said nasty things about him on the reading circuit. But our man gave as good as he got. Pratt described MacDonald as "the god-damnedest ass in Canadian history. He is such a shit that I would even pity his own poems if they were shoved up his ass." Now that's talent!

In 1941 Sir Charles G.D. Roberts decided to publish an anthology, Voices of Victory, to aid the wartime British Bomb Victims Funds. Pratt was one of a panel helping Roberts make selections from among the large number of lady poet contributors. When the panel threw out poems, Sir Charles immediately reinstated them. Pratt commented to a friend that, "For including their stuff, Charley probably got a fuck a page." And that, ιͺo, takes talent!

My own ambiguous feelings about Pratt remain, despite the human and rather likeable man emerging from his biography. I disagree profoundly with his marching metrics and monotonous rhymes. But I admire the man's thoroughness: he researched his epics of sea and land like a historical novelist, strove for accuracy and verisimilitude. Remove certain short passages, and they become little lyrics. This from *Brébeuf*:

> But not in these was the valour or stamina lodged;
> Nor in the symbol of Richelieu's robes or the seals
> Of Mazarin's charters, nor in the stir of the lilies
> Upon the Imperial folds; nor yet in the words
> Loyola wrote on a table of lava-stone
> In the cave of Manresa—not in these the source—
> But in the sound of invisible trumpets blowing
> Around two slabs of board, right-angled, hammered
> By Roman nails and hung on a Jewish hill.

That takes you there emotionally, and almost physically.

But in many ways Pratt strikes me as a poet-engineer. There was no first period in his work; he never dealt with relations between men and women in any meaningful way; he had no personal voice. And yet, but, still—he heard those "invisible trumpets blowing."

All the reviewer-friends and academic admirers of the years 1927 to 1964 who thought Edwin John Pratt a genius are now at least middle-aged or dead: the poems must stand on their own. This biography with its engaging minutiae will ensure the name survives a little longer. But there seems to me something essential about Pratt that is missing in David Pitt's book. And the engineer poet remains for me something like his own description of the iceberg that sank the Titanic:

> The grey shape with the paleolithic face
> Was still the master of the longitudes.

—as Pratt remains the master of the Canadian literary field.

*(1988)*

# Rudyard Kipling

IT WAS A MAGICAL CHILDHOOD. The *ayahs* with jewelled nostrils loved him; the white-robed male servants held his hand for trips about the city streets, past Hindu shrines, through heat-choked smelly slums, and to the sunset beach where Parsees, "standing in the scarlet waters, bow down before their God." And he heard the tales of "Shere Khan," the man-eating tiger, before he knew the English language.

Rudyard Kipling was born in Bombay in 1865. His father, John Lockwood Kipling, was a minister's son from Yorkshire, who became an artist and pottery designer; later the director of an art school in Bombay; later still, curator of an art museum in Lahore. Kipling's mother, a minister's daughter, was said to be "the wittiest and most talented" of four sisters.

The boy Kipling lived in India, cossetted and coddled by his *ayahs* (female servants), and spoke the "native" vernacular. He remembered going with one of the male servants "into little Hindu temples where, being below the age of caste, I held his hand and looked at the dimly seen friendly Gods," and "Near our little house on the Bombay Esplanade were the Towers of Silence, where the Dead are exposed to the waiting vultures on the rim of the towers, who scuffle and spread wings when they see the bearers of the Dead below."

Then everything changed. When he was six the boy and his sister, Trix, were sent to cold and gloomy England to escape the enervating topical climate. They lived with the wife of a retired naval officer at Portsmouth. In later years, Kipling wrote about that period in his short story, "Baa Baa, Black Sheep," in the novel *The Light That*

*Failed*, and in *Something of Myself*, a book which appeared a year after his death and which included autobiographical notes and memoirs.

It was an establishment run with the full vigour of the Evangelical as revealed to the Woman. I had never heard of Hell, so I was introduced to it in all its terrors—I and whatever luckless little slavey might be in the house, whom severe rationing had led to steal food. Once I saw the Woman beat such a girl who picked up the kitchen poker and threatened retaliation. Myself I was regularly beaten. The Woman had an only son of twelve or thirteen as religious as she. I was a real joy to him, for when his mother had finished with me for the day he (we slept in the same room) took me on and roasted the other side . . .

I was made to read without explanation, under the usual fear of punishment. And on a day that I remember it came to me that "reading" was not "the Cat lay on the Mat," but a means to everything that would make me happy. So I read all that came within my reach. As soon as my pleasure in this was known, deprivation from reading was added to my punishments. I then read by stealth and the more earnestly . . .

My troubles settled themselves in a few years. My eyes went wrong, and I could not see well to read. For which reason I read the more and in bad lights. My work at the terrible little day-school where I had been sent suffered in consequence, and my monthly reports showed it. The loss of "reading time" was the worst of my "home" punishments for bad school-work. One report was so bad that I threw it away and said that I had never received it . . . I was well beaten and sent to school through the streets of Southsea with the placard "Liar" between my shoulders.

Some sort of nervous breakdown followed, for I imagined I saw shadows and things that were not there, and they worried me more than the Woman . . . A man came to see me as to my eyes and reported that I was half blind. This, too, was supposed to be "showing-off," and I was segregated from my sister—another punishment—as a sort of moral leper. Then—I do not remember that I had any warning—the Mother returned from India. She told me afterwards that when she first came to my room to kiss me goodnight, I flung up an arm to ward off the cuff that I had been trained to expect.

This, from *Something of Myself*, strikes me as the kind of horror typical of the nineteenth century. But I wonder also: this man Kipling is such a writer as to make a reader see black where only white exists.

Could such terror and awfulness actually have been practised? However, I'm inclined to believe Kipling. It was like being taken from a warm bath as child and doused in ice-cold water. And it was much worse than that. Heaven and hell as concepts can only be appreciated and understood in relation and closeness to each other. I remember the terrors of my own childhood that are now overlaid with a thick palimpsest of good things, a coverlet that conceals and a memory that diminishes.

It is a curious part of the "horror" at Portsmouth (or Southsea) that Kipling's sister, Trix, was the adored little angel in the "Woman's" establishment. Three years younger than her brother, she was the favourite. She slept in the owner's bedroom, was catered to and presumably loved.

Kipling held nothing against his parents because of this ordeal. They placed him, at age twelve, in the United Services College, called Westward Ho, a name calculated to make one remember one's own childhood and the stories of Charles Kingsley. The school's purpose was to coach the children of service people, enable them to pass examinations and follow their fathers into the British Army or Navy. It was not co-educational, needless to say.

The headmaster—a friend of Burne-Jones, Rossetti and William Morris—became almost a surrogate father to Kipling, who made friends with boys named Dunsterville and Beresford who were athletes, almost bons vivants by comparison. Kipling was an aesthete who fancied himself a writer and became editor of the school paper. The three boys roomed together; they protected and appreciated him; he certainly reciprocated.

Not that Westward Ho was paradise. "Bullying was rampant," Kipling wrote later. "One amusement of older boys was to hold the little ones out of the top storey windows by their ankles." (I'm tempted to digress here, and mention the boys at Albert College, Belleville, who read stories in Chums about "ragging" and "fags" in English schools. But I will not digress.)

The school chaplain, if not a monster, was a ferocious bully. When he left the school, he preached an emotional farewell sermon and wept during the course of it. Kipling commented: "Two years' bullying is not paid for with half-an-hour's blubbering in a pulpit." Writers—and it is a kind of silly reward for scribbling—generally have the last word. The Reverend Campbell is remembered, but not the way he would have liked.

At Westward Ho Kipling wrote poems, read Swinburne and Browning (he had actually seen Browning "plain"), Poe, Dryden, Chaucer, the Elizabethans, and Whitman. (I can't understand how he could possibly have liked Whitman.) He copied his poems in a leather-bound notebook. (So did I at a similar age.) He supervised the redecoration of the room he shared with two friends with all sorts of exotic stuff that sounds like a description by Oscar Wilde. They searched surrounding junk shops for treasure, unregarded things that glowed in their minds. Dunsterville, who became a major-general, said later in his published memoir that the treasures they searched for were in the end not as valuable as the rough drafts Kipling threw away in the waste basket.

Young Kipling became the school poet, a boy man-of-letters. He imposed his own values on his friends. He grew a moustache. His eyebrows even then were great black caterpillars, paralysed by the million-horsepower brain behind them or by a dream of India and its Towers of Silence. (I refuse to say at this point that I was once "the school poet," somewhere west of Suez. I will not digress!)

For a writer, busy writing and developing his monster-minuscule ego, what a lovely place Westward Ho was! The flowers bow down, drunk with hearing their only-dreamed names spoken by alien tongues.

Buy my English posies
Kent and Surrey may—
Violets of the Undercliff
Wet with Channel spray
("The Flowers")

The other kids look at you nervously and fearfully and admiringly. You might include them in a poem. And they, marooned there, act very strangely and un-Britishly. "You'll die in a garret as a scurrilous journalist," one master predicted. Kipling might have used the much-later rejoinder by Brendan Behan about critics: They're like eunuchs in a harem. The eunuchs watch closely every night, see how it's done, figure it all out; but when the moment comes, can't do it themselves. And die sorrowfully.

Kipling was in his element at Westward Ho, despite occasional tiffs and almost humorous quarrels with masters. Crofts, the Latin master, gave him extra work because of a bad Horace translation. Kipling returned the favour with a version of "Donec gratus eram tibi" in Devonshire dialect. Imagine writing Latin in a Devonshire dialect! How could one do it? I'm glad to remember that I failed Latin badly.

The headmaster allowed the boy wonder to explore his own private library, where he got acquainted with Hakluyt, Peacock, Pushkin and Lermontov (I never heard of these guys till I was in my thirties), and also revived the school paper in order that Kipling might have an outlet for his writing. Kipling grew a moustache, wore pebble glasses; no doubt people looked at him oddly. After all, *they* read *Jack Harkaway*, or *Ned Kelly, the Ironclad Bushranger*—if they read at all.

In 1882, when he was nearly seventeen, Kipling had a choice of going to university or back to India. He chose India, and went to live with his parents there. He became a sub-editor on the *Civil and Military Gazette* at Lahore. *Stalky & Co.*, a version of his life at Westward Ho, was published seventeen years later. By that time Kipling was famous.

In India Kipling wrote *Plain Tales from the Hills* at age twenty, publishing most of them in the Civil and Military Gazette with its mostly European readership. Later, Kipling joined *The Pioneer*, a weekly paper with an all-India readership. *Departmental Ditties* appeared, and also "six small paper-backed railway-bookstall volumes embodying most of my tales in the *Weekly*."

"Till I was in my twenty-fourth year," he wrote, just before his return to England, "I no more dreamed of dressing myself than I did of shutting an inner door or—I was going to say turning a key in a lock. But we had no locks. I gave myself indeed the trouble of stepping into the garments that were held out to me after my bath, and out of them as I was assisted to do. And—luxury of which I dream still—I was shaved before I was awake!" Just imagine, coming out of sleep to find a sword at your throat!

Despite his privileged condition, Kipling associated with all "classes" of the Indian people. Sometimes he was not popular because of that. And he got to know the British Army from private to general and even the Governor General of India. In fact, he nearly worked himself to death, writing and editing; a couple of bouts with fever attest to his multiple activities. After six years he went back to England with a small but growing reputation.

Wars have been fought all over the world since Kipling died in January 1936, and each generation since has had different thoughts about him. Remember the princess? She slept on thirty mattresses, with a small pea underneath the first mattress. The princess was so sensitive she felt that pea against her back under all that ten or fifteen foot distance. It kept her awake. She was sensitive to the pea, and thus proved herself a genuine princess, not the Hollywood variety. As a sensitive and possibly intelligent reader, do you read critics? Or do the unheard of, read Kipling himself?

Today, nearly everyone seems to hate Kipling. No one reads him but everyone hates him for his use of phrases like "the lesser breeds" and "he drilled a black man white" and for the racist attitudes that pervade his work. Sometimes he sentimentalised, many times romanticised. He was an admirer of power, of the *box wallahs* who wielded power. Sure, Kipling was a racist. He was an imperialist. In his late nineteenth-century heyday, imperialism and racism were not uncommon, were even somewhat fashionable in some areas of society.

Among my own personal prejudices is a dislike of obvious rhyme and metre among modern poets. (I had great difficulty breaking myself of this "habit" and way of writing at one time.) But the older poets, they grew up that way; it was their world. Who could be contemptuous of Chesterton's "Lepanto" or Anon's "Tom O'Bedlam"? I still love some of those older poets, of whom Kipling is not the least.

So I proselytize here. And cite a couple of Orwell's Kipling quotes, for which he has replaced Kipling's excised aitches. The first about a funeral:

So it's knock out your pipers and follow me!
And it's finish up your swipes and follow me!
   Oh, hark to the big drum calling.
     Follow me—follow me home!

("Follow Me 'Ome")

again:

Cheer for the Sergeant's wedding—
    Give them one cheer more!
Grey gun-horses in the lando,
    And a rogue is married to a whore!

("The Sergeant's Weddin' ")

Nothing softened, no fucking euphemisms there! I don't know what "lando" or "swipes" are, and don't really care. But "Follow me—follow me home!" Is that poetry? And is Kipling primarily a ballad-maker, as Eliot (the condescending s.o.b.) called him? It's Kipling, imperialist and racist, who said:

Buy my English posies!
    You that scorn the May,
Won't you greet a friend from home
    Half the world away?
Green against the draggled drift
    Faint and frail but first—
Buy my Northern bloodroot—
    And I'll know where you were nursed!
Robin down the logging-road whistles, "Come to me!"
Spring has found the maple-grove, the sap is running free.
All the winds of Canada call the ploughing-rain
Take the flower and turn the hour, and kiss your love again!

("The Flowers")

The critics have had an enjoyable and puzzling time with Kipling over the years, and there have been many imitators, the most notable being Robert Service. Somerset Maugham said Kipling was the finest English short story writer; T.S. Eliot said Kipling wrote verse, not poetry. But the two critics I appreciate most are Randall Jarrell and George Orwell. The latter is repelled by Kipling's undoubted imperialism, but fascinated nevertheless. Jarrell, who admires many people I don't admire—such as Whitman and W.C. Williams—says:

An intelligent man said that the world felt Napoleon as a weight, and that when he died it would give a great *oof* of relief. This is just as true of Byron, or of such Byrons of their days as Kipling and Hemingway: after a generation or two the world is tired of being their pedestal, shakes them off with an *oof*, and then—hoisting onto its back a new world figure—feels the penetrating satisfaction of having made a mistake all its own. Then for a generation or two the

Byron lies in the dust where we left him: if the old world did him more than justice, a new one does him less. "If he was so good as all that, why isn't he still famous?" the new world asks—if it asks anything. And then when another new generation or two are done, we decide that he wasn't altogether a mistake people made in those days, but a real writer after all—that if we like "Childe Harold" a good deal less than anyone thought of liking it then, we like "Don Juan" a good deal more. Byron was a writer, people just didn't realize what sort of writer he was. We can feel impatient with Byron's world for liking him for the wrong reasons, and we are glad that our world, the real world, has at last settled Byron's account.

Kipling's account is still unsettled. Underneath, we hold it against him that the world quoted him in its sleep, put him in headlines when he was ill, acted as if he were God . . .

George Orwell, whose feelings are ambiguous, says Kipling never did understand that empire is a business proposition, something late nineteenth-century England itself did not understand: one fires a Gatling gun at coolies and natives, then robs their country. But, says Orwell, the totalitarian countries well understood this business principle. To which I add: and so does the United States of America, since their new-style empire is founded upon profit and loss (with a modicum of glory for the Marines).

Orwell says that Kipling is the only writer of our time ("our time" being mostly prior to World War II) who has added phrases to the language. He gives a list of them:

East is East, and West is West.
The white man's burden.
What do they know of England who only England know?
The female of the species is more deadly than the male.
Somewhere East of Suez.
—And probably the word "Hun."

John Middleton Murry quotes the following lines:

There are nine and sixty ways
Of constructing tribal lays,
And every single one of them is right.

Murry attributes this quote to Thackeray, which I think is hilarious.

Almost everyone would agree that Kipling had a gift for the felicitious phrase, the word that fits, the thought that strikes and wounds and stops the reader in mid-sentence. He talks about a lion cub his family had on the cape: "He dozed on the stoep, I noticed, due north and south, looking with slow eyes up the length of Africa."

In referring to the bad years between age six and twelve, when he was being bullied by the "Evangelical Woman" at Portsmouth, Kipling says: "In the long run these things and many more of the like drained me of any capacity for real, personal hatred for the rest of my life." On the basis of his work, prose and poems, one would have to say that Kipling was mistaken about himself. Read the short story, "Mary Postgate," for instance.

When I read these lines of Kipling's:

> I 'eard the knives be'ind me, but I dursn't face my man,
> Nor I don't know where I went to, 'cause I didn't stop to see,
> Till I 'eard a beggar squealin' out for quarter as 'e ran,
> An' I thought I knew the voice an' it was me!

I see Kipling had learned well the truth of William James' words:

> The normal process of life contains moments as bad as any of those which insane melancholy is filled with, moments in which radical evil gets its innings and takes its solid turn. The lunatic's visions of horror are all drawn from the material of daily fact. Our civilisation is founded on the shambles, and every individual existence goes out in a lonely spasm of helpless agony. If you protest, my friend, wait till you arrive there yourself!

(The Varieties of Religious Experience, "The Sick Soul")

When Kipling died his reputation was in a long decline. The world had shaken him off with an *oof*, replacing him with someone else. The British Empire as well had entered a long decline, and England had become a second-rate power.

Robert Conquest, a contemporary English poet, says: "All that Eliot and Orwell are quite truly saying, in fact, is that Kipling's is a poetry of clarification rather than of subtlety and suggestion." Eliot comments: "We expect to have to defend a poet against the charge of obscurity: we have to defend Kipling against the charge of excessive lucidity."

Orwell claimed Kipling was a "good bad poet" who had a sense of responsibility, was vulgar, but nevertheless vital. That "good bad" appellation bothers me. It's an ambiguous distinction, between two warring opposites. Orwell, one of the best critics, does not really account for the fact that it is impossible to dismiss the best of Kipling's poetry and prose.

But Orwell gives credit for Kipling's "not seriously misleading picture of the old pre-machinegun army—the sweltering barracks in Gibraltar or Lucknow, the red coats, the pipeclayed belts and the pillbox hats, the beer, the fights, the floggings, hangings and crucifixions, the bugle-calls, the smell of oats and horse-piss, the bellowing sergeants with foot-long moustaches, the bloody skirmishes, invariably mismanaged, the crowded troopships, the cholera-stricken camps, the 'native' concubines, the ultimate death in the workhouse . . . " In Orwell's mouth, the list becomes literature.

Eliot says he judges Kipling's poetry and prose in combination, not separately, that he expressed unpopular views in a popular style. Kipling was "the inventor of a mixed form," he says, "so a knowledge of his prose is essential to the understanding of his verse, and a knowledge of his verse is essential to the understanding of his prose." He is also much troubled whether the verse is poetry or whether the poetry is verse, and claims that "the starting point for Kipling's verse is the motive of the ballad-maker." He is bedevilled by a need for definitions, a condition with which Canadians are very familiar: "What is a Canadian?" "Do I dare to eat a peach?"

But the critics grow tedious. One returns to *Kim*, and to some of the short stories, for sustenance. Kipling's poems are such a complete world! They not only mirror the real world, they are another real world. One must accept the imperialism and occasional intrusions of racism, or at least try to ignore them, as one also ignores bad poems like "If," so loved by mothers and boys, and probably sneered at by the British tommy. Eliot included it in his Kipling selections, along with "The White Man's Burden," but left out most of my own personal favourites. Paradoxically, Kipling also wrote "The Gods of the Copybook Headings," which can be read as a complete refutation of "If":

On the first Feminian Sandstones we were promised the
   Fuller Life
(Which started by loving our neighbour and ended by
   loving his wife) . . .

To me, one of the most interesting things about Kipling is that he left his six years of mental and physical torture at Portsmouth and immediately afterwards assumed a fairly dominant position at

Westward Ho. Did that six-year period leave no trace on the twelve-year-old boy and succeeding youth and man? Witness "Mary Postgate" and *The Light That Failed,* and the ghost of the anonymous Woman at Portsmouth walks again. His own son died in World War I, *after* "Mary Postgate" was written, which perhaps accounts for his hatred of the "Hun."

Kipling's poetry, *especially* his poetry, was always close to the bone. It was about life and death, essentially. If he didn't like something he was downright nasty about it.

I dislike the ding-dong metrics of some of Kipling's poetry, even if they suited his methods. But other poems allow you to forget rhyme and metre. I think they are superb. And so, in this piece, I have done what Kipling has forbidden us to do:

If I have given you delight
   By aught that I have done,
Let me lie quiet in that night
   That shall be yours anon:

And for the little, little span
   The dead are borne in mind,
Seek not to question other than
   The books I leave behind.

("The Appeal")

The final poem here I also quote in its entirety. I have typed out this poem and have it on my workroom wall. It is a mystery-poem, and leaves questions in your mind. "The Way Through the Woods" reminds me of De la Mare's "The Listeners." But De la Mare's poem does not stay in a corner of my mind and speak to me at unexpected moments the way Kipling's does:

They shut the road through the woods
Seventy years ago.
Weather and rain have undone it again,
And now you would never know
There was once a road through the woods
Before they planted the trees.
It is underneath the coppice and heath
And the thin anemones.
Only the keeper sees
That, where the ring-dove broods,

And the badgers roll at ease,
There was once a road through the woods.

Yet, if you enter the woods
Of a summer evening late,
When the night-air cools on the trout-ringed pools
Where the otter whistles his mate,
(They fear not men in the woods
Because they see so few),
you will hear the beat of a horse's feet,
Steadily cantering through
The misty solitudes,
As though they perfectly knew
The old lost road through the woods...
But there is no road through the woods.

*(1989)*

# On Bliss Carman

FOR THE LAST DOZEN YEARS or so I didn't think anyone but me considered Carman to have much value. Most people who've written about him recently have sounded negative; few would admit they enjoyed him for fear other people would think they had no taste or modern sensibility. By contrast, many of those who wrote about him when he was alive were worshipful and embarrassing in their praise.

And now I am—let me admit it at the outset—quite surprised at the interest in Bliss Carman demonstrated by this volume. It seems I am not alone in my ambivalent admiration and less than unstinted praise for the man. And I wonder if my careful ambivalence about him resembles yours—

I was thirteen in the early 1930s when I first read Carman's "Peony." I don't have any of his poems before me at this moment while I process these words with two fingers on my manually operated Olympia typewriter, but the poem goes like this:

Arnoldus Villanova
Six hundred years ago
Said Peonies have magic,
And I believe it so.

There stands his learned dictum
Which any boy may read
But he who learns the secret
Will be made wise indeed.

Astrologer and doctor
In the science of his day

Have we so far outstripped him?

What more is there to say?

And et cetera. But you know, that poem stiffened me, enchanted me if you like. The words hummed through my head like hydro wires in winter, when you first realize the whole countryside is alive and talking under the snow. And I realized other people were talking to me as well—in books I'd never seen—when I read that one poem of Carman's. All this wasn't conscious though, of course, but it was there just the same.

I'd read a lot of books before this happened, but none I remember in the same way. And I suppose it was Carman who led me to R.L. Stevenson ("Home is the sailor, home from the sea/And the hunter home from the hill"), G.K. Chesterton ("Old Noah he often said to his wife as they sat down to dine/I don't care where the water goes if it doesn't get into the wine"), W.J. Turner ("I have stood upon a hill/and trembled like a man in love/A man in love I was/and I could not speak and could not move"), and eventually to Oliver St. John Gogarty ("I will live in Ringsend/With a red-headed whore,/And the fan light gone in/Where it lights the hall door/And listen each night/For her querulous shout/As at last she streels in /And the pubs empty out") . . .

And I'll bet some of you don't know at least one of those names. I could quote much more, but I'll spare you that ordeal, though I am tempted, since this selective memory of loved poems is something I treasure.

I wrote my own first poem right after Arnoldus Villanova. It was certifiably awful, but got published in our high school magazine, *The Spotlight*. I got paid a buck for it, thought it an easy way to make a buck, and kept on writing.

All because of Bliss Carman? I think yes, it was; but that story gets mixed up with the one about me playing football and not getting enough attention—so I wrote a poem. They've both become personal anecdotes of mine; the truth in them varies, according to the accuracy of my memory.

At the end of grade nine I was still writing, publishing poems in *The Spotlight* and the local newspaper, the *Trenton Courier Advocate*. I was committing book-length effusions about the Norse myths and Robin Hood, using a neighbour's machine to type them; and I stapled them together with leather covers into small books. I was hooked on the stuff—poetry, I mean. And all because of Bliss Carman? I'm not sure.

I became, of course, the "school poet" at Trenton High School. And came close to regretting this cultural status when one Wilson MacDonald visited us to read his own poems. I was solemnly ushered into his presence in the principal's office—another unfortunate who had contracted the metric disease.

MacDonald was in his fifties in the early 1930s. I remember most his long thin nose and black hair brushed sideways across a bald skull. I forget what we said to each other—but that MacDonald was a great poet was taken for granted by everyone. He admitted it himself.

In the school auditorium with a captive audience, he read "Whist-Wee"; something about tug boats in English Bay, Vancouver; and "Song of the Sky": "Norse am I when the first snow falls;/Norse am I till the ice departs/The fare for which my spirit calls/Is blood from a hundred viking-hearts." (I don't have MacDonald's poems in front of me either; but if I make mistakes, who would know?)

Anyway, the point is: Bliss Carman, whom I never met, is probably responsible for me meeting Wilson MacDonald. Visiting the Soviet Union in 1976, I came across a Russian edition of MacDonald in a Moscow bookstore—and expostulated mildly to my hosts. Still later, when they translated some of my own stuff here, I wondered if they'd compared me to MacDonald and Joe Wallace—the latter also Russian-published.

Reverting back to the mid-1930s, I was playing football at high school and enjoying the twin status of poet and athlete (I was a lousy football player, too), reading novels concealed inside textbook covers in class. Not surprisingly, I failed to pass into grade ten.

But I liked football, weighing about 180 pounds and being more than six feet tall; and I liked poetry. Therefore, I stayed another year at school to play football and write poems. You can see immediately the deleterious effect of Carman on young minds.

In the mid-1930s I quit school for good, and rode the freight trains west at age seventeen during the Great Depression. At one point I left the boxcars in Toronto and picked up a copy of Carman's *Collected Poems* at a second-hand bookstore. The book was bound in maroon leather, and probably marked the beginning of my bibliographic obsessions. I hugged it to my bosom as the train's wheels imitated Carman's iambic pentameters or dactylic hexameters or whatever the textbooks say they are.

As you've undoubtedly noticed, all this has been very personal. But I've never attempted to analyze my feeling for Carman until this moment, and I don't think I'll do that at this moment either. Strangely enough, W.H. Auden had something relevant to say relating to feelings about Carman:

Time that is intolerant
of the brave and innocent,
and indifferent in a week
to a beautiful physique,

Worships language and forgives
everyone by whom it lives...

("In Memory of W.B. Yeats")

Bliss Carman is an integral part of the history of Canadian writing. Beyond that, he lives for me as incantation; and I can't possibly escape him even if I wanted to—and I don't want to. His music shadow is in my head—"The Shambling Sea," "Make Me over Mother April," "The Nancy's Pride," and so on.

Carman's mysticism and solemnity I consider nonsense. Two paragraphs inside those three prose books he did with fancy titles, and I can read no further. They bore hell outta me. But his poems echo in my mind, like a remote counterpoint to what I write myself. And that sounds ridiculous to me, even as I get it down on paper.

I carry his stuff with me into the future, as possibly someone else may carry what I write into a more distant future. All of us do that, of course—update the past into the present. And Earle Birney once made Carman's past even more contemporary for me. He told me a story about Carman in New Canaan, which I believe is a town somewhere in New England.

It seems Carman had a mistress named Mary Perry King. She lived with her husband in New Canaan: Carman too lived, rather fortuitously, in the same small town. And each of these three must have made generous allowances for the other two.

Carman used to walk to his mistress's house every morning. And Doctor King walked to work as well, at the same time on the same street. They would pass each other on opposite sides, each with different objectives. Carman's personal objective need not be explored further. But as they passed each other in that small New England town, is it possible that Doctor King lifted his doctor's hat or Carman the poet's sombrero he affected? Did either sneak a look sideways as they passed, or Doctor King snort, "Ridiculous poseur!"? And did Carman ever consider including his mistress's husband in a romantic poem?

Not to quote Auden again, I doubt that time will be any more intolerant than it has been already of Bliss Carman. It's unnecessary to mention his shortcomings—we all have some of those; he is still in the company of Eliot, Dylan Thomas, Yeats, Lawrence and the rest. They will not be snobbish about his intellect, even though most writers are very noticeably snobbish about such things. They will all be silent together, those famous writers, for obvious reasons.

*(1990)*

# POETRY CHRONICLE:
# 1958–1990

# Louis Dudek: *Laughing Stalks / En Mexico*

**F**OR THE UNINFORMED, LOUIS DUDEK is one third of the Toronto-Montreal triumvirate consisting in unequal parts of I. Layton, R. Souster and L. Dudek—with no apologies to the earlier Latin triumvirate of Caesar-Pompey-Crassus, and certainly as vociferous unless Cicero is included.

Those were the Roman days when Catullus' verses were being scribbled on the walls of urinals and public baths in the Eternal City. It may have been a prurient age, for we don't do that with our poems—but sometimes make urinals the subject or focal point of a poem itself. As Louis Dudek has occasionally. In *Laughing Stalks:*

> De gustibus non disputandum?
> While some are living on artificial meringue,
> and some on the scrapings of toilet seats?
>
> ("To the Absolute Relativists")

Certainly the natural functions are receiving their due share of publicity; perhaps all we can hope for is some form of literary constipation—or a succeeding wave of Puritanism wiping out the past?

But make no mistake, I think Dudek's brand of humour is wonderful, makes excellent fall and winter fare (leaving out the toilet seats). And *Laughing Stalks* runs the gamut from social satire to sardonic philosophy and sexual hilarity. Nothing seems to be left out—but if so the author will include it in the next edition.

Many of the poems read as if they were entries in some contemporary diary: written in coffee houses (the Riviera?), parked cars, walking on the street—in fact they read as if composed in all the places where life is (lived). What about this?

> I praised his art
> And he praised me for praising his art.
> I never could get him to start
> To talk about my art.
>
> ("Closed Circle")

It is interesting to note that Dudek has come some distance from the direction of *East of the City* and *The Searching Image*—has become much more positive (not to say strident) in his opinions, is fond of throwing in a Latin or French tag in the manner of Pound and Eliot. It seems to me that much of the introspection has gone down the drain, the quiet tone when trees were "green clichés" and black girls evoked astonishing sensitivity. Perhaps he no longer wonders about "this unsteady stone in space on which we cross."

However, the present tense Dudek still writes surprisingly well in *Laughing Stalks*. There are parodies of Birney, Scott, Smith, Layton, etc.—just in time to prevent those authors from writing the same poems as Dudek has written. There is also the "Sequel to Browning's Last Duchess," and the short "Word for the Living"—

> Certainly nothing we can say
> can remove the necessity
> of decrepitude and decay;
> but having said all that, everything
> is still to see and say . . .

A previous reviewer has said some rather unpleasant things about Louis Dudek. Among them: he isn't the kind of poet he thinks he is. On the contrary, he is the kind of poet he thinks he is—and sometimes that's just the trouble. Which signals our arrival *En Mexico*. Not to beat around the typewriter, the poems of *En Mexico* are not my dish.

In format the book is a rather imposing creation. Lilac cover, facsimile of the author's signature, large, blank pages between which are interspersed short rhapsodic bursts, and two drawings of nude women languishing coyly among the poems. These are capsule, chile con carne philosophy and observation, good or bad depending on your perspective to Popocatepetl or Montreal. They are not trivial, downright bad, to be dismissed light. (A good poet wrote them.) But they're not my dish.

Perhaps Dudek is doing a travel diary of the world in our time, as in *Europe*. He may have a grand, overall theme, apparent only to a PhD, and perhaps students may one day write theses on the subject of his poems. But I'm not concerned with that. The poems are too easy, too verbose (despite their brevity), too loose and too shapeless. (Maybe the Japanese hokku is a good analogy—except it has a rigid form and discipline which calls forth the best in a poet.) Here's one of the worst:

With tender affection
I flick an ant to the ground,
"Go along now."

And another:

I have learned to give freely to beggars
in Europe, en México.
I have learned to be.

To hell with that sort of thing. I think Dudek can do much better, and I wish he would. Poetry demands sweat under the arm and on the forehead as well as the navel and anus. It seems silly to ask a poet to treat death and old age and the timeless problems of personal existence when men like Yeats, Pound ("In Tempore Senectutis"), Turner, and many "old fashioned poets" have done it so well. So the fashion in poetry is to talk of the brotherhood of man (communism), the crazy, demented, hell and fission-bound culture in which we live (politics?). So what? The old questions are still to be answered; the hell and heaven of individual life; the puzzles and paradox of human love, etc.

But I suppose we get too old to change, be something else suddenly; we harp on the same old themes, become rigid in our agitation at the current state of human affairs, yap and bray in static character. So I don't think Dudek is trying hard enough or sweating in the right places. He probably could and would if he weren't so sure of himself.

Last quotation from *En Mexico:*

I would not pretend to explain
but learn a stoic silence,
a little joy.

Well!

(1958)

∞

# Roy Campbell: *Collected Poems, Vol II*

I SUPPOSE THERE IS SOMETHING admirable—awesome if you like—about any elemental force: hurricane, earthquake, volcanic eruption and Roy Campbell. He rushed around Europe all his life with energy enough for ten men, writing poetry, breaking horses, fighting bulls, skindiving, shooting lions and buffalo, soldiering in both world wars (and the Spanish Civil War), and getting into all sorts of mischief. Perhaps he lived in a sort of delirium of adventure—a prolonged adolescence, someone has said.

At any rate all that now remains is poetry—the second volume of the collected edition in particular. Because Campbell died in May, 1957 in an auto accident.

Having some opinions of my own about Campbell I was interested in the press comments the publisher used for blurbs. Richard Church in *John O'London* says:

> At his best he has written poems that will surely live as long as
> English poetry lives.

G.S. Fraser in the *New Statesman* says:

> Mr. Campbell's place...among the dozen or so more important
> poets of our time is assured.

Robert Speacght in *The Tablet* says:

> . . . his mastery of traditional metre is matched by the inspiration of
> traditional themes.

So there we are. It would seem we have a ruddy genius on our hands. So let's take a look at the poetry—and it should be said that Campbell's later work is a polemical, satirical, and unabashed malevolent attack on certain individuals and groups (particularly everyone but Wyndham Lewis). In Memoriam of "Mosquito," a partner in the horse trade, gipsy of the Lozoya Clan,

> I never felt such glory
> As handcuffs on my wrists.
> My body stunned and gory
> With tooth marks on my fists:
> The triumph through the square,
> My horse behind me led,
> A pistol at my cutlets
> Three rifles at my head:
> And four of those Red bastards
> To hold one wounded man . . .

I think this trifle has some element of reality—quite apart from the political viewpoint. It is false-heroic, I would say, because that picture is false as well as true. And the ambiguity is not resolved.

Another excerpt:

The ivory, the jet, the coral,
The dainty groove that dints her back
To take the sting from every moral
And make each jealousy or quarrel
The fiercer aphrodisiac

("The Clock in Spain")

But the poem Campbell himself regarded as his major work is "Flowering Rifle," which deals with the Spanish Civil War—as if it were fought yesterday in your own backyard. In fact the author behaves as if this is the precise psychiatric worm burrowing beneath his fingernails, the one most important living event in his life—as perhaps it was. Campbell fought in that war on the Franco side and if you believe him, all the detestable elements in the world were gathered to oppose him personally on the other: Jews, Communists, intellectuals, etc.

Open the 120 page poem anywhere, excerpt a line, any line: "Even as now in this stupendous fight."

Notice the ding-dong beat? This metre is Campbells' star pre-dominant. If he varies it by placing two stressed syllables back to back it must be regarded as a radical departure. Needless to say the style becomes very tedious (it just about drives me to Dudek's theory of prose metrics). Indeed I found the poem's scattered multitude of foot-notes much more interesting.

Campbell refers to his earlier poem, the "Georgiad:" " . . . now a classic, and this poem—which soon will be."

Referring to Maeztu, de Rivera and others:

...they were intellectuals on a higher scale, and died better than the
cowardly Lorca. If the author of this poem, a better poet than
Lorca, so Borges the leading S. American critic points out, had not
been resourceful, he would have died like Lorca, but at the hands of
the Reds.

A few years prior to the publication of this collected volume Campbell translated Lorca into English and I regard the result as accidentally the best of all Lorca translations. But it would appear that Campbell changed his mind about Lorca between the date of that translation and this collected edition.

Well, he is dead, and we cannot question him about such things. But even dead, I should like to think his ghostly, present-day opinions of Lorca as a man and a poet would be a little more generous than that. I hope so.

*(1959)*

∞

# Raymond Souster: *The Colour of the Times*

T HESE POEMS ARE SELECTED FROM a dozen previous books, ranging from *Unit of Five* in 1944 to *A Local Pride* in 1962. Taken together (although nearly 700 poems are omitted from Souster's total production) they constitute an impressive achievement. I have strong doubt that any other book of poems published in this country in 1964 will equal them. From my highly personal viewpoint, Souster deserves the Governor General's bauble for *The Colour of the Times.*

Let's talk about the man himself first. In a country where the poets are nearly all critics of each other's work, and where "isolation" and "parochial" are words used to spank minor nationalistic versifiers, Souster performs a nearly impossible feat: he loves Toronto. It is a phenomenon unexplainable by any other inhabitant of that city except Pierre Berton. Souster has been employed by a Toronto bank for nearly twenty years; and barring a wartime stint in Europe and a yearly escapist holiday in Montreal, hardly ever leaves the place.

However, this terrible isolation is more apparent than real. Souster has edited international magazines (*Contact* and *Combustion*); he is an editor of Contact Press; along with Layton he is perhaps the best known of Canadian poets outside his own country. At one time he was closely involved with Cid Corman, editor of *Origin*, which magazine provided one of the first outlets for the "new" W.C. Williams and Charles Olson propelled poetry, now boiling south of our most frequently invaded border.

But for all this extroverted activity, I find Souster something of a personal enigma. He is no-man and everyman: a handy medium-sized poet (they come in other sizes) of such anonymity that he takes his colour from his surroundings. A modest poet (that unbelievable anachronism)—you might talk to him all night and never know he wrote poetry. But he is impossible to know unless you read it.

His hobbies are jazz, softball, being married and people-watching. None are exclusive of the others. A. M. Klein wasn't thinking of Souster when he remarked about some abstract poet:

> It is also possible that he is alive
> and amnesiac, or mad, or in retired disgrace,
> or beyond recognition lost in love.

It would be ludicrous to apply any of that to Raymond Souster except the last phrase.

> To find a new function for the *déclassé* craft
> archaic like the fletcher's;

Well, this I doubt—and hope there are a few fletchers around as skilled as Souster. The function of poetry through history has been to serve as primitive magic, social criticism, exploration of selfhood, and the so-called "archetypal myths" of mankind etc. etc. I suppose this Toronto poet contains all these things. In fact I wouldn't be surprised to see a line from one of his poems appearing on a poster illustrating some facet of the Toronto CNE: poetry as advertising—

In considering the poems, I have also to mentally include Eli Mandel's essay (*Canadian Literature*, Summer, '63) which opened up some new areas of understanding. Mandel believes that Souster's approach to poetry is formalistic: i.e. that he has created his own "formalism" and works within those limits, just as older and more traditional poets worked within the rigid stereotypes of sonnet and quatrain, etc.

I would add to this my own opinion that Souster's homogeneous poems, most of an amazingly high level of competence, result from a recognizable "tone" and some very "normal" human reactions rather than actual verse forms and conventions.

Consider, for instance, a man who always talks through his nose; another who continually talks at the top of his voice (Dylan Thomas); a third who speaks calmly and with certain long preformed attitudes (Souster). All these men would be immediately recognizable if you read 250 of their poems at a sitting, as I have of Souster's.

But after a while you begin to pick at the man's characteristics like a sort of literary detective—which is not a very human attitude considering the richness of the poems and the rewards of reading them with simple appreciation. Not excitement in the verse, for I find little of that. Violence in the lower register perhaps, as if overheard a few doorknobs away.

For Souster has achieved his own adjustment to the violence and injustice of living. He observes it, with not exactly detachment, but the belief that he can't do much about it. And this attitude bequeaths a curiously guilty sound to some of the poems. One of them ends: "I who have made my peace with the world." Souster's peace is a partial, violence-echoing quiet peace in his mind, abstracted from the real thing. And there are many others like him who have achieved this mental calm, for sometimes good and valid reasons.

Among Souster's most admirable characteristics is an occasional intensity: not a roar of anger or a scream or fear, but "intensity" so muted that the word most curiously doesn't quite fit.

> "Well, I'm not chicken..."
> that skinny ten-year old girl
> balanced on the crazy-high railing
> of the Dorset bridge:
> > suddenly let go
> down
> fifty feet into the water.
>
> "That one will never grow up
> to be a lady," my mother said
> as we walked away,
>
> but I'll remember
> her brown body dropping like a stone
> long after I've forgotten
> many many ladies . . .

("Lake of Bays")

I dislike such typical clichés as "crazy-high" and "dropping like a stone" (which nevertheless produce their own effect): but I admire the sheer magic blend of nostalgia and scorn in "many many ladies." It is Souster's own unique wave-length. Poetry at its best does this: finds the words to remember both trivial detail and the pain-poignance of all the varieties of love and living.

One thing I never expected to see in Souster is an echo of W.B. Yeats:

surrendered to that boundless air,
caught up in the great mystery.

And from "Leda and the Swan":

So mastered by the brute blood of the air—

But perhaps my own imagination is playing tricks, for Souster echoes humanity at large—and small.

Seen from a ponderous literary detective angle, Souster is an aborted moralist. But he has made his peace, and stays within his own boundaries of "formalism" and morality, observing evil and cruelty from across the fence and down the corridor. And it is one of the extraordinary wonders of language that his stereotypes and clichés actually work (used as he uses them). They do mean something—something familiar and valid. And yet, given practically any of the frames of reference in Souster-poems, I would describe things differently. And be wrong, which is perhaps only a slight indication of this poet's excellence:

Here's "The Old Tin Kettle":

If I'd pointed it out to you
I can almost imagine you saying
with your twin gifts of fantasy and humour,

"Some lost warrior of Champlain's
must have shed it to lighten his escape
from a band of blood-thirsty Iroquois."

So there it sits on the lawn,
no helmet, no shining headpiece, just
an ordinary kettle, very ordinary, old,

with that discarded look which moves me to pity
in people, animals, things: and I go outside, pick it up
almost tenderly, bring it inside with me.

I can imagine no other poet having exactly this thought and feeling and then putting it into words—except possibly Doug Jones. But the actual thought and feeling in this particular poem, once possessed, do not need Souster's own words to be remembered. It may be carried away from the book by any casual reader.

Well—I find myself a little at a loss, having said this much. I come to the sudden conclusion I've really said very little about

Souster. For within his open-shuttered world are an infinite number of fixed stars, most of the same magnitude and none in orbit. All quite still. Which is accounted for by Souster's homogeneous consistency from 1945 to 1964, and possibly and hopefully for many more years. It is also attributable to his reasonable and conversational "tone" of voice, that does not leap to exciting conclusions, states no certainties, delivers very few magisterial judgments.

But for all the minus signs you place beside individual poems, the only identification of the total is an enormous PLUS. They give you a picture of the poet: not a world-view—but Souster's own particular colours of the times. I think some of them are fast. They will not fade until humanity changes, fading slowly, changing slowly—worse to better or better to worse?

*(1964)*

∾

# John Newlove: *Moving in Alone*

IN A NARROW PARTICULAR SENSE poets are in competition with each other, despite the fact each one is supposed to be unique. In another sense entirely, quite apart from the material rewards for poetry (which don't happen to be very bounteous any way), a good poems acts as spur, incentive and springboard for another poet. It is something he can learn from, somebody else's step ahead, whereby he too can take a step ahead still farther in a direction he may not have known existed. Maybe also a catalyst, a thought-trigger which affects more than one person. And because it is these things it enables others with the right mixture of humility and insufferable egotism to learn.

Well, in this book I think John Newlove has learned from people with something to teach, though in no pedantic sense. His rhythmic style is smooth, not jagged. It flows, rolls ahead with the certainty of a poet having something to say. And what Newlove has to say seldom ventures far from fact or concrete incident. The people and place names seem familiar, though not commonplace. Even the few quietly speculative poems have this hard, solid base. The one really imaginative poem of Newlove's I've seen was published in the magazine

*Evidence*, and is not included here. The rhythm is conversational in tone, but has a "metric feeling," even if you can't always prove it.

The title, *Moving In Alone*, characterizes quite accurately the sort of poems the book contains. Isolation, alienation and aloneness. In some degree also it is poetry of self-pity, the confessions of a man who is perfectly aware of the dangers in his confessional stance (i.e., confession implies some sort of guilt, and gets close to the basic idea of religion).

In Newlove's poetry one is bound to think of the problem of human communication; the struggle to express nuances, hints and half-formed thoughts; the implicit premise that all of us are alone essentially, despite the small twitters of sound we make, the flutter of hands reaching out for something—

So faithless one, I in despair
turn from myself to you: Crying
I am the desperate faithless one,
I am the unbeliever, the liar
always confessing, have faith in me!

Though unconstant as the wallowing sea,
I will not move from about your rock:
stay in this poem, stay with me!

("Stay in This Room")

Newlove achieves power and grandeur in the above excerpt, which mere quotation conveys very imperfectly. It matters little that I disagree with many of the things the poems actually says, and that therefore the positive statements are pretty rhetorical to me. The important thing is: it's a fine poem, probably Newlove's best.

Not to be one-sided, I'd better mention some of the things I don't like about John Newlove. For instance, he ends one short piece entitled "Kamsack" with: "but I found it arid, as young men will." I think this is a derivative stereotype, almost Housmanish. But poets, like lovers and actors, are liable to strike an attitude sometimes. It's the very natural fault of settling for a smooth, complete-sounding phrase, without thinking about it any more, or wondering why it has that peculiar echo of having been said already.

In addition, there is the inherent fault of all confessional and personal poems, which is "I-I-I-I" ad infinitum. And you begin to wonder if the poet was ever merely an observer, someone you never noticed, who witnessed a murder or a withered blade of grass by the traffic light moving or seeming to move when cars rushed by.

If only as device or technique to prevent boredom in a reader, the poet should sometimes get the hell out of his own poems, at least seem to present the facts and nothing else. As device or technique only, mind you: for even an observer slants and arranges his material.

However, those are minor points. I want to emphasize one thing very strongly: *Moving In Alone* is a fine book, Newlove's best to date (and I hear the endless echo of other reviewers saying the same thing about now-forgotten volumes).

Despite a few false notes the book has the quality of an integrated personal testament. Perhaps in future Newlove will call to question some of the attitudes and stances in particular poems. I think he must in order to write better ones. In the meantime, from the perspective of a not-neutral observer, the sum-total of these poems looks very large to me.

*(1965)*

## ∞
# *The Cave*

SOMETIMES I THINK IF I SEE that word "honesty" used to describe a poet just once more, I'll grow talons and claw the blurbwriter until he emits shrieks of pain that are nothing if not "honest." The way blurbwriters use the word, it becomes a rank and smelly cliché, and it certainly doesn't describe John Newlove's poems in *The Cave* nearly as well as a wolf-whistle on a street corner encircles and worships a pretty girl.

Neither do Newlove's poems "speak plainly about plain themes," however much they may appear to do so. Superficially, perhaps, the human realities and politics of love are simple, but only from the outside. Newlove is inside. Take this line from "A Young Man": "I still dream of the perfect moment occurring": then later, in the same poem: "But I saw the dead bodies floating on the river."

That kind of thinking destroys placidity and the calm surfaces of things for ever.

John Newlove has always used a stripped-down language, in which decoration played small part, and in *The Cave* this quality is even more in evidence. In earlier books there was a brooding under-current of domesticated despair, along with recurrent gaiety and intensity. There was self-pity and navel-watching, and nearly complete awareness of these things in himself. There was also derision at his own weakness that becomes a metamorphosed strength.

All these things are carried to a near ultimate in *The Cave*, except that I think any trace of gaiety has disappeared. Bryan McCarthy, in *Smoking the City*, dived into these blackest places of the human psyche, and has not surfaced with another book since. One might speculate that the reason for this failure is McCarthy's own failure as a writer, or else that joylessness carried to its extreme is a dead end, a blank wall confronting the mind. I hope Newlove's present attitudes do not lead to this blank wall; he is only 32 years old, and his poetry has not quite become merely bitter philosophy, if only because it has more flesh attached.

But there is also wit attached to some of Newlove's bitterness, as in "Never Mind":

Never mind your jealousies and leavings;
she is beautiful and kind to you;
if you took hers, she took your leavings,

To be jealous of a loving woman for loving
is foolishness—she'd not love you
if she were not; and where'd your jealous loving be?
These meetings and lovings and leavings
ought to be comfort, not distress, to you.

It is a greedy man who acts as you,
one who cannot have enough of loving
and always plans his leavings.

And what is one to make of this autobiographic fragment: "I act the part/my youth derided: half-success/in a limited circle?" I feel an odd embarrassment reading that line, and wonder if Newlove feels he is hypnotized and trapped by this "half-success" which he probably accounts failure. But I've never thought Newlove a failure, for his poems have always seemed to me to bypass such words as failure or success. The very act of writing a poem or a novel or whatever, is an act of faith that makes whatever happens to the end-writing-product rather irrelevant when set beside the writer's own pride in his work.

Many of *The Cave* pieces are love poems, of a grinding intensity one can expect from Newlove. The themes are black, admittedly, but sometimes leavened by wit and such plays on words as the aforementioned "leavings." And there is a vision of existence in the title poem that seems to alleviate the blackness somewhat, unless this reader is deceiving himself. That poem ends:

> Beyond the planets,
> beyond the dark coffin, beyond the ring of stars,
> your bed is the shining tree-lit cave.

However, I remain dissatisfied with this book, despite its merits. Despair and bitterness are sometimes good material for poems; but some kind of magnificence and/or profundity has to come out of them. Poems are refracted in each case from a particular personal life, and taken in total I suppose it's possible to reconstruct that life. When the poems are one-sided, this seems to me due to the limitations of the writer—which I hope is not the case with Newlove.

*(1971)*

# ∞
## *Lies*

JOHN NEWLOVE RECEIVED THE Governor General's Award for this book in 1973. The jacket blurb, which quotes Margaret Atwood, says Newlove is a master of form, epigrams to lyricism to "something like a grand manner." I dunno about that. He is master of a blunt subtlety, hits you so suddenly over the head that you don't quite believe it and walk around pretending not to be unconscious. But this technique is a modern one, does not include such troglodyte forms as sonnets, etc. Nor are Newlove's rhythms easily scanned. He is not a poet of imagery. Things are so stripped down, with such muscular syntax, adjectives like outriders of a storm (he would never make such an image as that), and whatever he says is so simply stated that sometimes it seems more like telegram than poem. And yet the implications are not so simple. One could almost say, "The man who writes like this is a puritan ascetic who lives in the desert and writes verses to match his own temperament and character."

Newlove's subject matter is quite simply an indictment of all mankind as well as a personal indictment—for Newlove spares no one. Poem after poem parades grimly for the reader: "and I wish I were dead/or kissing the ocean's lovers/brown foam on their opened eyes . . ." Almost immediately afterwards: "and all time stopped/world without end/and I was as a tree is, loathing no one . . ." That last phrase makes me shiver under the warm bedclothes of optimism. Again: "There's a strange dog/puking in my sink/where I wash the dishes/I wish I were blind . . ." At this I wonder, is Newlove really human, the way we, humanity, are supposed to be? For he denies humanity except in cruelty, blood and oppression. Kindness? What's that? Love? Here's what love is: "Accept my suffering, which is all I have made of my life/which is all the love I want to offer you . . ."

Newlove is allied to all the verse pessimists who ever lived because of this black outlook; and yet he is like no one else, as nearly unique a poet as any I know of. Robinson Jeffers parades somberly beside him, condemning the corrupt and useless world. A.E. Housman works his bitter nostalgia by which we gain pleasure from our own pain, joyfully watching the progress of disease in mad humanity. These poets have all created a world; but is it a mirror held to the real world, or a mirror to their own minds, i.e., how close is Newlove to reality, if there is such an objective thing?

Few believe in Dante's *Inferno* any more, or in any of the other hellfire prescriptions. Few are religious—at least not many of the people I know—and subscribe to heaven and hell, except the one of their own making. But Newlove's human hell is a far worse inferno than Dante's, because he does not postulate a heaven as counterbalance. Hope there is none, pain is all; and the modulations of pain, lessening and intensifying, are among the few grim consolations of being alive. And one more consolation: the pleasure of taking one's own pulse to ascertain the degree of suffering. (I suffer, I hurt, therefore I am.)

Having made a few comments on Newlove's technique, I still don't quite know how he does it. A poem called "Company"—is marvelous in its verisimilitude to what we are sure we have known—specifically, the useless bum who inhabits all our fears of what we might become ourselves. Because, cunningly, Newlove allies himself and us to all the failures, all the hatred, all the pain . . . : "To remember without lying is difficult/With friends, drinking beer, there is a set of rules/a code of telling—that covers the errors/the cowardice and stupidities/turning them into weak amusing virtues/anecdotes in which no one really wins or loses." Migawd, one says, that's me, the me I am or was or will be.

Newlove's world, which one presumes to be the real world for him, in which goodness is only slightly higher gradations of evil, and history and morality and religion are nursery rhymes—is that a real place for the reader as well? And one must decide. I think it is real, to the extent that we all partake of it; but we all envy it with one part of our minds. Denial is self-deception, and the participation is sharing and hence guilt for what we share. But the obvious question for Newlove and all of us is, if things are so bad all over, why don't we give up our small pleasures and just commit suicide?

Here I interrupt my own uncertain discourse on morality. I want to be unfair to the rules of the reviewer's game, and irrelevant to the poems, since I have more information in this situation than the ordinary reader. Re Newlove's own character which, as I know it personally, is at variance with any of these poems. So I'm breaking some rules, so what the hell . . .

Okay—Newlove is ferocious sometimes, tolerates no fools, is scornful, sarcastic, laughs sometimes, sometimes helps other people, has been known to be sympathetic, has friends and values them. One part of him is like and matches these poems; one part of him does not.

Therefore, the black world he writes about is only one part, perhaps not even half, of his own personal existence—all of which he interprets differently than I would if I were able to live his life. So let me be explicit as possible: Newlove is a formidable person, but not a monster. Yet his poems are about monsters and inhabited by distorted devils.

Why the paradox? It is a real world Newlove writes about, but not the only real world. Is Newlove's real-written-about-world then a phony and false world, and blessedly imaginary? I think not. The place exists. And from it there is no built-in escape hatch whereby you can say the magic words, Bethune, Guevara, Gandhi etc., and make yourself feel good. Newlove does not see himself as having nicey nicey qualities. (I will not accuse him of them; it would make him mad.) He prefers to write about the world of cruelty, weakness and blood, which in poems is far more believable than sainthood. Not just "prefers"—but in some strange way makes his home there inevitably. The dichotomy between person and poems is very striking, and has more to do with philosophy than day-to-day life. And if the black, hopeless philosophy invades your daylight house, it is terribly dangerous. I think of John Clare and others who lived on the edge of madness.

Anyway, Newlove's reality is a marvellously effective one of poems, verses that appal, strike like sledgehammers, that say stop here and look at yourself, that say we are mad, whose message of pain is so one-sided the slightest alleviation is like the guy who kept hitting himself on the head with a hammer because it felt so good when he stopped. Poems that point up goodness like a bright but flickering light just slightly glimpsed, because the quality is so rare. If you exaggerate a thing enough, then the opposite becomes more prominent and real than the exaggeration, omnipresent just under the surface.

Newlove does not exaggerate, except insofar as he is selective in subject matter, interpretive re surface appearance and motives, and deeply, blackly philosophic. Take the girl who was raped a week ago in Toronto, whom many heard crying for help, but no one helped. Then a couple of days later on a subway platform, there was another attempted rape. But this second time someone came to her rescue. Add up the people in these two incidents whom you would label "good" and "evil." Evil has it by a large margin. And that is Newlove's reality. *Lies* is the reality we all live in, to whatever degree we can stand it, a reality that sends us searching for other kinder worlds, which must exist even if only by implication.

Of course, *Lies* is a good book of poems too. We've all been where it was written.

*(1973)*

∞

# New Wave Canada
## Raymond Souster, ed.

IN 1953 OR '54 I WAS IN VANCOUVER when A.J.M. Smith came to town to look over the farm system—poetry farm system, that is. He was editing another edition of *The Book of Canadian Poetry* for an American publisher, and was keeping his eyes open for a good minor leaguer or two, and there was a party and—

However, in 1966 the farm system is pretty well all included in Raymond Souster's *New Wave Canada*, though it leaves out some potential .300 hitters and good utility players I'll mention later. Souster says: "I contend in all seriousness that within the covers of this anthology is the most exciting, germinative poetry written by young Canadians in the last hundred years of this country's literary history."

That sounds like a large claim but when you consider that only in the particular series (preceded by *Poetry 62* and *Poetry 64* with both Fr. and Engl. poets) have the young poets been published en masse at all—then the claim doesn't seem to mean as much.

When Ryerson Press (as I understand it) decided not to continue its series, then Souster along with Contact Press stepped into the breech, and for this I am grateful. There definitely is more good poetry being written today than ever before, much of it having a homogenized revivalist character due to south-of-the-border origins.

But I have some reservation about Souster's large claim. Are the poets in his anthology better (for instance) than Smith, Scott and Klein were at the same age and placed in their particular time? Are they better than the Dudek-Layton-Souster triumvirate of the Forties? Well, probably such comparisons are silly and meaningless, but I make them because Souster brought up the question himself.

Is Souster's book (which leaves out the French Canadians) better than the first two volumes of the series? *Poetry 62*, edited by Eli Mandel, looks rather old-hat now. But it wasn't then, and not very long ago, including Jones, Acorn, Reaney, Cohen, Nowlan etc. (Will New Wave also look a bit passé in a short time? In *Poetry 64*, edited by John Colombo, the Tish-Black Mountain poets of Vancouver, whose roots are in the US, got their first hearing in an anthology of Canada-wide distribution, since they couldn't manage publication anywhere else. Does *New Wave* also surpass that anthology?

I suppose that to raise such questions is to demonstrate how senseless they are. But one thing is very clear about the Souster book: it's much more difficult to judge as to excellence than the others. Why? The reason, I think, is the changing style of poetry itself. It's getting better in some ways, and it's also getting much closer to prose rhythms—i.e., it's getting clearer, easier to understand, as prose generally is easier to understand than poetry. And one might think that the poetry being easier to understand would enable the knowledgeable reader to pick out the phony, separate the wheat from chaff and similar clichés. But there's a "mystique" of "inspiration" and "holiness" that has always been a corollary of poets and poetry. A mystique that inhibits criticism.

In Canada especially, one isn't supposed to say a poem is shit, even if it is. It might hurt somebody's feelings. Young poets always want to be treated with serious respect, and of course always deserve serious respect. Some of them. And in this book are enough fairly good ones to merit a hearing, though I think few of them will hold you enraptured (unless you badly want to feel enraptured), or lure you away from stock quotations or the hockey game.

About that mystique I mentioned: it's probably always existed. Poets have always been thought strange wild slobs, and most of them have taken pleasure in such a self-regarding, attention-getting concept of themselves, (i.e. I'm a genius, you ignorant insensitive clod!) Such innocent narcissistic pleasure in our own abilities we all need, whether poets or men of solid worth in the community.

But I think the mystique has been strengthened, and has been casting a longer shadow over us (us non-geniuses) during the last few years. And like most of our best imports the strengthening quality of the mystique comes from the US.

It's very likely the same mystique of holiness which attaches to the Beats, poetry writing ones or not. It's the mystique of—when you don't like something, such as the Viet Nam war or feeling yourself being turned into a cliché—retreating to another anarchistic world, instead of trying to do something about the world you're already in.

(For instance, where are the Beats in the Negro civil rights movement?) And the Black Mountain verse technique, so-called, is allied spiritually with the Beats. Both groups, if they are that, have an innate feeling of being a minority and outsiders, as many poets and neurotic children have had in the past.

Anyhow, the Beat and Black Mountain mystique has much in common with the poets' mystique, the latter having been in existence for centuries, ivory towers and all. And so all three have coalesced to some degree. But the first two have pretty well lost sight of an end or goal, lost it in the delightfully new self-importance of being outsiders. The fact and technique of actually being Beat poets or Black Mountain ones IS the goal. (The word "goal" is meant in the general sense of something worthwhile.)

All the above is not to say there is nothing valuable in BM methods. There is. But it's over-balanced and corrupted in narcissistic love of technique itself. Just as there is something valuable in beat withdrawal from the nasty world—as a demonstration of principle, not as end in itself.

To get back to New Wave Canada, most of the poets included use the conversational understatement rhythms of Pound, Williams, and Black Mountain—which are not new, nor were they new when used by Pound and Williams. One of the results of the Tish-poets and their explicit undeviating methods, is that a small wave of enthusiasm for poetry has come into existence in Canada. No one could deny that this is good. But is the poetry-product of such enthusiasm good or bad: Well, I say cautiously, poetry is indeed better than it was, but carries along with it the defects of over-enthusiasm: that is, suspension of the critical faculty: to some extent, in favour of the method itself.

In *New Wave*, the poets I like best are those I think have learned from Williams and BM without being overwhelmed by technique-mystique. Among them, Nichol, Buckle, Gilbert, Gill, Hawkins, Jonas, MacSkimming, McFadden & Ondaatje (a poem of his in *Canadian Forum* called "Elizabeth" knocks me over). Call it my square-wrong headed orneriness or what you like, but I think work of the remaining poets is fragmented in such a way that I don't know what they're getting at or don't care even if I should suspect. (Nor will they care much if I don't know.)

The poets left out of this anthology are nearly as impressive as those included: Ball, Mayne, Pat Lane, Marshall, Eadie, Bissett & Jim Brown—four of those named repairing the omission by publishing books in the Very Stone House series in Vancouver. I don't like all of them either, but think they should have been included in an anthology such as this one. However, I'm sure any poet with something to say will emerge sooner or later, and that omission may hurt but doesn't mean much.

To end a dull review I'd like to say something portentous. What? Well, dammit, I'd like to see young poets start to be themselves, find out themselves what they are, using techniques of any kind selectively, judiciously, for whatever their purpose may be. Even though I know most of us appear to have no purpose other than the navel-self, till we suddenly find one outside ourselves. In the meantime we imitate. (And I do mean the BM do-it-yourself kit with warm douche.) And certainly there are many Americans, tall and cast in heroic mold, not unwilling that we should imitate them, or even follow.

*(1967)*

∞

# Group Review I

IN 1943 A.J.M. SMITH PUBLISHED *The Book of Canadian Poetry* which contained most of the best-known Canadian poets of that time. In 1947 John Sutherland, as a kind of rebuttal, published *Other Canadians*, which included some writers omitted by Smith, and attacked the latter's critical terms of reference in a pungent foreword.

The 1966 parallel to the Smith book is *New Wave Canada*, the Contact Press selection of new poets, edited by Raymond Souster and which he contends in his foreword contains "the most exciting, germinative poetry written by young Canadians in the last hundred years of this country's literary history." But in 1966 as in 1943 some poets were left out of the new anthology. And I would hazard to guess that the new publishing venture, Very Stone House of Vancouver, is a direct result of the four writers reviewed here being omitted from *New Wave Canada*.

Seymour Mayne (originally from Montreal) is, to my mind, a

young professional. I'm sure he will be writing poetry all his life. In *From the Portals of the Mouseholes* (his third book) the language is loose and easy, and stems from both the Williams-Pound-Olson-Creeley progressions and the submerged lyricism of metric traditionalists—not to mention Irving Layton. Mayne's poems include some undoubted prose and posturings, but in others, when perhaps he forgets himself, his cleverness is fused with the subject matter. Despite the seeming openness of Mayne's love poems, I don't think he really wants the reader to know what he is like personally and he presents no clear and consistent image of himself (not that I think he is obligated to).

> Someone will build on us,
> Your children, mine, if I have any.
> Leave scratches on furniture
> Kick the walls of your suite
> Scar the bathroom mirrors
> leave a mark      leave it
> That I was here

("The Time")

The above version of Seymour Mayne is not performing, despite the injunction for breakage. And the excerpt is only one reason why I think his poems are a map of loneliness.

*Fires In the Temple*: Bill Bissett's poems are something of a puzzle to me, and perhaps to himself as well. He writes a great deal, intends many poems to have the effect of songs, performs wild typographic experiments on the page, uses his own brand of phonetic spelling, and occasionally indulges in the "Oh ain't it wonderful" type of exclamatory holiness. In short, Bissett has a rather marvellous inconsistency of style, which I think is rare and good in a young poet.

However, these various intriguing qualities have not jelled into coherence and power. Bissett rambles (probably without knowing where he is going or caring), and has very little self discipline. I think that even the wildest rhetorical experiments need a measure of control, require that the writer possess a cool brain which observes dispassionately all the body's most passionate excesses. And since I seem to be pontificating, let me add one more quality a good writer should have: the ability to see his own mistakes and turn them into positive virtues.

Pat Lane's poems in *Letters from the Savage Mind* are again a reversion to the commonplace: except that here the "commonplace" is streaked and veined with insights. Language: straightforward and communicating directly (except in the title poem, which is diffuse). Subject matter: everyday life of a Vancouver workman.

The above comments may not appear to add up to much, yet the poems do. As in certain other writers, Lane's sum is more impressive than the parts, though the worker is much less in evidence than the other two-thirds of his life. Excerpts are difficult to come by from a man who writes even-quality and fairly lengthy poems, but here is a recurring scene in any city:

a long blue arm
asking me
where I'm going
and
    no answers

hard looks
questions

    no identification
    nothing
        "Just walking—
        taking in the scene!"

    without excuse
    a wrong answer

WARNING
get inside
out of darkness

("Christmas 65")

Jim Brown's *The Circus in the Boy's Eye* has some fine erotic drawings (Bissett again), but the poems are easily good enough to stand by themselves. If Mayne is the professional, Lane the everyday chronicler, Bissett the wild experimenter, then Jim Brown is the rather shy and introspective prototype of the non-public poet: probably influenced by Leonard Cohen, the public opposite of himself.

Brown's language is tough and modern, but this is deceptive.

The poems are by turns sensuous, gentle, warm, and musing. Here's the last part of "Waitin for th Bus":

waitin for th bus
me in my university disguise
sayin as if I (and
the world is my oyster)
owned the fuckin country
,sayin that this modern art
on the fences is just as good
as art ever was
and explainin how poetry
is doin this and doin that
and old Tom sayin
its shit

waitin for th bus
and old Tom
laughin
cause I'm so serious
about nothin

The poems of these four poets are very different from the school book literary ritual drummed into our heads by tone-deaf teachers when some of us were children. All four young, groping and earnest—only Seymour Mayne has much sense of humour.

Of the four I'm most interested in Jim Brown's development. There seems to me little doubt that Seymour Mayne will continue to write and improve—his ego demands it. About Pat Lane, however good his poems are now, to continue in that everyday-poem-diary vein is a dead end. And Bill Bissett, just possibly, has the most potential—if he begins to pay attention to someone (not necessarily me) besides his own admirers, who are not likely to be very critical.

But these are young poets, well worth reading now; and in the future one of them may write something that will freeze you right inside your clothes. Any one of the four. And I think *New Wave Canada* made a mistake in omitting them.

*(1968)*

# Group Review II

WHAT CAN ONE POSSIBLY SAY OR FEEL when confronted with twelve books of poetry to be reviewed inside a couple of weeks? I feel profoundly shallow and inadequate. Why isn't Milton Wilson doing this, or Eli Mandel? Maybe F.R. Leavis? Most fortunately, I brewed a couple of batches of wine this fall, and will probably need every bottle before finishing the review.

What if I don't like any of these books? That would be equivalent to tearing maple leaves into little bits and dropping them on John A.'s tomb, or brutally strangling 1967 baby beavers. But if I like all the books, that's obviously nepotism or something, and I can be booked for incest.

However: among my scholarly remarks in this preface I would like to attack some other reviewers. Graciously, of course. In reviewing books, many reviewers look for greatness, compare the author to Yeats or Eliot, always to the detriment of the man they're dealing with. Which is silly. One kind of greatness doesn't point the finger at another. Besides, what is greatness, that it can be used as a yardstick? Nobody knows what the stuff looks like anyway.

I'm aiming very low in this review: all I'm interested in is what interests me. Whatever low standards I have have already been formulated by reading Yeats, Eliot, and Pogo (among others), so it isn't possible to entirely escape the great dead. But the quick and living interest me far more: they can still surprise the hell out of a poetry reader, occasionally jolt him right out of his seat, and knock over the wine bottle. (It's one of the things I live for, I suppose.) But all the dead can do is repeat themselves endlessly, saying the same things forever.

George Jonas. He's about 6'3" tall and wears coloured glasses. Sort of a Don Juan in a porsche. A CBC editor in the Script Department, when I read scripts part-time. While listening to Jonas talk about poems in Basel's Restaurant in Toronto, never once did I feel that he could write the poems in *The Absolute Smile*. I've read his older poems in *Tamarack*, and thought they were dull. They were too. But somewhere between then and now Jonas hit on something, felt something, thought something.

His Absolute poems are an expression of deliberate withdrawal, touching some of the things A.M. Klein did in "Portrait of the Poet as a Landscape," but without Klein's nice up-beat endings. That a man is surrounded by violence, deceit, and people who think different things than they say. But the individual can still live his own life, watching the whole thing happening and being protected by his own awareness—which is pretty idealistic. Jonas has somehow acquired insight and knowledge into wordless situations. To some extent he knows other people's thoughts in the love/hate relationships that make life interesting.

The impression that comes out of the book as a whole might be interpreted by some people as nihilism. As Baudelaire was a nihilist? Or Bryan McCarthy in his recent book, with its black dead-end? No, Jonas is Jonas. Unlike anyone I can think of—and very good.

As a sidelight, *The Absolute Smile* was rejected by three different publishers before House of Anansi finally said yes. Talking to a co-editor of one of these publishers recently, he mentioned that he thought the book was very good and so did the other two editors. "Then why did you reject it?" I said. It turned out the editors didn't like Jonas' outlook, his cynical approach to life, and the quality that might be called nihilistic.

This shocked me. It means the book was rejected because merit and excellence were not the first considerations. ( And I know this is naive on my part.) Perhaps it means that if you write a bad book it might be accepted if it's nice and cheery and appeals to the editor. I'm afraid it does mean that.

Doug Jones. *Phrases from Orpheus.* I have a recent memory of him riding water skis like a young valkyrie, skimming over Paudash Lake with the sun about to set. And it's a totally misleading and out-of-character portrait. In looking at a man' poems, I generally see the man himself reflected or refracted behind them (which is why my reviews can't be relied on). For Jones' poems are not written by a young valkyrie, with all that this term implies. They are tough and rather innocent testaments to his own survival, no matter what. They are also poems of withdrawal, not from life but to a prepared position (somewhat like Jonas' perhaps) where the poet can see what will happen next and not be hurt too badly by what happens. The poems accept what is, whether good or bad—to me a fatalistic outlook.

The first poem in the book, rather surprisingly, supports this view.

The mind is not
Its own place
Except in Hell.

It must adjust, even
When the place is known.

Only time
Will tell the mind
What to think,

What birds to place
On what boughs:
("The Perishing Bird")

Roy Kiyooka. I met him for the first time during a party at his pad in Vancouver. He had a stringy goatee on his chin and kept saying things like "Great man, you dig?" This bewildered me, since it utterly destroyed my conception of how Japanese-Canadians talked. My education is still continuing.

*Nevertheless These Eyes* is Kiyooka's second book. He is a painter, but his poems are not representational: they see things behind object and event. Here's a quote:

I'm on the side of the angels
and dirt . . .

("Nevertheless these Eyes")

Striking, but not true in Kiyooka's case. He's on the side of mysticism, philosophy, and psychology. And makes such elusive painting shadows in his poems that I want him to keep on writing them.

A.J.M. Smith's *Poems, New & Collected*. One picture I have of Smith is that of a stocky figure in a thick sweater, reading a poem in his boathouse at Lake Memphramagog in 1965. For some reason the man, a convivial and occasionally bubbling person, doesn't jibe with his poems. They are said by some, including himself, to be classic, reserved, ascetic, etc., etc.

In many ways Smith seems a figure out of the past, not a

seventeenth-century man but one whose present diction and metrics seem slightly wrong in a modern poet. Yet Smith and Scott in the 1920s signaled the inception of modern poetry in Canada. And there is no rule that says a poet must use slangy diction, or imitate Creeley and Olson. Smith is his own man, but I think he has remained nearly identically the same for many years. It's true that his language has loosened up slightly, and he now seems more preoccupied with death. But the tone and stance seem interchangeable with the early Smith.

Some have called him a minor poet. This seems to me very nearly irrelevant in a judgment of his poems. They are a solid, if not monumental, achievement. But then, who among poets today amounts to a monument? I think only Pablo Neruda. Smith's value is triple—as poet, anthologist, and critic. Among his poems are ten or twelve that I will always read with pleasure, and more that retain some interest.

If any good thing has been with us long enough, we are liable to grow tired of it. Masterpieces, for instance, require that the viewer or reader should grow and change enough to secure a different aspect of them. Smith's good poems have been around a long time (and with this edition are included twenty-two new ones). They give one sharp insights into Smith's character and thinking, but I think not about his particular life. The man in the boathouse reading his poem is another person entirely. Poems and poet have never quite matched. The conflict and dichotomy does not show, but I think it is there.

In *Kingdom of Absence*, Dennis Lee is a black poet, but not unrelievedly so. He has a very wry humour, is academic and slangy at the same time, and while often very good has still a distance to go before reaching full development. One doesn't know if any poet ever will, but in Lee the solid base for it is there.

> Eliot as he passed me
> sent up word: the crowd was just behind,
> there was going to be a parade, did I care to join them?
> But I was trying to extricate my left testicle from the trapeze cord,
>     and I had to decline.

What does one say of that verse? It's clever, trivial, and readable, perhaps a little too clever. It may mean that the poet is too involved in the agonies of life to leave it for anything else. Or it may mean bugger all. It's one of the irritating qualities of modern verse that the writer is liable to scream misinterpretation if you should be so rash as to ascribe any meaning at all to his verse. Anyway, I like much of the Lee I see in this book, and hope he keeps on going.

Raymond Souster's *As Is* is as was, only better. Souster is the old reliable, as to both quantity and quality. Everyone tells him how to write poems: write longer masterpieces, Hayden Carruth advises. I think all the advice worries Souster a little. So he writes a longer masterpiece, and says there now, a little defiantly perhaps. ("The Farm Out the Sydenham Road" picked up a deserved medal.) And goes back to work from nine to five every day in his bank (it ought to be his bank), plays no more softball now he's getting older, and is slowly becoming an absolute trademark of his home city of Toronto. (Quick, Cyril, name me another Toronto poet! You can, but Souster's has got to be the first name that comes to mind.)

This book of poems is easily traceable to all Souster's other books. Except—that he grows a bit more expert with diction and phraseology over the years, and his percentage of slightly marvellous poems rises as time passes. As others have pointed out far too often, Souster is not a go-for-broke poet, but a man who fits and adjusts all he sees to his own narrow focus, wraps a cloak of technique around the events. His typical stance is that of a man trapped by his job and the circumstances of his life. He dislikes the evil he sees around him, but believes little can be done about it. Underlying most of his poems is an innate fatalism, which comes close to being a method of writing poems, Perhaps if Souster looked too closely at his subjects he would see too many things, and hence be forced to exercise a different kind of selectivity, with the poem in danger of disappearing as a result.

But I'm glad to accept Souster as he is, a man who comes along rarely, perhaps once in a hundred years. He's embedded in the Toronto of 1967 as William Lyon Mackenzie was in 1837. I'd never ask him to change—leave the bank, go for broke, sign a non-absti- nence pledge, take a world cruise with a blonde, train a squadron of gulls to shit simultaneously on Toronto City Hall. If he did any of those crazy things, as busybodies like Carruth keep advising, he might not be able to write poems any more. Souster's life is reflected in his poems, and we're both satisfied with both. Right.

*Cry Ararat!* P. K. Page (What a silly title!) I fell in love with P. K.

Page the first time I read "Stories of Snow." The following are two excerpts from that poem.

> In countries where the leaves are large as hands
> where flowers produce their fleshy chins
> and call their colours,
> an imaginary snow-storm sometimes falls
> among the lilies.
> And in the early morning one will waken
> to think the glowing linen of his pillow
> a northern drift, will find himself mistaken
> and lie back weeping.
> And there the story shifts from head to head,
> of how in Holland, from their feather beds
> hunters arise and part the flakes and go
> forth to the frozen lakes in search of swans—
> the snow light falling white along their guns,
> their breath in plumes.
>     \*   \*   \*
>
> And stories of this kind are often told
> in countries where great flowers bar the roads
> with reds and blues which seal the route to snow . . .

Page had, and I guess still has, a marvellous gift for the dreamy stuff that borders childhood, but can still surprise you by veering off to the terrible starched robot "Stenographers" and the equally alien "Portrait of Marina."

I don't actually believe in any of Page's people, but that isn't necessary. They are created nearly full-length on paper, and the poet's own drawings match them in this beautiful book. Plants spring off the page, eyes peer at you, odd birds gawk, and one is lost and forgotten in these strange landscapes. I think if a hold-up man confronted Page with a revolver, she'd confound him with a geranium.

Always around her poems for me are the beautiful myths: the sleeping prince, the princess who finds a pea unbearable despite twenty mattresses underneath, Rapunzel who let down her long heir and died intestate . . . but never Mother Goose.

It's so long since I've seen new poems by P.K. Page that the seventeen recent ones in this book are an especial pleasure. They do not surprise me. I am not so entirely enthralled as I was the first time:

but then I am much older and sadder. I remember Page as I remember the Wizard of Oz and Dr. Doolittle, for she is instantly rememberable. Not urgent and pressing, loud-mouthed and vulgar, booming and majestic, cactus-tongued and satiric. Sensuous, heavy, and drama-like as the great flowers that always seem to bar her roads. I wonder where she would have gone otherwise.

Lionel Kearns has always looked like a pirate to me, and does still in the portrait on the back of *Pointing*—except his gold earring is missing there. In fact, he looks like Errol Flynn with a university degree, and Flynn did read the Kama Sutra. Of course Kearns denies this resemblance, quite vehemently. And it is undeniable that he teaches English at Simon Fraser U.

As a poet, Kearns subscribes—at least partly and with piratic reservations—to the Black Mountain dictums of "in the field composition" and W.C. Williams' ordinary speech rhythms. Perhaps he'd deny that too, but I think a little less vehemently. I agree entirely with Kearns' choice of subject matter: the actual feelings of a man alive today, and the recorded events of his life, without embellishment. (The last bit sometimes makes things difficult.) I'm not always sure that Kearns hits on any vital points in his treatment of those things, but sometimes he certainly does.

This time in the darkness
a twelve-foot pleasure-launch
sleek and gleaming white

The crew (both male
and female) in bikinis
laughing

And in tow
two water-skiers
doing acrobatics

At the back of the boat
instead of an outboard-engine

A man
has been bolted into place

Maybe that poem means people are serving the function of

machines, maybe it means people don't give a damn. In any case it's good.

Several years ago Kearns was experimenting with what he called "stacked verse," with vertical lines running down somewhere near the middle of the poem. I notice one or two relics from those stacked verse days in this collection—without the vertical line. And that indicates something. Kearns is moving and changing. I don't know where he's going, but it seems worthwhile to me just to see him move and watch the interaction of light and landscape; and for Kearns to accept and reject (I believe the old cliché that accepting one thing means rejecting another), explore and consolidate. It's a pleasure to watch him grow and change, as it is to watch any young poet who is doing that. I like pirates.

*The Unquiet Bed.* Dorothy Livesay went to Africa on a teaching stint a few years ago, and came back quite a different person. At least she seems different to me, both in her poems and as a person: a brown, middle-aged woman with an easy smile, one of the most attractive people I know.

At one time her writings had, in Milton Wilson's words, an "imagistic and epigrammatic quality"; and in the thirties she added to this "a new expressiveness of form and style, and a new range of social and industrial material." Milton Wilson is a wise man, but I have to say that I think Livesay's early poetry was dull, despite all the sweet nice things said about it and two G.G. Awards. She is a much better and more human poet now.

> *And what fantasies do you have?*
> asked the psychiatrist
> when I was running away from my husband.
> Fantasies? fantasies?
> Why surely (I might have told him)
> All this living
> is just that
> every day dazzled
> gold coins falling
> through fingers.
> So I emptied my purse for the doctor
> See! nothing in it
> but wishes.
> He sent me home

to wash dishes.

("Ballad of Me")

If, as Livesay says, verbalizing techniques of Creeley and Duncan have given her this human dimension, I applaud them—but prefer to give a little credit to Dorothy herself. The love poems in this book strike a wise, witty, and warm counterpoint to the woman herself. I really doubt that Kiyooka's drawings do anything for the poems. Dorothy Kiyooka and Roy Livesay don't mix. (Whereas Page's drawings go with her poems perfectly.)

Livesay is nearly sixty years old now, but I am hopeful (you condescending bastard, Purdy!) that this very human poet will go on to another plateau of personal discovery with poems to match—almost. As it is, there's a brown metamorphosed butterfly hovering on the cold window sills of Fredericton at UNB, where she is writer-in-rez. Strange too, I thought she was washed up years ago, and what pleasure I take in being wrong.

*Selected Poems.* George Woodcock's young face on the dust jacket of the first book of his I read looked peculiarly English, in a way I could never explain. Years later Woodcock's face looks Canadian, older, hair grizzled, the cockiness of intellectual youth replaced by calmness, and what I might call acceptance. It's a Canadian face now, and I can't explain that either.

As a small child Woodcock went to England, grew up there, and was mostly self-educated. He wrote poems during the thirties, edited the little magazine *Now.* And also began to write that series of books from William Godwin in 1946 to others on Kropotkin, Proudhon, etc., etc., that out-scholar the scholars. In 1949, Woodcock returned to Canada with his wife, lived in a cabin in the deep forest-jungles of Vancouver Island, tried to live by writing, and came close to starving.

All this has a familiar ring. Malcolm Lowry did the same in a squatter's shack on Burrard Inlet. And the "Walden Pond" bit of Thoreau. Countless others. But I speculate on the motives that impelled George Woodcock home to Canada after so many years in literary England. I suppose them to be some kind of reaction against cities, perhaps against the sense of dirty doom inculcated by politics, bombing planes, and war. He may also have felt nostalgia for something half-remembered, the semi-mythical country of birth, where renewal of self was possible in the great rain forests of BC.

The dust jacket of this book shows those forests, and they bear no apparent relationship to the poems inside. I suppose the drawing is meant to contrast with the "total involvement" of the poems, in politics and social anger of the thirties. Then and now, peace of the forest as against dribbling sordid politics, etc.

Poems in the book are selected from three previous books, published in the forties, but which bear a direct relation to the poems of Auden, Day Lewis, and MacNeice of the same period. I don't include Stephen Spender's poems in this comparison, for Woodcock seems to me to have little in common with Spender. In short, the Woodcock of this *Selected Poems* is not quite the contemporary Woodcock, and his poems seem fragments torn from that earlier time—the thirties in England. And yet, there is that drawing of rain forests on the dust jacket.

There are all sorts of literary allusiveness in the poems. Like a later Wordsworth, Woodcock also has his bridge, though he isn't as optimistic.

> This is the preposterous hour when Caesars rise,
> Bleeding, from their beds in the burning sea.
> The dead are cashing in on all our follies.
> They are not men and women, they are not divine,
> These spirits bred of our own villainy.
> It is ourselves who gibber at the pane,
> Clanking across our age magnetic fetters,
> Skywriting madness in incandescent letters.
>
> This evening aviators crumple on killing earth,
> This evening Trotsky is dying. Blood for blood
> Seeping from birth and cataclysmic death
> Mars the pale sky where gulls and flags are flying,
> And love is failing where but hate is good.
> This evening, I perceive, we are all dying,
> We are all dying, like Wilde, beyond our means,
> Dying, as sheep, for our folly rather than sins.

I am not saying that Woodcock is identical with Auden, Day Lewis, and others, for his personal vision is perhaps even darker than theirs. But in poems like "Sunday on Hampstead Heath" his is leavened by—hope?

> In the dead, grey streets I hear the women complain,
> And their voice is a spark to burn the myth of the state.

I suppose that to be the anarchical Woodcock speaking; the man who wrote *Prince Kropotkin (1950)* and *Anarchism (1962).*

It may show through in my own writing about Woodcock that I have a great deal of respect for him. He is the complete scholar, the many-faceted writer, who seems to me in himself to have achieved personal peace and his own kind of wisdom. But the era in which he wrote these poems is his time of testing, passionate acceptance or rejection, the terrible disillusion of the intellectuals, before the cocky English face changed into something like serenity.

His poems here exist for themselves, but also as part of his record, a milestone in time. A few are awkward, with that strange awkwardness which passion translated into poems sometimes has. Others have the quality of still-living myths.

> Imagine the South from which these migrants fled,
> Dark-eyed, pursued by arrows, crowned with blood . . .

What the present collection does for me, apart from appreciation of the Woodcock of the thirties, is make me want to see his now-poems. They would be in some sense his total self, in which pain and fury are blended into peace, as I think happens in the man himself.

Alden Nowlan's *Bread, Wine and Salt* is his first book in five years. It's a good book, as all his books have been good. Nowlan's early poems were nearly all rigidly metrical, but he has moved from that stage to a point where perhaps only one in three relies on metrics, the rest being in free verse forms.

Regional subjects still make up the bulk of Nowlan's poem material, but there are enough pieces dealing with childhood, Ottawa, his own illness, etc., to destroy any pat generalization of him as a strictly regional poet. His style is now tough and realistic, but some of his personal attitudes strike me as oddly naive, perhaps verging on the sentimental. I don't mean mawkish, sloppy sentiment, but the sad lonely feelings that genuinely do exist in people, and which is a human quality in which Nowlan feels his own involvement.

I've felt the same way myself at times. During a visit to Cuba in 1964, I listened to Fidel Castro speak, and afterwards a million people joined hands together and sang the "Internationale," swaying from side to side as they sang. That was a genuine moment, though I think also that it's sentimental as hell.

The best poem in Nowlan's book, for my money, is "The Wickedness of Peter Shannon," which I must quote in full.

> Peter had experienced the tight, nauseous desire
> to be swallowed up by the earth, to have his blue
> eyes plucked out of his fourteen-year-old head,
> his arms sliced off, himself dismembered and the
> remnants hidden forever, his shame was so unanswerable
> Oh, God, God, God, it was so he could take any part
> of Nancy Lynn O'Mally and lie open-eyed and stark
> in the darkness with it—her lilting backsides
> in the candy-cane shorts—and bring his thighs together
> like pliers, muttering, and it was so like the taste
> of peach ice cream and the smoke of leaves burning
> and the wanton savagery of a pillow over his face,
> breaking him, until he swung out over the seething
> water and the limb went down and down and down and
> the rain was a thousand horses urinating on the
> fireproof shingles and he whispered...Ohhhhh,
> Jesusss...mad as a turpentined colt among the rockpiles
> in the north pasture; what are your breasts like
> Nancy Lynn O'Mally, how is it that no matter how much
> I'm ashamed I don't blush, except in company...my cheeks
> burning as though Christ slapped them!

Nowlan's hospital operating room poems—concerning experiences when he didn't know if he was going to live or not—are a new dimension for him. But he is still the same Nowlan as before, with improvements added. Only in "Peter Shannon," with its dangling articles and conjunctions, its rushing verisimilitude of adolescent sexual feelings, does Nowlan show signs of technical change.

I've used those dangling prepositions, conjunctions, and articles myself, along with the rushing rhythms, and I don't say they're good in themselves. But sometimes they are the weightless, cut stone building-blocks of a little masterpiece like "Peter Shannon." And perhaps they prefigure other and rather more startling mental leaps forward. *Bread, Wine and Salt* is a very good book, Nowlan's best to date. But I think he is capable of still better poems, and may write them soon.

*The Making of Modern Poetry in Canada: Essential Articles on Contemporary Canadian Poetry in English* is an odd mishmash of a book. According to the editors, "it seeks to offer essays and documents intimately involved in the literary history of the period, rather than exemplary or autotelic show pieces of criticism." But critical these essays are. And the editors would have it both ways: if the criticism is bad, they can readily point out, as they have already in the preface, that the articles are not meant to be criticism, but historical documents only. If the criticism is good, the editors can then take credit for something that wasn't supposed to be there in the first place.

What Louis Dudek and Michael Gnarowski have supplied here (along with connective material) is their own choice and selection of articles which (they believe) best represent the growth of Canadian poetry. And I think some of their choices are bad. For instance, a piece about myself from *Time* magazine—which is ephemeral journalese and should not have been reprinted. That is personal, and I shall bear Dudek and Gnarowski a burning grudge till my dying day next week. But it's useless to put the finger on this and other pieces, for the editors will blandly say that the book isn't meant to be "exemplary" either.

That's okay, but just what is the book meant to be? I know, I know—the subtitle tells all, "Essential articles on Contemp—"etc. Nevertheless, the system imposed by the editors makes for a great deal of unevenness and the hodge-podge effect in this book of articles—let's not call them "documents." To which Dudek and Gnarowski supply the inevitable retort: "There is a scarcity of good writing dealing with some of the particular literary periods involved." This is true. And I am speechless—damn near.

On the other hand, there is also some extremely good writing in the book. I find John Sutherland's "Introduction to *Other Canadians*" very interesting, especially for a vitriolic attack on A.J.M. Smith that is reminiscent of Layton belaboring Dudek. (Bad manners or attacks of any kind are rare in CanPo.) I like Dudek's own "Patterns in Recent Canadian Poetry," though I disagree like hell with some of his opinions, including (again) those about myself. Dudek,

Gnarowski, and Davey are all good on little magazines. But the book still resembles a thrown-together hodge-podge. To which the editors will retort...etc.

In the Beginning was the Word, and it wasn't Jehovah's. It was Arthur Stringer's, John Murray Gibbon's, Frank Oliver Call's, and crap like that. Exodus was Frank Scott and Arthur Smith (the news just reached me) with the inception of the "modern movement" in Montreal during the twenties. Follow various prophets and high priests of the order of Klein, Layton, Birney, Souster, and Dudek himself. etc. The New Testament is *Tish* magazine in Vancouver, spawned by another prophet named Olson out of Black Mountain which begat begat...begat what? It is not possible for BM to begat or beget anything, so far as I can see, which isn't far. They are a dead-end in themselves, both ends.

But anyway, that's what Dudek and Gnarowski are trying to "document," with articles relating to all these "movements." I admit grudgingly and generously that they have done what they set out to do. But I don't like it. Despite the undeniable interest and value of some pieces, the shape of the book is blah.

I reviewed *The Making* after the poetry books, thinking it might give me something to push against, agree or disagree with, provide insight into the historical sequence of the other books. The trouble is that I disagree about the choice of articles (I probably couldn't do any better), as well as many of the editors' expressed opinions. I disagree with them so much, especially Dudek's, that I find the genealogy of the poetry I've just reviewed perfectly irrelevant. It isn't, of course. But I still feel that way. For instance, what does Souster's, Smith's, Woodcock's, and Livesay's Canadian literary genealogy consist of? My own reaction is Ah-r-r-r!

But doesn't the fact that I disagree with Dudek and Gnarowski so strongly make their book interesting for just that reason? Stimulating, that is. Yes, of course, within limits. The book is very interesting in spots. It's also a drag! To think the profs will use this as a textbook on CanPo in universities—where it will be extremely valuable. Yes, really valuable! But I hope the profs will also disagree, and students will disagree, everyone will disagree and that might be interesting. Maybe some of the dissenters will write articles, better ones, which Dudek and Gnarowski may/might perhaps include in the next edition.

*(1968)*

∞

# Poets Between the Wars
## Milton Wilson, ed.

**T**HIS BOOK IS THE THIRD IN A SERIES that has presented the work of better-known Canadian poets in large-sized chunks, in opposition to the usual practice of a few poems each from many poets. In this latest book there are five poets, and the title has the implication for me that poets were writing frantically before the inevitable war stopped their writing.

Of these five poets, Smith and Scott are associated with the beginnings of modern poetry in Canada. They collaborated in the 1920s on the *McGill Fortnightly* (the inevitable English-sounding title), with Smith becoming since then the grand panjandrum of anthologists and critics, and Scott achieving fame as lawyer and civil rights leader as well as poet.

Looking at their poems now, Smith seems to me more closely bound to the restrictions of techniques than Scott. The latter had an amazing variety of themes and construction, and shifts from metrics to loose speech rhythms with practiced ease. His ability to extract snobbish quotations from the invitation sent to prospective members of the Canadian Social Register and blend them with his own sharp asides, makes an hilarious poem.

I see F.R. Scott as a nationalist poet, but also humanist in a wider sense, satirist and lyricist. His "Lakeshore" is still, after many years, a magnificent portrait of humanity. And "Laurentian Shield" is clear and explicit, a poem realizing that the perennial possibilities of Canada have always remained unfulfilled in the north. Scott has never been anything else than clear and easy to understand, a quality difficult to achieve and which certain unperceptive critics have derided. If only through the sheer variety and diversity of his poems, I think Scott will be around for a very long time.

A.J.M. Smith is, of course, a proponent of classicist diction and philosophy, as perhaps exemplified by his poem "Like an Old Proud King." Smith's poetry, however, has moved from this ascetic stance to something more personal which surely amounts to a late blossoming. But the selection in this book does not fully indicate Smith's poetic renaissance.

E.J. Pratt, from the time of his first emergence in the 1920s, has achieved the greatest reputation of any Canadian poet. The selection here of "The Great Feud," "Towards the Last Spike," and three shorter poems, is probably the best that could be made in keeping with space limitations. Any description of Pratt I ever read labels him as one of those grand-sounding creatures, "epic poets." He deals with large themes, man against nature, scaly breeds versus mammals, disaster and triumph on sea and land. His lines are generally marked by a heavily stressed metric beat; he avoids entirely anything personal in his own poems. In this minority view, Pratt's metric beat and reiterative polysyllabic habits have the effect of making many of his poems excruciatingly dull. Some do not share this opinion, but even apart from method I find little to interest me in an imaginary battle between the race of reptiles and the clan of mammals.

However, in Pratt's narrative poem of the CPR's construction, the aforementioned heavy beat becomes softer and not so obtrusive. One hears of Scots whose "oatmeal was in their blood," and the food bequeathed "The power to strike a bargain with a foe,/ To win an argument upon a burr—." And the Canadian Shield above Lake Superior is conceived in the well-known lines:

> On the North Shore a reptile lay asleep—
> A hybrid that the myths might have conceived,
> But not delivered, a progenitor
> Of crawling, gliding things upon the earth.

Also a picture of John Macdonald getting drunk and hearing part of a contemporary song in his imagination:

> "We'll hang Riel up the Red River,
> And he'll roast in hell forever,
> We'll hang him up the River
> With a yah-yah-yah."

That fragment of song from the past retains a curious authenticity across the years.

"The Last Spike" seems to me the most readable of Pratt's poems. Certain others have brilliant and memorable passages, but remain indigestible as a whole. I think Pratt's large reputation will gradually subside until it finds its proper level, that of something more than competence, but something far less than genius.

Milton Wilson says in his note on Dorothy Livesay that she has an "imagistic and epigrammatic quality" in her earlier poems. And that in the Thirties "she added to this a new expressiveness of form and style and a new range of social and industrial material." At one time I thought that accurate and slightly forbidding description of Livesay's earlier self would apply forever, and that it was all that could be said for her. But on her return in 1963 from a teaching stint in Rhodesia, she encountered the so-called "Black Mountain" verbal and idiomatic techniques, and adopted them, with some personal variations, as her own.

In some ways Livesay was always a deeply personal poet, though her language was not particularly original in those early days. But recently a new frankness and more modern idiom have resulted from both experience and encounters with "new" techniques whose prime concern is the live "sound" of poems.

A.M. Klein has written no poems since 1951, but he remains a compass point and beacon of comparison for other Canadian poets, particularly Jewish ones. Layton has learned from him, and probably Leonard Cohen has too. Klein wrote poems of tremendous "Jewishness" with an erudition and knowledge of his own tradition that is probably without equal. He used conventional metrics, but varied them in surprising ways so that monotony is rarely present in his poems. And above all, his poems contain transmissible emotions:

> And those assembled at the table dream
> Of small schemes that an April wind doth scheme,
> And cry from out the sleep assailing them:
> *Jerusalem, next year! Next year, Jerusalem!*

This vivid Zionist emotion is one reason why I would place Klein near the top of any list of Canadian poets. It is a quality entirely absent in E.J. Pratt, whose persona seemed to remain always aloof from his poet's voice.

All the poets in this book are nearly 60 years of age or well past it. (Of course, Pratt is dead.) It is doubtful if any of them will add very much to the quality of work already written; but their total quantity of work will probably increase. None of them is great, but all are more than competent. They compare, I think favourably with a similar group of poets from any other country—unless such a group should include one of the very few outstanding figures like Neruda or Quasimodo.

The reader is not likely to be enthralled or fascinated or carried away by these poems, but he can and should be very much interested by what has been done in the past. For that is the key: all these poets seem to me to belong a little behind the present moment, embalmed just five minutes ago. They recede while you look at them (and this is not a writing-off or dismissal). Their work is both achievement and monument. I think that none now will break from the self-imposed bonds of style, idiom and personal mentality. At least it seems unlikely, despite Livesay's recent mutations of style.

And that is not to take anything away or lessen this body of work. But in some way, fulfillment negates potential. The trails have all been blazed, the roads cut through the jungle, and one stays on the known paths.

And since this is an odd way to end a review, here's another incident that might be relevant. A few weeks ago at Kingston, Irving Layton told me he was going to the Far East, and planned to remain there for some time—in an attempt to break out and away from the paths and trends of his previous poems. After the first vital rush and the authentic unselfconscious voice falters, such a break (not a retreat) might be the way to do it—find something somewhere that may trigger the undiscovered reality in your mind.

*(1968)*

# Group Review III

FOUR BOOKS OF POEMS. The only connection I can see between them is a remark by George Bowering in the Intro to his *Touch: Selected Poems* about reading poems aloud. "A woman in Barrie told me that she didn't like my poetry before she came to my reading and then she liked it—that was because she hadn't really read it, not all of what she had." And I wonder how many more "Women of Barrie" there are, who need to hear a writer aloud before they think he is good?

Bill Bissett (*Nobody Owns th Earth*) also reads before audiences a great deal; Bill Howell (*The Red Fox*) does sometimes; I've never heard Doug Fetherling (*Our Man in Utopia*) read at all. Interjecting myself into the discussion: I read at universities too, and can remember the "Woman of Barrie" saying much the same thing to me. Well, I've always felt that one of these people's senses was badly impaired, because I read poems on the page and hear their sound simultaneously in my head. However, it's apparent that some people do not, and these must depend on the performing poet declaiming from the platform. But despite the number of poets doing this, most people will only read verse from the printed page. Which I've always thought was a good thing.

Why? Because many fine poets are lousy readers of their own work. But a bad poet may be partly redeemed by having an excellent voice, with a dramatic personality adding things to his poems that are not really there at all. In fact I've seen people nearly hypnotized by some of the worst poetry ever written, simply because the reader was a cross between Alec Guinness and Dylan Thomas. I'm inclined to think most people listened to Thomas principally for his ocean-tidal-melodious voice, only secondarily for his poems.

The above is prelude to saying that Bill Bissett is probably the premier "performer-reader" in the country. A record I have of his, called "Awake in th Red Desert," is the most caterwauling cacophonous vowel-crazy collection of dissonance I've ever experienced. Therefore, look at Bissett's poems on the page. Notice the almost endless repetitions of line and phrase, the more or less phonetic spelling, the childlike obviousness of many things he says. In short, they are verbal spells and incantations.

Bissett is a poet-prophet, or at least believes he is. Legalized marijuana, universal love, and the undeniable fact that "nobody owns th earth" are three of Bissett's urgent requirements for Utopia or Heaven on Earth. And the very naiveté of his language and themes, the earnestness and complete personal belief he brings to poems— these make him oddly touching and, I think, worthwhile. Bissett's screaming crying moaning caterwauling on lecture platforms I dismiss—and isn't that condescending of me? Of course, but isn't discrimination selectivity, catholicism (what you like) integral in all of us, whether in the choice of beer or friends?

But there is a core of integrity about poet-prophet-Bissett one can't ignore. The reasons why one can't ignore him would be difficult to explain to (say) a panel of fifty middle-aged English profs never entirely weaned from Chaucer, Eliot and alcohol. In many ways, and in my own way, I agree with the things Bissett says in his poems and life. Universal love is the best contraceptive I can think of. It's also agreeable to me that nobody should own the earth, or even 65 per cent of Canadian industry. But Bissett isn't trying to convince me, just the world.

I have a strong feeling that Doug Fetherling may soon be a very good poet, if he doesn't lose the neuroses forced out into poems instead of lapsing into agonized moans. That seems melodramatic, but is the reverse side of many calm and urbane love poems. The book's dust jacket shows "Our Man" about to preach a sermon at the church in Utopia (I presume there is a Utopia, Ont., and Fetherling couldn't resist the opportunity), peering coyly insecure from the church door.

But Fetherling is not *my* man nor, apparently, that girl's to whom he addresses a suitable suite of poems. These involve descriptions of physical feelings and the hard circumstances of being in love—hotel rooms, beds, the female body, and being left in the lurch in Utopia. But the actual doomed-glorified feeling of being in love and hence immortally miserable doesn't come across, except once:

> Your absence has not taught me
> how to be alone, it merely has
> shown that when together we cast
> a single shadow on this wall.
> The wall I suppose is as a wall
> should be: plain and bare and
> final as a cliff. And when I
> stretch, my hands find it instead
> of you and I invent truths men
> thought of years ago without
> telling me.

("Your Absence Has Not Taught Me")

Much of Fetherling's work is written in a deliberate analytical-cum-vivisectionist method and tone of voice. (Incidentally, a complete change of style from his first book.) And perhaps this method increases the cold heat when such a genuine poem as "Your Absence" is discovered. And others are almost as good. But many of his poems repel me as device, rather than whatever a poem actually is. For instance, one mentioning "the effect (after the poet's suicide) his brains are to have upon the wallpaper design." (Who cares, except him?) Others are blank cartridges of the imagination.

However these adverse comments should prevent no one from reading *Utopia*. Poets may arrive like a world's possible ending: "not with a bang but a whimper." Fetherling's whimper holds a certain grandeur.

Bill Howell is 25, with many of the faults and virtues some poets have at that age. For instance, I'm sure Howell would defend "I can't wait to get home for Christmas and be hugged by Mom," which sentiments cause me to wriggle with extreme nausea. But then, "After finally Reading Camus Through to the End" ends:

> For the record again, I'll tell you how
> I'm going to end:
> I'm ninety-seven
> in my Ferrari on an Alpine roadway (or equivalents)
> when I miss a hairpin
> turn with my sixth or seventh wife, age 18
> beside me (again or equivalents),
> when a ball of living fire
> crowns my charisma.

At which point I chuckle, thinking he has a "good idea" for a poem there. Howell has a lot of good ideas, and sometimes he makes use of them. Sometimes.

Ten years ago, when Bowering, Frank Davey, Frederic Wah and others were schoolboys of the Vancouver Group—these being embryonic Black Mountain adults—I noticed phrases and passages in Bowering which I thought indicated a developing poet in his early stages. It's a pleasure to see that development carried much farther in his *Selected Poems*, and become solid achievement. But I retain the same reservations I've always had (somewhat differing from his own reservations about me) re Bowering's methods and loyalties to the in-group whose far-out gods are still Olson, Williams and Creeley. However, it's rather picayune to mention such ideologies in the face of Bowering's undeniable merit. I don't really give a damn how he manages to write his poems, although I'm sure he'll tell me if I don't ask. The best way to illustrate this merit is to quote a poem in full, "Poem Written for George":

> Poetry with politics in it
> is small men answering back to volcanoes.
>
> Volcanoes are upside down grails
> knights look for
> walking on their hands.
>
> I never met a poet yet
> who was a knight.
>
> Knights are ignorant men with strong arms.
>
> I never met a soldier yet
> who was a poet.
>
> Poets don't look for grails.
>
> They want to drink from
> the cups at hand.
>
> Sometimes they climb mountains
> to look down the middle
> where mangled kings lie in a heap.

But come to think of it, I've met one Black Mountain climber who was a poet. For my money, Bowering has not written a better poem than that—straightforward, clear, no waste wordage, and with implications for undeparted captains and kings. The poem also says: how wonderful to write poems! Or does it say: how wonderful to be a poet? I hope the first.

Bowering's methods are fairly easy to analyze unless you're the "Woman of Barrie." He uses good grammatical English, rarely any slang or throwaway lines. In fact this correct English seems to me *too* correct at times, not quite real or natural as Bowering believes speech should be; and he gives his poems a dead-pan seriousness, broken only occasionally, as in a poem called "Cold Spell" (not included here). And given that word-picture, one might think of him as an Eliotish sort of bloke, feeding cats and watering roses in his old age.

Despite writing poems like "Baseball," Bowering's colloquialisms occasionally seem contrived to me. "Lugging" means carrying, and "rooting" means cheering, which is about as close as he comes. If anything he tends to understatement, as in "The Silence":

> The silence
> that some days
> brings itself between us
>
> fools my heart,
> it thinks there is
> a loud constant noise.

But method apart, I call that a little masterpiece.

Well, having praised Bowering so highly (and I have), another side of him should be mentioned: triviality (again occasionally). I think it's trivial to write an eleven-page poem about baseball (and life too, of course): unless the poem isn't trivial. Bowering can immediately retort that I myself wrote a poem about hockey players, and he may very possibly judge that to be trivial. Obviously, a good poem can be written about anything, including the politics he says is "small men answering back to volcanoes."

But a good poem about baseball seems to me very difficult to write, perhaps because of the superficial nature of the game. Superficial because such games are the froth and entertainment of daily life, and because one game is really interchangeable for another. And there are dozens of others, including chess and parcheesi. The integral things of life are, life, death and sex (which last includes love among its other implications), and possibly taxes. Therefore, even a good baseball poem is bound to be trivial froth—unless its umbilical cord connects with something much more important. (To digress: Bernard Malamud wrote the only good novel I know of about baseball: *The Natural*—which is nevertheless a badly flawed novel.)

Bowering has three other long poems in his *Selected*: "Windigo," which is descriptive with symbolism engrafted; "Hamatsa," about Kwakiutl Indian "cannibal" societies, with its repeated delightful use of "the poet among us"; and "Touch," philosophic, trying to enclose all Bowering thinks and feels about—about everything, I suppose. All of these, while entertaining in part, are never wholly successful. Other long poems Bowering has omitted; and I think that's just as well. I make the dangerous judgment here that he is most effective in comparatively short pieces, which by his "natural" method and prosody he might think alien to him.

Employing throwaway lines and phrases for their "natural" effect as a break, as a voice-chuckle in a written tone of voice, supplies the human verbal quality cold print ordinarily prohibits. Speech is extempore, a quality that poetry seldom possesses—but should try to possess, at least sometimes. Bowering's continual lack of such ingredients sometimes gives his poems a rhetoric and solemnity I am sure he would deny having, even a faintly Biblical sound for me. This being an ingredient of his "method," which he might also deny having. But to make an end: I think Bowering is an "important" poet who should be read—even listened to as he demands. (Even the disagreements I have with him do not seem dead ends for me, but reasons to re-examine my own reasons for writing as I do.) He has written some half-dozen quite marvellous poems in this book—which means to me a very high lifetime batting average. And I join with the "Woman of Barrie" in my own kind of homage.

*(1972)*

∾

# Ralph Gustafson: *Selected Poems*

INTERESTING TO SEE THE BOOK BLURBS on Gustafson. Michael Hornyansky says, "He is the heir of civilized centuries." Michael Yates says, "It would be difficult to name a man who has done more to put Canada on the international map of literature." (I hadn't been aware Canada was on the international litmap, but it's probably a good thing for geography.) *The Performing Arts* says, "It is interesting to see, in the age of anti-sophistication and cult of the pseudo-primitive, a poet who is highly cultured and gets away with it." Whoever wrote that must be referring to people like me in the early part of the sentence. Anyway, I agree that Gus is certainly cultured.

Sometimes he's so damn cultured that I am impressed without

a clear understanding of what he means. In "Prefatory," Gus says that poems which lie are a bad thing. Ordinarily I'd be forced to agree, except that poems are presumably works of art in which truth and lies seem somewhat irrelevant to me. It's a highly dubious compliment to be told you tell the truth in your poems, whether higher truth or lower. For we are not statisticians or witnesses in a court case. It's probably possible to pick out dozens of stated facts in Gus's poems, and say, "These are lies." Earth is purple, earth is red, earth is on fire, the sun reads books . . . Those particular lies are not present in Gus tho. In any case, who cares? For in the midst of moral discussions in "Prefatory" there's an interesting cat: "The boop of a tuba arouses the cat from an illusion/ Of pheasants . . ." Now was that cat really thinking of pheasants or the sun reading books?

Anyway, Gus dallies and hobnobs with Daedalus, Theseus, Ariadne and Helen of Troy on pretty free and easy terms. But his language is intentionally stilted, twisted into things like "Helen had Paris' yarde"—a good example of the interesting uses of measurements outside the metric system. And sonnets are another example of Gus's culture, but I've forgotten the difference between Spenserian and Shakespearian, so can't comment. Influences, if not omnipresent, are emphatically belly-button omphalos. "Star-dazed dare" strikes me as Hopkins. I suppose if you can pick out such things as influences they are not sufficiently integrated.

Gus is a kinda romantic realist—which means what? Well, he starts from a base on the firm ground of reality in "Legend" ("ocean rinsing from flank and belly"), and at the end of the poem someone knows "what's left/ of Helen naked drag between his toes." I'm probably ruining my own example of romantic realism here, because I occasionally do something like that myself. Although there are better uses for the gal than to drag her naked between your toes.

As well, Gus can change tone and mood. The farewell to Ned Pratt is jovial and light: "Here's a farewell to you, Ned? How many of us have fed/ In your time there at York/ On roast beef, lamb chops, pork . . ." Sounds Chaucerian, or what people refer to as that. But such poems have a virtue beyond themselves of changing the mood of an entire book, adding variety and—tho I don't like the word much—perhaps also grace.

Sometimes too, Gus can be downright hilarious, as in "Four

thousand saints surround me/ My soul is utterly taken by the man/ Selling Cokes from a red refrigerator/ On the roof of Milan Cathedral . . ." Which might have been a little more effective if he hadn't anticipated himself by using the name of the cathedral in his title.

Anyway, let me use the phrase "romantic realist" again; also a lover, which means much more than the flesh and souls of women, includes the earth. But I think the aforementioned culture enters into Gus's philosophy a little too much; sometimes his bones do not include flesh. I mean by reason of the sheer emphasis and repetition of his archaeological and historic catalogue.

But just when I think I've got Gus pegged to a *t*, and that copulation is a four-syllable word he'd never condense to one, he says: "Chorion left poems and never knew when they were published/ he'd screw Helen/ On the top of Pelion he'd seen/ scorched snow . . ." Okay, that's kinda successful. And Pelion brings my childhood mountain in Trenton to mind. I didn't think the town fathers there ever read a book, let alone Greek mythology, or is it the Iliad. I can't remember. Well, no doubt about it, Gus has me there: fucked by superior culture.

In order to stop these meanderings: Gus is an excellent poet. But more like olives than apples, less like beer than wine. I think he probably should be read in not more than ten-page batches. He is extremely rewarding in that dosage; but the deliberately, slightly stilted, language clogs the brain if taken too rapidly. And he is a poet for the reader's reverie, perhaps more complement than instigator. And I don't mean "A Book of Verses underneath the Bough,/ A Jug of Wine, a Loaf of Bread—and Thou . . ." Not for him to instigate the stabbing wound, but rather the thoughtful look, the civilized reaction in pseudo-primitive reviewers. On top of that, Gus is rare: O Rare Gus. His particular amalgam is not present elsewhere in this country. Of course I wouldn't want more than one of any kind of poet. But Gus completes his own circle, of a unique excellence.

*(1973)*

# George Johnston: *The Faroe Islanders Saga*

**I**T BEGINS WITH MURDER. Two Faroese brothers, Brestir and
Beinir, are killed by one Hafgrim and his men, assisted by Thrand
for reasons of profit. Sigmund and Thorir, sons of the two brothers,
witness the killings. After it Thrand pays a ship's captain to take
Sigmund and Thorir so far away they will never return to the Faroe
Islands for revenge on reaching manhood. The two boys arrive in
Norway far northeast, are given haven by an outlaw, Thorkell Dry-
frost. Thorkell schools the two orphan cousins in all the Norse warlike
arts, treats them as if they were his own sons. The outlaw's daughter,
Thurid, falls in love with the heroic Sigmund, and is pregnant by him
when the two young men depart from Thorkell's mountain hideout
for the court of Earl Hakon.

At this point, which is really only a prelude, it's plain what is
about to happen. Sigmund and Thorir will become mighty men, sea
raiders in service of Earl Hakon and later King Olaf Tryggvason.
They will then seek "father-atonement" from Thrand, who by that
time has become the most prominent man in the Faroes. Earl Hakon
has made judgment against Thrand, demanding sovereignty and
tribute from the Faroes. Later the Norse King Olaf Tryggvason also
requires that the Faroese forsake their heathen ways and become
Christians. All this is said to have happened a thousand years ago.

But Thrand is a fox in other ways than his red hair. He does not
welcome Christianity, nor do the independence-minded Faroese
have any desire to be subjects of Norway's King Olaf. Thrand equivo-
cates and delays payment of the "father-atonement" judgment. Eventually he is responsible for the deaths of both Sigmund and Thorir.
The two cousins are forced to swim for their lives to escape Thrand's
men, reaching another island where a sea-weakened Sigmund is
murdered for his gold ring.

The *Saga* has several other sub-plots, but Sigmund and Thorir's
"father-atonement" battle with cunning Thrand, anti-Christian and
Faroese nationalist, remains central. The two cousins are conventional stock figures, but attractive since sympathy generally runs

toward such desperate survivors of their father's murder. And yet Thrand is a nationalist, apparently wants the Faroe Islands to remain independent. He is also anti-Christian. And these are two qualities with which I feel some kinship myself. But Thrand's nationalism and anti-Christianity are suspect by reason of self-interest: he is reluctant to part with "father-atonement" money or relinquish his own high position in the islands. And the death of Sigmund, his head cut off by Thorgrim the Bad for the sake of a gold ring—that is incongruously reminiscent of Christopher Marlowe being murdered with a three-penny knife.

We learn from George Johnston in his introduction that the *Faroe Saga* is a fiction, despite inclusion of definitely historic characters like Earl Hakon and King Olaf Tryggvason. It may have been written by an Icelander, but was not a dramatic version of history, such as the Icelandic settlement of Greenland by Erik the Red and Leif the Lucky's Vinland discoveries. Says Johnston: "It must now be found only as a series of interpolations in other sagas."

The *Saga's* fictional character and other inaccuracies come as a considerable letdown for me; but I console myself with its apparent authenticity, murder, blood feud and revenge. Those last things run through all the Icelandic sagas, in fact through all human history. But as a definite romantic, I sympathize more with Sigmund and Thorir than fox-like Thrand, differing in this feeling from the translator himself.

*The Faroe Saga*, in George Johnston's version, seems both modern and archaic. There are abrupt shifts of tense from present to past in the same paragraph. And we get lovely archaic-modern language like, "The bigger mare's cunt you if you can't bring down two men with two dozen . . . " I can hear George Johnston's own chuckle behind the phrase.

All this gives the saga an odd feeling for the reader, as if it were an experimental short novel surfacing in another time continuum. There are no heroic posturings or speeches; nobody stands in a Norse great hall thundering and thirsting for revenge. All the more chilling then, when Sigmund says to Thorir after watching their father's murder: "Let us not cry cousin, and remember all the longer."

Unless you're a scholar or immortal Viking, you cannot know the ancient Norse language, and must compare one translated saga with another to make any judgment as to accuracy of translation and literary excellence. I did read some of the Icelandic sagas a few years ago, and my memory of them is that they were more orotund, complicated in plot, generally less readable than the *Faroe Saga*. Now that may be because of differences in general character of the other sagas, perhaps less expert translators. I don't know. But whatever the reasons, this Faroe Islanders *Saga* seems to me remarkably interesting.

It moves. There is scarcely any extraneous material; everything is functional. One passage describes sea-raider Sigmund discovering enemy Norse ships in harbour: "the fifth of these was a dragon ship." Reading that I stiffened for some reason, thinking of the Gokstad Ship and Coleridge's "There was a ship, quoth he." And while the *Saga* may be fictional, it does translate one back to that thousand-year-old era, scarcely less violent and bloodthirsty than now.

Few people reading the *Faroe Saga* or this review are likely to know where the Faroe Islands are located. I did not myself, had barely heard of them. Therefore: the Faroes are between Shetland and Iceland, "a small archipelago in the North Atlantic." There are eighteen islands of different areas, and no trees grow there except those planted by the people themselves. The fifty thousand islanders live by fishing, are now under Danish rule, and their language is Norn, a variant of the old Norwegian. Modern novels and poems have been written in this survival-language from the past; it is the language of learning in Faroese schools.

But back to the *Saga* itself. The characters in it, those Norse who later became Faroese, strike me as supra-human, much larger than life. And I suppose the reason for that impression is the Saga-writer's method and art: stripped of all but things he regarded as essentials. Among those were loyalty, honour, friendship, love, endurance, treachery and courage—things that have endured since time's beginning.

*(1976)*

∞

# Alden Nowlan:
## *An Exchange of Gifts: Poems New and Selected*
## John Steffler: *The Grey Islands: A Journey*

IN THE COURSE OF MY OWN WANDERINGS across Canada, I encountered Alden Nowlan several times. He worked for a newspaper in Saint John, NB, in 1965, and was almost too shy to speak to me: I was embarrassed into a thunderous silence that seemed as much my fault as his. At Fredericton, when he was writer-in-residence at the University of New Brunswick, we sat together in a fancy restaurant where Sunday booze was *verboten*, and he plied me with not-very-surreptitious drinks from a 40-ouncer of rye under the table. At the Blue Mountain Poetry Festival near Collingwood, Ont., a few years ago, Milton Acorn, Nowlan, and I ate lunch together, Acorn ranting untranslatable PEI lobster jargon, Nowlan making sounds like an air conditioner badly in need of repair, me listening, shocked into a rare silence.

And now Nowlan is dead. I knew him and yet never knew him. The newspapers said he died of heart failure, but I think the cancer that haunted the last 20 years of his life was the real killer. And here in front of me are the essential poems that made his reputation. What reputation? How long will his poems endure and survive into the future? What do I really think of his poems? Where would I place them on the eternity totem pole?

But a word more about Nowlan's background. He was born near Windsor, NS, and regarded his childhood there as "a pilgrimage through hell." At 12 he left school to work as a pulpwood cutter. (His father was that as well, a labourer and mill-hand.) His childhood was—much of it—an escape from reality and into a fantasy world, in which he dreamt of being king of Nicaragua like the legendary William Walker; he even ordered a book from Eaton's catalogue, *Spanish Self-Taught*, in order to speak to his subjects.

Such fantasies permeate Nowlan's poems, even the later ones.

He started writing them at age 12. At 19 he finagled a job as a newspaper reporter in Harland, NB, and began corresponding with poet-editor Fred Cogswell of UNB. He worked as a reporter in Saint John then, in 1968, became writer-in-residence at UNB. And a reputation grew; a star rose in the East.

That background seems to me a necessity for understanding Nowlan's poems, and the man himself. He was self-educated, an autodidact, and escaped poverty through the fantasy land of his poems. Robert Gibbs has edited them for this book, and written a long introduction. It begins with 23 new poems. It then works forward in time from the past to near-present, including selections from each of his books. The result is a compendium that seems to me representative of Nowlan's best.

Most of his early poems are metrical and rhyming, but not all. Subject matter is backwoods and small-town incident, or comes from family and university environment and the books he read. Hero-fantasy is still present; it even usurps reality at times. For Nowlan was a romantic, a believer in sentiment (which I think permissible and even necessary in a poet), but was also very often sentimental in poems (which I think is not permissible—there is a tightrope between sentiment and sentimentality that a poet must straddle precariously).

Many of his poems are obvious and pointless, with small reason for existence. However, over the years Nowlan developed a facility and ingenuity with words, a strange kind of "knowing" how to write poems, which is partly instinct. (It is also a mental habit, not something that shrieks from the guts and shivers in your soul.) He developed a conversational, near-prose style that was easy to read; he talked of things in such a way as to allow the reader to feel that he too had sensitivity and feeling. No fireworks. I suppose that he mistrusted them, and fantasy worked well in their stead.

Nowlan wrote a certain kind of anecdotal poem extremely well. As insight into them: he admired Ray Souster, and he spoke well of John Wayne, the actor who loved violence and died of cancer. I believe he stopped developing, stopped changing from man to beast and beast to man. What remained was a poet who could write very good poems with practiced ease.

You have to be a little nuts to write the best poems—I will not say great ones. Like Milton Acorn, a ranting madman who wrote shit, then marvellous stuff in the next breath. Nowlan never wrote shit, but never rose above a certain practiced mid-excellence either. (But few can do that.) This review is a way of saying farewell, and I say it now more personally: Goodbye.

The subject matter of a book sometimes commands respect, even before the book is read. Such as the theme of the next book: spending the summer on a deserted island off Newfoundland, searching for something valuable in yourself. Such a theme unites philosophy and human emotion: it almost demands that the writer be given a fair chance to expound them.

John Steffler tells of a summer spent by a young man on one of the Grey Islands near Englee and the Great Northern Peninsula of Newfoundland. I believe the place was Bell Island, although it is nowhere named apart from a map. The narrator's reasons for doing so include boredom with his job, a marriage that seems precarious at the time, and probably also the feeling that such a book as this one is possible. (A writer almost always has a double motive for doing anything, the surface reason and another that he may not admit, the exploration of an experience in his writing.)

A fishing village once nested on 10-mile-long Bell Island. For unknown reasons (probably scarcity of fish) the people left. Their abandoned houses mouldered and decayed in the ceaseless breezes, gales, and cyclones, not to mention passing seasons. An old man named Carm Denny became the island's only occupant; but Denny was removed by Newfoundland authorities before Steffler's protagonist arrived.

In adventures like this, there is the sense of being Robinson Crusoe (despite the deserted village), of stripping yourself down to basics, and wanting to push yourself into some kind of ultimate condition you suspected in yourself but couldn't be sure existed. (The old questions: Who am I? Where am I? What am I doing here on earth?) Steffler assumes the personae of dozens of people inside his character's body, as well as those of people he meets or has heard about.

Carm Denny, the hermit of Bell Island, becomes real fantasy. Then reality as mundane as codfish takes over. The fisherman-ferryman, Nels, tells stories; Cyril and Ambrose Wellan, fishermen visiting the island, speak in Steffler's voice. Ghosts flit here and there among the ruined houses. A girl named Jewelleen slips into the character's bed at Englee in a dream and becomes real enough to leave daylight bruises.

This story that was real-life experience alternates in the telling between prose and verse, and slips naturally from one to the other without any jar of literary transition and changed rhythm in the reader's mind. Anecdotes, musings, remembrances, and time that is a clear liquid into which we insert our floating, mind-suspended impurities of self—these are the fabric of *The Grey Islands*.

Excerpts will not convey a completely accurate impression (when do they ever?) of the book. Still, they are fragments of Steffler's reality. Icebergs: "you suddenly see them as giant polar bears craning their necks to spy on you. Shamans' creatures. Come from a far time." A Carm Denny fantasy:

> The dozen or so ducks I still had, skinned and cleaned from the ones I got in the winter. I had them froze out in the pantry in a big wooden tub. At least they used to be froze. That damn south wind. So I lit a candle and went to the pantry and lifted the lid of the tub, and the stink that came out of there belted me like a loose boom, and there was a white flash at my hand and the next thing I knew I was down on my arse on the kitchen floor with a dozen skinned ducks zipping around the room with long blue flames shooting out of their hind ends.

About codfish:

> We are possibilities they cannot admit. We have broken the one train of thought they are capable of, and now they wallow sideways to the surface gaping and gulping like sleepwalkers fatally awakened. Even those that have slipped over the net and are free remain too deeply astonished to ever use their gills and dive again.

This is a book of such excellence that someone in future is liable to say about the author: "Steffler—Steffler, oh yes, he wrote *The Grey Islands*, didn't he?" Yes, he certainly did, and reading it I feel like a "deeply astonished" codfish.

*(1985)*

# Anna Akhmatova: *The Complete Poems*

A BEAUTIFUL WOMAN SHE WAS NOT, on the evidence of nearly a hundred photographs in these two books. She was majestic instead, her nose imperial Roman, unsmiling for every camera. She possessed immense natural dignity. Men fell in love with her continually. She married three times. Even in old age, her face and carriage were striking and received homage. Indeed, she expected homage, almost demanded it according to some who knew her well; and accepted it without surprise. The Grande Dame, yet rather pitiful in old age—although she rejected pity fiercely.

Anna Akhmatova. Born in 1889 of a well-to-do family, she was told by her father when she began to write poetry that he did not want his name (Gorenko) associated with "that trade." She changed hers to Akhmatova, the Tartar name of a maternal ancestor, and made the new name famous.

Prior to the First World War, in St. Petersburg (which became Leningrad after the Revolution), Akhmatova sometimes read her poems at a bohemian cabaret, "The Stray Dog." So did Alexander Blok, reverenced by a flood of admirers, and "the cloud in trousers," Vladimir Mayakovsky. In 1903 she met a young poet, Nikolay Gumilyov, and married him in 1910. Gumilyov and his group of poets, which included Akhmatova, rejected the current craze of Symbolism; instead they founded a group called "The Acmeists," which stood for a poetry of real experience and tangible objects.

Between 1905 and 1908 Gumilyov attempted suicide several times. At one point he was found lying unconscious in the Bois de Boulogne, in Paris. In 1906, Akhmatova tells of her own suicide attempt in a letter to her brother-in-law. "To die is easy," she said. "Did Andrey tell you how I attempted to hang myself in Evpatoriya and the nail pulled out of the plaster wall? Mama cried and I was ashamed—it was awful."

Over the 10-year period between 1912 and 1922, which included the First World War and the Russian Revolution, Akhmatova published five books of poetry. These were mostly love poems, and were very popular with young people at the time. She claimed, of course, that the poems did not reflect her own life (most poets do claim that), and were not autobiographical—which is true, in a sense. But one learns much about the woman from these poems: her romantic yearning for the perfect human relationship, her work growing in intensity and depth of feeling, and expanding in its subject matter.

In 1922 Mayakovsky denounced Akhmatova's poetry publicly, although she was as non-political as it was possible to be after the Revolution. Mayakovsky's mistress of that time said later that he read Akhmatova constantly, every day. But the Communist regime, growing ever more puritanical and repressive, could not abide Akhmatova's love poems: at least that seems to be one possible reason for her disfavour. Also: some of her friends were actually engaged in "alarums and excursions" of counter-revolution. After 1925 she was not allowed to publish in the Soviet Union. Zhdanov, one of Stalin's obedient minions, called her "half nun and half harlot." A critic, one Pertzov, said of her, "We cannot sympathize with a woman who did not know when to die."

I find this quite incredible! And horrible!

These two enormous books amount to a completely galaxy of Akhmatova's poems, and much else besides. There's a full-length biography by Roberta Reeder, the editor; several memoirs by people who knew her well; a chronology; and many, many photographs. The translator, Judith Hemschemeyer, learned Russian for the task, and devoted several years to it; receiving encomiums for her work.

I have previously read several other books related to Akhmatova: Nadezhda Mandelstam's memoir, *Hope Against Hope*; Olga Ivinskaya's reminiscences (she was Pasternak's friend); and, more important, Olga Carlisle's anthology of Russian poets, *Poets on Street Corners* (1968). There are many of Akhmatova's poems in the anthology, translated by various hands, including Stanley Kunitz, Adrienne Rich, Rose Styron, Richard Wilbur, and Robert Lowell. Lowell "adapted" Akhmatova's "Requiem," written after her son Lev's last arrest and imprisonment in Leningrad.

This long 11-part poem is regarded by many, including myself, as Akhmatova's best. "Requiem" was first published, long after its composition, in Munich, Germany, in 1963. Lowell included his adaptation of the poem in his *Imitations*. It begins in prose, with Akhmatova waiting, along with many other relatives and friends of the prisoners, in "the prison lines at Leningrad." Another woman, apparently recognizing the poet, whispered in her ear, "Could you describe this?" Akhmatova answered, "Yes, I can."

Lowell used quatrains, off-rhymes, and rough metrics in his adaptation; Hemschemeyer free verse in her translations. Using the latter method, I think it's much more difficult to make a poem memorable and meaningful. As a study in comparative translation then, here are the last five verses of Akhmatova's "Requiem" as adapted by each writer.

Lowell:

> Friends, if you want some monument
> gravestone or cross to stand for me,
> you have my blessing and consent,
> but do not place it by the sea.
>
> I was a sea-child, hardened by
> the polar Baltic's grinding dark;
> that tie is gone: I will not lie,
> a Tsar's child in the Tsarist park.
>
> Far from your ocean, Leningrad,
> I leave my body where I stood
> three hundred hours in lines with those
> who watched unlifted prison windows.
>
> Safe in death's arms, I lie awake,
> and hear the mother's animal roar,
> the black truck slamming on its brake,
> the senseless hammering of the door.
>
> Ah, the Bronze Horseman wipes his eye
> and melts, a prison pigeon coos,
> the ice goes out, the Neva goes
> with its slow barges to the sea.

And Hemschemeyer:

> And if ever in this country
> They decide to erect a monument to me,

I consent to that honor
Under these conditions: that it stand

Neither by the sea, where I was born,
My last tie with the sea is broken,

Nor in the tsar's garden near the cherished pine stump,
Where an inconsolable shade looks for me,

But here, where I stood three hundred hours,
And where they never unbolted the doors for me

This, lest in blissful death
I forget the rumbling of the Black Marias,

Forget how that detested door slammed shut
And an old woman howled like a wounded animal.

And may the melting snow stream like tears
From my motionless lips of bronze,

And a prison dove coo in the distance,
And the ships of the Neva sail calmly on.

Lowell called his version of "Requiem" an "imitation," a free
adaptation of Akhmatova; Hemschemeyer's is probably truer to the
original, but nevertheless still only an approximation.

After Stalin died in 1953, Akhmatova's verse was again published in the Soviet Union; and a reverence for her began. Most of her
friends were long dead, from imprisonment in Siberia, as victims of
execution, or simply old age; but a new generation loved her poems.
Joseph Brodsky, before he emigrated to the United States, was one
of her protégés. Some critics have called her the greatest woman poet
since Sappho; but it is impossible to judge Sappho's work accurately
since so little of it remains. In any case, Akhmatova left behind a
legend as well as her poems when she died in 1966, a woman who, in
the minds of some admirers, is emblematic of the soul of Russia. And
the "Requiem" suite (Lowell's version )is indelible in my own memory.

In a country where most of the citizens were prisoners, incarcer-
ated or not, Akhmatova was a free woman and lived her life as one. I

admire her immensely. During her lifetime she rarely had very much money. When her poems were banned she translated foreign literature for small remuneration. Her friends—Pasternak among them—helped her; she helped them. It may be thought that her life was tragic. Perhaps, but it was also a triumph: *Yes, I can.*

*(1990)*

# Acknowledgments

## Part I

"The Cartography of Myself," *No Other Country* (Toronto: McClelland and Stewart, 1977), ["Al Purdy's Canada," *Maclean's*, May 1971]; "The Iron Road," *NOC*, [*Canada Month*, July 1963]; "Lights on the Sea: Portraits of BC Fishermen," *NOC*, ["Caught in the Net," *Maclean's*, May 1974]; "Cougar Hunter," *NOC*, ["In the Shoes of the Fisherman," *Weekend* Magazine, 28 Dec. 1974]; "Tofino: A Place by the Sea," *Imperial Oil Review*, Fall 1992; "Ghost Towns of BC," *Imperial Oil Review*, Spring 1995; "Imagine a Town," *NOC*; "Dryland Country," *NOC*, ["The Grassland Question: Who Shall Inherit the Earth: —People or Prairie Dogs?" *The Canadian*, Nov. 1977]; "Streetlights on the St. Lawrence," *NOC*, ["The Rime of the Fledgling Mariner: Retracing the Route of Canada's Early Immigrants Along the St. Lawrence," *Weekend* Magazine, 10 Aug.1974]; "Angus," *NOC*, [*Weekend* Magazine, 1974]; "Norma, Eunice, and Judy," *NOC*, ["How the Salvation of Canadian Literature May Rest on the Good Deed of Three Toronto Prostitutes: Jim Foley's Unlikely Path to the Classroom," *Weekend* Magazine, 15 June 1974]; "Bon Jour?" *NOC* ["Lévesque: The Executioner of Confederation?" *Maclean's*, May 1971]; "Aklavik on the Mackenzie River," *NOC*; "Harbour Deep," *NOC*, ["A Village out of Time," *The Canadian*, 12 Feb.1977]; "Argus in Labrador," *NOC*, [*Weekend* Magazine, 1975]; "Her Gates Both East and West," *NOC*, ["A Feast of Provinces," *Maclean's*, April 1972]; "Introduction to *Moths in the Iron Curtain*," *Moths in the Iron Curtain*, [Sutton West, Ont.: The Paget Press, 1977]; "Birdwatching at the Equator," Birdwatching at the Equator, 1983; "Northern Reflections," *Imperial Oil Review*, Winter 1993; "Jackovich and the Salmon Princess," ["King Tyee and the Salmon Princess," *Weekend* Magazine, 3 May 1975].

---

## Part II

"Autobiographical Introduction," *The Poems of Al Purdy* (Toronto: McClelland and Stewart, 1979); Charles Bukowski, *It Catches my Heart in its Hands*, Evidence, No. 8 (1964); "Leonard Cohen: A Personal Look," *Canadian Literature*, No. 23 (Winter 1965); Leonard Cohen, *Beautiful Losers, Canadian Forum*, July 1967; Irving Layton, *Balls for a One-Armed Juggler, Canadian Literature*, No. 16 (Spring 1964); *The Collected Poems of Irving Layton, Quarry*, 15, No. 3 (1966); Constantine Fitzgibbon, *The Life of Dylan Thomas, The Tamarack Review*, No. 38 (Winter 1966); Farley Mowat, *Westviking*, Helge Ingstad, *Land Under the Pole Star, Canadian Literature*, No. 33 (Summer 1967); Farley Mowat, *Sea of Slaughter, Canadian Literature*, No. 106 (Fall 1985); Introduction to *I've Tasted My Blood*, (Toronto: House of Anansi Press, 1969); Margaret Atwood, *The Animals in That Country, Canadian Literature*, No. 39 (Winter 1969); Margaret Atwood, *The Journals of Susanna Moodie, Canadian Literature*, No. 47 (Winter 1971); "Malcolm Lowry," *NOC*, ["Let He Who is Without Gin Cast the First Stone," *The Montreal Gazette*, 17 Aug. 1974]; Introduction to *Notes on Visitations: Poems 1936–1975*, (Toronto: House of Anansi, 1975); "George Wood-cock, 1912–1995," *Queen's Quarterly, Summer 1995; The Literary History of Canada*, 3 Vol., *Books in Canada*, Jan. 1977; Introduction to *Ragged Horizons* (Toronto: McClelland and Stewart, 1978); Introduction to *Everson at Eighty*, (Ottawa: Oberon, 1983); Earle Birney, The Creative Writer, *Canadian Literature*, No. 31 (Winter 1967); Afterword to *Turvey*, (Toronto: McClelland and Stewart, 1989); Introduction to *Last Makings*, (Toronto: McClelland and Stewart, 1991); F.R.Scott, *The Dance is One, Books in Canada*, July/Sept. 1973; Sandra Djwa, *The Politics of the Imagination: A Life of F.R.Scott, Canadian Literature*, No. 121 (Summer 1989); David Pitt, *E.J.Pratt: The Master Years, Books in Canada*, Jan./Feb. 1988; "Rudyard Kipling," *Brick* 36 (Summer 1989); "On Bliss Carman," *Bliss Carman: A Reappraisal*, Gerald Lynch ed., (Ottawa: University of Ottawa Press, 1990).

## Poetry Chronicle

Louis Dudek, *The Canadian Forum*, Nov. 1958; Roy Campbell, *The Canadian Forum*, Jan. 1959; Raymond Souster, *Canadian Author & Bookman*, 39, No. 4 (Summer 1964); John Newlove, *Canadian Literature*, No. 25 (Summer 1965); John Newlove, *Canadian Literature*, No.

48 (Spring 1971); John Newlove, *Wascana Review*, No. 8 (Fall 1973); *New Wave Canada*, *Quarry*, 16, No. 3 (March 1967); Group Review I: Seymour Mayne, Bill Bissett, Pat Lane, Jim Brown, *Canadian Literature*, No. 35 (Winter 1968); Group Review II: George Jonas, D.G.Jones, Roy Kiyooka, A.J.M.Smith, Dennis Lee, Raymond Souster, P.K.Page, Lionel Kearns, Dorothy Livesay, George Woodcock, Alden Nowlan, The Making of Modern Poetry in Canada, *The Tamarack Review*, No. 49 (Spring 1968); Poets Between the Wars, *Canadian Literature*, No. 37 (Summer 1968); Group Review III: George Bowering, Bill Bissett, Doug Fetherling, Bill Howell, *Canadian Literature* 54 (Autumn 1972); Ralph Gustafson, *Wascana Review*, 8 (Fall 1973); George Johnston, *Canadian Literature*, No. 67 (Winter 1976); Alden Nowlan, John Steffler, *Books in Canada*, Oct. 1985; Anna Akhmatova, *Books in Canada*, Aug./Sept. 1990.

# Index